RaeAnne Thayne finds inspiration in the beautiful northern Utah mountains, where the *New York Times* and *USA TODAY* bestselling author lives with her husband and three children. Her books have won numerous honors, including RITA® Award nominations from Romance Writers of America and a Career Achievement Award from *RT Book Reviews*. RaeAnne loves to hear from readers and can be contacted through her website, raeannethayne.com.

New York Times and *USA TODAY* bestselling author **B.J. Daniels** lives in Montana with her husband, Parker, and three springer spaniels. When not writing, she quilts, boats and plays tennis. Contact her at bjdaniels.com, or on Facebook at facebook.com/pages/bj-daniels, or Twitter, @bjdanielsauthor.

New York Times Bestselling Authors

RaeAnne Thayne
and
B.J. Daniels

A THUNDER CANYON CHRISTMAS & CLASSIFIED CHRISTMAS

◆HARLEQUIN® THE COWBOY COLLECTION

Special thanks and acknowledgment
are given to RaeAnne Thayne
for her contribution to the Montana Mavericks series.

ISBN-13: 978-0-373-60189-9

A Thunder Canyon Christmas & Classified Christmas

Copyright © 2015 by Harlequin Books S.A.

The publisher acknowledges the copyright holders of the individual works as follows:

A Thunder Canyon Christmas
Copyright © 2010 by Harlequin Books S.A.

Classified Christmas
Copyright © 2007 by Barbara Heinlein

Recycling programs
for this product may
not exist in your area.

HARLEQUIN®
www.Harlequin.com

Printed in U.S.A.

CONTENTS

A THUNDER CANYON CHRISTMAS

RaeAnne Thayne

Chapter 1

Rock bottom was one thing. This had to be a new low, even for her.

Elise Clifton hunched onto the bar stool at The Hitching Post, painfully aware of her solitary status. She wasn't sure which made her more pathetic—showing up alone at Thunder Canyon's favorite watering hole or the fact that she would rather be anywhere else on earth, including here by herself, than home with her family right now.

She sipped at her drink, trying to avoid meeting anyone's gaze.

So much for the girls' night out she had been eagerly anticipating all week. She was supposed to have met her best friend, Haley Anderson, here for a night of margaritas and girl talk, accompanied by a popular local band.

Two out of three was still a winning average, she supposed.

The band was here, a trio of cute, edgy long-haired

cowboys belting out crowd-pleasing rockabilly music. Margaritas, check. She was almost done with her second and heading fast toward number three.

But the girl talk was notably lacking...maybe because Haley had called her twenty minutes ago, her voice hoarse and full of apologies.

"I'm so sorry I didn't phone you earlier," Haley had rasped out. "I completely zonked and slept through my alarm. All day I've been hoping the cold medicine would finally kick in and I would be ready to rock and roll with you at The Hitching Post. No luck, though. It's only making me so sleepy I'm not consciously aware of how miserable I feel."

"Don't worry about it," Elise had answered, trying to keep any trace of her plummeting mood out of her voice. She couldn't really blame Haley for her bad luck in coming down with a lousy cold on a night when Elise was particularly desperate for any available diversion. She would be a poor friend to make a big deal about it, especially when Haley probably felt even worse than she sounded, which was pretty bad.

"We can reschedule as soon as you're feeling better," Elise had said. "The Hitching Post will still be here in a week or two."

"Deal," Haley croaked out. "If I ever get feeling better, anyway. Right now that doesn't seem likely."

"You will. Hang in there."

That was about the time Elise had gestured for her second margarita as her plans for the evening went up in smoke.

"Thanks for understanding, honey. First round is on me next time."

Elise sighed now as the band switched songs to one she hadn't heard before. She watched the blinking of Christmas lights that some enterprising soul had draped around the racy picture of Lily Divine adorned in strategically placed gauze that hung above the bar.

Even Lily Divine was in a holiday mood. Too bad Elise couldn't say the same.

Usually she enjoyed coming to The Hitching Post. Once rumored to be Thunder Canyon's house of ill repute, the place was now a warm, welcoming bar and grill. Locals loved it for its enduring nature. Unlike the rest of Thunder Canyon, The Hitching Post had remained unchanged through the ebbs and flows of the local economy.

With hardwood floors, the same weathered old bar and framed photos from the 1880s on the walls, the restaurant and bar likely hadn't changed much since the days when Lily Divine herself used to preside over the saloon she'd inherited from the original madam.

Elise had never been here by herself, though, and was quickly discovering how that created an entirely different dynamic. She felt more alone than ever as she sipped her drink and tried to avoid making eye contact. With a lone woman in a bar like The Hitching Post, it probably looked as if she was on the prowl, in search of some big, strong cowboy to help her while away a cold winter's night.

One such cowboy—a little heavy on the outdoorsy aftershave—sat three stools away. He'd been eyeing her for the past ten minutes and she was trying her best to pretend she didn't notice.

Maybe if she had stayed at Clifton's Pride, she might have been snuggled up right now in a fleece blanket watching some movie on the big-screen television at her family's ranch house instead of perched here at the bar like some kind of sad, pathetic loser.

She took a healthy swallow of her margarita and gestured to Carl, the longtime bartender, for another one as she swung her foot in time to the music.

Who was she kidding? If she had stayed at the ranch, she wouldn't be snuggled up with a movie and a bowl of popcorn. Not when her mother and brother had company—hence her escape to The Hitching Post, so she wouldn't have to smile and nod and make nice with Erin Castro. Right this moment Erin was having dinner with her miraculous, newfound family—Elise's own mother, Helen, her brother Grant and his pregnant wife, Stephanie Julen Clifton.

Escaping the family gathering had probably been cowardly. Rude, even. Helen and John Clifton had raised her to be much more polite than that. But the truth was, she wasn't sure she was capable of spending a couple of hours making polite conversation just now, even though she liked Erin.

She couldn't blame this twisted tangle on the other woman. It wasn't Erin's fault that a nurse's error twenty-six years ago during an unusually hectic night at Thunder Canyon General Hospital and a string of mistakes had resulted in two baby girls—born on the same night to mothers sharing a room—being inadvertently switched.

Erin might have set into motion the chain of events that had led to the discovery of the hospital mistake—and the shocking truth that Elise's birth parents were a couple she had never even met until a few weeks ago—but she had only been trying to look into a mysterious claim by a relative that the truth of her birth rested somewhere in Thunder Canyon. She had come here several months ago to investigate why she looked nothing like her siblings and had finally discovered that she was in reality the child of Helen and the late John Clifton, while Elise—who had spent her lifetime thinking she knew exactly who she was and her place in the world—had been stunned to learn she was the biological child of Betty and Jack Castro.

Elise understood the other woman hadn't set out to drop an atomic bomb in her life, only to find answers. But every time Elise saw how happy her mother and Grant were now that they had found out the truth about the events of twenty-six years ago—and in effect gained another daughter and sister—Elise felt more and more like she didn't belong.

She took another healthy swallow of her drink, welcoming the warm, easy well-being that helped push away that sense of always being on the outside, looking in.

The funny thing was, she couldn't really blame Erin for that, either. She always felt like an outsider whenever she came to town because she *was* an outsider. Oh, she had lived in Thunder Canyon through elementary and middle school. She had loved it here, had thought she would stay forever—until the horrible events of that day more than a decade ago when her father and a neighboring rancher were murdered by cattle rustlers.

She couldn't say she was exactly a stranger in town. She and her mother came back occasionally to visit family and friends. Scattered throughout the bar and grill were various people she recognized. Her family's ties here ran deep and true, especially since Grant and Stephanie had revitalized Clifton's Pride, in addition to her brother's work as general manager of the Thunder Canyon Resort.

Grant certainly belonged here. Her mother, too, even though Helen had escaped the bad memories after her husband's violent death by moving with Elise to Billings when Elise was thirteen.

Elise didn't feel the same sense of connection. She had

come back temporarily with her mother for the holidays while their family absorbed the shocking developments of the last month. But she was beginning to think she might have been better off booking a month-long cruise somewhere warm and exotic and an ocean away from this Montana town and all the pain and memories it held.

The desire was reinforced when The Hitching Post door opened with a blast of wintry air. Like everybody else in the place, she instinctively looked up to see who it might be, but quickly turned back toward Lily Divine, her stomach suddenly as tangled as those wisps of material covering Lily's abundant charms.

Matt Cates.

She averted her face away from the door, mortified at the idea of him noticing her sitting here alone like some pathetic barfly.

He didn't seem to be on a date, which was odd. From the rumors she heard even after she moved away, Matt and his twin brother, Marlon, both enjoyed living up to their wild reputation.

Marlon was apparently reformed now that he was engaged to Haley. She didn't know about Matt, though.

Out of the corner of her gaze, she spotted him heading over to a booth in the corner where several other guys she vaguely recognized from school years ago had ordered pizza and a pitcher of beer.

Some of her tension eased. From his vantage point, he wouldn't have a direct line of sight to her. Maybe he wouldn't even notice her. Why would he? She had always been pretty invisible to him, other than as an annoying kid he always seemed to have to rescue.

She crossed the fingers of her left hand under the bar and reached for her third—or was it fourth?—margarita with her right.

"How'd I get so lucky to be sitting next to the prettiest girl in the place?"

Elise turned at the drawl, so close she could practically feel the hot breath puffing in her ear. She had been so busy hiding from Matt, she hadn't realized the cowboy had maneuvered his way to the bar stool next to her.

She definitely should slow down on the margaritas, since the ten gallons of Stetson cologne he must have used hadn't tipped her off to him.

"Oh. Hi." Her cheeks heated and she cursed her fair skin.

"I'm Jake. Jake Halloran."

She should just ignore him. She wasn't the sort to talk to strange men in a bar. But then, everything she knew about herself had been turned upside down in the last two weeks, so why not? It had to be marginally better than sitting here by herself.

"Hi, Jake. You from around here?"

"I'm working out at the Lazy D." His heavy-eyed gaze sharpened on her. "You sure you're old enough to be in here? You must have used a fake ID, right? Come on, you can tell me the truth."

"I—"

"Don't worry, darlin'. I won't say a word."

He smiled and mimicked turning a key at his lips. He was good-looking in a rough-edged sort of way, with tawny blond hair beneath his black Resistol and a thin, craggy, Viggo Mortenson kind of face.

She supposed she was just tipsy enough to be a little flattered at his obvious interest. Not that she had the greatest track record where men were concerned. She sighed a little. Her one and only serious relationship had been a total disaster. Kind of tough to see it any other way after the man she'd considered her first real boyfriend—

and had surrendered her virginity to—introduced her to his lovely fiancée.

She'd dated on and off over the three years since then, but most guys tended to see her as a buddy. Jake Halloran obviously didn't. Though she thought it was more than a little creepy that he would be willing to flirt with somebody he thought might be underage, she figured there was no harm in flirting back just a little.

"I appreciate that, Jake," she answered. "But I've known Carl, the bartender over there, since I took my first steps. He knows exactly how old I am and would be the first one to tan my hide if I were caught trying to pass a fake ID in The Hitching Post."

"Is that right? So how old are you?"

"Old enough," she answered pertly.

"Well, however old you are, you are about the prettiest thing I've seen in this whole town."

"Um, thanks." She forced a smile.

"How come I haven't seen you around before now?"

"I'm from out of town, here visiting family for the holidays." Or at least visiting the people she had always considered her family.

"What's your name?"

It was a simple question, really. Just about the most basic question a person could be asked. She still hesitated before answering, for a whole host of reasons.

"Elise. Elise Clifton."

The words came out almost defiantly. She *was* Elise Clifton. That's who she had been for twenty-six years, even if it turned out to be a lie.

She gestured to Carl for another margarita, even though she was usually a one-drink kind of gal.

"Well, Elise Clifton," Jake said. "This is goin' to sound

like a cheap line but what's a sweet-looking girl like you doing in a place like this all by herself?"

Now that was a very good question. She took a swallow of the new drink Carl delivered as the music shifted to a cover of a rocking Dwight Yoakam song. "Listening to the guys," she finally answered. "They're one of my favorite bands."

At just that moment, she spied Matt over Jake's shoulder. He stood at the other end of the bar, talking to a middle-aged man she didn't know.

He was so gosh-darned gorgeous, with that streaky brown hair and warm brown eyes and broad shoulders. She sighed. She'd always had more than a bit of a crush on Matt, ever since the day in first grade when he had taken down a big third-grade boy who had pushed her into a mud puddle.

Matt didn't see her as any sort of romantic interest. She knew that perfectly well. To him, she was small-for-her-age Elise Clifton, bookish and shy and clumsy, always in need of some silly rescue.

He turned in her direction and she quickly angled her body so she was hidden by the cowboy's big hat and his broad shoulders.

Jake's eyes widened with surprise at her maneuver, which also happened to put her closer to him, then she saw a gleam of appreciation spark there and he tilted his head even more closely.

"They are a mighty fine band," he agreed. "Makes you want to get up there and dance, doesn't it?"

"The bass player went to school with me," she said, trying her level best to act as if practically sitting in a stranger's lap was an everyday event. "He used to play tuba in the school band."

"Is that right? What did you play?"

"Clarinet," she answered. "I'm really good at blowing things."

He choked on his drink. It took her several beats of listening to him cough and splutter to figure out what she'd said and then she gasped. Her face flared—she wanted to sink through the floor. She was apparently a really cheap drunk. After three and a half margaritas, she excelled at unintentional double entendres.

"That's not what I meant," she exclaimed. "I really did play the clarinet. Oh!"

He laughed roughly, wiping his mouth with a napkin he'd grabbed off the bar. "I'd love to see you...play the clarinet."

Okay, she should really leave. Right now, before Jake Halloran got any ideas about checking out her embouchure.

Despite her discomfort, she laughed at her own joke but when she looked up, Lily Divine seemed to be undulating up there on the wall like a snake dancer. Elise blinked. Maybe she needed to switch to water for a while. Apparently the fourth margarita hadn't been her greatest idea.

"Hey, you wanna dance?" Jake suddenly asked. Either he was slurring his words or her ears weren't firing on all cylinders.

She considered his invitation, taking in the small dance floor that had been set up in front of the small stage where the band had now switched to a bluegrass version of "Jingle Bells." Only a handful of couples were out there: an older man and woman doing a complicated Western swing like they were trying out for some television dancing show, another pair who weren't really even dancing, just bear-hugging like they were joined at the navel, and a couple about her age, dancing with a painful awkwardness she instantly pegged as a first date, even through her bleary brain.

Ordinarily she loved to dance. But since she had probably spent enough time in the Thunder Canyon spotlight the last few weeks, she decided she didn't need to be the center of attention by dancing out there in front of everyone. Everyone being primarily Matt Cates.

"I'm not much of a dancer," she lied. "Why don't we just talk? Get to know each other a little better?"

"Talking's nice." Jake grinned and put his hand on her knee. Through the material of her favorite skinny jeans, his hand felt uncomfortably hot. "Gettin' to know each other better is even nicer."

Drat Haley and her stupid rhinovirus.

She tried to subtly ease her knee away, wondering if she ought to ask Carl for a cup of coffee.

"Where are you from, Jake?" she asked a little desperately. "Originally, I mean."

"Over Butte way. My daddy had to sell off our little ranch a few years ago so I've been on my own since then. What about you?"

"Um, I live in Billings most of the time. I'm only in town for the holidays. I think I said that already."

"You did. And doesn't that work out just fine for me?"

She barely heard him. Out of the corner of her gaze, she saw a woman in tight Wranglers and a chest-popping holiday sweater approach Matt's table and a moment later, he headed out to the dance floor with her. Elise refused to watch and shifted a little more so her would-be Romeo was blocking her from view.

He didn't seem to mind. "Hey, what do you say we get out of here? Take a little drive and see the Christmas lights?"

She might be tipsy, but she wasn't completely stupid.

She wouldn't go with him, even if his breath *wasn't* strong enough to tarnish the frame on Lily's picture.

"I'd better not. I don't want to miss the music. That's the reason I'm here, after all."

Just her luck, at just that moment, the lead singer stepped up to the mike. "We're going to take fifteen, folks. Meantime you can keep dancing to the jukebox."

"What do you say? Want to at least walk outside and get some air?"

Air might be nice. Even cold air. The faster she worked the margaritas out of her system, the faster she could leave. Where she would go until the dinner party with Erin was over was a question she didn't want to consider yet.

Though she was leery about going anywhere with a man she had just met and didn't trust, how much trouble could she get into walking out into the snowy parking lot on a frigid Montana night? Anything had to be better than sitting here trying to avoid being seen.

"Sure. Let me grab my coat."

The coat and hat racks at The Hitching Post lined the hallway on the way to the restrooms. She decided to make a quick stop at the ladies' room first to check her lipstick and maybe splash a little water on her face to clear her head.

It helped a little, but not much. When she emerged a few moments later, she found Jake lurking in the hallway.

"I thought you might be having trouble finding your coat," he murmured. For some reason, she thought that was hilarious. As if she was so stupid she couldn't recognize her own coat, for heaven's sake.

"Nope. I just stopped to fix my lipstick."

"It looks real pretty."

"Um, thanks." Maybe going outside with him wasn't

such a great idea. Actually, she was beginning to think walking through The Hitching Post doors tonight ranked right up there with her worst decisions ever. Second only to her ridiculous lapse in judgment in ever agreeing to date that cheating louse Jeremy Kaiser in college.

Jake cornered her just to the edge of the row of coats. "Bet that lipstick tastes as good as it looks," he said in what he probably thought was a sexy growl. Instead, he sounded vaguely like a cat whose tail just had a close encounter with a sliding door.

He leaned in closer and she edged backward until her hands scraped the dingy wood paneling.

He dipped his head but she managed to shift her face away at the last minute. "Um, I think I changed my mind about going outside. Too cold. Let's go dance."

"I reckon we can do a pretty good tango right here," he murmured.

He tried again and she planted her palms on the chambray of his Western-cut dress shirt. "No, I really want to go dance," she said and realized her voice sounded overloud in the still-empty hallway.

Where was everybody? Didn't anybody in the whole place need to use the bathroom, for Pete's sake?

They struggled a little there in the hallway and she started to feel the first little pinch of fear when she realized she wasn't making a lick of headway against those cowboy-tough muscles.

"Come on, darlin'. A little kiss won't hurt nobody."

"I don't think so. I don't know you."

His face hardened and she wondered why she ever thought he looked a little like Viggo. More like Ichabod Crane. "You sure knew me well enough to be all snuggly over at the bar," he snarled.

"Hey," she exclaimed when his hand slid behind her

to hold her in place. She pushed at the pearl buttons on his shirt. "Let go."

"Come on. Just a kiss. That's all."

"No!" She wriggled and squirmed but was faced with the grim realization that her 110-pound, five-foot-four frame was no match for somebody who wrangled tons of Angus cattle for a living. "Let me go!"

"Looks to me like the lady's not interested, Halloran."

The familiar steely voice managed to pierce both her sudden attack of nerves and her muzzy head.

She swallowed a curse. Matt. Her miserable night just needed this. Her face blazed and she knew she must be more red than a shiny glass Christmas ornament. Of every single person out in the crowded bar, why did he have to be the next one who happened into the hallway to come to her rescue?

Chapter 2

Matt stood a few feet away from them in the otherwise empty hallway, an almost bored look on his rugged features.

Jake Halloran had muscles, but he was no match for Matt, who helped run his family's construction business. He loomed over the other man, big and dark and dangerous.

"This ain't none of your concern, Cates," the wrangler currently trying to wrangle *her* snarled. "You don't know what you're talkin' about, so just walk on by."

"I don't think so." Matt stepped forward, looking tough and dangerous and heartstoppingly gorgeous. Elise slammed her eyes shut.

"Hey, Elise."

She opened them to find him watching her, a slight smile playing around his mouth. She certainly wouldn't be wriggling and squirming like a lassoed calf if *that* mouth had been the one coming at her.

"Hi," she whispered. She was never drinking again. Never drinking and certainly never talking to strange men in bars again.

"Let's let the lady decide, why don't we?" Matt said calmly. "Elise, you want me to walk on by and leave the both of you to whatever was going on here that you didn't particularly appear to be enjoying a minute ago?"

What kind of choice was that? She didn't want him here, but she certainly didn't want to be the star attraction in octopus cage fighting anymore.

"No," she whispered, then cleared her throat when she heard that pitiful rasp. "No," she repeated more firmly. "Don't go."

"That sounded pretty clear-cut to me, Halloran. The lady isn't interested. Better luck next time."

Matt reached around the cowboy to grab her arm and extricate her from yet another humiliating situation. With a tangled mixture of relief and trepidation, she reached to take his hand.

She wasn't sure exactly what happened next. One moment she was stuck to the cowboy's side, the next Matt had her elbow firmly in his grip and was leading her away.

"Come on, Elise. Let's get you something to eat."

They took maybe three steps away from the situation when the wrangler grabbed her other arm and yanked her back. Pain seared from her shoulder to her fingers and Elise gave an instinctive cry.

Why in *Hades* hadn't she just put on her big-girl panties and stayed at the ranch to deal with Erin? Anything would be better than this. She did not want to be here right now, caught in a tug-of-war between two tough, dangerous men.

Something dark and hot flared in Matt's expression

as he eyed the other man. "You're going to want to let go of her arm now," he said in a low voice, all the more ominous for its calmness.

"I saw her first," Jake muttered, just as if she were the last slice of apple pie in the bakery display case.

Elise managed to wrench her wrist out of his grasp and after a moment, Matt continued leading her back toward the bar, but apparently Jake didn't get the message.

"I saw her *first,*" he said more insistently and shoved his way in front of them to block their path.

A muscle flexed in Matt's firm jaw. He certainly didn't look like the kind of guy *she* would want to tangle with. "Come on, Halloran. Take it easy. The lady wasn't interested, but I'm sure there are plenty more back at the bar who will be."

"Want this one," he said, reaching for her arm again. This time Matt stopped him with a sharp block from his own arm. In the tussle for her appendage, Matt shoved the wrangler away. Halloran stumbled back, but came up swinging with a powerful right hook that connected hard with Matt's eye.

Elise gasped and jerked away from both men in time to evade Matt's defensive punch in return.

And that was it. Halloran leaped on him, yelling and swinging.

"Fight!" somebody yelled inside the bar, resulting in a mad rush of people into the narrow hallway. The only thing patrons of The Hitching Post liked better than a good band was a rousing brawl.

Matt's buddies at his booth joined in to pull the wrangler off. As soon as he was clear, he grabbed Elise and pushed out toward the nearest booth and out of harm's way, but apparently the cowboy had friends at The Hitching Post, too, and soon it was a free-for-all that spilled from the restroom hallway into the main room of the bar.

Everybody seemed to be having a grand old time until Carl took matters into his own hands.

"Knock it off, you idiots," the bartender yelled out, working the pump action of an old Remington shotgun, just like he was out of some cheesy old Western like the kind her dad used to love to watch.

Another voice joined in. "What the hell is going on here? Who started this?"

About a dozen hands pointed toward Matt and Jake, roughly equally divided between the two, as Elise recognized Joe Morales, a Thunder Canyon sheriff's deputy, who didn't look happy to have his dinner interrupted when he was obviously off duty.

"Cates. Should have known you'd be involved," he grumbled, his brushy salt-and-pepper mustache quivering. "What the hell happened?"

Since he seemed to be focusing on the two of them, the rest of the crowd seemed happy to slip away from any scrutiny and return to their drinks and their food. Elise really wanted to join them all and started easing away, but Matt pinned her into place beside him with a glare, as if this was all *her* fault.

"Sumbitch stole my girl." A thin trail of blood spilled out of the corner of Jake Halloran's mouth and he wiped at it with a napkin.

The deputy frowned at Elise. "You his girl?"

She shook her head, grateful she was still sitting down in the booth when the room spun a little. "I just met him tonight."

"You're Elise Clifton, aren't you? Grant's sister?"

Wouldn't her brother just love to hear about this little escapade? She couldn't wait to try explaining to Grant why she had let herself get cornered in an empty hallway by a drunk cowboy. "Yes."

"Well, Ms. Clifton, the guy seems to think there was more to it than a little chatting at the bar."

"He's wrong," she said, then was appalled at the note of belligerence in her voice. Must be the margaritas. She normally was not a belligerent person. Just another reason she needed to swear off drinking for a long time.

"We were only talking, Deputy Morales," she went on in what she hoped was a much more cooperative tone of voice. "I met him maybe half an hour ago. We talked about walking outside for some fresh air while the band was taking a break. I came back here to get my coat and he just…kissed me."

She drew in a shaky breath, more mortified than she ever remembered feeling in her life. Even more embarrassed than the time she had been bucked off by her horse in the junior rodeo for Thunder Canyon Days when she was eleven and Matt had been the first one to her side.

"I tried to tell him I wasn't interested but he didn't listen," she said. "Then Matt came into the hallway and saw I was having a tough time convincing him to stop, so he stepped in to help me and Jake hit him."

"How much have you had to drink, Ms. Clifton?"

She looked down at the speckled Formica tabletop then back up, drawing a breath and hoping she sounded more coherent than she felt. "Not so much that I don't know how to be perfectly clear when I'm saying no to a man, sir."

"That what happened?" he asked Halloran. "Did she say no?"

"I heard her say no, Joe," Matt said. "Loud and clear."

"I don't believe I asked you," the deputy growled. Elise suddenly remembered he had a younger sister who had once carried a very public torch for Matt back in Matt's younger, wilder days when bar fights probably weren't an uncommon occurrence.

"Did the girl say no?" he asked Jake again.

"Well, yeah. But you know how women can be."

The deputy gave him a long, disgusted look, then turned back to Elise. "Do you want to press charges for assault?"

She gave him a horrified look. "No. Heavens no! It was just a misunderstanding." Yes, the man had been wrong to paw her, especially when she'd made it clear she didn't want him to. But she had been wrong to flirt with him back at the bar, to use him only so she could hide from Matt.

"What about you, Cates? You want to press charges?"

Matt shook his dark head. "I know how things can get out of hand in the heat of the moment."

"Fine. All of you get out of here, then, so I can go back to my wife and my steak. Can you make sure she makes it back to Clifton's Pride okay?" he asked Matt.

Matt gave her a look she couldn't decipher, then nodded.

The moment the deputy ushered Jake over to the other Lazy D cowboys who had come to his rescue, Elise rushed back to the hallway, grabbed her red peacoat off the rack and twisted her scarf around her neck. She had to escape. What a nightmare. As if she needed more gossip about her flying through town.

She heard someone call her name but she didn't stop, only pushed through the front door out into the cold night.

The streets of Thunder Canyon glittered with brightly colored Christmas lights. They blinked at her from storefronts and the few houses she could see from here. A light snow drifted down, the flakes plump and soft. Away from the front door, she lifted her face for a moment to feel their light, wet kisses on her face.

She found a strange sort of comfort at the realization that she'd been seeing the same holiday decorations in Thunder Canyon since she was a girl. Her entire life may have changed in the last few weeks, but some things remained constant.

"You're not thinking about driving in your condition, are you?"

She opened her eyes, somehow not very surprised to find Matt standing a few feet away, looking big and dark and dangerous in a shearling-lined ranch coat. His eye was beginning to swell and color up and he had a thin cut on his cheek she very much feared would leave a scar.

"Thinking about it," she admitted.

"Sorry, El, but I can't let you do that. You heard what the deputy said. I need to take you home."

"And how are you going to stop me?" she asked, with more of that unexpected belligerence.

He smiled suddenly and she blinked at the brilliance of it in the dark night. That must be why she was taken completely off guard when he reached for her purse. After a moment of fishing through the contents, he pulled her keys out, dangled them out for a moment, and then pocketed them neatly in his coat.

"I can give you a ride back to the ranch and find somebody later to take your car home. Face it, Elise, you're in no shape to drive."

She couldn't go back to Clifton's Pride yet. Just the thought of walking inside the ranch house in her condition made her queasy.

She didn't need to see that same wary look in everyone's eyes she'd been dealing with since before Thanksgiving, as if she were somebody who had been given some kind of terminal diagnosis or something. Her mother hugged her at the oddest moments and Grant and his wife, Stephanie, went out of their way to include her in conversations.

She especially didn't want to show up tipsy when Erin was there in all her perfection, the daughter they *should* have had.

"I don't want to go home yet," she whispered, grimly aware the words sounded even more pathetic spoken aloud.

"No?"

"Not yet. I'll only be in the way. My...my mother and Grant have...well...guests for dinner."

He gave her another of those long, considering looks and she could feel herself flush, certain he could guess what—or rather whom—she meant.

"Want to go back inside?"

She shook her head. "I don't think I need to see the inside of The Hitching Post for a while."

Or ever again.

"Fair enough. Do you want to go grab a bite to eat somewhere? I'm sure we can find somewhere still open."

"Not really."

He gave a half laugh. "Well, I'm running out of options. You'll freeze to death if you sit out here in the parking lot for another hour or two until your head clears."

"I know."

After another pause, he sighed. "My place is just a block or two away. If you want to, I can get cleaned up and fix you something to eat and we can hang there until you think the coast is clear back at Clifton's Pride."

She hated that he had to come to her rescue, just like when they were kids. She had been a clumsy kid and it seemed like every time she fell, he had been right there to help her back up, brush off the dirt, gather her books, whatever she needed.

From the time he had fought two schoolyard bullies bigger than he was—and won—he had been stepping in to protect her from the world.

She was twenty-six years old. Surely it was high time she found the gumption to fight her own battles. Still, the idea of somebody else taking care of her for a few minutes sounded heavenly.

"Don't you ever get tired of rescuing me?" she asked.

Instead of answering, he laughed and tucked a strand of hair behind her ear. His hand was warm in the cold December air and she wanted to lean into him, close her eyes and stay there forever.

"Come on. Let's get you out of the snow."

Chapter 3

Though Matt only lived a few blocks from The Hitching Post, Elise dozed off beside him in his pickup truck before he reached his house—a small, run-down cottage on Cedar Street he had purchased a few months back to rehab in his spare time away from his work at Cates Construction.

Before the first snow a few months earlier, he'd rushed to put new shingles on and managed a new coat of white paint and green shutters. From the outside, the place looked fresh and tidy.

Inside was an entirely different story.

He thought about driving around for a while to let her sleep off the alcohol in her system, but he had a feeling she probably needed food more than sleep. Back in the day when he used to enjoy the wild weekend here or there, that's what always helped him most.

He pulled into his driveway and put his truck in gear,

though he left his engine running to keep the heater blowing. He shifted his gaze to her and shook his head.

Elise Clifton.

She was still as sweet and pretty as she had always been, blonde and petite, with delicate features, a slim little nose and her cupid's bow of a mouth.

She always looked a year or two younger than the rest of their grade. Now she probably considered that a good thing, but when they were kids, he knew she had hated being mistaken for a younger kid.

Maybe that was why she always stirred up all his protective instincts. She was right, it seemed like he was always coming to her rescue. He hadn't minded. Not one damn bit. He only had brothers—a twin and two older ones—and didn't know much about dealing with girls back when he was a kid. But his father had taught them all that a guy was supposed to watch out for those who were smaller than him.

Elise certainly fit the bill—then, and now. She looked small and fragile with her blond hair fanned out on the pickup's upholstery and her bottom lip snagged between her teeth.

Elise had always seemed a little more in need of rescuing than others. Even before the terrible events when she was thirteen, something about her seemed to stir up all his protective impulses.

Her long lashes fluttered now as she blinked her eyes open. For a brief instant, she smiled at him, her eyes the soft, breathtaking blue of the Montana sky on an early summer morning. As he gazed at her, he felt as if he'd just taken a hit to the gut from a three-hundred-pound linebacker.

He drew in a breath, trying to shake off the unexpected sensation. This was Elise, he reminded himself.

Little Elise Clifton, whose junior-rodeo, barrel-racing belt buckle had nearly been bigger than she was.

Except she wasn't little. She hadn't been in a long, long time. Though still petite, he couldn't help but notice she was soft and curvy in all the right places.

"Feeling better?" he spoke mostly to distract himself.

Her brow furrowed a little, as if she were trying to figure that out herself. After a moment, she nodded a little shyly, a trace of color on her cheeks. "Actually, I think I am. At least there's only one of you."

"Until Marlon shows up," he joked about his identical twin, and was rewarded with her sweet-sounding laugh.

"I hope he's with Haley right now, tucking her in and bringing her tissues and chicken soup. She and I were supposed to have a girls' night out to see the band at The Hitching Post together tonight but she bailed on me at the last minute."

She sat up and stretched a little and he tried not to notice how her sweater beneath her unbuttoned coat hugged those soft curves. "Since I was already there and…well, didn't really want to go home yet, I decided to stay and listen to the band."

Ah. That explained why she'd been sitting by herself at the bar. He had spied her the moment he walked in and had been keeping an eye on the cowboy she'd been sitting beside. At first, he thought maybe they'd been on a date. The little spark of inappropriate jealousy had come out of nowhere, taking him completely by surprise.

When she walked down the hall toward the ladies' room, he had watched the cowboy follow her. When neither of them emerged after a moment, he'd gone looking for her. And just in time.

"Poor Haley," he said now. "Being sick bites anytime,

but especially at Christmas. Still, I'm sure Marlon loves the chance to baby her. He's crazy about her."

"He'd better be," she said darkly. He hid a smile at the belligerent tone he'd noticed her adopting earlier. He didn't know how much she'd had to drink. With her small frame, it probably wasn't much, but he definitely recognized the signs of somebody on the tipsy side.

"Let's get you inside and find you something to eat."

"I'm really not hungry."

"Humor me, okay?"

After a moment, she shrugged and reached for the passenger-side door handle. He climbed out of the truck and hurried around the front of the pickup. His work truck was high off the ground so he reached inside and grabbed her hand to help her to the ground.

Her fingers felt small and cool inside his and when her high-heeled boots hit the ground, she wobbled a little. He reached out to steady her and found he was strangely reluctant to release her.

He held her, gazing into those blue eyes far longer than he should have while the fat snowflakes drifted down to settle in her hair and cling to her cheeks.

He hadn't seen her much over the years since she and her mother moved away from Thunder Canyon. Last time was probably over the summer when she'd come for a visit and he had ended up pulling over to help her change a flat tire.

Every time he saw her, he was struck again how lovely she was.

He had missed her, he suddenly realized. More than he ever could have imagined.

She shivered suddenly and the delicate motion jolted him back to his senses. "Let's get you inside."

"Thanks," she murmured.

He gripped her arm so she didn't slip on the skiff of snow covering his sidewalk as he led the way up the porch. He twisted the key in the lock and was greeted by one well-mannered bark that made him smile.

As soon as he opened the door, a brown shape snuffled excitedly and headed toward them. Elise took a quick, instinctive step backward on the porch, wobbling a little again on her dressy boots.

He reached for her arm again, feeling the heat of her beneath the red wool coat she wore. "Sorry about that. I should have warned you. Tootsie, sit."

His chocolate Labrador immediately planted her haunches on the polished wood floor of the entry, her tail wagging like crazy.

Elise reached down to pet her head. "Tootsie?"

He winced. "When she was a puppy, she looked like a big, fat Tootsie Roll. My mom named her."

Tootsie waited patiently until he gave her the signal to come ahead, then she hurried to his side and nudged his leg for a little love.

"She's beautiful, Matt."

"The sweetest dog I've ever had, aren't you, baby?"

She snuffled in response and he obediently scratched her favorite spot, right behind her left ear.

He loved having a dog to keep him company. When the weather wasn't so cold, she rode with him to construction sites. After the cold weather set in, his favorite evenings were spent at home watching a basketball game with her curled up at his feet.

Used to be Marlon would join them but these days his twin had better ways to spend his time.

Matt supposed it was only natural that lately Tootsie's company didn't seem quite enough anymore, especially since it seemed like everybody he knew was pairing up.

"How long have you lived here?" Elise asked.

He shifted his attention from the dog to his house and winced again at its sorry shape. The place was a work in progress. He had stripped years' worth of ugly wallpaper layers, down to the lath and plaster. He'd finished mudding the walls a few weeks earlier but had been so busy rushing his crew to finish Connor McFarlane's grand lodge in time for Christmas, he hadn't had time to paint.

At least the kitchen and bathroom were relatively presentable. He had started with the kitchen, actually, installing hand-peeled cabinets, custom tile floors and gleaming new appliances.

He had also taken out the wall of a tiny bedroom to expand the bathroom into one big space and he was particularly satisfied with the triple heads in the tile shower and the deep soaking tub.

But he couldn't exactly entertain his unexpected guest in his bathroom. Maybe he should have spent a little more time working on the more public areas of the house.

"I've got lots of plans but I have to fit the work around the jobs I'm doing with my dad," he said.

She nodded. "That's right. I heard you were working for Cates Construction these days. Do you like it?"

He was never sure how to answer that question. Most of the time, he was only too aware of the subtext behind the question. *You really dropped out of law school to work construction? Couldn't hack it, huh?*

That hadn't been the truth at all. His grades had been fine after his first year of law school. Better than fine. Great, actually. He'd been in the top ten percent of his class and had fully intended going back for his second year—until he realized after he came home to Montana for the summer that he was much happier out at a work site with his dad, covered in the satisfying sweat of putting in a hard day's labor, than he'd ever been in a classroom.

"I do like it. There's always a new challenge and it's great to watch something go from blueprints to completion, like the McFarlane Lodge."

"Haley told me about that. It sounds huge."

"It is. More than 10,000 square feet. It's been a fun project but a little time consuming. That's why I only have bits and pieces of time to work on this place. This is the third house in town I've rehabbed on my own."

She cast her gaze around the room. "Um, it looks good."

He smiled at her obvious lie. "No, it doesn't. Everything's a mess out here. As soon as we wrap up the Mc-Farlane Lodge, I'll have more time for the finish work here. But come on back to the kitchen and see what I've done there. I'd love a woman's perspective."

Surprise flashed in her eyes. "Mine?"

"You see any other women around?"

"Not right this very moment," she muttered. "I'm sure that's not typical for you."

He shouldn't be irritated by her words but he was. Yeah, he'd been wild in his younger days. Not as wild as Marlon, maybe, but he'd had his moments. How long and hard did a man have to work to shake off a wild reputation?

"Come on back," he said again and led the way through the compact cottage to the kitchen.

When she saw the room, the shocked admiration on her features more than made up for the dig about his reputation.

She did a full three-sixty, taking in the slim jeweled pendant lights over the work island, the stainless-steel, professional stove, the long row of paned windows over the dining area.

"Wow! You really did all this by yourself?"

"You sound surprised. Should I be insulted by that?"

She made a face. "I guess I just never realized you were such a...what's the word? I can't think. Artisan, I guess."

"Nothing so grand as that," he protested. "I'm just a construction worker."

She slicked a hand over the marble countertop and he was suddenly entranced by the sight of her long, slim fingers sliding along his work.

He cleared his throat. "How does pasta sound? I've got some lemon tarragon sauce in the fridge I can heat up while I throw a pot of water on to boil."

"You cook, too? I guess with a kitchen like this, you must."

"Not much," he was forced to admit. "The kitchen's for whoever eventually buys the place. I've got a few specialties and know enough so I don't starve. That's about it. My mom sent over the pasta sauce. She thinks I live on fast food and TV dinners."

"I don't want you to go to any work."

"How much effort does it take to boil a pot of water on the stove and push a few buttons on the microwave? Have a seat. If you'd rather go in and watch something on TV, the family room isn't in too bad a shape, as long as you don't mind a few exposed wires."

"I'll stay here. Could I have a drink of water?"

"I can make coffee. That would clear your head faster."

"Water is okay for now."

He pulled a tumbler out of the cabinet by the sink and dispensed ice and cold filtered water from the refrigerator. When he handed it to her, she took a seat at one of the stools around the work island. Tootsie, always happy for someone new to love, settled beside her and Elise smiled a little and reached down to pet her before the dog curled up on the kitchen floor.

"Maybe you ought to put something on that black eye, don't you think?"

How had he managed to block out the throbbing from both his eye and his cheek where Halloran had gotten off a cheap shot? She was a powerful distraction, apparently. "Right. Let me get the fight washed off me first and then I'll fix you something to eat."

"Do you need help?"

He thought of those fingers, cool and light on his skin, and felt his body stir with interest. This was Elise, he reminded himself. Not some bar babe looking for a good time.

"I think I can handle it," he finally answered. He wasn't sure he trusted himself around her right now. "Hang tight. I'll be back in a minute."

It took him about ten to wash away the blood, most of it belonging to the idiot who had mauled her, and to change his shirt. When he returned to the kitchen, some of the tension had eased from her features. She was leafing through a design book he'd left on the kitchen desk and she looked sweet and relaxed and comfortable.

As if she belonged there.

She looked up and he watched her gaze slide to the bandage he'd applied just under his colorful eye.

"Does it hurt?"

"I've had worse, believe me."

That didn't seem to ease her concern. "You could have been really hurt. He might have damaged your vision."

"He didn't. I'm fine."

She closed the book, her fine-boned features tight and

unhappy. "I'm really sorry about…everything. I feel so stupid."

"Why? You didn't do anything wrong except maybe pass the time of day with a cowboy who'd had a few too many."

"I can't really blame him for getting the wrong idea," she admitted. "I might have…acted more interested in him than I really was. If you want the truth, I was using him to hide from you."

He raised his eyebrows. "Why would you need to hide from me?"

She suddenly looked as if she wished she'd never said anything. "I was embarrassed about being there by myself. It's not something I usually do."

"I'm glad you were there," he said as he headed to the refrigerator for the sauce. "Except for your little episode with the jerk, it's great to see you. So are you back in Thunder Canyon to stay?"

She sighed and sounded so forlorn that Tootsie must have sensed it. She nuzzled her leg. "I don't know. Everything's in…limbo. My mother wanted to come home for the holidays and begged me to come with her so I took a temporary leave from my job until the new year. After that, I don't know what I'll do."

He really hoped she would decide to stay. He liked having her around. He started to say so but she spoke before he could get the words out.

"I guess you heard about my…about what happened twenty-six years ago."

"Who in town hasn't?"

Her sigh this time sounded even more forlorn and he cursed himself for his tactless response.

"Sorry. Was that the wrong thing to say?"

"I really hate having everyone gossiping about me. I

hated it after my dad's murder and I hate it more now. Everything is such a mess."

He couldn't begin to imagine what she must be going through. "How are you holding up?"

"Not too great," she confessed softly.

He set down the box of pasta he'd just pulled from the cupboard and crossed to give her a reassuring squeeze on the shoulder.

Instead of comforting her, as he'd intended, his gesture made her big blue eyes brim with tears.

"My mom wants the family together for Christmas. Everyone, including Erin."

"And that's a problem?"

She sighed. "I feel like I don't even belong at Clifton's Pride anymore."

He stared. "You most certainly *do* belong at Clifton's Pride! It's your home and the Cliftons are your family. Why would you feel otherwise, even for a moment?"

"I'm not a Clifton. Not really. If not for a quirk of fate and a moment's mistake by a nurse, I never would have known any one of them. I'm not a Clifton. But I'm not really a Castro, either. I barely know those people. I don't know who I am."

A tear brimming in her eyes dripped over and slid down the side of her nose and his heart broke.

He grabbed a tissue box and couldn't resist the compulsion to pull her into his arms. She felt small and feminine and he wanted to hold tight and take on all her demons for her.

"You're the same person you've always been. You're Elise Clifton, daughter of John and Helen and sister to Grant. Blood or not, that's who you are."

"I wish it were that easy."

"Why isn't it? They're your family."

She frowned. "They're not my parents! I don't belong in Thunder Canyon at all!"

A dozen arguments swarmed through his head—he hadn't been in law school without reason. But then, she wasn't a hostile witness on the stand, either.

"So blood and genetics is everything? According to your reasoning, anybody who's been adopted into a family should always feel like an outsider."

"I wasn't adopted!" she exclaimed. "I was switched for their real daughter. For the child Helen and John should have had. They didn't choose to be stuck with me. My whole life is a mistake! *I'm* a mistake."

"Do you really think that's what your mother and Grant think?"

"I don't know. They're so happy about Erin," she whispered.

Her tears started flowing in earnest now and she added a few sobs in there to really twist the knife.

Nice, Cates, he thought. *Take a vulnerable woman who has already had a rough night and reduce her to tears.* He had definitely lost his touch.

"Hey. Easy now. Come on." He pulled her back into his arms.

"I'm sorry. I'm so sorry." She sniffled.

"For what? Being human? Anybody would be upset."

"Oh, I'm making a big mess of your shirt and you just changed it for a clean one," she wailed.

He tightened his arms. "No worries. I've got a good washing machine."

His words only seemed to set her off again and Matt held her, hating this helpless feeling. With no sisters and a mother who rarely lost her cool in front of her boys, his experience with crying women was extremely limited.

This was a novel experience, trying to offer comfort instead of instinctively seeking any handy escape route.

She clutched his waist as if he was the only thing keeping her from floating away on her wild emotions, her cheek pressed against his chest. Her hair smelled like fresh raspberries just plucked from his mama's garden behind their house and he inhaled, doing his best to ignore how soft and curvy she felt in his arms and feeling powerless to do anything but hold her.

He moved into his half-finished family room where he could sit down on the sofa, pulling her with him.

After a few moments, her intense sobs quieted. She took a few slow, hitching breaths and he could feel the shudders against him subside.

With vast relief, he felt her regain control until some time later when she eased slightly away from him, though she didn't seem any more eager to leave the shelter of his arms than he was to let her go.

"This is the single most embarrassing night of my life," she finally said, her cheeks flaring with color. "Apparently, I'm a maudlin drunk. Who knew?"

He laughed a little roughly, still unnerved by the intensity of his attraction to her, which somehow far outweighed all those protective impulses.

Elise always had the ability to make him laugh, he remembered. She had a funny, quirky sense of humor and he remembered back in school feeling privileged to be among the few she revealed it to.

"I haven't cried once since…well, since Erin told us all what she suspected."

"Then you are probably long overdue, aren't you?"

She said nothing for a long moment and then she smiled at him and he felt like he was seeing his first taste of springtime after weeks of fog and gloom.

Even with her reddened eyes and tear-stained cheeks, she was beautiful. He gazed at her upturned face a long moment, then with a strange sense of destiny or fate or inevitability—he wasn't sure—he leaned down and pressed his mouth to that smile.

Chapter 4

Elise froze at the first warm touch of his mouth. He tasted delicious, like fresh-baked cinnamon cookies, and his arms around her seemed the safest place in the universe.

She couldn't quite believe this was happening and wondered for a moment if she was hallucinating. No, she hadn't had quite *that* much to drink. She wasn't sure about a lot of things but she knew that, at least.

Matt Cates, who had never looked twice at her all these years, really was kissing her, holding her, like he couldn't get enough.

Elise would have laughed at the sheer, unexpected wonder of it if she wasn't so preoccupied with the sexy things his mouth was doing to hers.

This all seemed so surreal. She wasn't exactly a femme fatale. Most guys tended to think of her like the girl next door, somebody sweet and fairly innocent. Blame it on her blond hair or the blue eyes or her small stature. She didn't know exactly what, she only knew that she wasn't the kind of girl men considered for a quick fling.

Now, twice in one night in the space of only an hour or so, she found herself in a man's arms. Not that the two things were in any way comparable. Kissing Matt Cates was a whole different experience than trying to fight off Jake Halloran in the hallway outside the ladies' room at The Hitching Post.

Then, she had been doing everything she could to avoid the man and wriggle away from him. With Matt, she had absolutely no desire to escape. She wanted to stay right here forever, where she was warm and safe.

She should be curling up behind the sofa with a blanket over her head. Even as he kissed her, she couldn't shake her lingering embarrassment when she remembered her emotional breakdown.

Definitely must have been the margaritas. Why else would she spill everything to Matt when she hadn't talked to another soul about her emotional turmoil over learning of the hospital mistake? She hadn't told her mother or Grant or even Stephanie, Grant's wife, who along with Haley Anderson had been her closest friend when they were kids.

Matt only had to show her a little sympathy in those brown eyes and she started blubbering all over him.

Her stomach muscles quivered as he shifted his mouth over hers. What was the matter with her? After all these years of wondering what it might be like to kiss him, she finally had her chance and she was wasting the moment being embarrassed about the events leading up to this. Was she completely insane?

She leaned into that hard, solid chest and opened her mouth for his kiss. He made a sexy little sound in his throat that rippled down her spine as if he'd run his thumb from the base of her neck to her tailbone.

He wrapped his arms more tightly around her and slid his tongue inside her mouth and she forgot everything else but Matt.

She slid her hands in his hair. Funny, she might have expected his thick dark hair to be short, coarse, but it felt silky and decadent against her skin.

Time seemed to shift and slide and she had no idea how long they stayed there on his sofa, wrapped together. She only knew she didn't want him to stop. Matt suddenly felt like the only solid, secure thing she had to hang on to since Erin Castro shook the foundations of her world.

His hand burned through the cotton of her sweater and she ached for closer contact. As if in answer to some unspoken request, his hand slid beneath her sweater and glided to the small of her back. She shivered at the heat of him and murmured his name.

Well, that was a mistake, she thought as he froze. Next time she would keep her lovesick murmurings to herself.

He wrenched his mouth away and she felt even more like an idiot. His breathing was ragged and he looked like he'd just been kicked off a prize bull.

He stared at her for a long moment, then raked a hand through his hair. He didn't move, though, and she was still sprawled against him.

"I'm sorry, Elise. That was the last thing you needed, another stupid cowboy pawing you."

"Was it?" she murmured.

"Yes! You're upset and vulnerable and I completely took advantage of that."

"No, you didn't." She was exhausted suddenly, her muscles loose and fluid, as if his kiss had been the only thing keeping her upright. "I'm glad you kissed me.

You're a great kisser. All the girls used to say so. I'm glad I finally had the chance to find out. You really were. Great, I mean."

He gave her a skeptical look but she thought she saw a hint of color over his cheekbones. She was too tired to know for sure, though. She just wanted to close her eyes and ease into sleep like she was sliding into sun-warmed water.

"I never did rustle up something for you to eat."

She opened one eye. "I'm not hungry. Do you mind if we stay here like this for a minute?"

He looked startled for only a moment, then shook his head. "What man with a brain in his head would mind having a chance to hold a pretty girl for a while longer?"

She smiled, though the last remaining rational part of her brain was sending out a whole host of warning signals. Matthew Cates was exactly the sort of man who could make a woman completely lose her head.

She was definitely going to have to take care around him.

The thought slid through her mind but she pushed it away. She wouldn't worry about a little detail like that. Not right now. For now, she only wanted to stay right here, savoring the warmth of his arms around her and the steady rhythm of his breathing, and indulging in this rare, precious moment of peace.

It was her last thought for some time.

This should have been the perfect way to spend a December Friday night. The lights on his Christmas tree glistened brightly and through the window, he could see those plump snowflakes still drifting down.

When Elise had first fallen asleep, he had taken a chance and reached with his free hand for the remote.

Somehow he had managed to turn the TV on low without waking her and had turned to one of the digital music stations offered by his satellite provider, this one playing soft, jazzy holiday music.

Matt shifted on the sofa. His legs tingled and he was pretty sure he'd lost all feeling in one arm.

He didn't mind any of that. What worried him was this unaccustomed tenderness coiling through him as he held the slight woman in his arms.

He had always cared about Elise and considered her a friend. Maybe he'd been more protective of her than most of his friends over the years, in part because she'd been small for her age and had appeared delicate, even if she really wasn't, and in part, of course, because of the terrible event in her family when she was still a girl—her father's brutal murder.

A desire to watch out for her was one thing. This desire for *her*—to taste her and touch her and explore every inch of that delectable skin—stunned him to the core.

He had never been so aroused by a simple kiss. If he hadn't suddenly remembered that she'd had a little too much to drink, he wasn't sure just how far he might have let their kiss progress.

Just remembering her sweet response—those breathy sighs, the trembling of her hands in his hair—sent a shaft of heat through him now.

He tightened his arms around her. What a hell of a mess. He didn't want to hurt a sweet girl like Elise, but his track record at relationships wasn't the greatest. He usually leaned toward women who preferred to keep things casual and that was exactly what he told himself he wanted. Fun, easy, no strings.

He thought briefly of Christine. She was the perfect example. The last thing she wanted from him was a serious commitment. The only reason they started seeing each other in the first place was because neither of them was romantically interested in the other. She wanted to avoid a persistent ex-boyfriend and he wanted to escape his mother's transparent matchmaking attempts.

He had enjoyed taking Christine around town for the last couple of months and they had a good time together, but the few experimental kisses they'd shared just to see if things might progress in some sort of natural order had left both of them shaking their heads and wondering why they just didn't spark the magic in each other.

Christine was far more his usual type than Elise. His few long-term girlfriends had each been dark-haired and tall like her, funny and social.

Elise couldn't be more different from what he had always considered his usual taste, yet he'd never known a kiss as explosive and stirring as theirs, or this soft, easy tenderness flowing through him, just from holding a woman in his arms.

He shifted on the sofa and finally drew his legs up along the length of it, sliding as far as he could to the side to make room for both of them. She murmured something in her sleep then nestled against him, her arm around his waist.

Her straight blond hair reflected the Christmas lights and he watched them for a moment, then closed his eyes. He would let her sleep for a little while until the effects of the alcohol she'd consumed were out of her system and then he would take her back to Clifton's Pride.

He was only thinking of her, he told himself. Not about how terrifyingly perfect she felt in his arms.

So much for good intentions.

When Matt awoke, Elise was still asleep snugged up

against him, her arm across his chest, her hair brushing his chin and one of her legs entwined with his.

As he slid back to consciousness, he became aware of her first, small and soft against him. Not a bad way to wake up, he thought, with the sweet scent of raspberries surrounding him and a beautiful woman in his arms—and then he heard a little well-mannered whine and noticed Tootsie stretched out in front of the door, waiting to go out, something she usually only did first thing in the morning.

He shifted his gaze to the window. That couldn't be right, could it? It looked as if the first pink rays of dawn were sneaking through the slats of his window blind. Had they really slept here all night?

He was going to have a crick in his neck all day from sleeping like this and he could only hope he would regain feeling in his arm one day. Working construction might be difficult if he didn't have the use of his right arm.

Tootsie whined again and Elise made a soft little sound in her sleep and he decided all his discomforts didn't matter—a small price to pay for the pleasure of holding her.

As he watched, her eyelashes fluttered against her skin and a moment later her eyes opened. She gazed at him for a long moment and her brow furrowed.

"Matt? What are you…"

The words were barely out before she groaned. "Ow," she muttered and squeezed her temples.

He suddenly remembered her excess the night before and winced in sympathy.

"Headache?"

She sat up and opened one eye to glare balefully at him. Her hair stuck up a bit on one side and her cheek was creased with a funny little pattern from the material of his sweater but he still thought she was just about the prettiest thing he'd ever seen.

"Headache," she groaned. "That's one word for it. If you like understatements. I don't suppose you've got coffee?"

"Sorry. I've been a little preoccupied all night."

She looked at him and then at the couch and color rose up her cheeks in a rosy tide. "I fell asleep."

"We both did. I hadn't planned a sleepover. Sorry about that."

She looked at the pale light outside the window with something akin to panic. "What time is it?"

He glanced at the clock above the gas fireplace. "Early. Looks like it's not quite six. I need to put the dog out."

"Oh. Of course."

He winced a little as he stood on numb legs but still managed to make it to the door without falling over. A few more inches had fallen in the night, but not enough to be more than an annoyance. Tootsie bounded out when he opened the door and he turned back to find Elise looking distressed.

"I've been gone all night. Mom must be frantic. And Grant is going to kill me."

He had a feeling if Grant had *anyone* on his hit list, Matt's name would be right there at the top after last night.

"You're twenty-six years old, Elise. Surely you've been out all night before."

"Of course I have." She spoke the words with more than a trace of defiance. "But not when I'm staying with my mother and my brother. Or at least not without letting them know I'll be late. Maybe they'll just think I stayed over at Haley's."

He sighed. "When I let Tootsie back in, I'll run a comb

through my hair and then I'll take you back to Clifton's Pride. We'll just explain what happened. I took you home to feed you after we left The Hitching Post and we both fell asleep."

"I'm sure that will go over just great."

"It's the truth. Or most of it, anyway."

She pressed her fingers at her temples again. "It's the 'or most of it' I think we might have a problem explaining."

"I wouldn't worry about it, El. Your brother knows me well enough to know I'm not the kind of guy to take advantage of a vulnerable woman."

No matter how much he might have wanted to. Okay, as much as he *still* wanted to.

Much to her relief, Matt was right. Grant hadn't kicked up any kind of fuss about her rolling in just after sunrise from a night on the town.

Her brother had just been leaving the house when they pulled up. He didn't say so but Elise suspected he'd been on his way to look for her since he generally didn't go to work at the resort this early in the morning.

She had feared some sort of scene. Grant could have a temper and was the only male she knew more overprotective than Matt. But Grant—the closest thing she had to a father figure since John Clifton's murder a dozen years ago—had given Matt one long, searching look, then apparently accepted the story.

"I really appreciate you keeping her safe," Grant said, clapping Matt on the shoulder. "Somebody without your scruples might have taken advantage of the situation."

Elise remembered that searing kiss and her intense reaction to it. She could feel a blasted blush creep up her cheeks and had to hope Grant didn't notice.

"Glad I could be there. We left her car at The Hitching Post. Need me to shuttle it home for you?"

"No. I can have somebody from the resort drive it out here later this morning."

Elise felt supremely stupid and about ten years old again. She was grateful when Matt said goodbye quickly and left, saying he needed to get to the McFarlane job site early that morning.

After the door closed behind him, she was faced with her headache and Grant, who watched her with a concerned frown.

"I don't get it. After Haley pulled out of your plans, why didn't you just come home and have dinner with us?" he asked. "Erin was sorry she missed you."

She didn't want to sound whiny or self-pitying, especially not when Grant and Helen were so happy about finding Erin. "I was already at The Hitching Post and you all weren't expecting me home so I just decided to stay and enjoy the band. In retrospect, maybe not the smartest decision I ever made, but it worked out okay in the end."

"You were lucky," Grant growled.

She sighed. "I know."

"I don't even want to think about what might have happened to you if Cates hadn't been there," Grant growled.

"If Cates hadn't been where?"

Her mother walked into the kitchen wearing her favorite green bathrobe and Elise mentally groaned. So much for her furtive hope that she might sneak away from Grant's lecture and climb back to bed to nurse her blasted headache before her mother came downstairs. She was in for it now.

"Elise had a little run-in with a drunk cowboy last night down at The Hitching Post. Matt Cates came to her rescue. That's why she's just rolling in at 6:00 a.m."

"What a nice boy. Those Cates brothers are always so thoughtful." Helen smiled. "They must take after their father. He's always been the nicest man."

Her mother tended only to see the good in people. Either that or she hadn't paid any attention to the Cates twins' antics over the years. Matt and his brother had been wild hell-raisers until recently.

They hadn't completely worked all the wildness out of their systems. She remembered the fierce way Matt had taken on Jake Halloran to protect her and then the stormy, wondrous heat of his kiss.

"Tell me again how you ended up spending the night at Cates's place instead of coming back here after you left The Hitching Post?" Grant asked pointedly, which she found the height of hypocrisy coming from a man who'd enjoyed a healthy reputation as a ladies' man before his surprise marriage to Stephanie three years earlier.

To her surprise and relief, her mother stepped. "I think that's really Elise's business, don't you?" Helen said with a reassuring pat to Grant's arm.

"I fell asleep on his couch. Relax, Grant. You can put your mind at ease. Matt was a perfect gentleman," she answered. Mostly.

"I would think a perfect gentleman would have made sure you spent the night safe and sound in your own bed."

"I'm here now. Look, don't blame Matt for any of this." Her head hurt and she was embarrassed and wanted nothing more than to crawl into bed and sleep the rest of the morning away but she had to set the record straight first.

"It's all completely my fault. The truth is, I'm embarrassed to admit I wasn't paying attention to my drink quota and I had a little too much on an empty stomach. You know I don't have much tolerance for alcohol."

Last night had truly been full of anomalies and she

would be wise to remember that. She rarely drank more than a glass of wine with dinner and the kisses she'd shared with Matt had been a fluke, something that wouldn't happen again.

"Where does the drunk cowboy come in?" her mother asked.

Elise sighed. Maybe they ought to go wake up Steph so she didn't have to go through the story again. "I struck up a conversation at the bar with a Lazy D ranch hand. He mistook our conversation for more of a flirtation than I intended and he…didn't take my attempt at brushing him off with very good grace. He tried to…to kiss me and didn't seem to believe my no really meant no."

"You could have been in serious trouble."

"I know. Believe me, I know." She shivered, remembering again that moment of fear when she had felt overpowered and helpless. "But Matt saw I was having trouble and he stepped in before anything could happen. The two of them got into it a little bit, mostly shoving, pushing, that sort of thing. When it was over, Matt took me back to his place so I could help him clean up and to grab a bite to eat. I'm afraid we both fell asleep. And here we are."

She was leaving out a few details, like how she had cried all over him and then kissed him until she couldn't think straight.

Some things were no one else's business but hers and Matt's.

"I guess I owe the man for looking out for you," Grant said.

"You don't owe him anything. I do."

"Well, you're home now and that's the important thing." Helen pulled her into a hug and Elise held on, closing her eyes and inhaling the clean, wholesome scent of lilacs and Tide detergent that clung to her mother.

Tears stung her eyes and not just from the headache pulsing through her veins. This was the scent of her childhood, when she had felt warm and safe and beloved.

Before she knew anything about wicked people who could kill men because of greed, or innocent hospital mistakes that would come back years later to destroy everything she thought she knew.

"I wish you had stayed," Helen said. "We had a perfectly lovely evening with Erin. Corey Traub came with her. They make such a wonderful couple."

Elise forced a smile and eased away from her mother. "They seem great together."

"She was sorry to miss you, too. I think she's looking forward to having a sister after growing up only with brothers."

But they weren't sisters. They weren't related at all except for the weird, sadistic twist of fate that had brought them all together.

Elise decided she must be a terrible person. Erin obviously wanted to be friends and Elise couldn't seem to put any effort forward in that direction.

She should have stayed home and tried last night, she thought again. A few hours of being polite seemed a small enough price compared to her humiliation at causing a scene at The Hitching Post and, worse, spilling her angst all over Matt Cates and then sharing a kiss with him.

Her mind replayed those stunning moments at his house—his mouth warm and sexy against hers, the strength of his arms around her, the safety and security she felt near him. The man could definitely kiss. She'd always suspected it and now she knew without a doubt all the whisperings she'd heard around town were based on fact.

For a few moments there, she hadn't been able to think

about anything but his touch. Not hospital mistakes or drunk cowboys or even her own name—Elise Clifton or Elise Castro or whoever the heck she was this week.

Chapter 5

"Nice bit of color you've got there, son. Thought I taught you how to duck a little better than that."

Matt made at face at his father, who leaned on the doorjamb of the bedroom at the McFarlane Lodge where they were putting up the last bit of finish trim around the windows and doors.

A guy got in one lousy fight and the whole town wanted to talk about it. He supposed it didn't help when he sported the worst shiner he'd had since he was fourteen, when he and Marlon had gotten a little too physical over a cute cheerleader from Bozeman.

He'd never realized he had a long and painful history of fighting over women.

"Heard you got into it with a drunk cowboy over a girl down at The Hitching Post," piped in Bud Larsen, one of their workers, as he carried in another load of trim from the truck.

Matt used the fine-planed black walnut he was measuring as an excuse to avoid the gaze of either Bud or his father.

"Something like that," he answered evasively.

"Was Christine involved?" Frank asked.

He supposed he couldn't blame his father for jumping to that conclusion. His parents thought he and Christine Mayhew were serious since they had been "dating" steadily for the last few months.

"She wasn't even there, Dad. She had a baby shower last night so I went to hang out with some of the guys."

Frank set the level on the trim to double and triple check, as he always did. "She know you got into a fight over another girl?"

His parents liked Christine. Now that both of his older brothers were married and Marlon was engaged to Haley Anderson, Matt often found himself the object of much teasing and speculation from his family about when he planned to take his turn on that particular merry-go-round.

He had tried to be evasive to his family about his and Christine's relationship but it was becoming more difficult without blatant prevarication, something he tried not to do to his parents very often since they always seemed to catch him at it anyway.

"I don't know if Christine has heard or not. I haven't had a chance to talk to her, but you know how the grapevine works around here."

"Women like to hear those sorts of things straight from the horse, if you get me," Bud offered with a wink.

"I'll keep that in mind," Matt said. He decided he didn't need to mention that he wasn't about to take relationship advice from a man who had been married four times, two of them to sisters.

"Anyway, it was just a misunderstanding."

"So if the girl you tussled over down at the bar wasn't Christine, who the heck was it?" Frank asked.

For some reason, Matt found himself strangely reluctant to tell his father the truth. He knew this was just what Elise had feared, that she would find herself the subject of gossip and speculation.

But he also knew that look in his father's eyes. Frank wouldn't stop until he'd extracted every ounce of available information out of Matt. Sometimes he wondered if his father had undergone interrogation training somewhere in his distant past or if he was just particularly gifted at squeezing information out of his reticent sons.

He should probably just blurt it out, rather than hem and haw and obfuscate, when Frank would just find out sooner or later.

He sighed. "Grant Clifton's sister."

"Elise?" His father registered a moment of surprise then he shook his head. "That poor little thing. She's had a rough time of it this last month, hasn't she?"

"She has."

"If some no-account cowboy was messing with her, you did the right thing, son. She all right?"

He thought of her sobbing out her confusion and pain in his arms and then the stunning, unforgettable kiss that never should have happened. "I think so."

"She's tough, our little Elise."

"Not so little anymore, Dad. We're the same age."

His father again looked surprised. "I guess you are at that. I always forget you went to school with her. Well, I'm glad you were there to watch out for her. Christine will probably understand."

"If she don't and throws you out on your butt, you mind if I have a go?" Bud asked eagerly. "That is one fine-looking woman."

The man was twenty years older than Christine. Hell, he had kids who were older than she was. Matt was trying to come up with a diplomatic response but his father didn't bother.

"Shut up, Bud, and get back to work now before I throw *you* out on your butt," Frank growled.

Bud grumbled but headed back out for another load.

When the other man left, Frank turned to him, his brown eyes uncharacteristically serious. "As much as I hate to say it, I think Bud's probably right about this, anyway. You might want to get out in front of the story. Call Christine and explain your side of the story before she hears a rumor and gets the wrong idea. Be careful there, son. She's a nice girl. You don't want to hurt her."

An image of Elise in his arms flashed through his mind again, a picture he hadn't been able to shake all morning. He didn't worry about hurting Christine. They were only friends. Elise was an entirely different story. "Yeah. I know."

His phone rang just a few moments after his father left to direct the other workers, leaving Matt alone with the work and his thoughts.

Matt pulled it from the holder on his belt and glanced at the caller ID.

"Hey, Christine," he said. "I was just talking about you."

"You're a busy guy, Matt. Rumor has it you pulled the white-knight act last night at The Hitching Post."

How the heck did rumors manage to fly so fast and furiously in a small town? "A guy might think nothing exciting ever happens in Thunder Canyon," he complained. "Doesn't anybody in town have something more interesting to talk about?"

She gave that rich, husky laugh he had always enjoyed.

"I guess tongues all over town are going to wag when one of the supposedly reformed hell-raising Cates boys comes out of retirement."

"Yeah, yeah."

She laughed again. "That's why I'm calling, actually. I'm just wondering if you want to cancel our plans for tonight."

"Why would I do that?"

"I just figured, now that you've apparently taken on the cause of some other damsel in distress, you might be too busy."

Elise might have returned his kiss the night before with a sweet passion, but for all he knew, that might have only been the margaritas talking. "I'm never too busy for you, Chris. As far as I'm concerned, we're still on."

"And the bar fight I'm hearing about? From what I understand, you whomped on a Lazy D cowboy."

"All a misunderstanding." He repeated what he'd told his father.

"And the girl?"

"Elise is just an old friend," he lied. "I'm definitely looking forward to dinner."

"So am I. I owe you. Taking you to The Gallatin Room is the least I can do to repay you for helping me out these last few months."

"How many times will I have to remind you I was happy to be able to help, before you start to believe me?"

"A few more, maybe."

He smiled. "It's been fun, Christine. And I think your devious plot worked. You haven't been bothered by Clay for a while, have you?"

"Not much. The stray email here and there and message on voice mail but I can always delete those."

"So does seven tomorrow still work?" he asked.

"Perfectly. Try not to get into any more barfights between now and then. I might have a tough time explaining why my supposed boyfriend is ripping it up down at The Hitching Post over another woman."

"Maybe because you won't give it up," he teased.

She laughed hard. "Ewww. Don't even go there, Matt. Don't get me wrong, you're gorgeous and all, but it's like kissing a brother."

He couldn't fault her for that since he'd had a very similar reaction.

"Sorry, I've got to run," she said a few moments later. "This place is crazy with Christmas shoppers today. I'll see you tonight, okay?"

After he hung up, he paused for a moment, gazing out the window at the spectacular view of the mountains from the McFarlane Lodge. Some part of him really wished he could stir up something more than friendship with Christine. She was perfect for him in many ways. Fun and exuberant and undeniably beautiful.

A few months ago, he never would have believed it, but he was beginning to feel ready to start thinking about the next phase of his life. Maybe it was Marlon's relationship with Haley that had set him on the road, but his life had begun to seem empty.

He loved the job. He loved the challenge of rehabbing houses on the side. He enjoyed hanging with the guys and going fly-fishing and watching basketball games. But something had been missing for a while.

His thoughts filled with Elise again—the softness of her mouth, the startling hunger racing through him, that incredible wash of tenderness as he held her while she slept.

He had a fierce desire to see where things might take them but it was tempered by the awareness that this was abysmal timing for her. She was dealing with a lot right now, stresses he couldn't begin to imagine. Maybe what she needed most from him was a little patience, something that had never been one of his strengths.

He sighed. He wasn't going to get this project finished in time for Connor McFarlane's grand lodge opening if he didn't focus.

He had to stop thinking about Elise. A pleasant evening with Christine would be the perfect diversion.

He hoped.

"We'll have your table ready in just a moment, Mr. Clifton."

"No problem, Sara. We don't mind waiting."

Elise felt a pang of sympathy for the hostess at The Gallatin Room at the Thunder Canyon Resort, who looked on the verge of a full-fledged panic attack that her boss and his family had to wait even thirty seconds.

Grant had been running the ski resort—now a four-season destination—for several years. He seemed to be highly respected by his employees, with perhaps a healthy amount of fear added to the mix.

She had a hard time reconciling his professional persona with her teasing, sometimes annoying older brother.

After her disaster of an outing the night before at The Hitching Post and the gossip she knew likely had galloped through town, her first instinct was to stay at the ranch where she was safe, to avoid showing her face around town. But her usually sweet mother could be stubborn about certain things.

"We've hardly had a moment with Grant and Stephanie since...well, since everything happened with Erin and since you and I came back to Thunder Canyon," Helen had said that afternoon. "With Grant's busy schedule from now until New Year's, who knows when we'll have time for a family dinner again."

Elise hadn't known how to wiggle out of it. As the hostess finally led them through the always-crowded restaurant toward the best table overlooking the snow-covered mountains, she wished she'd tried a little harder.

Many of the guests were tourists in town for holiday skiing but she recognized several locals, who all seemed to follow the Cliftons' progress through the restaurant with avid, hungry gazes.

"I hate this," she muttered under her breath.

She really hadn't meant to say the words aloud but she must have. Stephanie, Grant's wife, tucked her arm through Elise's. "Hate what, honey?"

"Everybody's staring and whispering at us," she finally said. "I feel like some kind of circus freak."

Stephanie's blue eyes warmed with compassion and she smiled, squeezing Elise's arm. "And here I thought they were staring at me, in all my voluptuous glory."

Elise had to laugh. Steph was seven months pregnant, due in February, but carried the baby well on her slim, athletic frame.

"You're right." Elise smiled back, grateful at Steph for yanking her out of her pity party. "What else would they be looking at but how utterly, gorgeously pregnant you are? How narcissistic of me to automatically assume I'm always the center of attention."

"Wait until you're either a bride or pregnant for that," Steph said.

By then they had reached their table and Grant pulled out the chairs for all three of the women. "Aren't I the luckiest guy here, to have the three most beautiful women in town at my table?"

"Suck-up," Elise muttered, earning a grin from her

older brother. She couldn't resist returning his smile. Elise reached for her water glass when the hostess filled it, then nearly dumped the whole thing over when she spotted the couple sitting only three tables away from them.

Matt Cates seemed to be enjoying a very cozy dinner for two with a slender, lovely brunette. The woman was laughing at something he said and leaning into him, her body language clearly telegraphing an easy, comfortable familiarity. While they spoke, the woman kept one hand on his arm as if she didn't want to let him go—the same arm that the night before had pulled Elise to him and held her close while she slept.

She told herself to look away. His choice in dinner companions was absolutely none of her business, and she would do well to remember that. She was not about to spend the evening gawking at him.

She had just started to heed her own advice and shift her attention back to her family when he suddenly happened to look straight at her. Rats. Caught. Just like in junior high when she used to moon over him in Mrs. McLarty's algebra class.

Something flashed in his eyes as he smiled at her. She jerked her gaze away, fumbling with her flatware and knocking her salad fork into her lap.

"Everything okay?" Stephanie asked in an undertone.

"Sure. Fine. Just great. Why wouldn't it be?"

She let out a breath. Naturally, she had a clear view of the two of them from her vantage point. If she didn't suspect it would spark a host of questions she wasn't in the mood to answer, Elise would have asked her mother to switch places so she didn't have to sit and watch him. Instead, she would just have to force herself not to stare.

There were plenty of other restaurants in town. Why

did they both have to choose tonight to come to this particular one? she wondered. His presence—complete with that spectacular black eye—was certain to generate plenty more conversation among anyone who might have heard even a whisper of a rumor about the altercation the night before.

Grant spied him at the same moment and lifted a hand. Matt returned the greeting before turning back to his companion.

"His shiner's looking even prettier," Grant said just as their waiter approached with an obsequious smile.

Grant cut him off at the pass before he could even go into his spiel welcoming them to The Gallatin Room.

"Listen, Marcos. I need you to do me a favor."

"Of course, Mr. Clifton. Anything."

"Send a bottle of our best Cabernet Sauvignon to table seventeen, with my compliments," he answered.

Curiosity flashed briefly in the man's eyes but he quickly concealed it and nodded. "Of course, sir. Right away, sir."

He hurried away and Elise rolled her eyes at her brother with an exasperated sigh. "Was that really necessary?"

Grant smiled. "He protected my baby sister from a sticky situation and has the battle scars to prove it. I'd say it is."

Would Grant be so amused by the whole thing if he knew about the heated kiss she and Matt had shared?

Elise snapped her napkin out onto her lap, trying not to remember the heat of his mouth and the strength of his arms and the liquid pool of desire seeping through her.

A moment later, the sommelier delivered a bottle to Matt's table. He acknowledged Grant's gift with a wry smile to her brother, which Elise pretended not to notice.

The next hour was a definite challenge. Through each course, she had to work hard not to gawk at Matt and his companion. She made a pointed effort to enjoy the delicious dinner, though each bite seemed a chore.

Halfway through the main course, she excused herself to use the restroom, located just outside the restaurant in the main lobby area. When she emerged, she was somehow not surprised to find Matt waiting for her.

He looked far more delicious than the roasted chicken and new potatoes she had ordered, in a cream-colored sweater that made him look dark and gorgeous in contrast.

"How's the head?" he asked.

She made a face. "Better. Just be glad you didn't ask me that a few hours ago or you would have a headache of your own after I bit yours off."

He smiled. "I'm glad you're feeling better."

Why did he make her feel so safe and warm just inhabiting the same air space? It was completely ridiculous, this yearning of hers to stand here and bask in his smile.

She suddenly remembered his companion. "Your date is lovely," she said, working hard to ignore the sinking sensation in the pit of her stomach, that pinch of jealousy she had no right to feel.

For an instant, he looked slightly taken aback, as if he'd forgotten all about the poor woman, then he nodded. "Do you know Christine Mayhew?"

"I'm not sure we've met."

They lapsed into awkward silence. She was just about to excuse herself when he gestured toward the dining room. "You look as if you're enjoying your dinner. How are things with your family? Better?"

She fidgeted, embarrassed at the reminder of her emotional breakdown at his house. "Yes. Fine."

"I've been worried about you today."

Her cheeks felt hot and she cursed her fair skin that revealed every hint of embarrassment. "Don't. I'm fine, mostly just embarrassed that I fell apart like that. I learned a hard lesson, that too much alcohol turns me into a bawl-baby. You'll notice I'm not having anything stronger than ginger ale tonight. I really am sorry, Matt, for putting you through that and dumping all my troubles on you."

"I'm glad I could be there. If you, you know, need to talk or anything, you know where to find me."

He looked completely sincere and Elise felt a tiny little tug on her heart. "Thank you. I appreciate that. I think I'm done feeling sorry for myself for a while. I've even got a job. Well, sort of. Haley called and asked me to help her with the ROOTS Christmas party next week. Staying busy will help."

"Good. That's great. I'll be there, too. Marlon has demanded—I mean, asked me in no uncertain terms—that I help out at the party."

Apparently she wouldn't be able to completely avoid him during the rest of her stay. She didn't know whether to rejoice or be depressed by that.

Elise glanced inside the dining room where the rest of her family members looked to be finishing up their meal. Stephanie was already gesturing for Marcos to take away her plate. "I should go. And you probably need to return to your date."

"Right."

He followed her gaze to the other diners, then shifted his attention back to her. He seemed strangely reluctant to leave her company, but she must be misinterpreting things. He was here with a date. A beautiful, vivacious date. Why would he want to hang around in a hallway with her when he could be sitting out there with a pretty brunette? She knew the thought shouldn't depress her so much.

"I guess I'll see you around ROOTS, then," he said.

"Enjoy your evening," she answered, then hurried back inside the restaurant to rejoin her family, trying hard not to wish *she* were the one sharing that bottle of wine with him.

"So that's Elise."

Matt returned his napkin to his lap, careful not to meet Christine's gaze. She was entirely too perceptive. For some reason, he was hesitant to let her see the depth of his attraction for Elise. Even though he and Christine were strictly friends, showing such blatant interest in another woman seemed rude.

"Yes. Grant's little sister."

"But she's not really, right? Grant's sister, I mean. She's the one who was switched at birth with Erin Castro."

"That doesn't make her any less Grant's sister," he answered, more curtly than he intended. He couldn't shake the memory of her anguish the night before as she had sobbed out her confusion in his arms.

Christine raised an eyebrow but said nothing and he squirmed. Yeah. Entirely too perceptive. So much for concealing his growing feelings for Elise.

"She's very pretty," Christine said after a moment. "Has she moved back to Thunder Canyon for good?"

He was wondering that same thing. "Not sure yet."

She was quiet for a moment then she touched his forearm. "Whenever you want to stage a breakup, you only have to say the word. You've been wonderful these last few months but this arrangement of ours was never supposed to be open-ended."

"Why do we need to change anything?"

She smiled. "I don't know. Maybe because you haven't stopped sneaking glances over at the Clifton table all night."

He took a sip of the delicious wine Grant had sent over to thank him for doing what any decent man would do. "I'm sorry," he murmured.

"Why are you sorry? This isn't a real date, Matt. You're not breaking any unwritten rules here. I'm just saying, I'll step out of the picture whenever you want me to."

He mulled her offer, not sure exactly how to respond. How was it possible that one crazy evening with Elise seemed to have changed everything?

"What about Clay?"

Christine shrugged. "I'll deal. If he hasn't gotten the message by now that I've moved on, the man needs serious help. I don't know what more I can do."

He had thought more than once that Christine was too softhearted. From the moment she broke up with Clay Robbins, she should have been clear that she was breaking up with him because he was clingy and obsessive. Instead, she had tried to let him down gently. When that didn't work, she had enlisted Matt's help to convince the other man she had moved on.

In Matt's opinion, the man needed somebody to knock him ass over teakettle until he clued in that Christine wasn't interested. Sort of like Jake Halloran the night before at The Hitching Post.

They finished their dinner not long after that. A surreptitious peek at the Cliftons' table while he was waiting for their server to return the check revealed they were lingering over dessert. He supposed it would be better to leave before they finished to avoid any awkwardness with Elise or the embarrassment of having to endure more unwanted gratitude from her family over the events of the night before.

He and Christine walked out into the lobby of the resort, with its leather sofas and life-size elk sculpture. He grabbed her coat and was helping her into it when her shoulders suddenly tensed beneath his hands and she inhaled sharply.

"Sorry. Did I pull your hair?" he asked, feeling big and fumbling.

"No," she whispered with a panicked look at a group that had just entered the lobby carrying holiday presents, obviously out for a night of festive celebrating.

"That's Kelly Robbins, Clay's cousin."

"Which one?"

"The one in the plaid sweater."

He saw exactly when the thin-as-a-rail other woman recognized Christine. Her eyes widened and jumped between the two of them, resting on his hands still at Christine's shoulders as he finished helping her with her coat.

"She's the biggest gossip in the whole blasted county."

"Is that right?" Some spark of recklessness must still be lingering in him from the tussle the night before at The Hitching Post. Heedless of the consequences, he threw an arm over Christine's shoulders.

"She's coming this way," he muttered. "Smile. It's about damn time Clay got the message once and for all."

"What are you going to do?"

"Just play along," he said. "Let's go say hello."

"Matt…" Christine said in a warning tone, but before she could finish, Matt dragged her over to the group of chattering women, who happened conveniently to be located near the entrance to the valet parking, anyway.

Christine gave a polished sort of smile. "Hi, Kelly. I thought that was you."

The other woman gave a high-pitched squeal, just as if she hadn't already seen them five minutes earlier. He could already tell she was exactly the sort of woman who always grated on his nerves, plastic and gushy.

"Christine! Hi! You look *gorgeous!* I haven't seen you in *ages!* Not since you and Clay…well, not in *forever.* How are you?"

Christine sent him a help-me sort of sidelong look as if she were waiting for his grand master plan.

"Good. Great. Um, Kelly Robbins, this is Matt Cates. Matt, Kelly lives over in Bozeman. I used to…um, date her cousin."

"You're Clay Robbins's cousin?" he asked, forcing a note of intrigue in his voice.

"Yes," she said slowly with a wary sort of look.

"How is Clay these days?" Matt asked. "I guess I should feel sorry for the poor guy but I just can't."

He squeezed Christine's shoulders, laying the cheese on as thick as he dared.

"Why is that?" the other woman asked, her overbright friendliness beginning to show a few hairline fractures.

"He really did me a favor, breaking up with Christine. If things had worked out with the two of them, I wouldn't be about to become the luckiest guy in the world."

He kissed her temple, lingering there with his mouth in her hair as if he couldn't bear to lose contact with her, in exactly the sort of public display of affection that always gave him the creeps.

He was probably going overboard here. Christine obviously thought so, at least judging by the heel of her boot that was currently digging into his instep.

"You're getting married?" Kelly squealed. She yanked Christine out of his arms and pulled her into a hug and even from here he could smell the spicy holiday-scented perfume she must have spritzed heavily before walking out the door. "When is the big day?"

Christine slanted him a sour look over the other woman's shoulder and Matt grinned back at her.

He tried to dissemble as much as he could manage to get away with. "You know how it is. Nothing's official yet. We're, uh, still working out the details. Keep it to yourself though, okay?"

Kelly gushed for a moment or two more. "I'm happy for you. Really I am." She frowned as if she'd suddenly thought of something, when Matt knew damn well she'd only been trying to figure out a way to work it into the conversation. "It's just, well, Clay's gonna be pretty upset, you know."

Christine sighed and then sent Matt a swift look. "I'm sorry for that but I guess it's time he moved on and found someone else, like I have."

"I s'pose," she said.

She looked as if she might say more but the hostess at that moment came out from The Gallatin Room to let her party know their tables were ready.

"Congratulations again," Kelly said. "Let me know when the big day is, won't you?"

"Nothing's official," Christine protested, with another sideways glare at him.

"That ought to do it," he said, dropping his arm as soon as Kelly was out of view inside the restaurant. "If Robbins doesn't get the message after that, he's more of an idiot than I thought."

Christine somehow managed to look relieved and upset at the same time. "You're crazy, do you know that?" she said, shaking her head. "What are you going to do when the rumor starts flying around Thunder Canyon that we're engaged?"

"Who's going to talk? I didn't recognize a single one of those ladies and I know everybody in town. They must be from Bozeman. Who are they going to tell?"

"Don't you think Clay will figure out something's hinky when this engagement of ours never materializes?"

"Who knows?" Matt shrugged. "By then, he'll hopefully have found some other poor woman to cling to."

She was quiet for a moment as they walked out of the lodge and into the December night, starry and cold and lit by little twinkling gold lights adorning the lodge.

"What about Elise Clifton?" she asked as they waited for the valet to bring his pickup. "What if she hears rumors we're engaged?"

"There's nothing going on between Elise and me," he said, even though the words weren't precisely true. What would it matter if she did find out? She probably wouldn't care, even if it were true. Elise was a friend—that was all.

Yet he was suddenly shocked to find himself wanting much more.

Chapter 6

"You need to march straight home and climb back to bed, missy. I'm not going to listen to any more arguments."

Elise stared down at Haley. Her best friend, who was currently huddled at her desk at ROOTS with a blanket over her shoulders, a nearly empty box of tissues at her elbow and complete misery on her features.

"I can't be sick another minute. I have way too much to do!" Haley wailed, then gave a wretched-sounding cough. "The Christmas party is only four days away and I still have to finish the decorations and make sure the caterers are ready and organize the swag bags from all the donations we've received."

"And if you don't get some rest and take care of yourself, you're going to be in a hospital bed while the rest of us throw a party. Go home, Hale."

"I can't just dump it all on you."

"I don't mind. Knowing you, I imagine your notes are extensive enough that I can figure out everything."

"It still doesn't seem right."

Elise wasn't always the most firm person on the planet, but she wasn't going to budge about this. "Go home," she repeated. "If not for your own sake, think about all these kids you love so much. What if you pass on all your pesky little germs and make them sick for the holidays?"

Haley opened her mouth to answer, then closed it again and slumped a little further down in her chair. "You're right. Darn it, you're right."

"Of course I am. Come on, I'll help you to your car."

Haley sighed heavily as if the very idea of moving just then was far beyond her capabilities. She lifted her hands to the arms of her desk chair but before she could rise, the door to ROOTS opened with a blast of cold air.

For a moment, Elise felt her heartbeat skitter at the tall, muscled figure who walked through, then she shook herself. Not Matt. Despite the fact that he shared the same brown hair and eyes and those sturdy, cry-on-me shoulders, this was Marlon, Matt's twin brother. She could tell in an instant, though she wasn't exactly certain how she knew.

He stood inside the renovated storefront that now housed Haley's volunteer organization aimed at helping Thunder Canyon's troubled youth. Marlon looked between the two of them. "What's going on?"

"I'm trying to convince your stubborn girlfriend that she needs to be home in bed."

He raised his eyebrows. "Funny, that's exactly what I told her when she managed to crawl out this morning."

"It's just a cold," Haley insisted, though her brown

eyes were bloodshot, her nose red, her skin pale. "I'll be fine."

"Sure you will," Elise said briskly. "You'll be good as new in a day or two. In the meantime, I can handle things here. I don't want you to worry for a single moment. I think I can manage to answer phones and make some Christmas decorations without ROOTS falling completely apart."

"It's such a lousy time to be sick. I have so much to *do*."

Elise shared a sympathetic look with Marlon and was struck again by the similarities yet differences between him and Matt.

"Nothing that's so important it's worth jeopardizing your health to accomplish," Marlon said sternly. "Come on, I'll drop you back at home and tuck you in with a cup of tea and a good book."

Was she a terrible person that she actually envied her friend? Oh, not for the lousy cold. She would happily leave that to Haley since Elise hated being sick worse than just about anything. But Marlon's tender concern for the woman he loved touched a chord somewhere deep inside, left her with a nameless ache in her chest.

Though she dated here and there, she had avoided any serious entanglements the last few years after a nasty experience with her ex-boyfriend. As she watched Haley and Marlon together, Elise had to wonder if she'd been wrong. A broken heart—or more accurately, probably, bruised ego—from one cheating louse didn't mean she had to give up all hope of finding what Haley and Marlon shared.

"Go home and go back to bed," Elise said again. "When you wake up later today, you can email me your to-do list. Meantime, I can start with the Christmas decorations for the party."

"Are you sure?"

"Positive. Go home. If you don't go on your own, I have a feeling Marlon over there will toss you over his shoulder and haul you out of here."

"Really?" Haley shifted her gaze to the man. For the first time since Elise had walked into ROOTS a half hour ago, she saw a tiny smile on her friend's face.

Marlon grinned. "In a heartbeat, sweetheart. Want to try me? Come on, let's get you home."

Though Haley still looked far from convinced, Elise and Marlon finally managed to usher her out the door and into Marlon's vehicle.

After they left, Elise turned around to survey this place her friend loved so much. The place wasn't fancy but Haley had managed to turn it into a comfortable hangout for troubled local teens. The wall facing the street was covered in a mural that Haley painted—kids with books, computers, sports images. A couch covered with a slipcover took up one wall and in a corner was a TV with video games.

Haley loved it here and was passionate about helping her teens. Elise knew Haley came up with the idea after her own brother Austin ran into trouble and was helped through it by some local ranching folk. Haley had more than paid it forward by providing a foundation for kids who might be feeling similarly rootless.

Elise envied Haley her dedication and determination. She wasn't sure she had ever cared as passionately for anything.

Oh, she had worked hard to earn her bachelor's degree in business and had enjoyed her job managing a bookstore in Billings. She wanted to think she had been good at her job—good enough that her district manager had assured her he would only accept a temporary leave of absence rather than a full-on resignation when she made the decision to come to Thunder Canyon for the holidays after Erin's stunning revelation.

While she had enjoyed the challenges of running a small bookstore, she couldn't say she really missed it. What she *had* missed was the chance to do something constructive. The last two weeks, she had tried to stay busy by helping out at the ranch but Stephanie had everything running so smoothly there, Elise had mostly been in the way.

She actually relished the chance to help Haley out at ROOTS for a few days, if only to provide a distraction from everything that had happened in the last month.

If the work also helped divert her mind from Marlon's gorgeous twin brother, she considered that a definite bonus.

Several hours later, Elsie was questioning her sanity. Her fingers had a dozen pinpricks from stringing popcorn and cranberries for the tree garlands, her neck had cramped about an hour ago and her eyes were blurry and achy from concentrating.

Added to that, all afternoon, ROOTS had been a madhouse with people coming in and out to make deliveries of donations for the party and the phone had been ringing off the hook with people asking questions she couldn't answer.

Since the high school let out, a couple dozen teens had descended to do homework or play video games or just to hang out.

Now, near 6:00 p.m., they had all dispersed, leaving her alone again to finish up the Christmas decorations.

Night came early at this latitude as Montana was headed for the shortest day of the year in a week, and outside the Christmas lights up and down the streets of Old Town Thunder Canyon had slowly flickered on.

There. One more cranberry and she was calling this one good. She tied the knot on the string then carried the garland to the back room to go with the rest of the decorations, twisting her neck from side to side as she walked, to stretch her achy muscles. She laid it carefully across the folding table she had unearthed from a corner and had set up to hold the decorations. She flipped off the light to return to the front when she suddenly heard the jingling bells on the door.

So much for locking up. Who would be coming this late? Probably somebody with another donation. The generosity of the townspeople had been a definite eye-opener.

Elise gave a weary sigh and headed out to greet the newcomer.

As soon as she spied the tall, dark-haired man near the door, her heart gave a ridiculous little leap and this time she didn't even wonder for an instant which Cates brother it was.

"Matt. Hi!"

He entered the room with that long-legged, loose-hipped walk of his and her stomach sizzled.

Surprise and something else—something that left her hot and edgy—flashed in his eyes. "Oh! You're not Haley."

"No. She's a few inches taller and her hair is brown and quite a bit longer. And you're not Marlon."

He sent her a sidelong look and she saw the teasing sparkle in his eyes. The Cates boys had been notorious in school for playing tricks on people, pretending to be each other at the most inconvenient moments.

"You sure about that?" he asked.

She stacked stray papers on Haley's desk so her workspace would be neat in the morning. "Completely. Marlon's the good-looking one."

Surprise flickered in those brown eyes again and then he laughed. "Wow. A little harsh, don't you think?"

All the stresses of the day seemed to shimmer away like silvery tinsel on the wind. How did he have that effect on her? she wondered. She had no idea—but she was very much afraid she might become addicted to it.

"You know I'm joking. You're identical twins, both of you too gorgeous for your own good."

As soon as the words were out, she couldn't believe she had actually spoken them aloud. She wasn't exactly the flirty, lighthearted type. Actually, she had always been a little on the shy side when it came to men, especially big, sexy men like Matt Cates.

He didn't seem to find her remark out of character but it did seem to make him uncomfortable. He rolled his eyes and she thought she detected a slight hint of color on his features. Really? Could he honestly not be aware of his effect on the opposite sex? He had been breaking girls' hearts since grade school.

"Seriously, how can you tell?" he asked her with a quizzical look. "Sometimes our own parents aren't sure."

"Besides the black eye, you mean? I'm not quite sure. I just know." She studied him, trying to figure out the signs she took for granted. "Your chins are shaped a little differently, I guess. Your hair's just a little more streaky than his. Oh, and your lashes are just a bit longer."

He still looked baffled and Elise could feel herself blush. How could she tell him she had spent a long time staring at him when he wasn't paying her any attention, from the time she was old enough to even notice him?

"However you do it, it's amazing. Not many people can tell us apart." He looked around. "So is Haley here?"

"No. Your brother—"

"You mean the good-looking one?" he interrupted.

She smiled. "Right. Marlon took her home earlier. She's got a bad cold and is feeling lousy. She tried to tough it out here at ROOTS for a while but seemed to be getting worse, not better. I offered to step in to help her with the Christmas party Friday so she could recover and keep her bad juju to herself."

"Oh, right. I forgot about the party."

She pointed to the boxes of donations. "If you'd like, I've got about a hundred gift bags to fill that might jog your memory."

"Tonight?"

He sounded as if he was completely willing to sit right down and start throwing bags together, which she found rather wonderful.

"No. I'll probably work on them a little later in the week once all the donations come in. But thanks for the offer. Haley might take you up on it if she comes back in time to crack the whip over all the volunteers." She paused. "Sorry, you must have had a reason for coming in to see Haley. Is there something I can help you with?"

He didn't say anything for several beats, only looked at her with that glittery look in his eyes again, until her skin felt achy and tight.

After a moment, he cleared his throat. "Actually, I had a good excuse to come visit Haley but that's all it was. An excuse. In reality, I was trying to be sneaky."

"You? Sneaky? Imagine that!"

He ignored her dry tone. "You know, finding you here

instead of Haley works out even better for me. You're the perfect person to help me out."

"Am I?"

He sat on the edge of the desk and she tried not to feel overwhelmed by all that rugged strength so close to her. "You've been friends with Haley for a long time, right? So you know her pretty well."

"She and Steph have been my closest friends forever."

"Great!" He grinned and she had to remind herself to breathe. "This is perfect. You can come to Bozeman with me tonight."

She blinked. "Excuse me?"

"I'm trying to find a Christmas present for her. Not just any Christmas present, the perfect Christmas present. She's the only one left on my list."

That he had a list in the first place struck her as odd. That he was enlisting her help to cross Haley's name off that list was even more surreal. "She's really the only one whose present you haven't bought yet? You still have another week and a half before Christmas. I thought most guys tended to wait until the last minute."

He manufactured an affronted look. "That is a blatant stereotype, Ms. Clifton, and I am personally offended by it."

She couldn't help herself—she smiled. She couldn't remember the last time she had felt this, well, happy. "Oh, sorry to be a reverse chauvinist. But every man *I* know waits until the last minute. Grant and my cousin Bo are the worst."

He shrugged. "I happen to love Christmas and the whole giving-presents thing. I've had almost everything done and even wrapped for a while now, except for Haley's gift. She's still fairly new to our family circle and since this is her first Christmas with us, I wanted to find something special. I'm heading into Bozeman right now before all the stores close and dropped by ROOTS hoping I could finesse a few hints out of her about what she would like before I leave."

"I'm sorry she's not here."

"Not at all. Now you can come with me, which is even better. I'll even spring for dinner. What time are you closing up shop here?"

"I was just about to. But I can't just…"

"Sure you can," he said over her objections. "Come on, it will be fun."

She could think of a dozen reasons why she shouldn't go with him. She was tired. She had a headache. She wasn't thrilled about her silly, futile crush on him and had been warning herself since Saturday morning when he dropped her off back at Clifton's Pride that she needed to keep her distance so she didn't make an even bigger fool of herself over him.

But her words to Grant that morning after he drove away still echoed in her mind. She owed him for coming to her rescue the other night at The Hitching Post—and he still had the vividly colored eye to show for it.

Without him, she might have found herself in serious trouble with Jake Halloran. He had stepped in to rescue her from a jam at considerable risk to himself. All he wanted now was the simple favor of helping him select a gift. If she went with him to Bozeman, perhaps she wouldn't feel quite so indebted to him.

The trick would be making it through the evening alone with him without completely humiliating herself while the memory of that stunning kiss simmered under her skin.

"Fine." She spoke quickly before she could change her mind. "But since you apparently love Christmas so much, I'm still going to expect you to help me fill those gift bags."

"It's a deal." He grinned and helped her find her coat.

"Are you sure about this?"

Two hours later, they stood inside an art gallery just before closing time looking at an elaborate—and elaborately priced—needlework sampler that depicted an old, gnarled oak tree. In the thin, topmost branches perched a stately, magnificent eagle with its wings outstretched, gleaming gold as if reflecting sunlight.

"Positive. Oh, Matt. It's perfect. Haley will love it."

He studied the piece. It was lovely, in an artsy sort of way. He could see where Haley would probably enjoy it. Elise seemed convinced, anyway. The moment they had walked into the gallery after searching fruitlessly through three or four other crowded stores, she saw it hanging on the wall and gasped with delight.

"You're the expert, I guess," he said now.

"Trust me, she's going to love it. It's perfect," she said again. "So perfect it might have been custom made for her. You know that's the reason she named her teen organization ROOTS, right? Because of a sampler her mother had hanging on the wall. It said something about how there are but two lasting bequests we can give children—roots and wings. This covers both of those things. I mean it. With this present you're going to win the best future brother-in-law race, hands down."

"Well that's something, at least," he said dryly. "I wouldn't want her favoring Marshall or Mitch over me."

"Haley's going to love it," she assured him. "In fact, she just might wonder if she's marrying the wrong twin."

He made a face as they headed to the salesperson seated behind a discreet counter. "I doubt that. The two of them seem to forget that anybody else on earth even exists when they're together."

He paid for the needlework, gulping a little at the price tag but grateful again that Cates Construction had managed to avoid the worst of the economic downturn so he could splurge a little for his twin's future wife.

"Would you like this gift wrapped?" the saleswoman asked.

"Please. Gift wrapping isn't one of my particular skills."

While the salesclerk carried the piece over to a nearby table where wrapping supplies were neatly organized, Elise picked up their conversation.

"Do you mind? About Marlon and Haley, I mean? The two of you have always been so close. Do you worry she'll interfere with that bond?"

He thought about Haley and the changes she had wrought in his brother. She was sweet and loving, as different as he could imagine from his formerly wild twin. Somehow the two of them managed to still perfectly complement each other.

"Haley's been great for Marlon," he answered honestly. "She centers him, you know? Before she came along, the only thing Marlon really cared about was having a good time and making the next deal. Now he's as passionate about ROOTS as Haley is. They're crazy about each other."

"I noticed." She smiled a little and gave him a considering look. "I guess that leaves you the last Cates standing, which is probably exactly where you want to be, right?"

He gazed at Elise, bright and lovely in the recessed lighting of the gallery. Whenever he looked at her, something soft and tender lodged just under his chest.

Maybe he ought to be a little uneasy about how quickly everything he always thought he wanted had shifted in the last few days, but all he could manage to drum up was gratitude that she had come back to Thunder Canyon.

"I don't expect that particular situation will last long," he said, purposely vague. A guy had to hope, right?

She gave him an uncertain look but he decided not to explain yet. He could be patient, give her time to figure out her feelings.

"Well, whoever manages to capture the last Cates will be a very lucky woman, I'm sure. Especially if you're always so generous with your gifts."

Now would probably be a really good time to change the subject, he decided, before she started to probe too deeply into areas he wasn't quite ready to discuss.

"What about you?" he asked her. "What's on your Christmas list this year?"

She shrugged. "My gifts are already all wrapped this year. When you work in a bookstore, it's easy to find something perfect for everyone on your list."

"I meant for yourself. What are you asking Santa to bring you?"

She looked reluctant to answer and he saw relief in her blue eyes when the saleswoman brought back his wrapped gift for Haley before he could probe a little more.

"Will there be anything else?" the woman asked in the brisk, tired tone of someone who had spent hours on her feet dealing with holiday shoppers.

"Not tonight. But thank you. This is perfect," he said.

He held the door open for Elise and they walked out into the frosty night. A light snow was falling and a few flakes landed on her crimson knit hat and then on her eyelashes.

"You were saying about your Christmas list…" he prompted.

She made a face. "You're about the most persistent man I know."

"I haven't even gotten started yet."

She sighed. "I'm not a big Christmas fan, if you want to know the truth. I haven't been in a long time. Probably since my dad's murder. It's always a difficult time but I'm afraid this year I feel even less like celebrating."

He studied her there in the fluttery snow and that soft tenderness swelled up inside him again. She had certainly been faced with a rough road to walk. He thought of his own family, the parties and traditions and craziness of a Cates family Christmas.

So much had been taken from Elise. He wanted to give her something back but he didn't have the first idea how to help her enjoy Christmas again.

"Come on," he said suddenly. "Let's lock Haley's present in my truck and then take a walk through town before we grab a bite to eat."

She stared at him in the light reflected from the gallery's front window. "Take a walk? It's got to be fifteen degrees out! Are you crazy?"

"Maybe. Probably." He grinned at her. "Come on, let's enjoy some of the Christmas decorations and then I'll buy you dinner at my favorite steak house."

She laughed, though he saw a little lingering sadness in her eyes. "You're in a very strange mood tonight."

"What's strange about being happy? It's Christmas and I'm with the prettiest woman in Bozeman. What guy wouldn't be happy about that?"

Rosy color climbed her cheeks and he knew it wasn't from the cold. Her blushes fascinated and charmed him. On impulse, he pulled her toward him with his free arm for just a moment, leaning in to kiss her forehead. Up close, her eyes were wide and startled and impossibly blue.

He wanted to stay there holding her for a long time while the snow eddied around them and the Christmas lights twinkled in the storefronts, but he sensed she needed a cautious approach.

He eased away and took her hand. "Come on. Let's see if we can find you a little holiday spirit."

They took their time dropping off the package for Haley in his truck then wandering through the streets of Bozeman, listening to the carols playing from speakers out front of the businesses and peering into the all the storefronts like they were children dreaming about the biggest, best bicycle in town.

He found every moment magical, especially watching her eyes lose a little of that lost, haunted look. She laughed and joked with him like the girl he remembered and through the knit of her gloves, her fingers curled inside his as if she didn't want to let go.

By the time they reached his favorite restaurant, his toes were numb from the cold but he wouldn't have changed an instant.

Though the popular steak house could be crowded, business was slow this late on a weeknight and they didn't have to wait long for a table.

She looked lighter somehow, he thought as the hostess seated them and rattled through the evening's specials. Maybe that's what she needed most. Someone to make her smile and help her forget her troubles for a moment.

He wanted to give her the gift of a happy, lighthearted evening where she could forget her worries—and this was definitely one present he didn't need anyone else's help to deliver.

Chapter 7

How did he do it?

Elise studied the man across the low-lit table from her, strong and dark and gorgeous. Though both Cates twins had been wild, Marlon had always been the charmer while Matt had always seemed more the studious type—one reason he had gravitated toward law school, she supposed.

But tonight, he was making every effort to charm her...and it was definitely working. If she wasn't careful, she would fall hard and fast for him.

She would just have to be careful, she warned herself as her insides trembled from another of his smiles.

"So you never really answered me the other night. How long do you think you're staying in Thunder Canyon?" he asked, in a tone of voice that made her think he had genuine interest in her answer.

She refused to let him fluster her. Matt might be the

studious one but he had a reputation as being every bit the player that Marlon used to be.

"I'm not sure," she answered. "I promised my mother I would spend the holidays in town. For now that's what I'm focusing on, just spending time at the ranch and helping Haley at ROOTS while I'm here. Once the holidays are over, I don't know. I'm considering my options."

"What are they? Maybe I can help."

"My job is still waiting for me in Billings if I want it. That's a definite possibility. My life is there. My friends are there. For now, I still have a house until my mother decides whether to sell it or rent it out."

She paused, then added reluctantly, "Jack and Betty Castro haven't exactly made it a secret that they would like me to go down to San Diego for a while so they and…their sons can get to know me beyond phone calls and emails."

He studied her out of those surprisingly perceptive brown eyes. "You're not so sure about that one, are you?"

She sighed, moving her undeniably delicious pasta around on her plate. At the reminder of the Castros, the happy bubble around them she suspected he had carefully nurtured seemed to fizzle and pop.

"It's all so difficult. They're strangers to me, you know?"

"Sure they are." He paused and reached across the table to entwine his fingers around hers. "You know, they're going to stay strangers to you until you make an effort to get to know them better."

"You sound like my mo—like Helen."

"Your mother," he said, squeezing her fingers lightly. "Helen is your mother, no matter what the DNA says."

His words brought a lump to her throat and she had

to reach for her water glass. "My mother is urging me to spend more time with them."

"Don't you like them?"

"Sure I like them. They're very nice people."

How could she explain that spending time with them, coming to know them, would make this strange, twisted journey seem more real, somehow? She didn't understand her tangle of emotions, she only knew she wanted everything to go back to the way it was a few weeks ago, before she'd ever even heard of Erin Castro.

She couldn't continue in this limbo, she knew. Something had to change. She just wasn't sure she was ready yet.

"Jack and Betty are coming back to Thunder Canyon as soon as school lets out in San Diego to spend the holidays in Montana with Erin. Betty is a teacher there. History. Jack's a police officer. They have two sons in addition to Erin, one who's a police officer like his father and one who is a student."

"Are the brothers coming, too?"

"As far as I know, only Jack and Betty. They want to get to know me better while they're here."

"That's a start."

"We'll see."

She didn't want to talk about the Castros. She wanted that bright, happy bubble back. "What about you? What are your plans? Do you think you'll ever consider going back to law school?"

"Right now, I doubt it. I like working with my dad. I've discovered I really love the whole building process, seeing a place take shape under my direction. I'm not sure I'd get that same high from practicing law.

"So you think you'll be sticking around Thunder Canyon, then?"

He gave her another one of those intense, unreadable looks that made her blush, for reasons she didn't fully understand. "I guess you could say I'm pretty content with my life right now. For the most part, anyway."

She wondered if he was serious about the woman she'd seen him with the other night at dinner. Probably not. Matt probably had a dozen beautiful women like that, all eager to hang on his every word.

That probably shouldn't depress her so much, she thought. She wasn't doing a very effective job of protecting herself around him.

They finished eating a short time later and somewhat to Elise's surprise, she found she was grateful he'd parked some distance away so she could stretch out the enjoyable evening. He took her hand to help her over a patch of ice, then didn't release her. They walked hand in hand through the quiet streets.

She was fiercely aware of his heat seeping through her gloves, of his solid strength beside her.

She sighed, knowing perfectly well she shouldn't find such comfort just from his presence. Matt made her feel…safe. He had a tendency to watch out for anything smaller than he was but for some reason he had singled her out for extra protection.

She didn't know why but it seemed as if every time she found herself in trouble, Matt was there to help her out. Whether she was falling off a swing at the playground, tripping in the halls, schoolyard bullies, even suffering that flat tire last summer. Whenever she needed him, he seemed to be there.

What a comfort that was, she realized. A girl could definitely find herself getting used to that.

She had missed him after she moved away. Oh, she had made several good friends at her new high school in

Billings, friends she kept to this day, but none who would step up to look out for her like Matt.

This time, they walked back to his truck by a more residential route, passing the small, close-set houses of downtown Bozeman. All seemed to be adorned with holiday decorations, from elaborately lit facades to a simple Christmas tree in the window and a wreath on the door. They were still a block from his pickup when Elise suddenly grabbed Matt's arm, peering around him to the shadows near a white clapboard house.

"What was that?"

He looked around. "What's the matter?"

"I saw something out of the corner of my eye. Something huge." She squinted in the direction of the blur, vaguely aware even as she did that Matt had moved his body protectively in front of her, even though he didn't know what she was talking about or even if anything posed a threat.

Maybe it was just a shadow. No. There it was again.

Her gaze sharpened and she gasped. "Do you see it?" she asked him. "Over there by the corner of that house across the street. Near that big pine tree."

He scanned the area and then laughed. "A moose! Right in the middle of town. Think he's Christmas shopping?"

"How cool is that?" she exclaimed. "I've seen plenty of mule deer in town, even in Billings, but never a moose."

She stood with her hand in Matt's, heedless of the cold seeping into her bones as they watched the massive creature leisurely nibble on a bush as if he were standing at the buffet at a Christmas party.

They watched for a long time, until Matt suddenly snickered. "He'd better watch out for the colored lights on the next bush or he's going to find himself a not-very-merry crisp moose."

She groaned and laughed at the same time. "Oh. You had to go and ruin a lovely moment with a lame joke."

"Sorry." He smiled at her and reached to push a loose strand of hair away from her face, his suede gloves caressing her skin.

"You need to do that more often," he murmured.

"What? Complain about your corny jokes? Sure. Anytime."

"I meant laugh. I've always thought you had the sweetest laugh of anyone I know."

She stared at him for a long moment, her heart pulsing. What would he do if she kissed him? Just reached up on tiptoe and pulled his head down to hers? The moment stretched out between them, as bright and hopeful as those fairy lights dripping from the eaves of the nearby house. She drew up on her toes inside her boots…then chickened out and slid back down to the ground.

"The people inside have no idea he's even out here," she said, her voice hushed.

He was quiet for a moment, then he spoke in an equally hushed voice. "It's amazing what you can miss when you're not paying attention."

Her gaze flashed again to his and her stomach trembled at the intensity in his eyes and a moment later, his mouth brushed hers.

His lips were warm and firm and he tasted of chocolate and mint from the piece of gourmet candy their server had delivered with their check at the restaurant.

She closed her eyes and leaned into his strength. The night seemed magical. The lights, the moose, the easy flutters of snow. She felt so safe here, warm and content, a slow peace soaking through her.

She finally followed her impulse of earlier and rose up on her toes so she could wrap her arms around his neck, savoring the heat of him.

She was in deep trouble. Since Friday night she had wondered what it would be like to kiss him again. To really kiss him this time, not when she was slightly tipsy from too many margaritas but when she was completely clearheaded and rational.

Now she knew exactly how his mouth tasted and his arms felt around her, exactly how silky his hair was sliding through her fingertips and the strength of his muscles against her body.

What she didn't know was how, in heaven's name, she would manage to endure the rest of her life without more of this—without more of *him*.

She shivered suddenly, cold despite his heat engulfing her, and Matt immediately slid his mouth away.

"You're freezing," he murmured. "I'm a brute to keep you out here in the cold."

She couldn't tell him her reaction wasn't from the temperature but from reality slapping her around. Better to let him think she was in danger of freezing to death than to admit she was afraid of having her heart broken.

"That's probably a good idea."

They left the moose to his browsing and Matt grabbed her hand to lead her the rest of the way to his truck.

A single kiss shouldn't leave him feeling as if his world had been rocked off its whole foundation.

A half hour later as Matt drove back to Thunder Canyon, his heartbeat still hadn't managed to settle. Every time he looked at Elise in the seat beside him, blonde and delicate and lovely, he felt that little tingle of awareness, the urgent throb of hunger.

He felt as if everything in his world had changed. A week ago, he thought he had everything figured out. He was happy with his life in Thunder Canyon, content working for his dad.

And then Elise Clifton blew back into town and everything he thought was important seemed to have shifted.

For a few moments after they had returned to his pickup, they had made small talk. But even before they left the Bozeman town limits, she started to yawn. Now she appeared to be fast asleep.

He risked another quick glance across the cab of the truck. She seemed comfortable enough with her cheek pressed against the upholstery but he still had to fight the urge to ease her onto his shoulder and tuck her under his arm, which wasn't the most safe position when the roads were slick and icy from the light snow.

He sighed. What was he supposed to do with her now?

He hadn't missed that when she was talking about her options for the future, not once had she mentioned staying and settling down in Thunder Canyon for good. She had talked about returning to Billings and about spending time with her newly discovered birth parents, but never anything about staying in town.

What would he have to do or say to convince her to add that to her plate of possibilities? he wondered.

He had a feeling he would have to take things slow and steady with her. Anticipation curled through him. He didn't mind. He could be patient when the payoff promised to be everything he had never realized he wanted.

He was still mulling his options when he finally drove up to the Clifton's Pride ranch house.

"Elise? Sweetheart, we're back."

Her eyes blinked open. For a few seconds, she stared at him with a disoriented look in her eyes and then she

gave him a slow smile that made him wish he was seeing it from the comfort of his own bed, with her on the
pillow next to him, instead of in the cramped cab of his
pickup truck.

"Hey," she murmured. "Sorry I fell asleep. It was a
crazy day at ROOTS today. I never realized just how
exhausting a bunch of teenagers could be. I guess I was
more tired than I thought."

"No problem. It was warm and cozy in here. I don't
blame you a bit. I would have liked to sleep, too."

"I'm really glad one of us decided to stay awake."

She reached to open her door, but he quickly held out
a hand to stop her. "Thank you again for your help picking out Haley's gift. I don't know what I would have done
without you. I think she's going to be very happy with it."

She smiled. "You're welcome. I... It was really a lovely
evening."

He couldn't help himself. Despite all his plans to give
her time, he had to kiss her again, especially when she
looked so soft and sleepy and adorable.

He leaned across the width of the pickup and cupped
her chin, then lowered his mouth to hers. She seemed to
sigh against him, just about the sexiest sound he'd ever
heard and after a long moment, he felt her arms around
his neck.

The kiss was slow and gentle, like an easy ride into
the mountains on a summer evening. He intended to keep
it that way, but then her mouth parted slightly and he
couldn't resist deepening the kiss.

She froze for just a moment and then she was kissing him back, her mouth eagerly dancing with his, her
curves pressed against him.

After several long, delicious moments, she finally
jerked away, her breathing ragged. Her knit cap had fallen

off and her hair was tousled. She shoved it away from her face with fingers that trembled slightly.

Her mouth was swollen from his kiss and he drew his fingers into fists to keep from reaching for her again.

She stared at him for a long moment, then she shook her head, that curtain of hair swinging with the movement. "This really isn't a good idea."

He pretended to misunderstand, even as he felt a hard knot of unease lodge under his breastbone. "I know. Been a long time since I made out in the cab of a pickup truck. Seems a lot harder than it used to be."

"You know that's not what I meant."

"Elise—"

She shook her head. "Don't. Let me finish. I'm obviously attracted to you. I have been for, well, a long time. But I… I'm not in a very good place right now for a casual fling. I need to tell you that."

He opened his mouth to argue that he wanted much more than that but she again cut him off.

"I'm still trying to sort out everything that's happened the last few weeks and I'm afraid I really can't afford this sort of…of distraction right now."

"I can wait."

She looked stunned by his words but quickly shook her head. "I'm not asking you to wait. That's not fair to either of us. Matt, you've always been a great friend to me. I don't want to risk losing that by complicating everything."

Now there was a tidy little bit of irony. He eased back into his seat. How many times had he used similar phrases while trying to let a woman down gently? He didn't know quite how to react. Mostly he was confused. How could she kiss him with such sweet passion and then try to brush him off in the next moment?

"I think you're just trying to come up with any excuse to run away," he finally said.

She narrowed her gaze. "Oh?"

"I think you sense we could have something really fantastic together and that scares you right now so you're taking the safe road."

She looked out the window. "We might have been friends in grade school, Matt, but it's been years. I'm not the same person I was then. Don't make the mistake of thinking you know anything about me or about what I feel right now."

"I know enough to recognize when someone's running away. Believe me, I've been doing it long enough myself that I recognize all the signs. You're scared."

"And you're unbelievable." She reached for her door.

"Elise, don't. I'm sorry." He was blowing this. Hadn't he just vowed to give her whatever time and space she needed? Now here he was jumping on her for being cautious. He needed to back off. He could be patient, especially with something this important.

"Forget I said anything. You're right. The timing is lousy. You want to be friends, we'll be friends. I'm fine with that. Come on, I'll walk you to the door."

"That's really not necessary."

He gave her a pointed look that seemed to shut her up in a hurry. They trudged through the thin skiff of snow to the porch of the ranch house. It was past midnight and most of the windows were dark, though someone had thoughtfully left a light burning on the porch for her and a colorful Christmas tree blazed from the front window.

"Please don't be mad at me, Matt," she said in a low voice when they approached the front door. "I really did have a great time with you tonight. More fun than I've had in…a while now."

"I'm not mad," he protested, though it wasn't quite true. He was mad at circumstances—at Erin Castro for stirring up the past, at her family for not seeing how upset and lost Elise was, at himself for the lunacy at falling for her right now when she had other things to cope with.

He would deal, he told himself. What other choice did he have?

"Good night." He forced himself to give her only a kiss on the cheek, even though he wanted much, much more, then he turned around and walked back through the cold.

While she removed her coat and scarf and slid off her boots, Elise kept her gaze fixed out the window, watching Matt turn his truck around in the driveway then head back in the direction of Thunder Canyon.

She watched until his taillights faded pink in the lightly falling snow and then disappeared.

She wanted suddenly to be the sort of woman he was probably used to, someone who could flirt and laugh and kiss without thinking anything of it. But kisses meant something to her. Especially *his* kisses. She couldn't pretend otherwise.

A month or two ago, she might have been happy just for the chance to indulge her foolish daydreams about him, even at the risk of a little inevitable heartbreak. He was Matt Cates, for heaven's sake.

But she didn't have room in her life for that sort of mess and chaos right now.

She made the right choice, she told herself as she walked into the kitchen for a glass of water before heading to her room. Friendship with him was a much more safe option than these tantalizing kisses and terrifying emotions.

She saw a light glowing from the kitchen and just assumed her mother or Stephanie had left it on for her. She walked in to turn it off and discovered her sister-in-law sitting at the kitchen table with a mug bearing a silly blue snowman in front of her.

"Hey, you!" Elise exclaimed softly. "What are you still doing up?"

Stephanie gave her a quick smile and Elise thought how happy she was that her brother and one of her dearest friends had found love together. They had been married for three years now and seemed happier than ever.

"I couldn't sleep," Steph said.

"Everything okay?"

Stephanie made a face. "The baby's restless tonight. He's rolling around like he's calf roping in there."

Elise forced a laugh. "Maybe the kiddo is practicing the pre-Christmas hijinks to get the parents psyched and ready for all the sleepless nights a few years from now when he's a little kid waiting for Santa."

"Oh, don't remind me of that." Steph gestured to her mug. "I'm already having nightmares about putting together toys on Christmas Eve. I had a craving for cinnamon hot cocoa and thought it might help me and the baby relax a little. Want to join me?"

"Think I'll pass on the cocoa but I'll keep you company for a minute."

She sank into a chair across from Stephanie, thinking again how very much she had always loved the kitchen at Clifton's Pride. After she and her mother moved to Billings, Elise had missed many things about the ranch. Moonlit rides into the mountains, the excitement of roundup, the thrill of watching a newborn foal come into the world.

One of the things she had missed most of all was this kitchen, warm and comfortable and homey.

Steph and Helen had decorated the kitchen for Christmas, with greenery and lights and pinecones covering every unused space. As she sat with her sister-in-law in the hush of a December evening, she could fully understand why Steph and Grant loved it here so much.

She reached down and rubbed her feet, sore from her long day at ROOTS and then their snowy walk through Bozeman. Better not to think about that, she told herself, especially if she wanted to stick to her resolve to be only friends with Matt.

"How was your evening?" her sister-in-law asked.

Her mind flashed to the two kisses she and Matt had shared, both very different but equally intense.

"Nice." She paused, then added in what she hoped was a casual tone, "I went to Bozeman with Matt Cates."

"Helen mentioned you left her a message on her cell phone that you were going with him."

Elise heard the curiosity in her friend's voice and she purposely avoided her eyes. Steph and Haley both knew she'd had a major crush on Matt when they were girls. They had all giggled about him and Marlon and the other cute boys often enough at recess and sleepovers.

"Matt was trying to pick out a Christmas present for Haley and he asked for my input," she said.

"Did you find something?"

"Yes. I took him to that gallery near Grand Avenue, the one with all the embroidery. We found a gorgeous piece with an eagle alighting with outstretched wings in an oak tree. It will go beautifully in the ROOTS clubhouse."

Stephanie's eyes lit up. "That does sound perfect. Haley will be thrilled."

"I think so. It fits perfectly with her concept for

ROOTS, a place where teens can stretch their wings while remaining rooted to values and traditions."

"I didn't realize art galleries stayed open this late," Stephanie said.

Elise shot her a quick look but her sister-in-law merely sipped at her hot cocoa with an innocent look. "We went to dinner afterward at that steak house you and Grant took me to a few years ago."

Stephanie was quiet for a moment, then she looked at her with concern in her eyes. "I guess Matt's fiancée must be an understanding sort."

Elise froze as her heart gave one hard, brutal kick in her chest. "Sorry. His...what?"

Stephanie looked apologetic. "Well, I'm not sure it's official yet, but someone in town asked me about it today."

"I'm sure it was a mistake." Oh, heavens. Let it be a mistake. Fate wouldn't play that particularly nasty trick on her twice.

"I don't know. My source sounded pretty credible. Remember we saw him at dinner last night with Christine Mayhew? Tall, leggy brunette?"

"Yes," Elise said, her voice low. She remembered the woman vividly and the way she and Matt had appeared so cozy together.

"The mother of one of my riding students works at the front desk of Thunder Canyon Resort. Joanie Martin. After the lesson today, we were chatting about the party next week at the McFarlane Lodge and about how hard Matt and his father had rushed to finish it. In the course of the conversation, she asked me if I'd heard about Christine and Matt yet. She said she overheard Matt telling someone after dinner last night that he and Christine were making plans for their future together.

Speculation is they're going to announce it at Connor's big party on Christmas Eve."

The dinner she had barely touched at the Bozeman restaurant seemed to congeal into a hard, nasty ball inside her stomach. She thought of his kisses and the tenderness in his arms.

We could have something really fantastic together.

Had that just been a line? She tried to remember their conversation and realized he had never once said anything that implied he wanted anything more from her than the fling she'd accused him of wanting except for that—which in the abstract was vague enough it could mean anything. He could have just been talking about great sex, since they seemed to strike such sparks off each other.

Engaged. How could he be engaged? She wanted to deny it, to chide Stephanie for listening to gossip. But Steph wouldn't lie and she wouldn't repeat something unless she considered the source credible. Elise had seen them too, talking and laughing, had seen Matt's arm around the other woman.

Hadn't she always known he was a player? Oh, he might kiss her with breathtaking intensity but it obviously meant little to him.

She felt nauseous, remembering another time, another place, when she had been forced to stand politely by while the man she thought she loved, the one she had given her virginity to just a few weeks earlier, had introduced her to his very lovely bride to be.

Was it really possible that she had completely misread the situation with Matt? Now she couldn't meet Stephanie's concerned gaze, afraid of what her sister-in-law might read in her foolish, foolish eyes.

"Matt and I are just friends," she mumbled, wondering why her lips suddenly felt numb and achy.

Friends. The word rang hollow. She certainly couldn't consider any man a friend who would put her in this position—and worse, when he would betray his fiancée with such callous disregard.

How foolish she was, still hanging on to childish dreams. That she would even consider for a moment that Matt might genuinely have feelings for her made her just about the most pitiful woman in the county.

For just a moment, she fought down a vicious stab of jealousy that some other woman would know the sweetness of those kisses, the strength of his arms, the tenderness of his lying, cheating smile.

"I'm sorry, El," Steph said.

She forced her own smile, hoping it looked more genuine than it felt.

"About what? Matt and I are friends," she repeated. Friends who neglect to mention an impending engagement. Who laugh and tease and kiss and betray.

"Whether he's engaged or not is no business of mine," she lied. "He needed a favor, I owed him one for rescuing me the other night at The Hitching Post. Now we're square. He's free to be engaged to a dozen women, as far as I'm concerned."

Steph didn't quite look convinced. Small wonder, since Elise couldn't even convince herself.

"You know, I'm beat. Think I'll leave you to your cocoa and the quiet. I wouldn't want to get the little one riled up again now that you've calmed him down."

Stephanie smiled a little but touched Elise's hand with concern still in her eyes.

"It's really been wonderful having you back here at

the ranch. Just like old times. I don't think I've told you that enough since you came back."

Tears pricked the back of her eyelids as she hugged her sister-in-law and friend. She told herself it was just exhaustion from the busy day. "It's fun to watch you growing that baby in there. You're going to be a great mom, Steph."

Stephanie made a face. "We'll see about that. I have a lot to learn. But at least I can make a mean cup of hot cocoa."

Elise forced a smile and said good-night, then headed for her bedroom—the same one she had used when she was a girl, before her father's murder, when life at Clifton's Pride was warm and joyful.

By the time she closed the door behind her and sagged onto her bed with its blue-and-violet quilt, she was shaking with anger and something else, something dark and forlorn.

The anger was wholly justified. But she had no business entertaining even for a moment this yawning sense of betrayal, of loss.

Matt had never been hers. Not a half hour ago, she had bluntly told him she wasn't interested in a relationship. How pathetic must that had sounded to him, when he obviously wasn't interested in anything so formal, anyway?

She had a lucky escape, she reminded herself. Some wise part of her had warned her not to let herself be swept away by the moment, by the seductive magic of being in his arms.

Good thing she had listened to it and hadn't done something supremely foolish like allow her heart to get tangled up with his.

Right?

Chapter 8

"You're sure everything will be ready by the end of the week so we can bring in the decorators?" Connor Mc-Farlane surveyed the kitchen where Matt was currently installing the knobs and handles on the custom cabinetry.

"That's the plan," Matt answered, carefully setting another hole. "Everything is on schedule. The carpet layers will be here tomorrow and we'll do the floor trim and hang the closet systems the day after that, and that should wrap it all up."

"Good. Excellent. I've got a team of designers coming in from McFarlane House hotels to finish up and they've informed me they need at least four days."

"We should be good," Matt said again. Better than good. He loved a job well done. Finishing that job ahead of schedule was icing on the cake.

Connor ran a hand over the Italian marble countertops. "Cates Construction has gone above and beyond to bring the work in early. I want you to know I won't forget the work you've done here."

"It's been a pleasure." The words might seem polite but Matt sincerely meant them and he hoped Connor knew it.

He was proud to have his name associated with this particular construction project. McFarlane Lodge would be a showpiece in Thunder Canyon, tasteful and well-crafted. More than that, it would be warm and comfortable, a home for Connor, his son, CJ, and his wife to be, Tori Jones.

The only thing he loved more than setting the last tile and hammering the final nail was the other side of any building project: that first scoop of dirt in the backhoe, those heady days of pouring the foundation and framing the first few walls, when everything was still only possibilities.

He was particularly pleased about the chance to be part of building McFarlane Lodge, with its expansive views and the massive river-rock fireplace that served as the focal point in the open floor plan.

"I've got other irons in the fire around Thunder Canyon," Connor said with a significant look. "I'm going to need a dependable contractor. I'd love to keep Cates Construction at the top of that list."

Matt experienced a sharp burst of pride and a not inconsiderable degree of elation. He didn't doubt that the hotel magnate had various projects underway. Connor always seemed to be cooking up something and in this economy, anything that allowed Cates Construction to keep its workers swinging a hammer was a blessing.

"If we can fit in the job with our other commitments, we'll be happy to consider whatever work you send our way," he said, moving on to the next cabinet.

Connor smiled and patted the countertop. "I'm sure we can work something out. I'll be in touch."

"Sure thing."

After McFarlane left the kitchen a moment later, Matt glanced toward the adjacent laundry room. A grizzled gray buzz cut bobbed there and he could see his father lurking, pretending not to listen.

"You catch all that, Dad?" he asked with a grin.

Frank walked into the kitchen. "I heard. He's right. You've done a hell of a job with the place."

"This isn't a one-man show. The whole crew worked their tails off to get 'er done by Christmas."

"Don't be humble, son." Frank gave him a stern look. "It doesn't fit you. You're the one who made it happen on time and under budget and every single man on the crew knows it."

Matt flushed at the unexpected accolades. Frank was a good man and a wonderful father but he wasn't one for outright praise—his style was more like subtle encouragement. Matt didn't know quite how to respond.

"You've done so well the last few years, you're starting to put ideas in your mother's head."

Matt looked up and found his father looking remarkably ill at ease. "Oh? What sort of ideas?"

"Crazy ones." Frank sighed. "She's talking about taking a cruise. Maybe even a couple of them. She's even brought up maybe heading somewhere warm for the winter. Southern Utah, maybe, or Arizona. You know how the cold bothers her."

The idea of a Thunder Canyon without his parents was just too strange to contemplate. "What do you think about her ideas?"

His father was silent for a long moment. "I'm considering them. I've been in this business a long time. I've got old habits, old ways. Maybe it's time somebody else shook some new life into Cates Construction."

"Dad—"

"Your brothers aren't much interested in construction, son. Marshall's busy at the hospital and Mitch and Marlon both have their own companies. I don't suppose it's a surprise to you or any of them that I would like you to take over for me. Hell, you're doing most of the work, anyway. I'd just like to make it more official."

Excitement pulsed through him. This was what he wanted, he realized. Taking over the operations of Cates Construction fit him much better than law school ever could.

"I would have asked you before but I didn't want you to feel tied down to Thunder Canyon. You're still young. Your mother and I have always wanted you boys to feel free to experience the world on your own terms, not ours. But now that it looks like you're settling down, I figured this would be a good time to get things out in the open."

Matt stared. "Now that I'm what?"

His father looked uncomfortable. "Your mother's got some crazy idea you're getting married."

"Where did you hear that?" he asked.

"Apparently Edie heard a rumor last night at her bunco club about you," he answered. "A couple different people dropped a bug in her ear that you and Christine are talking about tying the knot."

The hammer suddenly slipped out of his fingers and he barely managed to snag it before it would have clattered onto the Italian tile floor.

He mentally hissed an expletive he wouldn't dare say aloud in front of his father. He should have known his impulsive gesture Sunday at The Gallatin Room would come back to bite him in the rear one day. He hadn't been thinking clearly or he never would have started the charade.

What the hell was he supposed to say to his father now?

"Um, don't believe everything you hear, Dad. Christine and I aren't getting married."

Frank narrowed his gaze. "What are you up to, son?"

"Nothing. This is all a big misunderstanding."

"I thought I taught you boys better than to mess around when it comes to this sort of thing."

"You did. I haven't been messing around."

Frank cleared his throat, looking ill at ease. "A woman's heart is a fragile thing, son. It's like that tile down there. If you'd dropped your hammer a minute ago, you might have chipped one of them fancy tiles. We might have repaired it, filled it in a bit. On the surface, it might look good as new, but there would always be a weakness there."

His father gave him a stern look. "Christine is a nice girl. If you're not serious about her, you need to cut her loose so she can find somebody who will be."

He did *not* want to be having this conversation with his father right now. "I hear you, Dad. Thanks for the advice."

"So you're going to do the right thing by Christine?"

"If by doing the right thing you mean marry her, then no. Trust me, Dad. Christine is not expecting an engagement ring from me. We're good friends, that's all."

His father continued to study him. "I hope you're right. I guess I need to tell your mother she won't be planning another wedding anytime soon."

For one insane moment, Matt pictured Elise in a white dress, something feminine and lovely, flowers in her blond hair and her face bright and joyful.

Whoa. Slow down. He drew in a sharp breath, astonished at the yearning trickling through him.

He wasn't at all ready to go there yet. Even if *he* was—which he clearly wasn't, right?—Elise certainly had made it apparent the night before that she didn't want to have anything with him beyond friendship.

That seductive image faded like an old photograph under a hard western sun. He had his work cut out for him to convince her he wanted more. But Matt had never been the sort to back down from a challenge.

Three hours later, Matt drove through town on his way to drop off a bid at a restaurant in Old Town Thunder Canyon that was planning a big remodeling project.

If the restaurant just happened to be on the same street as ROOTS, well, that was a happy coincidence. It would give him a chance to implement his new strategy for winning Elise over.

She claimed she didn't want to lose their friendship. Great. Fine. He had decided he would be the best damn friend she'd ever had. He would offer a sympathetic ear, a helping hand, a shoulder—whatever part of his anatomy she needed, until she discovered she didn't know how she could survive without him.

Though it was a weekday afternoon, Christmas shoppers were out in force in town. He happened to spy Bo Clifton and his very pregnant wife, Holly, heading into a clothing store, and Tori Jones and Allaire Traub coming out of the florists with their arms full of what looked like poinsettias and evergreen branches.

After he dropped off the bid to the restaurant owner, he dodged holiday shoppers and slushy snow piles down the street a few storefronts to the ROOTS clubhouse.

Connor McFarlane's son, CJ, sat with Ryan Chilton

and a couple of other boys at one of the tables with text-books open in front of them, though they didn't seem to be paying them much attention. A couple of teen girls he didn't know looked bored as they leafed through magazines on the couch.

As he had hoped, Elise was at Haley's desk, the phone pressed to her ear. Her gaze lifted at the sound of the bells on the door chiming, a ready smile on her features.

The moment she spied him coming through the door, her smile slid away and her expression turned stony, much to his consternation.

He eased into the chair across from the desk. By the time she finished her phone call, her eyes were the wintry blue of the Montana sky on a clear January afternoon and her jaw looked set in concrete.

She hung up the phone, a muscle twitching in her cheek. "Can I help you?"

Not a good sign, when her voice was even colder than her eyes.

"Um, I was in the neighborhood dropping off a bid and figured I'd walk down and see if you need help filling the gift bags."

"They're done," she said curtly. "I finished them today."

This wasn't going at all as he'd hoped. "Okay, then. Any idea what my assignment might be for the Christmas party? Haley said something about needing some muscle for setting up tables, that sort of thing."

"I don't know. You'll have to ask her that."

"I'm assuming since you're here and she's not that she's still laid low with the flu," he hazarded a guess.

Elise jerked her head in a nod. "She sounded better this morning when she called. She should be back tomorrow. I'm sure you can talk to her then."

So much for his grand master plan. Elise was acting as if she didn't even want to share the same air space with him. The night before, she had said she didn't want to lose their friendship. Had he screwed that up now?

"What's wrong?" he finally asked warily. "You seem upset."

She made the same sort of sound his mother did when he tracked job-site mud on her mopped floors. "Do I?"

He looked around the ROOTS clubhouse to make sure none of the teens were paying attention to them, then he leaned forward. "Is this about last night?"

Her jaw hardened even more and for a long moment, he didn't think she would answer him. When she spoke, the chill in her voice was nearing arctic proportions.

"I suppose you could say that. You put me in a terrible position."

He glanced at the teens, who seemed to be arguing about some super-hero movie and paying absolutely no attention to them.

"Why? Because I kissed you?" he asked in a low voice. "You weren't complaining at the time."

Whoops. Wrong thing to say. The ice queen disappeared in an instant. Elise shoved her chair back and rose, her color high. He wouldn't have expected it, but apparently his quiet, sweet Elise could pack a pretty decent temper.

"You haven't changed a bit," she snapped. "You're the same wild, irresponsible cowboy who thinks he can use his charm to get away with anything!"

Where did that come from? "Hold it right there," he said, pitching his voice low. "What the hell did I do?"

"You kissed me!" she hissed.

That drew the attention of the teens. A couple of them—the girls especially—cast sidelong looks in their direction. Maybe this conversation would be better in private, he thought, about five minutes too late.

He gestured with his head to the teens and then pointed to a back room. Mortification replaced some of the anger in her eyes but she gave a short nod and headed into the back room, closing the door behind them.

"I guess I haven't read the Thunder Canyon town ordinances closely enough," Matt said when they had some measure of privacy. "I didn't realize kissing a beautiful woman had been outlawed when I wasn't looking."

Two high spots of color flared on her cheeks. "It might not be a crime, but it's wrong on so many levels I don't even know where to start."

"Why?"

"You're engaged to marry someone else!"

He stared at her for about twenty seconds. He closed his eyes, cursing his big mouth and the white knight syndrome he couldn't seem to shake.

"This is about Christine?"

"Of *course* it's about Christine! I can't believe you even have to ask! I always knew you were a player, I just never imagined you would take things this far."

He had a feeling this was a disclaimer he was going to have to provide a few times before the rumors around Thunder Canyon started to fade. "I'm not engaged to Christine. I never was. We're only friends."

"Funny, that's not the rumor going around town. The minute I walked in the house last night, Stephanie was bending my ear about your engagement. And she's not the only one. I've now heard it from more than one person."

He loved living in Thunder Canyon but life in a small town where everybody cared about your business had some definite downfalls. A stray bit of gossip could run rampant like an August wildfire. With just a little fuel, it would spread to every corner, wreaking havoc in its path.

And he had stupidly been the one to set the match to this particular rumor. He should have expected this, damn it.

The hell of it was, he couldn't go around putting out this particular fire completely, not if Christine was going to convince her jackass of an ex that they were done.

He might not be able to tell everyone, but he could certainly confide the truth to Elise, he decided. "Look, if I tell you something, I need you to keep it to yourself, at least for a little while."

She crossed her arms over her chest, obviously not at all in the mood to listen to anything he had to say. Still, she didn't toss him out so he figured he would take what he could get at this point.

"The truth is, Christine had an overenthusiastic exboyfriend a few months back who couldn't seem to get the message they were really over. I wouldn't exactly put him in the stalker category, but maybe a step or two down from that. She confided in me one night what she'd been going through and somehow we decided to pretend to be dating in hopes the ex would finally figure out it was over."

"So out of the goodness of your heart, you agreed to pretend to date a beautiful woman with absolutely pure and altruistic motives."

He fought down annoyance at her sharp tone. "I never said that. I'll be honest, it was a mutually beneficial arrangement. My parents stopped bugging me for a while about settling down for the first time since Haley and Marlon got together. And I enjoy Christine's company. She's a very fun person. But we're not engaged and never will be. Neither of us feels that way about the other."

She didn't look convinced. "For the sake of argument, let's say I was stupid enough to believe you. Don't you think becoming engaged to the woman is taking your charade a little too far?"

He sighed. How to explain this part without sounding like a complete idiot? "We bumped into a cousin of the ex-boyfriend outside The Gallatin Room the other night. Completely on the spur of the moment, I figured this was the perfect opportunity to convince the guy things were over, once and for all. I never really stopped to consider the consequences, that word might trickle out and we would have to explain the truth someday."

He thought he detected a slight thaw in her expression but it was barely perceptible so he pressed harder.

"I'm telling the truth, Elise. Come on, think about it. Do you really believe I'm the kind of guy who would announce his engagement one night, then spend the next night kissing someone else?"

She gave him a long, considering look. "I can't answer that, Matt. I guess that's part of the problem. I've been away from Thunder Canyon for a long time. All I know are the rumors I've heard about your wild past. Didn't you and Marlon get engaged a few years ago to twins you'd barely met?"

He winced. She *would* have to dredge up that little gem of a story, one of his less than stellar moments. "We were young and stupid. I think it was more of a joke than anything. Marlon and I have both changed over the years. Look at him, happily engaged to Haley. And he was always the reckless one, not me. I was mostly along for the ride."

He thought the ice thawed just a little more. At least she didn't look ready to feed him to the wolves yet.

"Trust your instincts, El," he said softly, reaching for

her hand. "We're friends. I wouldn't treat any woman like that, not Christine and not you."

She stared at him for a long moment and he could feel the tremble of her slender fingers. She swallowed hard and opened her mouth to say something, but at that moment the door was shoved open.

CJ McFarlane burst in, all auburn hair and lanky skater boy. He didn't seem to notice any of the fine-edged tension in the room. "We're starving, Miz Clifton. Okay if we nuke a couple bags of popcorn? Haley keeps a supply back here."

"Um, sure." She stepped away from Matt and tucked a strand of hair behind her ear. "Anything else you need?"

"No. Popcorn ought to do it."

She gave Matt a long look, then returned to the other room. He followed, frustrated and more than a little annoyed that she was being so stubborn.

"I guess I'll give Haley a call about what she needs me to do for the party. Sorry I bothered you," he said tersely and headed for the door.

"Matt. Wait."

He turned. "Yeah?"

She twisted her fingers together and chewed her bottom lip. "What was I supposed to think?" she finally said with a quick look at the kids. "Stephanie's not the sort to make up stories."

"And I'm not the sort to string two women along. You ought to know me better than that."

She sighed. "I've been in that position before, in college. The other woman, I mean. My first real boyfriend was a…well, a jerk. I dated him for three months and never knew he had been engaged for a year to marry a girl in his hometown right after graduation. Then I bumped into them one day while they were picking out wedding flowers and had to stand there, stunned and heartbroken, while he introduced me as some girl he had a class with."

She paused, fidgeting with a stapler on Haley's desk. "It was an awful situation. I hated thinking you could do the same thing to me or to Christine."

He sighed. He felt like he was doing nothing but taking one step forward and two or three giant steps backward with her.

"I'm sorry you were hurt that way. But I'm not some idiot you knew in college, Elise. You've known me for a long time. You should have given me a chance to explain before you jumped to all kinds of crazy conclusions."

He was hurt, he realized. It was a feeling he wasn't very accustomed to when it came to his dealings with women.

"I've got to go." He didn't want her to see it, didn't want to reveal the depth of his feelings for her just yet, not when she was fighting him every step of the way. "Tell Haley I dropped by and I'll do whatever she needs me to for the party."

"Matt—"

He didn't wait for whatever else she wanted to say, only pushed open the door and walked out of the ROOTS clubhouse and into the December afternoon that seemed to have lost all its good cheer.

Chapter 9

"Everything looks absolutely perfect!"

Haley slung her arm over Elise's shoulders and pulled her close as they stood in the doorway admiring the winter wonderland they had spent all day creating in the ROOTS clubhouse.

"You did a fantastic job with the whole thing. You should be a party planner, El. You didn't need me after all," Haley said.

"Not true. I never could have thrown it all together without you the last two days. I still think you're overdoing it, though. Are you sure you're up to this?"

"I'm feeling almost back to normal, if I can only shed this stupid cough." As if to illustrate her point, she suddenly had to step away from Elise in order to cough into the corner of her sleeve.

"Sorry. I really am feeling better," she said after a moment. "Those garlands you made are fantastic and the swag bags are perfect."

"The kids are going to have a great time." She smiled at her friend, noting all the changes in Haley over the last few months. Her friend glowed with happiness, even though she still looked pale and worn-out from her illness.

Elise was thrilled for her. Haley's handbag design business, HA! was taking off, she was passionately committed to the success of ROOTS and she was deeply in love with Marlon Cates, who loved her right back.

She deserved all those wonderful things and more after giving up her dreams early in order to take care of her younger siblings after her single mother's untimely death.

Elise wouldn't have begrudged her any of it and she refused to feel even a tiny niggle of envy that everything seemed to be coming together so perfectly for Haley when Elise's life seemed like such a tangled mess.

"What you're doing here is a good thing, Haley. It's been really cool to be a part of it this week, in my small way."

"Not small." Haley squeezed her arm with affection. "You know we would have had to cancel the whole thing if you hadn't stepped in to save the day. I can't begin to tell you how much I appreciate it."

"I had help," Elise said. "Your hardworking volunteers plus those amazing kids."

"They are, aren't they? Amazing, I mean. I think I get more out of associating with them than the other way around."

She looked at the clock suddenly. "And speaking of the kids, they're going to be here any minute now. You're staying, right? I won't let you leave, not after all your hard work."

Elise nodded. "I brought some party clothes to change into so I didn't have to go back to the ranch to change."

"See, that's why you always were the smartest girl I know."

Ha, Elise thought as she headed for the ROOTS women's restroom. If she were as smart as Haley thought, she would have stayed far away from Matt Cates the moment she spied him at The Hitching Post the other night. Instead, she had let her life become more and more entwined with his and now here she was fighting down completely inappropriate anticipation at the likely possibility that he would come to the party.

Not that he would be thrilled to see her. The last time she had seen him, the anger in his eyes that she had believed he was two-timing his fiancée by kissing Elise would have melted every inch of snow on the whole road out front.

She hadn't seen him in four days, since that tense scene here. His outrage still seemed unfair. If he was telling the truth—and she still hadn't managed to completely convince herself of that, despite every instinct that urged her to believe him—he and Christine Mayhew *wanted* people to think they were engaged, right?

Or at least one particular person, Christine's ex-boyfriend.

For him to be angry with Elise for believing the rumors they had started themselves seemed wrong, somehow.

She changed quickly, out of jeans and a hooded sweatshirt into a pair of black slacks and a shimmery white blouse, sheer at the neck and sleeves, then sighed as she replaced the utilitarian small hoops she'd put in her ears that morning with her favorite chunky, dangly crystals.

Why did it matter if Matt was upset with her? Engaged

or not, her reasons for stopping their kiss the other night at Clifton's Pride remained. Nothing had changed since Monday. If anything, things were more tangled than ever now that Jack and Betty Castro were returning to Thunder Canyon for the holidays.

She thought of the phone call she had received the night before from Betty and her stomach quivered with nerves.

Betty and Jack were back in Montana, staying with friends in Billings. Betty had sounded desperately eager for Elise to join them for dinner on Sunday. She knew they genuinely wanted to get to know her, to forge whatever relationship they could with her.

Elise had always considered herself a nice person. She tried to treat people with decency and respect. But the Castros' continued overtures made her want to saddle up one of the Clifton's Pride horses and ride fast and hard into the mountains to hide out somewhere she wouldn't be found for days.

Her reaction was ridiculous, she knew, and rather shameful. The Castros weren't trying to hurt her. They only wanted to become acquainted with the child who had been taken from them by circumstances beyond anyone's control.

After she applied a new coat of mascara, Elise gazed in the mirror at the face she had seen looking back for twenty-six years. She had inherited her cheekbones, her eyes, the curve of her mouth from Betty and Jack. Didn't she owe it to them to at least be cordial?

She had two brothers she didn't know, an entire family history to learn. She couldn't keep avoiding them, hoping this whole tangled mess would just sort itself out. It was time to face her angst.

But not tonight. This was a Christmas party and she wouldn't ruin it for the teens that Haley helped.

The first guests had started to arrive by the time Elise finished changing her clothes and makeup. Haley had started playing some holiday music and Elise could see a group of teens already taking to the small dance floor they had set up.

She could see Haley's siblings, Austin and Angie, as well as many of the volunteers and teens she had become acquainted with the past week, including CJ McFarlane, Roy Robbins and Ryan Chilton.

Marlon was helping Haley fiddle with the speakers.

And Matt. Her insides did a long, slow roll when she spotted him filling glasses with punch at the refreshments table.

He looked dark and rugged and absolutely gorgeous in a dark green sweater, tan slacks and boots.

He wasn't alone, Haley suddenly realized. Next to him was the lovely brunette she recognized from the restaurant the other night, though that seemed a lifetime ago.

Christine Mayhew.

They were talking and laughing but she had to admit they looked more friendly than romantic. Was it possible he was telling the truth? She wanted to believe him. The last three days she hadn't heard any more rumors about any engagement—but she hadn't heard anything about it being a sham, either.

Haley suddenly grabbed her arm, distracting her from any more pointless wondering. "Help! I can't find the MP3 player I spent hours loading with a Christmas dance mix while I was sick," Haley wailed. "Have you seen it?"

"Is it your pink one? I think I saw it on the table in the back room. Let me go see if I can find it."

She supposed it wasn't a very good sign when she

couldn't wait to leave a party not three minutes after she showed up. She hurried to the other room and emerged a moment later with the MP3 player in her hand.

Haley hugged her. "You're a lifesaver! We would have had to listen to 'Jingle Bell Rock' all night."

"Oh, horrors!"

Her friend laughed and headed back to Marlon and the sound system. Elise was just about to go talk to Austin and Angie when she saw Christine Mayhew heading in her direction.

The other woman was indeed beautiful, tall and curvy. Elise felt about twelve years old in contrast.

She wasn't at all prepared when Christine gave her a warm, friendly smile. "You're Elise Clifton, right?"

"Yes," she admitted warily.

"I'm Christine Mayhew. Matt's told me a lot about you."

"Has he?"

Christine's smile was warm and open and not the slightest bit jealous. "I have to tell you, I've never seen him like this about any other woman."

She stared. "Like…what?"

"Nothing. Sorry. Forget I said anything." Christine sent an amused look over her shoulder to where Matt was watching them intently. "I'm on a very important mission here tonight."

"Oh?"

"I'm under strict orders to convince you beyond a sliver of doubt that Matt and I are not engaged."

Elise cast a quick look at Matt then shifted her gaze away. She knew perfectly well she shouldn't have this little fizz of happiness welling up inside at the word.

"Matt is a great guy," Christine went on. "Don't get me wrong. I care about him and always will. But there won't be any wedding bells ringing for the two of us. We're friends, that's all. I swear it."

What was she supposed to say in response? *I'm really happy to hear that* didn't seem quite appropriate under the circumstances.

"He was doing me a favor," the other woman said firmly.

"Why are you telling me this?"

"Matt asked me to. He told me he explained it all to you but you still had some doubts."

"What about your ex-boyfriend?"

Christine shrugged. "Word on the street is that he's started dating someone else recently. I can only hope she turns out to be a keeper for him so he'll take my number off his speed dial."

She paused and studied Elise until she could feel her face heat in another of those blasted blushes. "Can I give you some advice?"

"Okay," she said slowly.

"I've been friends with Matt for a while now and as I said, I've never seen him like this over any woman." Christine gave her a careful smile. "I think you're more important to him than even he wants to admit."

Elise shot him another look. Though he was busy talking to his twin brother, he must have felt the weight of her stare because he shifted his attention to her. For a moment they stared at each other and the crowd, the decorations, the music all seemed to fade.

"Matt is a great guy. When he finally falls for a woman, I have a feeling he will move heaven and earth to make her feel happy and safe and loved."

Elise drew in a shaky breath. She didn't know what to say. She did know she shouldn't be fighting this powerful yearning to be that woman.

"Pretending to be his girlfriend these last few months has been great fun," Christine added, her glittery earrings reflecting the Christmas lights from the tree. "I can only imagine being the real thing would be a million times better."

With that parting shot, she walked away, leaving Elise floundering for a response.

For the next hour, she carefully avoided Matt as she circulated among the party guests and helped Haley with hostess duties. She knew she owed him an apology for ever doubting him but the middle of a noisy, festive party full of teenagers didn't quite seem the proper venue.

She was in the kitchen preparing another plate of appetizers when she finally couldn't avoid him any longer.

He walked in and something unreadable flashed in his gaze when he spotted her there. "I'm under orders from Haley to see if there are any more of those cheesy cream puff thingies in here."

"A few. I was just about to carry them out."

"Here, I can take them." She handed him the tray but instead of heading back out to the party, he stood in the doorway.

"It's a great party, Elise. Haley's giving you all the credit."

"Not true," she protested. "She had already laid all the groundwork. I only had to finalize a few details."

"Well, you did a great job. Everyone seems to be having a wonderful time, from the kids to their parents to the volunteers. And I know fundraising wasn't the intent of the party but Haley said donations have been pouring in."

She could barely focus on anything but Christine's words. *I've never seen him like this about another woman.*

She had to be wrong. He was treating her just like he

treated everyone else. Maybe even on the cold side of the politeness thermostat.

"More donations are always good."

He gave a short laugh and set the plate of appetizers back down on the counter. "Yeah, they are. Haley has done wonders with a small amount of money. Who knows what she can accomplish when her funds increase?"

He paused and gave her a careful look. "So do you want to tell me why you sound like I just told you somebody injected botulism into the cream puff thingies?"

She blinked, then flushed. "I'm happy about the donations. I just… I… I owe you an apology."

"I guess you've talked to Christine."

She sighed. "She was only corroborating what I already knew. I believed you that day you came here to ROOTS and explained about your sham engagement."

He winced. "It was never supposed to go that far, I swear it. I didn't expect anyone else to hear about it. I'm sorry you were caught up in it. The whole thing was stupid."

Christine was right, Elise realized. Matt was a good man. When he gave his heart, he would give it completely. He would never betray the woman he loved for some thrill *du jour.*

He couldn't be more different than her first boyfriend.

She drew in a deep breath, her pulse racing. "Christine basically told me I would be crazy if I didn't…give things with you a chance."

He gazed down at her but said nothing for several long moments. The party sounds were muted in here, just a throb of bass, and she could swear she heard her heart beating in her ears, keeping time to the music.

"Are you going to listen to her?" he finally asked.

She swallowed hard and realized just where they were

both standing—under one of the many clumps of mistletoe the kids had hung for the party.

"I'm thinking about it," she murmured, then without giving herself time to second-guess, she rose on tiptoes and brushed his mouth with hers.

He froze for just a moment, his mouth firm and delicious against hers, and then he made a low sound in his throat and kissed her back with a slow and aching gentleness.

Both of them kept their eyes open and she was hypnotized by the deep brown of his eyes as he stared back at her, unsmiling.

In that instant, she made a decision, what felt like a monumental one to her.

She eased away and gave him a tentative smile. "Would you like to go to Billings Sunday with me to have dinner with my…with Jack and Betty Castro?"

He looked as if he hadn't quite heard her right. "You want me to go with you while you have dinner with your birth parents?"

She nodded, feeling edgy and foolish and wondering if she was crazy to even ask. "To be honest, I think I could use a friend on my side there. But more than that, I really would like to…spend time with you. If you want to, anyway. I thought it would give us a little time to talk, on the way there and back."

She sounded like a complete idiot. Why couldn't she be smart and sophisticated, someone like Christine?

But Matt didn't seem to mind. His eyes were warm and he seemed to know exactly how difficult she had found it to ask him.

"That sounds terrific. Really terrific, as long as you're sure the Castros won't mind if I tag along."

"I don't think they will."

"Great. It's a date."

A date. She did a little mental gulp but it was too late to back down now.

"We'd better get these appetizers in there before those teenage boys start eating the popcorn strings I worked so hard on."

"Good idea."

He grabbed the plate and they headed back into the reception area.

Christine was sitting at a table talking to Erika Traub and a very pregnant Holly Clifton. She smiled when she saw them emerge from the kitchen together but Elise was painfully aware of a few speculative looks zinging between the two of them and Christine.

When news started to filter out of Matt's "breakup" with Christine, speculation was bound to fly that perhaps Elise was the cause of it. The thought of being the subject of more gossip filled her with dread and for a moment she was tempted to tell Matt to forget about everything.

No. She was tougher than that. She could withstand gossip. Hadn't she been doing it since her father's murder?

Matt smiled at her and she resolved to forget about everything for the rest of the night, to simply enjoy the party.

It was long past time she found a little holiday spirit.

Chapter 10

"What was your favorite subject in school?"

Elise took a sip from her water glass at the elegant restaurant in Billings, doing her best to handle what felt very much like an interrogation. Beside her, Matt nudged his knee against hers and out of the corner of her gaze, she took great comfort from his supportive smile.

"Um, English," she finally answered. "I've always loved to read. Working in a bookstore is a dream come true."

That was apparently the perfect thing to say to a high school teacher. Betty's eyes warmed and her smile widened. "You come by that naturally, my dear. Women on my side of the family have always been big readers. My mother, my aunts. All of us. They're all dying to meet you, by the way."

Oh, mercy. Elise hadn't given much thought to extended relatives she might have to meet. Aunts, uncles, cousins. Just the thought of it had her snatching up her water glass again and gulping it like she had just run a marathon through the Mojave.

Under the table, she felt Matt's leg nudge her knee again. He was doing it on purpose, she knew, offering her whatever physical comfort she could take from his touch.

"So Jack, tell me about being a police officer in San Diego. Harbor police, isn't it?" Matt asked as smoothly as the attorney he might have become, finessing a witness. "You probably deal with some really fascinating cases. What were you working on just before you came out to Montana?"

"My partner and I are trying to nail a money launderer working with the Mexican cartels. It's mostly legwork but we've had some close calls."

With Matt's subtle encouragement, all through their entrées Jack told stories about his work while Betty added her own perspective about what life was like being married to a police officer.

Elise liked both of them. They seemed to be a genuinely nice couple who loved each other and their family. That was one of the toughest things about everything that had happened. If circumstances had been different, she would very much have enjoyed the chance to get to know them.

Jack was just like the delicious cheese rolls they served at the restaurant…crusty on the outside but warm and gooey at heart. Betty was smart and funny with a deep streak of kindness Elise had already sensed.

They seemed great, two people she instinctively wanted to know better. But everyone just seemed to expect so much of her.

Maybe it was only her. Erin didn't seem to be having the same trouble adjusting to everything. From the moment Erin met Helen and Grant, she seemed to instantly love them and had melded into the fiber of their family with apparent ease, with none of this stiff awkwardness Elise felt around her birth parents.

Elise knew she couldn't love them as parents and probably never would. Helen and John were her parents and no amount of DNA testing would ever change that, just as Matt kept trying to tell her. She just wished she could relax and become more comfortable with Jack and Betty's eagerness to be part of her life.

She just had to try harder, she told herself. "How long will you be staying in Montana?" she asked at the next conversational lull.

Betty and Jack exchanged a look. "We don't have to be back for work until after the New Year," Betty said.

"We actually wanted to talk to you about that," Jack added.

Her nerves suddenly tightened. "Oh?"

"Erin tells us you've left your job at that bookstore here in Billings to spend some time in Thunder Canyon with your mother and brother."

"I'm not sure if that's a permanent leave or not. I guess you could say I'm on sabbatical."

Jack and Betty exchanged another look, then Betty reached across the table and gripped Elise's hand in hers. Her birth mother's fingers were long and slender, just like hers, Elise thought.

"I know we've mentioned this in passing before but we wanted to make more of a formal offer. We would really love you to come stay with us for a while."

Elise felt a lump rise in her throat at their hopeful faces and she didn't know how to respond.

Betty squeezed her fingers. "We have tons of room now. It's just the two of us, since your brothers..." She faltered a little and looked at Jack for help, then cleared her throat. "Since our sons are both back east now."

Elise had never lived anywhere but Montana. The idea of moving to California wasn't without some appeal, she had to admit, but beneath the table, Matt's long leg tensed next to hers and a muscle flexed in his jaw—reminding her of a very big reason she wasn't sure she wanted to leave Montana just now.

The Castros seemed to sense her hesitation.

"Don't worry about answering now," Jack said in that gruff tone she was beginning to recognize was characteristic for him when his emotions were involved. "You just think about it over the holidays. And you know, maybe you might enjoy just coming down for a couple weeks and testing the waters a bit."

"Which are lovely, by the way," Betty added. "The waters, I mean. Beach, sunshine, perfect weather."

"Beats scraping six inches of snow off your car every morning during a Montana winter," Jack said.

"I can see where it would." She managed a smile, more than a little charmed by this taciturn police officer.

She thought of her father, strong and honorable and handsome, always willing to listen to her troubles and offer her advice. She had desperately missed having a father in her life during her formative teenage years, when everything from boys to school to her future seemed so confusing. Grant had tried to fill a paternal role in her life, but an older brother's advice wasn't quite the same as a father's.

"I'll think about it," she promised them now, aware of Matt's continued tension beside her.

The conversation shifted to foods she enjoyed and stories about her childhood. By the time they finished dessert, some of the tautness in her shoulders had eased.

She was suddenly glad she had come—and immensely grateful to Matt for being so willing to step up and join them as her support system.

"Thank you for coming all the way to Billings just for dinner," Jack said after he'd picked up the check. "We would have been happy to come to Thunder Canyon, you know. We're going to be there anyway in a few days."

"I know. That's what Betty said when we discussed arrangements over the phone. But I really didn't mind coming here."

Actually, she had been the one to suggest they meet in Billings—she just hadn't told the Castros why—that she wanted to avoid all the prying eyes in Thunder Canyon and those who would be sure to gossip about Elise meeting up with her birth parents for dinner.

Since the Castros mentioned they planned to stay with friends in Billings before coming to Thunder Canyon in time for Christmas, she had jumped at the opportunity to meet them in relatively neutral territory.

"This was lovely," Betty said while they were finding their coats.

"It was." Elise shivered a little when Matt's fingers brushed her hair as he helped her into her coat.

"We'll see you again while we're here," Betty said. "Your mother invited us out to the ranch for Christmas Eve, then called back to say you were all going to a big party at some new lodge and we were invited to that as well."

Helen hadn't mentioned she had invited the Castros to Connor McFarlane's lodge opening.

"Everyone in town is talking about it," Elise said. "Matt and his father actually built it."

"It will be good to see some of our old Thunder Canyon friends," Jack said.

A few hours ago, Elise might have dreaded the idea of facing them again in a few days. Now she didn't find it nearly as overwhelming. She was making progress, she thought. Baby steps still made up forward motion, right?

"Have a safe journey back to town, my dear," Betty said. She wrapped Elise in a lavender-scented hug. When she pulled away, Elise was disconcerted to see tears in her eyes. She was more surprised when Jack also wrapped his arms around her.

"You think about what we said, about coming down to San Diego. We would sure love having you there."

"I will," she promised.

Matt took her hand when they left the restaurant. The sky was a starless matte black and the air carried the smell of impending snow.

Matt held the door of his pickup open for her. Acting completely on impulse, Elise brushed her lips along his jawline. "Thank you so much for coming with me tonight. It means the world to me. I'm not sure I could have made it through without you."

He shook his head and kissed her forehead. "You did fine, El. Great, in fact. I could barely tell you were nervous."

She eased back onto the seat while he walked around to the driver's side. When he climbed inside and started the truck, he immediately turned the heater on high to take away the chill.

"They seem like nice people," he said.

"They are." She closed her eyes and rotated her neck to ease some of the strain of the evening. "I think I suddenly realized tonight that letting them into my life and maybe my heart isn't really a betrayal of my family."

He gripped her fingers in his. "Of course it's not. There's room enough in there for everybody."

Including tall, dark-eyed cowboys with sexy smiles.

Elise shivered a little, suddenly stunned by how very quickly Matt had become such an important part of her life.

Despite the poor timing and the general emotional uproar in her life, she was falling in love with him. Real love, not some girlish infatuation. Each moment she spent with him, those ties binding her heart to him tugged a little more tightly.

She ought to be terrified, but somehow all she could manage for now was a little flare of panic, quickly squelched.

"I hate to ask after you've already been so wonderful to come all this way with me just for a steak…"

"A great steak. And wonderful company," he corrected.

She smiled. "Right. But I forgot one of my mother's Christmas presents at our house here in Billings. I bought it months ago and hid it in the back of the closet. Somehow I overlooked it when I was packing for the move to Thunder Canyon. The house is only a few blocks from here. Do you mind if we stop there before we head back?"

"Not at all."

She gave him directions and a few moments later they drove down the wide, tidy street where she and her mother had lived for more than a decade.

Neighbors along their street had always enthusiastically celebrated the holidays. Every house had decorations of some sort—from a couple of those big inflatable snow globe thingies to the discreet colored bulbs the sweet, elderly Mrs. Hoopes in the little house on the corner left up year-round.

By contrast, the small brick house she shared with her mother looked dark and cheerless against the dank sky, even though a few of the windows gleamed with the lights they had set on timers to avoid announcing to the world the house was empty.

They should have at least put up a Christmas tree before they left for Thunder Canyon. Neither of them had thought of it in all the craziness of discovering the mix-up at Thunder Canyon Hospital twenty-six years ago.

"So do you think you'll go to San Diego with the Castros?" Matt asked after he put the pickup in gear in the driveway of her house.

She shot him a quick look. Though his tone was casual, his brown eyes watched her intently. Her mind flashed back to that stunning kiss beneath the mistletoe, to the soft, tender peace that had wrapped around them like holiday ribbons.

"I need to give it more thought. I certainly wouldn't mind escaping the cold this winter but there are...other reasons I'm not sure I want to leave Thunder Canyon right now."

The silence seemed to seethe between them and she could feel her cheeks burn from more than just the pickup's heater. She reached for the door handle, needing to escape the finely wrought tension inside the cab.

"It should only take me a moment to find the gift in my closet."

"I'll come with you," he said.

"If you want, I'm sure I can find some cocoa or something before we start out back to Thunder Canyon."

"Sounds great."

He opened the door for her then took her elbow to help her through the snow. She and her mother had paid a neighbor boy to keep the walks clear and it looked as if he was keeping up with his responsibility. Still, Matt didn't let go and she was grateful for his warmth as he helped her up the steps to the small porch.

Inside, the house had that expectant feeling of a place that hadn't seen human interaction in a few weeks. The air was musty and still and a thin layer of dust that would make her mother crazy if she saw it had already begun to settle on everything.

Matt flipped on more lights, taking an obvious interest in the comfortable chic decor Helen favored.

Though small, the house had always seemed warm and bright to Elise, especially after the oppressive darkness that had descended on Clifton's Pride after her father's murder.

"Nice," Matt said.

She smiled as she untwisted her scarf and set it on the usual spot atop the console table in the entry.

"I think it became a haven of sorts for both of us after my father died. Grant was busy with his own life by then, so my mother and I just had each other. We made a pretty good life here."

"You didn't want to go off on your own?"

She shrugged. "I moved into an apartment for a year or so while I was in college but it seemed silly to pay rent when my mother and I have always had a great relationship and never seemed to get in each other's way."

She paused and gestured to the living room. "Go ahead and make yourself comfortable. It will only take me a minute to grab my mom's present and then I'll see what I've got in the kitchen."

"Why don't I do a walk-through of the house, check the pilot lights on the furnace and water heater, the pipes, that sort of thing?"

She smiled a little. Wasn't that just like him, to think about those sorts of guy details that probably wouldn't have occurred to her? "Thanks. Good thinking," she answered, then headed down the hall to her bedroom.

Her room was icy and she took a moment to flip on the gas fireplace for an instant warm-up. After she pulled her desk chair over to her closet, she climbed up to dig in the back recesses of her top shelf for the handcrafted necklace and earring set she had purchased for her mother at a summer art fair and then promptly forgotten about until the other day.

After she returned the chair to her desk, her gaze landed on a framed picture that had sat there so long it had become a usually overlooked part of the landscape.

She picked it up, the glass frame cold and heavy in her hands. The picture had been taken at Clifton's Pride a few weeks before her father's death. If she remembered correctly, one of her aunts had taken it near the horse paddock and it featured all of them—John, Helen, Grant and her, looking skinny and small with blond braids and a little freckled nose.

She looked absolutely nothing like the rest of her family. Everything was different—the shape of her eyes, the tilt of her nose. How had they all missed the signs for all these years?

She was a changeling, an interloper.

Her thumb traced John Clifton's strong, smiling features, frozen forever in her memory just like this. Raw emotions bubbled up in her throat, clogging her breath. She missed him so dearly.

What would he have to say about this whole mess? She couldn't even begin to guess. Then she thought of Jack Castro and his gruff eagerness to be part of her life.

It was too much. The stress of the evening, her conflicted feelings, everything. She sagged onto her desk chair and clutched the photograph to her chest, fighting tears and memories and this gaping sense of loss.

Sometime later, she heard Matt walking down the hall and hurriedly swiped at her stupid tears.

"Everything looks like it's running just fine," he said. "I nudged the thermostat up a little bit while we're here. Remind me to turn it back down when we go."

His voice trailed off as he entered the room and Elise winced. Why did he always have to see her at her worst? She felt like she had been an emotional mess since the moment she bumped into him at The Hitching Post.

He crossed to her quickly, his eyes dark with concern. "What's the matter? What happened?"

She gave a resigned sigh and held out the picture. "I thought I was doing so much better about everything tonight at dinner. Coming to terms with...all of it. I had a good time with Jack and Betty. They're very nice people, people I think I could grow to care about. Then I saw this picture of my family...the family I've always known as mine...and I just feel like I've lost something somehow."

"Oh, sweetheart. Come here."

He pulled her into his arms and she hitched in a breath, feeling foolish and weepy and deeply grateful.

"This is so stupid." She sniffled. "I'm such a mess."

"Anyone else would be in the same situation. You've had the rug yanked out from under you again, just like it was when your father was killed."

She stared at him, stunned that he could so clearly understand something she hadn't even put together in her own head. She felt as if she were reliving those terrible days of loss and uncertainty all over again. "That's it exactly! I'm not sure how to go on now that everything has suddenly changed."

"You're doing fine, Elise. Give yourself some credit."

His faith in her warmed a cold place deep inside. "Thanks, Matt. You must be so sick of me and my maunderings."

Yes. Exactly! She felt as if she were reliving those terrible days of loss and uncertainty all over again as she struggled to adapt to her changing situation.

"I don't know what that word means," he admitted with a soft smile. "But I'm not sick of you. I could never be sick of you, Elise."

His arms tightened around her and with a sense of inevitability, she lifted her mouth to his. When his lips slanted over hers lightly, the whole twisting, crazy emotional snarl inside her seemed to settle.

The kiss was slow and tender, and she closed her eyes and savored it.

"Thank you," she murmured after a long moment. "I don't know what I would have done without you here tonight, both earlier and just now."

"You would have made it through," he replied. "You're much tougher than you seem to think, El."

"When you say that, you make me want to believe it."

He kissed her, his arms a warm comfort around her. "I remember after your dad died, watching how you coped with everything you'd been hit with. I thought then what a strong person you were. I could tell you were hurting, but you survived it. I always admired that about you."

She was quiet for a long moment, her feelings for him a thick, solid weight in her chest, and then she stood on tiptoe again and kissed him, telling him with her mouth and her hands the feelings she was afraid to voice.

He pulled her against him and deepened the kiss and they stood wrapped together for long moments while the flame from her gas fireplace flickered and danced and tiny snow pellets hissed against the windows.

She wanted to be with him. The yearning blossomed inside her, fierce and powerful. She felt as if everything the last few weeks—okay, for years, if she were honest— had been leading them to this moment.

A low, sultry heat simmered between them and she could taste the change in his kiss, from tenderness to something more, something rich and sensual and delicious.

She pressed against him, tangling her fingers in his hair, stealing sensuous delight through the slide of her tongue along his.

He made no move to capitalize on the convenient queen-size bed behind them so Elise decided she would just have to take matters into her own hands. She eased down and pulled him along with her.

He made a low, sexy sound in his throat and stretched alongside her, his body hard and powerful. She could feel the heat of him scorching her, his tightly leashed strength, and for one crazy moment she couldn't believe this was really happening, that she was really here with Matt Cates.

Somewhere in her room amid the collected detritus of her childhood—maybe in a box of keepsakes under her bed?—was the diary she'd kept in elementary and junior high school, where she had poured out all her silly angst about him.

Why wouldn't he notice her?

He sat with that silly, brainless Jamie Fletcher at lunchtime.

He smiled and joked with her while they were standing in line for the drinking fountain.

She wondered how he would react if he knew about her girlhood crush. Would he be mortified or amused?

She didn't care. Not right now, with his arms around

her. This was so much more wonderful than anything she could have imagined back then.

His mouth trailed down her throat, his breath warm on her skin. Everything inside her seemed to sigh. If she had even an inkling back then how magical kissing Matt could be, she would have gladly tripped through the hallway every single day at school, if that was the only way to make him notice her.

His mouth slid just below the loose cowl of her sweater, and she shivered, aching for his touch.

"We'd probably better stop," he murmured.

"Why?"

His gaze met hers, clear reluctance there. "We've still got a long drive back to Thunder Canyon tonight."

"It's snowing," she pointed out in what she thought was a particularly reasonable argument. "Let's just stay here for the night. We can head back in the morning, can't we?"

He sat up and drew in a ragged breath, his eyes dark and hot. "I really don't think that's a great idea, Elise. In case you haven't noticed, I can't seem to keep my hands off you."

She could see his arousal in that slumberous look he wore, hear it in his ragged breathing. He wanted her, just as much as she wanted him, and the realization left her feeling sexy and feminine and powerful.

She hadn't experienced that particular heady mix of emotions very often in her life and she decided to revel in it.

"I don't want you to. Keep your hands off me, I mean. In case *you* haven't noticed, I happen to like your hands on me."

He closed his eyes on a rough-sounding sigh. "Elise—"

"Spend the night here with me, Matt. I want you to."

Chapter 11

Her low words sizzled through him, rich and potent, with a hell of a kick. Just like Christmas eggnog. He stared at her, slender and delicate and lovely, and he wanted her with a fierce hunger.

It would be so very easy to take what she was offering, to kiss her and touch her until they were both crazy with need.

But he thought of her tangled emotional state, the stresses weighing on her for the last few weeks and knew he couldn't take advantage of her like that, as much as he ached to taste the passion he sensed brimming just under the surface.

His entire strategy since that night at The Hitching Post had been one of patience. He intended to give her plenty of time to come to terms with everything that had happened the last few weeks with her family—and with the possibility of a deepening relationship between the two of them.

She was throwing that plan all to hell.

He wanted to devour her right now, just cover her body with his, slide beneath that silky-soft comforter on her bed and spend the night wrapped together while the snow clicked against the window and the world outside this room ceased to matter.

He wanted that so intensely he could barely hang on to a coherent thought, but he did his best, knowing this was too important for him to screw it up.

"I'm not sure this is the right time," he began valiantly.

She smiled that soft, reckless smile again and he wondered a little wildly what had happened to his sweet Elise and how this sexy seductress had taken her place.

Not that he was complaining or anything.

"This is the perfect time," she murmured, leaning into him. "I want to be with you. I want it more than I can tell you."

He closed his eyes, praying he could do the right thing here. Finally, he rose and stood beside the bed. When he spoke, his voice was low and tinged with sadness.

"I wish you were saying that because you meant it and not just because you want to forget everything for a little while."

She stared at him for a long moment and then she gave a low, throaty laugh. "Is that what you think this is?"

She rose until only a few inches separated them. He could feel the heat of her, smell the delicious raspberries-and-cream scent. She splayed her fingers against his chest and he could swear she would scorch through the material of his shirt.

"You're wrong, Matt. So wrong. I've wondered how it would be with you since I was old enough to even understand about the difference between men and women. You've never noticed me as anything but sweet little Elise." She sighed. "I guess it's confession time. My thoughts about you have always been anything but sweet."

She smiled again then leaned in to kiss him, her mouth soft and delicious, and he was lost.

This probably wasn't the smartest thing he had ever done but right now he didn't care. The only thing that mattered was Elise and the heartstopping promise of her kiss.

His body was yelling at him to rush, to rip off clothing and surge inside her fast and hard but he drew in a shaky breath and sought control. Not that way, not with Elise—at least not this time.

He felt as if he'd been handed a precious gift all wrapped up in pretty paper, and he wanted to savor every moment of discovering its secrets.

Without lifting his mouth from hers, he lowered them both to the bed again. Her breasts brushed against his chest and her thighs shifted on either side of one of his legs. He propped most of his weight on one elbow, worried a little about crushing her, but she wrapped her arms around him, nestling against him as if she wanted to be nowhere else in the world than right here with him.

"You tell me if you decide you've changed your mind," he ordered against his mouth. "I can't guarantee I'll like it, but I'll stop."

"I can take care of myself, you know," she said with that same enticing smile. "You can stop watching out for me now."

"Never," he said hoarsely.

He deepened the kiss, licking and tasting and exploring her mouth until he couldn't think straight. She tasted so good, sweetly delicious, and he couldn't seem to slake his hunger.

He wanted—needed—more. He slid his fingers beneath her sweater to the small of her back, and his insides trembled at the sensuous contrast of her soft skin against hard, calloused fingers that had driven a few too many nails.

"My hands are too rough," he murmured. "I don't want to hurt you."

"Never," she repeated his words earlier and eased into his touch.

They kissed for a long time, until she sat up a little and reached to pull the edges of her sweater over her head, leaving her in only a lacy red bra that barely cupped her lush little breasts and instantly ratcheted his temperature up about a thousand degrees.

He gulped. "Um. Wow."

She laughed. "I like sexy lingerie. It's a quirk, I know. I guess you'll just have to decide if you can accept it."

"It's going to be tough," he growled, "but I can probably manage."

He unbuttoned his own shirt and pulled it off, aware of her eyes watching every moment and the hot tendrils of hunger coiling through him. He knew he'd been attracted to her before, but he never expected this sort of wild, ferocious heat.

She spread a hand over his chest and made a sexy little sound in her throat and then she toppled him backward on the bed and kissed him, her honey-blond hair a silky, sensuous veil around them.

How the hell had he overlooked her all these years? What was he thinking, always considering her just a sweet kid he needed to watch out for? A smart guy would have seen the sexy woman inside all that sweetness and would have jumped at any chance to be with her like this much sooner. He felt like he'd wasted far too much time as it was and didn't want to squander another moment.

She was everything he had ever wanted, all those nebulous things he hadn't admitted, even to himself. Even as they kissed and touched, he was aware of that edge of uncertainty around them. Her life was in chaos right now—as she'd said, she wasn't in a good place for a relationship. Though he knew it would be difficult, especially after tonight, he would just have to dig deep for patience.

He could wait. For now he had this, he had her, and he wasn't about to waste time worrying about all those uncertainties.

He slid his hands to the sides of her breasts above the lace of her bra and she hitched in a breath, her stomach muscles contracting. "Oh, yes. Perfect," she murmured.

"Not yet," he said with a lopsided grin. "But heading there."

He was wrong. This was sheer heaven.

Elise felt powerful, sensual. He carefully flipped her back onto the pillow and danced his thumbs over her curves, then pushed one of her bra cups away before lowering his mouth.

She gasped aloud and gripped his head tightly, arching against him and holding him in place while he tasted and explored one and then the other.

With one hand, she slid her fingers through his hair, with the other she explored all that tantalizing skin stretched across his strong back.

The years of construction work had hardened him. He wasn't bulky but every inch was tightly leashed muscle and she wanted to taste all of it. She pressed a kiss to the muscles that corded between his neck and his shoulder and knew the exultant power of feeling his tremble of reaction.

Despite the fact that he was here, in her arms, in her bed, this still didn't seem real. She was afraid she would wake up and he would be gone.

She was almost more afraid that she would wake up and he would be right here, all those hard muscles and tender concern shoving their way into her defenseless heart.

"I care about you, Elise," Matt murmured after they had removed the rest of their clothing, after their bodies were entwined and all that hard strength surrounded her. "I want you to know, this is important to me. *You're* important to me."

His words seemed to sneak through whatever was left of her paltry defenses to nestle in next to her heart. As much as they scared her, in a weird sort of way they managed to calm her more.

She *was* in love with him. This wasn't infatuation or friendship with benefits but something she had never known before.

Maybe that's why she had been fighting her feelings so hard. She wasn't sure she was strong enough to survive the sort of heartache Matt could leave behind.

She thought of Grant and Stephanie, how deeply they loved each other. They only had to walk into a room together and you could feel it snap in the air like ions whirling just before an electrical storm.

Marlon and Haley shared the same sort of love and everyone could see it.

She supposed she had always expected that when she finally fell in love it would be a soft and easy sort of thing, like settling in near the fireplace with a good book—even as some part of her had yearned for exactly this sort of wild, consuming passion.

"You're important to me, too," she confessed, her voice low. She wasn't going to worry about heartbreak. Not now. For now, she only wanted to focus on this moment, this man, the incredible heat and wonder of being in his arms.

He gripped her hands in his and kissed her as he entered her with one powerful surge. Oh, yes. Now it was perfect. Her body shifted and settled to accommodate him and she wanted to lie here beneath him for the next week or two, just savoring this rare and beautiful connection between them.

"Elise," he murmured. "My sweet Elise."

She loved the sound of her name spoken in that rough-edged voice, the heat in his eyes as he kissed her.

She clutched his back as he surged inside her, every muscle shivering with delight. She felt as if she were like that eagle in the needlepoint they had bought for Haley, as if she were soaring and circling on currents of air with widespread wings, climbing higher and higher toward the sun. And then he kissed her, his mouth fierce and demanding, and reached a hand between their bodies, to the heat and ache at her core, and she climaxed in one mad, crazy instant that left her gasping and arching against him needing more and more.

When she glided back to earth, she found him watching her out of those hot, hungry, dark eyes.

"That was just about the sexiest thing I've ever seen," he said on a growl, then he kissed her fiercely and she held him while he found his own release.

After he had taken care of the condom—even in this, he protected her—Matt slid back into bed and pulled her close, nestling her against all his heat and strength. "You matter to me," he said again.

The snow continued to beat against the window and the sky looked dark and menacing, but here they were safe together. With her cheek resting on his chest, she listened to his strong, steady heartbeat in her ear and thought about love and fear, fantasy and reality and the strange twistings of fate, until she fell asleep.

For the first time in his life, Matt found himself reluctant to return to Thunder Canyon.

Usually he loved driving through town, that first glimpse of the mountains, the sense of homecoming, of belonging in a beautiful place.

Not today. Climbing out of Elise's bed in the predawn hours was just about the hardest thing he ever had to do. Unfortunately, though he would like to forget everything and stay right here, he had obligations waiting for him, the last few finishing details to the McFarlane Lodge, and knew they needed to make an early start.

Okay, he hadn't minded the early start—especially when he woke with a soft, sleepy Elise in his arms. She had kissed him, her body warm and pliant, and they had pleasured each other while dawn stretched across the sky.

He would have liked to think the incredible night and morning they spent in each other's arms could magically solve all the issues between them.

Unfortunately, reality wasn't always so cooperative. With each mile that he drove closer to Thunder Canyon, she seemed to pull away from him, until it was all he could do not to jerk the pickup around and head back to Billings.

Though she continued to make small talk with him—about the weather, about the Christmas gifts she was giving her family, about the things she had enjoyed at her job at the bookstore—she seemed distant, distracted.

Her words would sometimes trail off in the middle of a sentence and he would shift his attention from the road for a moment, to find her gazing absently out the window.

Finally, when they were only a mile outside the Thunder Canyon town boundaries, he knew he had to do something to try yanking her back toward him.

"Connor McFarlane's lodge is nearly finished," he said. "We should be wrapping it up today."

"I've heard it's beautiful. Haley said your dad gave her a tour and she can't stop talking about all the luxurious details."

"McFarlane's throwing a big party on Christmas Eve, inviting most of the town."

"Yes. My mother and Grant are planning on going. Remember, the Castros said they were going, too."

"That's right. I forgot we talked about it last night at dinner." He grabbed her hand and squeezed her fingers. "I guess I've been a little distracted."

He loved watching that little blush steal over her features. He had a feeling he would never tire of it.

"You and your father should certainly be the guests of honor for all the hard work you've put into the place."

He shrugged. "Like you said about the ROOTS party the other night, it was a team effort. But watching people enjoy a place you've built is a gratifying experience."

His hands tightened on the steering wheel. Nerves curled in his gut, something that didn't sit well with him.

"Listen, I want to take a date to the party. Specifically, you."

Her eyes widened and he didn't miss the barely perceptible clenching of her fingers in his.

"Matt, I'm not sure I'm ready for that."

He gave her a long look across the width of the cab. "Funny. I would have thought last night proved you were."

She sighed. "Everyone in town is already whispering that I'm the reason you broke your engagement to Christine. Yesterday morning before you and I left for Billings, I went to the grocery store with Steph and three people stopped her to ask if it was true the wedding was off. None of them would meet my gaze and I could practically feel the disapproval radiating off them. The two of us showing up together at the McFarlane Christmas party would certainly add considerable fuel to that rumor."

There she went, trying to find excuses again. Just how hard was a guy supposed to work before he gave a cause up as lost?

He thought about the connection they had forged together the night before, the sweet peace they had shared, and he was angry, suddenly, that she seemed willing to give that up without a fight.

"Who the hell cares about a little gossip? You and I both know it's not true and so does Christine. What else matters?"

She huffed out a breath. "That's easy for you to say. You've never cared about gossip. Good grief, you and Marlon spent your lifetime raising as much trouble as you could, gossip be hanged."

He acknowledged some truth to that, but those days seemed far away.

"I'm not like you," she went on. "I hate finding myself the center of attention—and I feel like I haven't been standing anywhere else since the day Erin Castro showed up in Thunder Canyon."

She paused and pulled her fingers away from his. "When my father was murdered, I know everyone talked about me all the time. I could feel the conversation stop.

Nobody talked to me about his murder except my few close friends. Haley, mostly, since Steph was in a pretty dark place with her dad's murder, too."

She sighed. "With everyone else, I felt like I had entered some kind of social black hole. I know they were kids and probably didn't have the skills to deal with such a rough thing. Nobody knew what to say, I guess, so it was easier to ignore me. But it still hurt, especially because I know everyone said plenty behind my back."

"I always talked to you," he said curtly, sick of her excuses and the whole damn situation. "*Always*. And I never let anybody say anything hurtful about you or your family, at least when I was in earshot."

He could feel her gaze on him. He shifted his attention from the road long enough to see her features soften. She reached a hand out and touched his thigh.

"You always did," she agreed. "You've been riding to my rescue since we were kids, haven't you?"

He couldn't have this conversation while he was driving, he decided. Since they were close to Clifton's Pride, he steered onto the shoulder and put the truck in gear so he could safely face her.

"Because I care about you, Elise. I always have. I convinced myself you were just a sweet girl, maybe a little naive, who needed somebody to watch her back. And then you showed up in town again and I realized my feelings for you ran much, much deeper."

She drew in a shaky breath. "I care about you, too, Matt. Last night was...well, you know what it was. I don't want to screw this up. But I don't have the greatest track record with relationships and I'm so afraid."

"You think I'm not? You scare the hell out of me, Elise."

She gazed out the window at a magpie scavenging for

berries on the stark, bare crimson dogwood branches along the ice-crusted creek. "I'm not bringing my best self to this," she finally said. "I don't think I can right now."

Those nerves in his gut coiled more tightly. "So instead of giving me the chance to show you I can be patient, you want to push me away, just as you've been doing since you came back to town."

"I don't know. Maybe." She sighed. "I told you I was a mess, Matt."

"I guess you have to decide what's more important to you. A little pointless gossip." He took a chance and reached for her hand, then drew her cool fingers to his mouth. "Or the way we feel about each other."

She narrowed her gaze at him. "Not fair."

He grinned and put the pickup in gear to drive the rest of the way to the ranch house. "Whoever said I was fair?"

When they reached Clifton's Pride, he could already see a few signs of life, though the day was just starting: A ranch hand hauling a bucket of something, a light on in the kitchen, the rumble of a tractor probably hauling hay bales out to hungry cattle in some distant, snow-covered pasture.

He moved around to open her door before she could climb out and helped her down from the high truck. "I'll swing by before the party. I really hope you'll be here."

She sighed. "You're not going to give up, are you?"

"I walked away from law school without a backward look and haven't regretted it for a moment. But something tells me if I gave up on you as easily as I did that, it would haunt me for the rest of my life."

Chapter 12

"Here we go."

Matt parked his pickup in front of the sprawling Mc-Farlane Lodge and Elise could do nothing but stare.

"Wow! It's gorgeous!"

The house was everything people in town had said, soaring and majestic like the mountains around it. Constructed of log and stone, it seemed part of the landscape, as if it had grown here amid the boulders like the Douglas fir and spruce surrounding it.

"We worked with a log home company out of Helena on the structure but Cates did all the work inside."

"I'm sure it's even more beautiful there than it is from the outside."

"You ready to go see?"

She gazed at Matt across the width of his truck. He must have showered and shaved just before he picked her up at Clifton's Pride. His brown hair appeared freshly combed, his jaw smooth, and all through the drive here the scent of his sexy soap or aftershave or whatever it was had been driving her crazy.

He wore a dressy black leather bomber-style jacket over a tan twill shirt that made him look rugged and masculine, darkly dangerous.

He looked like the sort of man who could take on dragons. Or at least a house full of curious friends.

"Yes. I think I am."

"I'm really glad you came with me," he said as he opened the door for her.

She had to admit, she had waffled back and forth all week long. Some part of her would have liked to stay back at Clifton's Pride—and not simply because of the potential for wagging tongues.

Since her father's murder, Christmas Eve had become one of her least-favorite days of the year. She didn't miss the irony. Like most kids, she had always loved the holidays when she was a girl. Her father had loved the season, too, and she had many wonderful, vivid memories of her girlhood: Christmas caroling, wrapping gifts, sneaking baskets of gifts and food onto needy porches.

If the weather wasn't too snowy, every Christmas Eve her dad would saddle horses for her and Grant and the three of them would take a long, snowy ride into the mountains while Helen stayed back at the ranch putting the finishing touches to their Christmas Eve dinner.

They were wondrous times for a girl, filled with laughter and excitement and breathless anticipation. After his death, all the joy and magic of the holidays seemed to die with him. Helen had tried to make an effort, but over the years Elise had come to the point where she wanted to just forget the whole day.

She'd even come to dread it, finding it too much of a

struggle to pretend to be bright and cheerful when she wasn't.

As they walked up the winding pathway to the house, Elise tried to tamp down her nerves. She was so tired of this wild tangle of emotions. She wanted to just enjoy herself today, to focus on family and friends.

And Matt, the man who had become so very important to her.

Now, on the porch of the home he had built, she looked around at the fine-crafted details. The outdoor lighting looked like something out of a museum and the massive front door was hand-carved, a sculpted, twisted design of a tree with curving branches.

She couldn't resist touching the polished wood. "Wow. This is really exquisite, Matt. Beyond anything I expected."

He looked pleased at her praise and that fragile tenderness fluttered in her chest.

She had missed him this week. Both of them had been preoccupied with family obligations and he was busy with the beginning stages of a new Cates Construction project. She had only seen him once, when he had picked her up two nights earlier for a quiet dinner at his house.

Afterward, they had bundled up and gone for a chilly walk through the darkened streets of town with his chocolate Lab bounding through the snowdrifts ahead of them. Though they didn't encounter a moose this time as they had in Bozeman, walking hand in hand through the snowy streets in the moonlight had been sweet and peaceful.

He had kissed her when he took her back to Clifton's Pride but not with the heat and passion she wanted. Rather, he had exhibited remarkable—albeit frustrating—restraint and had limited their embrace to a few brief moments.

She pulled her fingers away from the door and slipped them through his. "It's really stunning, Matt. I'm very impressed."

"Come and see the rest."

He pushed open the door and they were instantly assaulted by noise—shrieking children, jazzy holiday music playing through hidden speakers, laughter and the low, chattering hum of a dozen conversations.

She knew just about everyone. Her mother was talking with Steph's mother and Judy Johnson, owner of the Clip N' Curl. In another seating group, she spied Holly Clifton talking with Erika and Shandie Traub.

A few people looked up at their entrance and Elise thought she saw a few raised eyebrows, but she told herself she didn't care. Matt was right, a little gossip wouldn't hurt her.

They hadn't made it two steps inside when suddenly Christine Mayhew hurried over to them, her arms outstretched. To Elise's shock, Christine pulled her into a warm hug, laughing and talking about something one of the children had just said. She hugged Matt next and then looped an arm through Elise's.

Elise saw confusion on more than a few faces. She was confused, too, since she had barely met Christine but the woman was acting as if they were best friends.

Christine talked with them for several moments before excusing herself. "There's Tori. I need to ask her who did that incredible oil painting in the master bedroom."

Before she walked away, she gave Matt a sidelong smile. "Unless you think that wasn't sufficient to prove to everyone in town you didn't wrench out my poor little heart and drive over it with your backhoe, you beast."

He grinned. "That ought to do it. Thanks, Chris."

"Anytime," she said with another hug to Elise before she sauntered away.

"So that was all a setup?" Elise asked.

He shrugged, trying and failing to look innocent. "I figured the best way to shut off the gossip valve in a hurry was to show that this is not some torrid love triangle. Looks like it worked."

Oh, she was in serious trouble. That tenderness zinged through her again and she was immeasurably touched that he would make the effort to keep her out of the spotlight.

She should have expected it. He *was* her self-appointed protector, wasn't he? Apparently that covered everything from schoolyard bullies to social scandals.

She couldn't resist smiling at him. "You're a very sweet man, Matt," she murmured.

His brown-eyed gaze met hers and everything inside her sighed at the warm light there. "Guys don't like to be called sweet, El," he said with a mock growl.

She checked to make sure they were out of earshot of others at the party, then she spoke in a voice pitched low so only he could hear. "Okay. How about this. When you do thoughtful little things like that, I find it incredibly sexy. Even better than that thing you do with your tongue in my ear."

He gave a rough laugh. "Cut it out or I'll be dragging you out of the party before we even say hello to our hosts."

As much as the idea of that appealed to her right now, she knew this party was important to him. He had worked hard to create a showplace for Connor McFarlane and was justified in being pleased with his efforts.

"I want to see the house. Will you give me a private

tour? Show me all the secret corners and out-of-the-way closets?"

He sent her a dark look but grabbed her hand and led her up the staircase. On the way, he pointed out details like the hand-peeled banister and the imported light fixtures.

He kept up a running commentary as he led her from room to room. Though she wouldn't have thought she could find a discussion on the challenges of post-and-beam construction fascinating, he made it interesting and she admired the obvious care Cates Construction had put into the work.

In one of the bedrooms, he started discussing the relative merits of using alder or black walnut. He was so impassioned about it, she couldn't help herself, she wrapped her arms around his neck and pulled his mouth down to hers.

For an instant, he only stared at her and then he closed the door firmly, leaning against it so no one could interrupt them while he kissed her properly, as she had been wanting him to do since the moment he picked her up.

That sweet peace fluttered through her as he kissed her, the sense of rightness and home and everything wonderful. She held him close, heat churning through her and her emotions a thick, tangled clog in her throat.

By the time he eased away, both of them were breathing raggedly.

"You're killing me, Elise. Everyone in town is downstairs and all I want to do is lock that door and forget the rest of the world exists. Hell, look at me! I can't even leave this room until I'm a little more...under control."

She glanced down at his obvious arousal and smiled, thoroughly enjoying herself. "Well, then, I guess you'll just have to tell me more about exactly why black walnut is so vastly superior for its hardness and durability."

He stayed a safe distance away for several moments while Elise wandered through the bedroom and its attached bathroom, admiring all the thoughtful little luxuries in the design. Finally, he determined he could face polite company again.

When they left the room and walked down the stairs sometime later, Elise could sense something momentous happening. Excitement seemed to coil through the lodge like the silvery garlands on the tree.

"What's going on?" Matt asked the first people he saw standing at the bottom of the stairway—his brother Mitchell and sister-in-law Lizbeth.

"The craziest thing." Lizbeth's lovely features glowed. "Connor and Tori are getting married."

Matt frowned. "Haven't we all known that for months?"

"No, I mean right now. They decided on the spur of the moment that this was the perfect time to tie the knot, while all their friends and family are already here and everyone is celebrating. We're having a wedding in just a few moments! Won't that just make Christmas Eve perfect?"

"Oh, how wonderful," Elise exclaimed.

"Tori already has her dress and veil. Knowing her fashion sense, it's going to be gorgeous," Lizbeth said.

"What can I do to help?" Elise asked.

"I think everything is nearly ready. Tori's upstairs with Allaire getting dressed. I think Shandie's doing her hair."

"I'll help set up the chairs," Matt said.

For the next half hour the lodge was filled with a flurry of activity as the residents of Thunder Canyon rallied to help organize the last-minute wedding. Flowers and greenery were snatched from the elegant decorations for bouquets and corsages, slim white candles were gathered from various locations around the house and arranged along the mantel and someone shifted the music on the sound system from holiday carols to sweetly romantic songs.

Matt and his brothers and some of the other men had dragged every available chair into the huge great room and arranged them in rows, all facing the twenty-foot Christmas tree and the sweeping mountain views beyond from the floor-to-ceiling windows.

Now, Elise sat beside him while soft, romantic music played. He reached for her hand as Connor and his teenage son, CJ, walked up to stand near the Christmas tree. Connor looked handsome and successful in a gray designer suit that set off his distinctive auburn hair.

Everyone rose when Tori appeared at the top of the curved half timber staircase on the arm of her father, Dr. Sherwood Jones, with her best friend Allaire Traub and CJ's friend Jerilyn Doolin as her attendants.

She looked breathtaking, in an off-the-shoulder, three-quarter-length dress. Shandie had worked wonders with her strawberry-blond hair and it was coiled atop her head in a style both elegant and romantic.

While everyone admired the lovely bride, Elise found her attention shifting to Connor McFarlane, waiting near the windows. Something fragile and sweet tugged in her heart when she witnessed the soft light in his eyes as Tori glided down the stairs with her arm tucked through her father's.

The two of them radiated happiness and Elise wasn't the only one dabbing away tears as she listened to their heartfelt vows and saw their obvious joy in each other.

After the ceremony, Connor brought out magnums of

champagne and everyone lifted flutes in a toast to the glowing couple. When several toasts had been offered, Connor nudged Marlon. "You know, we're all set for a wedding now. Everybody's here. Trust me, you could save yourself a lot of trouble if you just took care of things now and tied the knot."

"A lovely offer—thanks," Haley said with a smile. "But I have my heart set on a spring wedding."

"Have you set a date?" Elise asked.

Marlon and Haley exchanged glances. "Yes," Haley answered. "Finally. We decided last night on April 11, if we can put it together that soon."

Tori hugged her. "If we could throw mine together in half an hour, I think a few months should be plenty of time."

"You'll still be my maid of honor, won't you?" Haley asked Elise.

Would she be in Thunder Canyon for the wedding? Elise had no idea what the future held, but she decided she would do whatever it took to help Haley have the most beautiful wedding in Thunder Canyon history. She deserved a wonderful happy ending of her own.

"You couldn't keep me away," she answered with a hug.

"I don't think you're going to be the only ones hearing wedding bells in the near future," Connor said with a gesture toward Erin Castro and Corey Traub.

They stood in a group with Elise's mother and Grant and Stephanie. Erin and Corey held hands and even from here, Elise could sense the bond between them.

Everyone around her was getting married. She swallowed hard with a careful look at Matt, who had left their group to talk to his father and a few other men.

He looked strong and gorgeous and everything inside

her seemed to sigh whenever she saw him. She wanted what it seemed everyone else around them had found but she was so afraid to dream about forever, especially right now when everything felt so topsy-turvy.

Mindful of the hazards of overindulging—hadn't she learned *that* particular lesson painfully well?—she took only a tiny sip of her champagne while she listened to the ebb and flow of conversation around her.

Out of the corner of her gaze, she spied Grant and Stephanie approaching Erin's group. As she watched, her brother slipped an arm around his newly discovered sister's shoulder and guided her to a couple of Thunder Canyon old-timers who must not have had the chance to meet her yet.

The champagne took on a bitter taste and suddenly the room felt close and airless.

Suddenly she thought of what Matt had said the other day, that there was room in her heart for everyone. She was definitely discovering that. She was already coming to care for the Castros. Didn't the same hold true? Just because her family had embraced Erin didn't mean they were pushing her away at the same time.

She let out a shaky breath. She had been acting like a spoiled brat, she realized. She wanted something—her life back, the one she'd known before Erin discovered the hospital mistake. Since she could no longer have it, instead of reacting with dignity and grace and looking for the good in the situation, she felt like she'd been throwing a pissy temper tantrum since Thanksgiving.

How had anybody been able to stand her?

As she gazed out the window, through the trees she saw a wide glimmer of white not far away from McFarlane Lodge. Silver Stallion Lake, she realized. Because

of the way the road curved, she hadn't realized it was
so close.

She glanced around the crowded room at everyone
celebrating weddings and engagements and Christmas
and then looked back at the lake, a favorite spot of locals.
The idea of clearing her head was suddenly immensely
appealing. Since she didn't think anyone would miss her
for a few moments, she headed for the room where they
had hung their coats earlier.

A moment later, she slipped out the lovely sculpted
door and into the lightly falling snow.

"No, I'm not joking." Bo Clifton, Elise's cousin and
the town's new mayor-elect, gave Matt's father a solemn
look. "Completely serious. I know it's hard to believe but
I just got the phone call from the sheriff that they've arrested him."

"Who's under arrest?" Matt asked, overhearing just
the tail end of the conversation as he approached them.

"Arthur Swinton," Frank said, eyes wide and shocked.

His father hadn't been a fan of the mayor, whom Bo
was supposed to be replacing after the new year. He
considered him a prosy old windbag, but he seemed as
shocked as Matt that the man had been arrested.

"What are the charges?" Matt asked.

"Multiple counts of embezzlement and fraud of public
funds," Bo said, his features grim. "You know how the
town budget has been struggling so much for the last few
years and revenue seems to have dwindled to a trickle?
Well, it turns out the soft economy is only partly responsible. Arthur Swinton has been dipping his fat little fingers into the city's coffers, maybe for years."

"I always knew he was difficult to work with," Frank
said with disgust. "Always making us jump through ri-

diculous hoops when it came to building permits and zoning regulations. I just never imagined he was crooked."

"I did," Grant Clifton said. "Everything makes sense now. I never could figure out where the redevelopment tax incentives we'd been promised to expand the resort had disappeared to. Now I know."

"We'll get everything straightened out," Bo promised them all. "I'm pushing hard for the swearing in to be held on New Year's Day so I can start cleaning up this mess and get this town back on track."

Grant clapped him on the shoulder. "Whatever you need, Bo, we'll help. I've been talking with Corey and Dillon Traub and we've got big plans for the resort."

"The Traubs are partnering with Caleb Douglas and Justin Caldwell?" Matt asked, surprised.

"That's the plan," Grant said. "They're looking for another investment and see nothing but good things for Thunder Canyon and the resort in the future. We're talking a major expansion here."

He paused and smiled at the Cateses. "You know, we're going to need a reliable construction company. Cates is at the top of that list."

Pride surged through Matt. His father had built a solid reputation in Thunder Canyon and he knew his work the last few years had only added to that, but his professional satisfaction was tempered by plenty of uncertainty.

Part of him rejoiced at the idea of the revitalization of Thunder Canyon and the role Cates Construction might play in that. But the other part was all tangled up with a woman who didn't even know if she wanted to be anywhere near the town he loved.

News of the mayor's arrest had spread through the party and several people approached Bo for more details. While the man was busy explaining everything he knew about the charges against Swinton, Frank pulled Matt aside.

"You think we can handle a big project like Grant and the Traubs have in mind?" Frank asked. "We might need to add to the crew."

"I'm not sure," Matt admitted.

His father stared. "What do you mean, you're not sure? Wrong answer, son. You're supposed to say, 'Sure, Dad. I got this. We can handle anything.'"

On a professional level, Matt knew the company could handle any challenge that came its way. Hadn't they proved it the last few months by bringing in this job for Connor McFarlane quickly and efficiently?

When it came to his tangled, complicated relationship with Elise, he wasn't sure of anything.

"Dad, I need to be up-front with you," he finally said. "Since we talked last week about me taking over the company, a lot has changed." He paused. "More than a lot. *Everything* has changed."

Concern furrowed his father's brow and Matt squirmed under his scrutiny.

"Let's go where we can talk in private," Frank said gruffly, leading the way through French doors to one of several covered decks off the back of the house.

The deck was warmed by an outdoor gas fireplace, flames dancing and weaving as they pushed away the heavy, expectant cold of an impending storm.

"What do you mean?" Frank said after Matt closed the doors behind him. "What's changed?"

He looked down at the town he loved and was surprised at the ache in his chest. "I might be leaving Thunder Canyon," he said quietly.

Frank stared at him and Matt saw a host of emotions

cross those expressive brown eyes, ending with resignation.

"It's Elise Clifton, isn't it?" he asked.

He shoved his hands in his pockets. "How did you… Why would you say that?"

His father shook his head. "I knew the moment I saw you two come in together. You've got that look in your eyes, the one I've seen all three of your brothers wear. Guess I shouldn't be so surprised."

Did he really want to be lumped in with his lovestruck brothers? He thought about it for a moment, then gave a slight smile. "Yeah, that about sums it up," he answered.

"Doesn't mean you have to up and leave. Your brothers seem to be happy enough sticking around," Frank said.

"You know I love Thunder Canyon, Dad. If I could figure out a way, I would in a minute. But Elise hasn't been back in a long time. Things here haven't been easy for her. She has some pretty dark memories."

His father was silent for a moment, watching the flakes drift down in the gathering twilight. "She has reason, I suppose. Poor thing. I guess you and she will have to figure out your own path."

"We're working on it. To be honest, it's a hell of a lot more rocky than I expected."

His father nudged him with his shoulder. "The best views always come after a long, hard climb. Don't worry, you'll figure things out. She's not stupid, our Elise."

"Not in the slightest. But she has a lot of things to work through."

"You know your help has been invaluable at the company the last few years," his father said gruffly. "But I'll figure out how to get along without you if I have to."

"Thanks, Dad." He was fiercely grateful, suddenly,

for his parents and the support and love they had always showered upon him and his brothers.

"You coming back inside to join the party?" Frank asked.

"In a minute. Think I'll watch the storm come in for a moment."

Sure enough, the snow already seemed a little heavier than it had when they walked onto the deck and those gray-edged clouds looked plump and full.

After his father left, Matt watched the trees twist and curl with the increasing wind. He could see downtown from here, cheerful and bright against the gathering darkness and felt another pang of regret. He would love to live here the rest of his life, to raise children, to help build the town and leave a legacy for those children. He could imagine many more Christmases spent here, filled with joy and laughter, friends and family.

But with something lost, something infinitely more precious could be found.

He was thinking about choices and growth and the future when he spied a slender figure bundled up in a red peacoat heading through the trees. He narrowed his gaze. He knew that coat. He had hung it himself when he and Elise had arrived.

Where was she going? The only thing in the direction of that trail was Silver Stallion Lake.

Of course. Crazy woman. Didn't she know it was dangerous to wander away on her own with that kind of storm brewing? Not to mention, with the above-freezing weather they'd had the last few days, more snow was bound to make the snowpack unstable and avalanche-prone.

All his protective instincts rattled around inside him. No way was he going to stand by while she put herself in possible danger. He hurried back inside the house and found his own coat quickly then headed outside to follow her trail in the gathering gloom.

The trail toward Silver Stallion Lake crossed the narrow road that ended in the box canyon where Connor had built his home. Some distance away toward town, Matt could see a huge cornice of snow blown by the wind now covering the peak at the canyon's edge.

He frowned. Add a few more inches on it and he could easily imagine the danger of a snowslide could potentially be high.

He would have to warn Connor when he returned to the house. But first, he needed to find Elise and make sure she was safe.

He walked quickly through the pines down a deer trail. The snow was soft and light for now and the air smelled of pine and winter. As he expected, he found her at the small lake, surrounded by pines and the pale ghostly skeletons of the winter-bare aspens.

In the few moments' head start she had, she must have unearthed a pair of skates from the small structure on the edge of the lake that was kept stocked with such things for locals' use. She sat on a log bench tying the skate. When she finished, she stood and glided out gracefully onto the ice.

Though he was aware of the need for haste and caution with the storm blowing in, he couldn't resist watching her from his concealed spot in the trees. She looked free and relaxed as she whirled and danced.

He thought of his father's words. He was lovestruck, just as his brothers. The realization should have scared him, sent him hurrying away. Instead, he was aware of a sweet, fragile tenderness.

He loved Elise. No matter what, he loved her. Nothing

else mattered. She was everything he had ever wanted, the only thing he needed. If she wanted to move away from Thunder Canyon, he would do it. Hell, he would go live in a hut in Borneo if it meant he could have Elise with him.

He finally emerged from the trees and made his way down the trail toward the bank of the frozen lake.

She toed to a stop when she spotted him and stood waiting as he carefully moved across the ice.

A thin trail of tears had left a mark down her cheeks and his heart ached for her. "Oh, sweetheart. Are you okay?" he asked.

She smiled and it took a few beats for him to realize what seemed so different about her. Despite the tear stains, she looked relaxed, happy.

At peace.

"My dad used to bring me to the lake all the time when I was a little girl. I had completely forgotten how much I love it here. It always seemed to me when I was little that the mountains appear to cup this valley like comforting hands. That sounds silly, doesn't it?"

"Not to me."

"I can see my dad clear as day, holding my hands and towing me along the ice while I slipped and slid and tried to find my skate legs for the first few moments. I wasn't the most graceful kid, as you might recall. I was so clumsy everywhere else but when I skated, it seemed like I forgot that."

He pictured her as a little girl, small and slender for her age, running so fast she often stumbled as she tried to keep up with all the other kids. He could visualize her father, too, strong and handsome, a man everyone in town had admired and respected.

Learning she wasn't genetically John Clifton's child

must feel to her as if she had lost her father all over again. He couldn't even imagine how difficult it must be for her.

He wanted to comfort her, to say something magical that would make her pain disappear. He couldn't think of any words so he reached out and gripped her mittens in his own gloves.

"Is this the way he did it?" he asked and began walking backward, pulling her across the ice.

"Be careful. You're going to fall," she warned.

His heart was a sweet, heavy ache in his chest. "I'm counting on you to catch me, Elise."

Her gaze locked with his, emotions churning there. Despite the party still in full swing back at the McFarlane Lodge, despite the storm hovering just out of view, despite all the turmoil, he wouldn't have traded this moment for anything.

Just the two of them in the quiet hush of a miraculous Christmas Eve.

After a few passes across the lake, he stopped in the middle of the ice and with a sense of destiny, he pulled her into his arms and kissed her.

Her mouth was cold against his but she sighed and wrapped her mittened hands around his waist, leaning into him.

The kiss was slow and lovely. Perfect for the evening and the moment.

"You should know something," he murmured against her mouth. "I told my dad just now that I might not be taking over Cates Construction after all."

She eased away from him, her expression perplexed. "Why? I thought you loved being a builder. Are you thinking of going back to law school?"

"No. I do love the work. But I figured I can do the

same thing anywhere. Billings. Bozeman. Even San Diego if that's where you decide you want to go."

He brushed his mouth over hers. His heart seemed to pound loudly in his ears. This was a risk he had never taken with a woman before—never *wanted* to take. With her, it was right. He knew it deep in his bones.

"I love you, Elise," he murmured.

She drew away from him sharply and nearly stumbled backward on the ice. Her hands flailed a little before she caught her balance. "You...what?"

He saw shock and disbelief and something else, a tiny spark of something bright and joyful that filled him with hope.

"I love you," he repeated firmly. "If you're not happy in Thunder Canyon because of the memories or your dad or what's happened with your family or whatever, I won't try to convince you to stay. I would never do that to you."

He moved forward to take her hands in his again while the fat flakes landed in her lashes, on her cheeks, in her hair. He pulled her across the ice into his arms again and kissed the corner of her mouth.

"You don't have to stay in Thunder Canyon, Elise. But I'm not about to let you go somewhere else without me."

She closed her eyes for a long moment. When she opened them, that tiny sliver of hope he had seen had been replaced by sadness.

"You can't love me, Matt."

"Why not?"

She didn't answer, only pulled her hands away from him and headed across the ice, her movements no longer full of grace and beauty but abrupt, forceful, each stroke digging into the ice.

He followed after her as she sat down on the log to remove the ice skates. "Don't tell me how I feel, Elise.

I've never been in love before but I know exactly what this is. I'm crazy about you."

"How can you be?" she asked, her voice bitter. "I'm such a mess and you seem to have borne the brunt of it these last few weeks."

He heard the despair in her voice, that sadness that had seemed such a part of her since she had come back.

But he had also seen that moment of joy in her eyes. He had tasted the heat of her kiss and sensed the suppressed emotions behind it.

She cared about him. They had something special here and he wasn't about to let her throw it away because of some misguided idea that she didn't belong here.

If he ever thought he might have had the skills to be persuasive in a courtroom, now would probably be a really good time to prove it.

He sat beside her on the fallen log, remembering when he and some buddies had dragged it over to the edge of the lake a few years back.

"You asked me how I can love you," he said quietly. "A better question would be, how can I not? Yes, you've had a rough few weeks. But no matter what you think, all I've seen is a woman facing a hard situation with strength and courage."

She flashed him a look, then returned to unlacing her skate. He hoped she was listening. All he could do was try.

"Despite your own turmoil," he went on, "you've reached out to everyone else in town. Just look at what you did for Haley last week and how hard you worked to make Christmas great for some needy kids at ROOTS, despite your own ambivalence about the holidays?"

"Haley's my friend. I did it to help her."

"I saw you with all those kids, Elise. You can tell yourself you were only helping Haley but I saw how excited you were to give them all their gift bags—the bags you spent hours preparing. And the Castros. You were so great with them at dinner, patiently answering all their questions about your childhood even though I saw how difficult it was for you to be there."

"You helped me get through that. I'm not sure I could have done it on my own."

"You could have," he assured her. "But don't you think it's significant that you asked me to come with you? That you turned to me for help when you needed it?"

He reached for her hand and brought it to his mouth. "I love you, Elise. No matter how much you've been fighting it, I know you have feelings for me, too. I want a future with you, no matter where and what shape that future might take."

Chapter 13

Elise listened to his words, low and fervent amid the snowflakes fluttering down, and that tiny, fragile joy curled through her again.

This couldn't be real. She couldn't really be sitting on the banks of Silver Stallion Lake with Matt Cates declaring his love for her. Things like this didn't happen to girls next door like her. Any moment now, she was going to wake up and discover this was only some surreal dream brought on by too much eggnog.

But now, if it were a dream, she wouldn't feel the wet snow in her hair, the cold of the ice seeping through her boots.

"I love you, Elise," Matt murmured one more time. "You trusted me out on that ice not to let you fall, just as I trusted you. Don't you think we can trust each other about this?"

She stared at him as the snow fell heavier, until his features were hazy, indistinct.

She didn't need to see him. She knew every line, every angle of his face.

She loved him.

The precious truth of it slid through her, filling and healing every battered aching corner of her heart.

She loved him—and she suddenly knew that if she threw this chance away, she would be the craziest woman who had ever come out of Thunder Canyon.

She gave a tiny, bubbling little laugh, unable to contain so much happiness inside.

"You're right. You're so very right."

"Elise—"

"I love you, Matt. I have loved you most of my life, if you want the truth. Those days when we were in school and you were always watching out for me, keeping me safe—you were my hero, Matt. Everything I ever dreamed about."

He made a low sound of disbelief and for some reason, that made her laugh again. She was so happy, she wanted to shout it to the trees, to spin around and around on the ice like she was a fearless, clumsy six-year-old again.

She took off her mittens then reached for his hands and slid his glove off so she could raise his warm hand to her cold cheek.

She held his hand there against her skin. "I had no idea back then how you would ride to my rescue again, Matt. You saved me."

"No, I didn't. You would have come through."

"Maybe. But I feel like I was falling through that ice, floundering in the cold, and you reached a hand in and yanked me back to light and warmth again. Thank you for that and for...giving me back myself."

She smiled tremulously. "I love you."

He stared at her and she saw heat and wonder and she

thought she might even see the sheen of tears there. "Are you sure you don't have dreams of being an attorney? That's quite a closing argument."

"No, thank you." She smiled.

He kissed her there amid the falling snow and she tasted a sweet tenderness and the promise of a beautiful future.

Her father would have approved, she thought. He would have been delighted she found someone who could make her so very happy, who could pick her up when she stumbled, brush her off, and give her a chance to soar across life like she skated across Silver Stallion Lake.

They kissed softly for a long time, love wrapping them tightly together against the elements.

Finally, he drew away from her. "We're going to freeze to death if we stay here much longer. Do you think you're ready to go back?"

She slid her hand into his, loving his heat and the solid strength of him. "No," she answered. "But I think I'm ready to go forward."

He smiled and kissed the tip of her nose then led the way through the storm.

The snow was falling in earnest by the time they made it back to the lodge. A good four inches had fallen, Elise realized. Not enough to make driving impossible for Montanans used to inclement weather, but certainly enough to make it challenging.

She saw that several vehicles that had been parked out front earlier were gone. Probably families with young children, returning to their own homes for their own holiday traditions—hanging stockings, telling stories, setting out cookies for Santa.

It was Christmas. Anticipation nudged her like an old,

familiar friend. Christmas, a time of hope and renewal, of miracles and second chances.

"Come home with me and spend Christmas Eve, Elise," Matt said just before they pushed open that beautiful door to Connor and Tori's home. "Will you?"

Through the windows, she could see her family inside. Both of her families. Her mother was chatting with the Castros and they all looked so happy together.

They wanted her to be happy with them, she realized. No one had been pushing her to the outside. She was the one who had refused all their efforts, the outstretched hands waiting to pull her toward them.

They would be sorry if she wasn't with them on Christmas Eve but there would be other years. This year, she wanted to be with Matt and she knew her entire crazy, complicated family would understand.

She smiled at him. "I just need to tell my mother so she doesn't worry," Elise said. She pushed open the door but before she could go inside, a huge rumbling roared above the sounds of the party coming from inside.

"What on earth?" she gasped, grabbing his shoulder.

"Avalanche," he said grimly. "Look."

Perhaps a quarter mile away down the road, she watched a vast, unrelenting sweep of snow tear away and pour down the mountain, breaking trees and moving boulders in its destructive path.

When it stopped, the only road back to town was completely covered with several feet of snow and debris.

Elise was still processing the shock of the slide as the other guests rushed out onto the wide porch.

"What the hell was that?" Connor McFarlane, still in his wedding suit, looked around. "It sounded like a hurricane."

"A slide blocked the road," Matt said. "I saw the cornice earlier and it looked unstable. I was going to warn you but got…distracted. I'm guessing all this heavy wet snow must have shifted the base enough to send the whole thing tumbling down."

"Did you see what happened? Is anybody down there?" Bo Clifton pushed his way through the crowd. "Do I need to call out search and rescue?"

"I don't think so. I didn't see anyone," Matt said. "A car had just driven through but they were a half mile down the road already when the snow came down."

"We'd better go check it out," Matt's brother Marshall said.

Several men hurried to find coats.

"By the looks of it, it's going to take several hours to dig out the road," Matt warned Connor.

"You mean we're stuck here?" someone said. "But it's Christmas Eve!"

"Oh, dear." Helen and Betty Castro exchanged distressed looks.

"I'm sorry about this." Connor immediately stepped in to take charge, as he was so good at doing. "We have plenty of food and blankets. It will be fun. We'll have a good, old-fashioned Christmas Eve."

He was being remarkably decent about sharing his wedding night with half the town, Elise thought. His words and his calm manner seemed to galvanize those remaining at the lodge into action. Immediately, people went in search of blankets and pillows and the party took on an even more festive air.

Elise was helping Haley organize an impromptu holiday classic film festival in the lodge's elaborate media room for some of the disgruntled teens when she suddenly became aware of Erin standing in the doorway, watching her with a wary expression.

"Do you guys need any help in here?"

She studied the other woman and was ashamed of herself for her small-minded jealousy of the last few weeks. None of this was Erin's fault and she had tried several times to forge a friendship. Elise had been the one pushing her away.

"Actually, I think Haley's got everything under control. I was just about to go to the kitchen and see if I can make popcorn. Want to join me?"

Erin looked surprised at the invitation but gratified. Together, they unearthed several bags of microwave popcorn in the elaborate kitchen and stuck one in each of the pair of gleaming appliances.

They talked casually for a few moments, until Erin suddenly blurted out, "I don't want your life, you know."

Elise stared at the other woman. "I'm sorry. What?"

Erin pushed a strand of blond hair out of her face. "I know you've been struggling to deal with what happened twenty-six years ago. I just wanted to let you know I'm sorry you've been hurt by everything. I never expected... well, what happened. I'm sure you probably would have preferred if I'd never come to Thunder Canyon looking for answers."

Elise traced the events of the last month. She thought of how her life would have been different if she had never come back to Thunder Canyon. She probably never would have reconnected with this place and the people who had been so important to her once.

Through the kitchen doorway, she heard Jack Castro's gruff laugh and she thought of how kind and loving Erin's parents were and of the two brothers she had scarcely met.

And Matt.

If Erin hadn't come to Thunder Canyon to dig into

the secrets of her past and discovered that fateful mistake, Elise would never have reconnected with Matt. She never would have discovered that sometimes silly girlish dreams could come true.

That secret joy shivered through her again, the love she would no longer deny, and on impulse she hugged Erin. The other woman froze for just a moment before Erin returned her embrace.

"I've always wanted a sister," Elise said. "In a weird sort of way, it almost feels like we were twins separated at birth."

Erin laughed. "Oh, please! Not twins. Isn't our past twisted and tangled enough?"

She laughed. "Good point."

Before she could say anything else, a thin, nervous voice interrupted them.

"Excuse me, have you seen Bo?"

She turned and found Holly Pritchett Clifton, her cousin's lovely new wife.

"I think he's down assessing the avalanche with some of the other men to figure out how to dig out the road," she answered. "Is everything okay?"

"Um, not really." She gave a nervous-sounding laugh. "We're stranded here with no way into town on Christmas Eve in the middle of a blizzard."

"I know," Erin said. "Things couldn't get much crazier, right?"

Holly gave that nervous laugh. "Want to bet? I think my water just broke."

"What is taking so long?" Erica Rodriguez Traub exclaimed. "I swear, I wasn't this nervous when my own baby was born."

The entire temporary population of McFarlane Lodge

seemed to be on edge, gathered in the great room while upstairs in a hastily arranged delivery room, Holly was attended by Drs. Marshall Cates and Dillon Traub—and, of course, Bo.

As the hours ticked away, everyone stranded at Mc-Farlane Lodge hovered in a state of excitement, even the teens who emerged from the media room every once in a while to check the status of the delivery.

And then, finally, at ten minutes to midnight, a thin, high cry wailed through the house. Everyone in the great room raised up a huge cheer.

A few moments later, Marshall emerged onto the landing. He looked disheveled and tired but Elise saw the quiet satisfaction in his eyes.

"It's a boy. Mother and baby—and mayor—are all doing fine."

"Good thing we've got plenty of champagne," Grant said, breaking out another magnum.

Elise declined to drink as she kept a careful eye out the window. Down below through the snowy darkness, she could see lights moving at the avalanche site.

Once it had been determined that the threat of more snowslides had passed, Matt had hiked down the mountain through the storm for one of the Cates Construction backhoes to begin digging out the avalanche.

Elise hated thinking about him out there in the cold, but she wasn't at all surprised. That was the man she loved, strong and dependable, always willing to help out those in need.

She was still watching sometime later when she spied those lights approaching the house and a few moments later, a bundled figure walked up the porch. Soon after, Matt walked inside and started stomping off snow in the entryway.

Her heart a sweet, heavy ache in her chest, Elise hurried to him and threw her arms around his neck, not caring at all who might be watching. She kissed him with fierce emotion and he responded with gratifying enthusiasm.

"What was that about?" he murmured after a few moments. "Not that I'm complaining."

"It's after midnight. Merry Christmas, Matt."

She helped him out of his wet gear and found hot cocoa for him. She would have thought he would want to stay right next to the fire, but he grabbed her hand and a blanket and headed out to the protected covered porch, where the gas fireplace still sent out its warmth.

He sank onto a cushioned lounger out there and pulled her onto his lap, wrapping them both in a heavy blanket until they were snug and cozy.

He kissed her deeply then, his mouth firm and demanding, and she clutched him tightly, shaken by the emotions churning through her. She longed for a little more privacy so they could make love but she knew she could be content to be with him like this, hearts and bodies entwined beneath the blanket.

The storm was lifting. Outside their safe shelter, Elise could see tiny scattered stars glimmering through the clouds.

She sighed, resting her cheek against his broad, muscled chest, his heartbeat in her ear.

"I don't want to leave," she murmured.

He gave a rough-sounding laugh. "I don't think we can sleep out here. Even with the gas fireplace and the blankets and your considerable body heat, I'm afraid we'll freeze."

She tilted her head to study his features. "I don't mean

right here, tonight, though this is pretty wonderful. I meant... I don't want to leave Thunder Canyon."

His arms tightened around her and he shifted so he could meet her gaze, his brown eyes intent and hopeful. "Are you sure? You don't like it here."

Her hair brushed his chin as she shook her head. "Not true. Part of me has always loved it here. And tonight while you were down clearing the road and we were up here waiting for Holly to have her baby, I... I can't explain it, but I was part of something. Something bigger than me, bigger than any of us."

She smiled. "It was wonderful. Really wonderful. Everyone was so concerned about each other and I realized how very much I have missed that in my life, being part of a community. I have enjoyed living in Billings but it's never felt like home. Thunder Canyon is home and it always has been. I want to stay."

His arms tightened again and he kissed her with a new intensity, his eyes filled with emotion. He had been willing to leave the town he loved for her, and his willingness to make that sacrifice meant all the more to her now, when she could see how very much her words meant to him.

"What will you do?"

"I thought I would see if Haley needs more permanent help at ROOTS. I was also thinking about opening a bookstore. Somewhere roomy and welcoming, with plump couches for people to stretch out in."

"It sounds wonderful, El." He nuzzled her neck. "I know a good builder who might be willing to give you a good deal."

"I may take you up on that."

"What about San Diego and the Castros?"

She shrugged. "Maybe I can go spend a few weeks with them once everything settles down a little."

He was quiet for a long moment. When he spoke, his tone was one of studied casualness as his fingers traced the skin at the small of her back, just below her sweater.

"You know, San Diego would be a great honeymoon destination."

She stared at him, her heart pounding. "Honeymoon?"

"Maybe not next week or even next month, but that's what I want. I figured it would only be fair to warn you."

She gave a disbelieving laugh, even as her heart continued to pound. Marriage. With Matt Cates. A future with his teasing smiles and tender kisses, with that strong sense of honor and goodness. A future with him watching out for her—and then transferring that strong protective streak to any children they might have.

She pictured Holly and Bo and the tiny baby they both loved. She could easily picture a little dark-haired version of Matt chasing after them, riding in the backhoe with him, skating across Silver Stallion Lake.

A few snowflakes blew into their cozy shelter and one landed at his temple. She kissed him there, letting the cold melt against her mouth.

"Now," she murmured. "Now everything is perfect. I love you, Matt. Merry Christmas."

And as he held her, more stars peeked out through the clouds to glitter above the quiet peace of Thunder Canyon.

* * * * *

CLASSIFIED CHRISTMAS

B.J. Daniels

This one is for Jody Robinson, for her encouragement and support and friendship.

Chapter 1

This year was different. Cade Jackson couldn't swear why exactly, just that he wasn't anticipating the anniversary of his wife's death with as much dread.

Maybe time *did* heal. Not that he didn't miss his wife. Or think of her. Especially with the anniversary of Grace's death only days away. He just didn't hurt as much when he thought of her. Nor after six years did he think of her as often.

There was something sad about that, he thought, as he watched the other ropers from the top rung of the corral. The thunder of hooves raised a cloud of dust that moved slowly across the enclosed arena.

Outside, snow continued to fall, promising a white Christmas. He breathed in the comforting scent of leather and horses, both as natural to him as the lay of the land beyond the arena walls.

Snow-covered open prairie ran to the deep cut of the

Missouri River as it wound its way through Montana, the dark outline of the Little Rockies that broke the horizon.

He felt as if he'd come of out of a coma. Everything looked and smelled and felt new and different. He'd missed a lot of holidays with his family, lost in that dark place that his grief had taken him. But this year he felt as if he might make it through the holidays without having to hide out at his cabin or in his ice-fishing shack until Christmas was over.

Cade felt an odd prickling just under his skin and looked toward the window. Snow fell in huge flakes that floated down blanketing the earth with both cold and silence. He frowned at the sudden sense of apprehension he'd felt just moments before. What had that been about?

He shook it off. He wasn't going to let the old ghosts get to him. He was finally feeling as if he might make it.

Andi Blake discovered a manila envelope on her desk when she got back to the newspaper from lunch. She'd spent her first morning at the *Milk River Examiner* cleaning off her predecessor's desk, only a little unnerved by the fact that he'd been murdered, thus the opening.

Glen Whitaker hadn't been neat. After boxing up all of his notes, she'd cleaned the desk, scrubbing away months if not years of grime.

She gave the envelope only a sideways glance as she slipped off her jacket and hung it over the back of her chair.

The envelope was addressed to her and had a Whitehorse postmark. Nothing unusual about that except for the fact that it was addressed to Andi *West,* the name she'd gone by as a television newscaster in Fort Worth, Texas.

She felt a shiver of trepidation. No one here knew her

as Andi let alone Andi West. Her full name was Miranda West Blake. She had been named after her father, Weston Blake. He was the one who'd nicknamed her Andi.

To put Fort Worth and the past far behind her when she'd applied for this job though, she'd used Miranda Blake and now wrote as M. W. Blake.

She'd thought by moving to Whitehorse, Montana, and using her real name that she would be able to escape from the terror that had run her out of Texas. Had it followed her?

Her heart pounded. All her old fears came back in a wave of nausea. Was it possible there was nowhere she could get away from it?

Fingers trembling, she picked up the envelope, turning it in her fingers. The contents felt light. And the package didn't sound like it was ticking. Something slid inside making her jump.

Her fear, though, gave way to anger. She was sick of being scared. She'd given up everything she loved because of some psycho. If he'd found her...

Taking out her letter opener, she sliced through one end of the envelope and carefully dumped the contents onto her desk.

She'd gotten enough of these at the television station that she knew what to expect.

A white cassette tape thudded to the desktop an instant before a piece of newspaper fluttered down beside it, surprising her.

She frowned and picked up the tape. It was file-card size. There was nothing written on it. She glanced at the CD player on her desk and wondered where she might find a cassette player that played this size tape.

Not that she would play it. She'd learned it was better not to listen to the calls although she'd read most of the letters before handing them over to the police. Except the police hadn't been able to find her stalker let alone stop him or the threatening letters and calls.

Putting down the tape, she turned her attention to the other item from the envelope. As she unfolded the newsprint, she saw that it was a clipping of a local newspaper brief about a woman named Grace Jackson who'd died in a one-car rollover south of town.

She felt a wave of relief. Apparently someone thought the story warranted a follow-up. That's all this was.

True it was odd because the accident had happened six years ago Christmas Eve.

But at least it wasn't connected to Texas. Or her. She tried to relax.

Still the fact that it had been sent to Andi West bothered her. Who besides the newspaper publisher, Mark Sanders, knew her television name?

Just then Mark Sanders came in the door.

She held up the clipping and he took it from her as he walked by her desk, glanced at the story and handed the clipping back saying, "Yeah, that was real sad. They hadn't been married long." He started to walk off.

"Do you want me to do a follow-up?" she asked his retreating back.

He stopped to glance over his shoulder and frowned. "Can't see any reason. It's been what—"

"Six years," she said.

"Right. No reason to bring it back up," Sanders said.

"Someone sent it to me."

"Just file it. You're covering the Parade of Lights tonight, right? It's a pretty big deal in Whitehorse. You sure you don't mind shooting it, too?"

"No problem." She didn't bring up the name thing. It was possible, she realized, that Mark Sanders had told someone who she was thinking no one in Whitehorse, Montana, would care let alone cause her any trouble.

"I've got it covered," she assured him, imagining what her best friend back at the television station in Fort Worth would say if he knew she was covering parades for a small-town weekly newspaper, taking the photographs as well as writing the stories.

She hadn't talked to Bradley since she'd left Texas. Maybe she'd call him. She was sure he was probably worried about her since he'd tried to talk her out of coming up here. She missed him and hadn't wanted to call until things were going better. She didn't want to hear him say I-told-you-so. Even though he was right. She feared this move had been a huge mistake.

But she had some time to kill before the Parade of Lights and she really needed her friend.

"Hello?"

Just the sound of Bradley's voice brought tears to her eyes.

"Hello?" The apprehension she heard in his voice surprised and worried her.

"It's me," she said quickly. "Are you all right?"

"Hey." Instantly he sounded like his old self again. "I'm fine. I just thought it was someone else calling. I've been getting some obscene telephone calls. I might enjoy them if I was straight," he said with a laugh. "I am so glad you called. I have been worried to death about you. I was beginning to think you'd forgotten about me."

"No chance of that," she said, tucking her feet up under her. It was almost like old times talking with him over a delivery pizza and old movies.

"So how bad is it?" he asked.

"It's…interesting."

"I told you not to take that job. You must be bored to

tears. You haven't been banished, you know. You can get on the next plane and be back in Texas in a matter of hours. I'll pick you up at the airport."

She laughed. It *was* tempting.

"So how horrible is it in the wild, wild West?" he asked. "You can tell me."

"It's freezing cold for starters."

"I know. I confess I've been watching the weather. I knew you were going to freeze your cute little behind off." He laughed. "Seriously, how are you?"

"Homesick for you, for warm weather, for Mexican food." She smiled. "There isn't any in Whitehorse."

"Imagine that," he said with a smile in his voice.

"So how are things at the station?"

"It's been bloody hell. There was practically a revolt over your job even though everyone knew the position was only temporary."

Her boss had promised to hold her job for six months.

"So who got it? Anyone I know?"

Bradley let out a dramatic sigh and she knew.

"Rachel," she said. Rachel was as close a female friend as she'd had at the station. "I'm happy for her."

"Oh, please," Bradley said. "You can be honest. It's *me,* remember?"

Andi laughed. It felt good. "You're just jealous because she won't let you try on her shoes."

"I miss you."

"I miss you, too." She hated to ask, but she had to. "Has the station received any more threats addressed to me?"

That telltale beat of silence, then, "I made sure they were turned over to the police."

Hearing this surprised her. She'd thought the threats would stop once she wasn't on the air anymore.

"I'll bug the cops until they find this freak and lock him up so you can come home."

She smiled through her tears. "You're a good friend." She hung up, glad she'd called him. She felt better about her decision to come to Montana. If the television station was still getting threatening letters for her, she was much better off being as far away from Fort Worth as she could get.

As she started to file away the news article about the woman who'd died in the single-car accident, she stopped to read it through again, still curious why anyone would have sent it to her.

The deceased woman, Grace Jackson, had apparently been driving at a high rate of speed when she'd lost control of her car south of town. The car had rolled numerous times before landing in a ravine, where it had caught fire.

As she had the first time she'd read it, Andi shuddered at the thought of the poor woman being trapped in the vehicle and burning to death. There were so few vehicles on the roads up here and miles between ranches let alone towns. Even if the car hadn't burned, the woman probably would have died before someone had come along.

According to the article, Grace Jackson had been married to a Cade Jackson. Wasn't the sheriff's name Jackson? Carter Jackson, as she recalled from reading back papers to familiarize herself with the town.

She wondered if Cade and Carter were related. Pretty good chance given their names. The sheriff's name had come up quite a lot in the news—including the murder of the reporter who'd had this desk, Glen Whitaker.

She looked again at the manila envelope the newspaper clipping and tape had come in, checking to make sure there wasn't a note that she'd missed. Nothing. The envelope had been mailed in Whitehorse so at least it was from someone local.

She filed the story, still a little anxious, though, that at least one person in town knew her other name.

As she pocketed the cassette tape, she wondered where she could find a tape player.

The Parade of Lights definitely was an event in White-horse, Montana. Andi stood on a curb with the rest of the county that had turned out, everyone bundled up for the cold, snowy December night, as one homemade float after another cruised by.

The air was filled with excitement, the stores along the main street open and lit brightly for the event. The smell of Christmas trees, hot cider and Native American fry bread wafted in the chilly air.

The streets were packed with not only townspeople, but also apparently ranchers and their families had come in from miles around for the event.

Andi shot a dozen photographs of the floats, surprised at how many there were given the temperature and how much work had gone into some of them.

She liked the small-town feel, which surprised her. It felt like an extended family as she heard people visiting and calling greetings from the floats.

Just as she was finishing up, she heard someone call out, "Cade!"

She looked up to see an attractive woman waving from one of the floats. Andi followed the woman's gaze to a man leaning against the building yards to her right. She could see only his profile, his face in shadow under the brim of his Western hat, but he was tall and all cowboy. He wore boots, jeans, a sheepskin coat and a Stetson, the brim pulled low, dark hair curling out from under the hat at his nape.

From the way he stood, back in the shadows, she got the impression he had hoped to go unnoticed.

Cade *Jackson?* The husband of the deceased woman from the newspaper clipping?

Andi lifted the camera and impulsively snapped his photograph. As she pulled the camera down, he disappeared into the crowd.

Cold and tired, she returned to the newspaper office just down the block, anxious to get her photographs into the computer. Warmer, she decided to go ahead and write up her story even though it was late.

She knew she was just avoiding the small apartment she'd rented on the other side of town. It wasn't far from the newspaper given that Whitehorse was only ten blocks square. She usually drove to work out of habit more than necessity, although she didn't relish walking through all the snow.

The apartment was small and impersonal to the point of being depressing. In time she would make it hers, but right now she preferred the newspaper office to home.

After she put in the photographs and wrote cutlines for each, she sat down at the computer to write an accompanying article.

Her mind wandered, though, and she found herself calling up the photograph of the cowboy she'd seen on the main street tonight, the one the woman had called Cade. How many Cades could there be in Whitehorse?

The publisher had said Cade Jackson and his wife, Grace, had only been married a short period of time before her death. That meant there should be a wedding announcement in the file, she thought, unable to shake her curiosity as to why someone had sent the cassette and clipping to her.

Five minutes later, she found the wedding announcement and photo. The two had married November 14—just weeks before her death.

Andi studied the photograph of the groom, comparing it to the one she'd taken of the cowboy she'd seen on the street tonight. Cade Jackson. The two were one and the same.

The cassette was still in her pocket. Now more than ever she was anxious to find a player and see what was on the tape.

Intent on the cowboy, Andi finally looked at the wedding photo of the bride, Grace Browning Jackson. Her mouth went dry, her heart a hammer in her ears.

She *knew* this woman.

Except her name hadn't been Grace Browning. Not even close.

Chapter 2

Andi Blake stared at the photograph, telling herself she had to be mistaken. But she knew she wasn't.

It *was* Starr, she'd stake her life on it. Starr Calhoun wasn't someone she could have forgotten even if the first time Andi laid eyes on her wasn't indelibly branded on her memory. They'd both been only young girls. Andi remembered only too well the look they'd shared before all hell broke loose.

And it wasn't as if Andi hadn't seen Starr Calhoun since, she thought with a chill.

It made sense, Starr masquerading as this Grace Browning woman and marrying a local yokel. Starr Calhoun had been hiding out here, using marriage as a cover, waiting. Waiting for what, though?

Her brother Lubbock! He'd been arrested only an hour away from Whitehorse six years ago. She felt a chill as she realized she was meant to come here. As if it had always been her destiny. As if Starr Calhoun had called her from the grave.

She shivered and glanced toward the front window of the newspaper office along the main street, suddenly feeling more than a little paranoid.

A few shoppers straggled past. The Christmas lights still glowed in the park across the street by the train tracks. Next to the old depot, a half dozen passengers waited by their suitcases. Whitehorse's depot had closed years ago, but a passenger train still came through. Passengers had to call for tickets and wait outside until the train arrived.

Andi got up and closed the front blinds, double-checking the front door to make sure she'd locked it.

It didn't take her long to find a more recent photograph of Starr Calhoun on the FBI's most wanted list. She printed the photo, standing over the printer as it came out. The copy wasn't great. But then the original had been taken from a bank surveillance camera.

That had been six years ago August. Wearing masks and carrying sawed-off shotguns, a man and woman had robbed a series of banks across Texas amassing an estimated three million dollars over a two-week period.

During what turned out to be their last robbery, there had been an altercation and the mask Starr Calhoun had been wearing was pulled off by a teller exposing her face to the surveillance camera.

A warrant had been issued for Starr Calhoun, but she and her accomplice had gotten away and had never been heard from again. Nor had the money been recovered.

The accomplice was believed to be her brother Houston Calhoun, a known criminal who'd done time for bank robbery.

The Calhoun family shared more than their distinctive

pale blue eyes and curly auburn hair. Nor was the robbery six years ago the first time Starr Calhoun had been caught on a bank surveillance video camera.

She was first filmed at the age of three when her infamous parents, Hodge and Eden Calhoun, hit a bank in Orange, Texas, with all six children in tow, ranging in age from fifteen to three.

Hodge and Eden had eventually been caught, their children put into foster care and scattered to the wind.

Andi made a note to find out the latest on the rest of the Calhouns. At least she had a good idea where Starr had disappeared to, she thought, studying the wedding photograph.

She couldn't help the small thrill she felt. Her instincts had been right. As a reporter, she'd made a point of keeping track of the infamous Calhoun family. Whenever a news story from any part of the country mentioned one of the Calhouns, her computer flagged the story for her.

That's how she'd seen the article about Starr Calhoun being ID'd in the bank surveillance tape six years ago. Also the lesser story about her older brother Lubbock Calhoun being arrested not long after that.

She'd forgotten about where Lubbock had been arrested, though. It wasn't until she'd been looking for a job away from Fort Worth that her job search had popped up a newspaper reporter position in Whitehorse, Montana, on her computer and triggered the memory of Lubbock's arrest.

Too excited to wait until she saw him the next day, she had called her friend Bradley. Bradley Harris worked in fact-checking at the news station. The two had become good friends almost at once. He loved Tex-Mex food and old movies and was safe because he was gay and Andi didn't date men she worked with. Actually she didn't date at all—too busy with her career, she told herself.

"Why Montana? It sounds like a one-horse town," Bradley had joked when she'd told him about the job, leaving out the part about Lubbock being arrested near there. "Surely there is somewhere closer you could disappear to. Wait a minute." He knew her too well. "How close is this town to where Lubbock Calhoun was arrested?"

Bradley was one of the few people who knew about her interest—or obsession as he called it—in the Calhoun crime family. She'd thought he wouldn't make the connection.

Reluctantly she'd showed Bradley on a Montana map on her computer. Lubbock Calhoun had been arrested for an outstanding warrant in a convenience store in Glasgow, Montana, six years ago—an hour away from Whitehorse.

"I think it's a sign I should check into this job," she said and waited for Bradley to talk her out of it.

And Bradley had tried, pointing out that it had been six years, Lubbock was probably just passing through Montana, and "What could you possibly learn after all this time? Not to mention, you'll be stuck in One Horse."

"Whitehorse," she'd corrected, the job having taken on more appeal with the possible Lubbock Calhoun connection.

"I'm worried about you and this thing with the Calhouns," he'd said. She suspected he knew why they held such interest for her because he was the best researcher she'd ever known. But he never let on.

He'd finally given up trying to stop her, knowing how desperately she needed to get out of Fort Worth. And how she couldn't turn down even a remote chance to learn more about the Calhouns.

Coincidence? Starr coming to Montana, marrying a cowboy from Whitehorse and Lubbock being arrested just miles away? No way. Andi felt her excitement building. There was a story here, the kind of story that had propelled Andi's rise in broadcast news. That and her instincts when it came to investigative reporting.

And while she might have had to give up television news for a while, a story like this would definitely assist in her return when the time came.

Eagerly she planned how to proceed. She had to get the whole story and that meant hearing Cade Jackson's side of it, she thought as she looked up his address in the phone book.

As she took it down, she couldn't help but wonder. Did Cade Jackson know who he'd married? Or was he in for the surprise of his life?

Cade Jackson walked home from the parade through the underpass beneath the tracks as the passenger train pulled in.

The night was cold and dark, the streets snowpacked and icy. He breathed in the air. It felt moist, the clouds low, another snowstorm expected to come in by tomorrow morning.

A white Christmas. He could hear carols coming from one of the cars' radios as it passed. He quickened his step, anxious to get back to his apartment behind the bait shop. Going to the parade had been a mistake. Now he felt antsy. He thought about driving out to his cabin on Nelson Reservoir, but it was late and he was tired.

The parade had brought back memories of Grace and the night they'd come to the parade together, cuddled close as music played on a float with a Western band. She'd looked over at him, her eyes bright with excitement, her cheeks flushed from the cold. And he'd kissed her.

He could still remember the way she'd tasted. Sweet and just a little pepperminty from the candy cane she'd eaten. He recalled the way she felt in his arms and how happy he'd been. Newlyweds. They'd been newlyweds and he'd thought they had years together ahead of them.

That was the night they talked about having children, he realized as he finally reached the bait shop. He started around back to his apartment in the rear when he saw that someone had left a note on the shop's front door.

He stepped over to pluck it free before going around to the back. While he locked the bait shop door, like most everyone in Whitehorse, he left his apartment door open.

Stepping inside, he flipped on a light glad to be distracted from his thoughts as he opened the note. Something fluttered to the floor, but he was busy looking at the note, surprised he didn't recognize the handwriting. He knew everyone in Whitehorse, having grown up in the area. He and his brother, Carter, had been raised down by Old Town Whitehorse to the south, but they'd both gone to high school here.

The town of Whitehorse had sprung up to the south closer to the Missouri River breaks, but when the railroad had come through in the 1800s, the town had moved north, taking the name with it.

The note read: "Mr. Jackson, I need to talk to you, M. W. Blake." There was a local phone number at the bottom. And four little words that ruined his night. "It's about your wife."

The word "wife" jumped out at him. He glanced down at the floor and saw the business card at his feet. Bending, he stooped to pick it up. This he recognized. The logo was from the *Milk River Examiner,* the local weekly newspaper.

Under it was the name: M. W. Blake

Under that was the word: Reporter

He crumpled both the note and the business card in his fist. He didn't have any idea who M. W. Blake was and he didn't care to know. The last thing he planned to do was talk to a reporter about Grace.

On the way home after leaving a note for Cade Jackson at his bait shop, Andi realized she couldn't wait until morning to find out what was on this cassette tape. She called the publisher and asked if anyone had a tape player that took regular-size cassette tapes.

His daughter just happened to have an old one she no longer used, he said. If she stopped by, she was welcome to borrow it. He also had a couple of tapes she could use if she needed to tape something.

Mark Sanders had bent over backward since she'd applied for the job. She'd told him she needed a change of pace. He, in turn, had needed a reporter after Glen Whitaker had been murdered. Not a lot of reporters wanted to come to Whitehorse, especially after they found out what it paid.

Sanders had been worried that Andi had too much experience and wouldn't be staying long.

"Whitehorse is nothing like Fort Worth," he'd said with a laugh. "Maybe you'd better come up here and have a look-see before you take my offer." He had already apologized for how little he could pay her.

She'd had to convince him that Whitehorse was exactly what she was looking for. She didn't tell him her real reason. Only her friend Bradley knew that.

Back at her apartment, Andi took the cassette tape

from her pocket and popped it into one side of the player. Hitting play, she turned up the volume and went into the kitchen to pour herself a glass of wine.

At first all she heard was static. She was beginning to think that the tape was blank as she took the wine bottle from the fridge.

But as she reached for a glass, she heard a woman's voice on the tape and froze.

Like a sleepwalker, she moved into the living room, the wine bottle in her hand as the tape continued.

She didn't recognize the voice—she'd never heard Starr Calhoun speak. Nor did the woman have much of a Texas accent. No, it was what the woman was saying that captured all of Andi's attention and convinced her that the voice was that of Starr Calhoun.

On the tape, the woman talked about robbing a series of banks. After a moment, a male voice could be heard on the tape. Her accomplice.

The tape went to static but Andi didn't move. Couldn't. She stood too shocked to do anything but stare at the tape player.

Who had sent this to her?

And why?

And where had it been the last six years?

She told herself not to look a gift horse in the mouth. Why not just revel in her good luck at having a story like this dropped into her lap?

But she knew that hadn't been the case. It was no coincidence someone had sent her this. Just as it was no coincidence she was here. Was it possible that someone had sent her the job notice, counting on her need to escape Fort Worth and her interest in the Calhouns? With Lubbock's arrest just miles from here the person who'd sent her the job notice knew she wouldn't be able to resist.

Just as she wouldn't be able to resist breaking this story once she had all the facts.

She stepped to the player, her fingers trembling as she rewound the tape and listened to it again before she went to the kitchen and poured herself a healthy glass of wine. She was shaking now, the realization of what she had in her possession starting to sink in along with the apprehension.

She needed to talk to her friend Bradley. He'd been her sounding board through the whole secret-admirer-turned-stalker trauma in Texas. She dialed his number, needing him to be home.

"So how's the weekly newspaper business," Bradley said after they'd exchanged pleasantries about the weather in Montana versus Texas and he'd told her the TV-station gossip.

She hesitated but only for a moment before she told him about the story she'd stumbled across. Bradley, being Bradley and a journalist at heart, was ecstatic.

"What an incredible story," he cried. "So you were right about there being something to Lubbock Calhoun's arrest up there. Well, that's why you're the hotshot news celebrity and I'm the lowly researcher," he joked. "And to have this story dropped in your lap…" He suddenly turned serious. "Oh, sweetie, I almost forgot. I saw on the news that Lubbock Calhoun was released from prison three weeks ago and has already broken his parole."

Her heart leaped to her throat. Lubbock was on the loose?

"You don't think he's the one who sent you the information, do you?" Bradley asked.

"Why would he?" she asked, although she already knew.

"Isn't it obvious? He figures a hotshot reporter like you will find the money," Bradley said.

She bristled at the hotshot reporter comment. "I work for a weekly newspaper."

"Now you do. Stop being so modest. You are a great reporter. Lubbock must have seen you on TV during one of your stories that made national news," Bradley said. "Sweetie, I don't like this. I think you should hightail it back to Texas. If Lubbock Calhoun's feeding you this information, then it's too dangerous. The man is a hardened *criminal*."

"You know I can't come back to Texas."

"But can you stay there? What if I'm right and he's hoping you find the money for him?"

"It would make quite the story," she said, only half joking.

"Sweetie, but what if you don't find the money?"

"For all I know Starr faked her death and has already spent all the money," Andi said and took a drink of her wine, unnerved by the news about Lubbock. "Don't forget Houston. He could have already blown the money. No one has seen him since he and Starr pulled off that last robbery six years ago."

"If Houston *was* her accomplice," Bradley pointed out. "We know it wasn't Lubbock. He didn't resemble the man in the bank surveillance photos. Plus he was arrested on an old warrant so he wasn't even a suspect in the robberies apparently."

Andi had been thinking about the millions of stolen dollars. "You can bet one of the Calhouns has already spent that robbery money."

"If that were the case, wouldn't Lubbock Calhoun know that—if he's the one who sent you the information?" Bradley asked.

He made a good point.

"Maybe he doesn't know what happened to the money—or Starr or Houston. Maybe he's winging it just like me," she said.

"Maybe. Or maybe Starr hid the money, planning to take off with her new identity, but hadn't planned on losing control of her car and dying."

"That's another possibility," she admitted. "That's the problem. There are too many possibilities."

"Oh, wait," Bradley said, "but if Starr had hidden the money, surely her husband would have found it by now. Unless he *did* find it!"

"Is there some way to find out if any of the stolen money ever turned up?" she asked.

"The robberies were during the day, right? Banks have what they call 'bait' money. It's traceable. So if any of it has surfaced… I'll see what I can find out and get back to you," he said, sounding as excited as she felt about the story.

She gave him her new cell phone number and they both promised to keep in touch.

After she hung up, she shot a glance at her front window as a car drove slowly by. Lubbock wasn't just out of prison, he'd already broken parole.

Quickly she stepped to the window and closed the curtains, telling herself that the smartest thing she could do was to take everything she knew to the local sheriff, Carter Jackson, Cade Jackson's brother.

But then the story would break prematurely. A story that belonged to her. And not the whole story. Not to mention that she might never find out who was sending her the information or what they wanted.

She checked to make sure her door was locked before she rewound the tape and listened to it again, her mind racing. She took one of the blank tapes Mark Sanders had given her and put it in the second cassette deck and made a copy of the original.

Wouldn't anyone who wanted the story to come out have gone to the sheriff? Or the FBI? Or if not that, a major television station?

Whoever had given her the newspaper clipping and the tape wasn't after a story—or justice. No, they wanted something else. Bradley had to be right. They wanted the money.

She took the tape out of the player and stared down at it. The big question was what was *she* going to do with this?

Chapter 3

The Jackson Bait Shop was on the edge of town. The sign was weathered, the building small. As Andi got out of her car the next morning, she wondered how Cade Jackson made a living in such a remote place selling bait.

Or was he living off the three million dollars Starr had stolen?

Andi had gone into the newspaper early, gathering everything she could find on Cade Jackson. There hadn't been much. A local cowboy, he'd grown up on a ranch south of here near what was called Old Town Whitehorse.

Since then he'd won some horse-roping events and caught a few big fish that had made the newspaper.

His only claim to fame just might turn out to be marrying Starr Calhoun, she thought as she saw that the Closed sign was still up in the bait shop window. There were no store hours posted. Did anyone even fish this time of year?

She knocked at the door and waited on the small landing out front, hugging herself, trying to keep warm. She guessed he was already up since the *Great Falls Tribune* newspaper box next to the door was empty. It had snowed again last night, coating the entire town with a couple of inches. The snow glittered so bright it was blinding. But it was the breeze that cut through her, chilling her to the bone. She'd had no idea it would be this cold up here.

As a gust of wind whirled snow around her, she instinctively reached for the doorknob. To her surprise, it turned easily in her hand, the door falling open.

She was hit with a blast of warm air. She leaned into it, stepping into the room and closing the door behind her as she tried to shake off her earlier chill.

Apparently Cade Jackson sold more than bait. The room was divided into four long aisles by three high shelves filled with lures and jigs, rods and reels, paddles and oars, nets and an array of boat parts and sporting equipment.

Cade Jackson was nowhere in sight but she thought she heard water running somewhere in the back.

She moved through the shop toward the sound. It was warm in here and she was in no hurry to go back outside into the cold.

But she reminded herself: for all she knew this man had known about the robbery, might even have gotten rid of his wife to keep all the money for himself.

But if he had the three million dollars or even some of it, he didn't appear to be enjoying it much, she thought as she saw his living quarters.

The shop opened onto a small apartment. The lack of stuff made her wonder if anyone could live this simply. Certainly not Starr Calhoun.

For a moment Andi considered what she was doing. This felt all wrong. Not to mention she couldn't guess what Cade Jackson's reaction was going to be to not only her being here, but also what she had to show him.

What if she was wrong?

She wasn't and she knew it.

But she still felt apprehensive. She had no idea what this man was like. The fact that Starr Calhoun had married him was a clue, though. Andi was wondering if she'd made a mistake coming here alone.

She was no fool, though. In her large shoulder bag, along with a copy of the cassette she'd made and the boom box, she had a can of pepper spray and her cell phone.

"Mr. Jackson?" she called from the doorway into the apartment. No answer.

She called his name again. The sound of running water stopped. "Hello!" she called out. "Hello?" She stopped to look at a bulletin board filled with photographs of fish being held by men, women and children. Some of the fish were as huge as the grins on the many faces.

When she looked up, she was startled to find the apartment doorway filled with a dark silhouette. She got the impression Cade Jackson had been standing in the doorway for some time studying her.

To make things even more awkward, his dark hair was wet and droplets of water beaded on his lashes as well as on the dark curls of his chest hair that formed a V to disappear into the towel wrapped around his slim hips.

"I'm sorry, the door was open," she said quickly.

He smiled either at the fact that he had her flustered or because of her accent. "The shop isn't open yet, but then again you don't look like a fisherman," he said eyeing her. "Nor do you sound local."

"No, I'm neither," she said, getting her composure back. He was even more handsome up close and personal.

He cocked a dark brow at her.

"I'm Miranda Blake. I left my business card and a note on your door last night? But I can wait while you dress."

He'd looked friendly before. He didn't now. "M. W. Blake, the new reporter over at the *Examiner?*" He was shaking his head and moving toward her, clearly planning to show her out. "I don't talk to reporters."

"You'll want to talk to *me,*" she said standing her ground as she put her hand on her shoulder bag, easing the top open so she could get to her pepper spray.

He stopped in front of her and she caught a whiff of his soap. Yum. He stood a good head taller. She had to tilt her face up to look into his eyes. Eyes so dark they appeared black. Right now they were filled with impatience and irritation.

"I'm afraid you're mistaken about that, Tex."

"I have some information about your wife," she said, determined not to let him intimidate her but it was difficult. The look in his eyes alone would frighten someone much larger than herself. She clutched the pepper spray can in her purse.

He was as big a man as she'd first thought, a few inches over six feet and broad at the shoulders. Solid looking, she thought. Not like a man who worked out. More like a man who worked. That surprised her given that selling bait and tackle couldn't be all that strenuous.

He settled those dark eyes on her. Everything about him was dark. She tried to imagine someone like Starr Calhoun with this man. Starr with her wild, curly auburn hair and those pale blue eyes, as fair as this man was dark.

"You're new here," Cade Jackson said as if roping in his irritation. "You don't know me. So I'm going to cut you some slack. I don't want another story about my wife's death. It's Christmas and I don't need any more reminders that she's gone, all right?"

"I think you'd better look at this," she said, slipping her hand from the pepper spray can to the copy of the photo taken from the bank's surveillance camera. It had gone out to all news media six years ago, but she doubted it had made it as far as Whitehorse, Montana.

Cade didn't take the photo she held out. He stood with his hands on his hips, dripping on the wood floor of the bait shop, the white towel barely wrapped around his hips showing way too much skin.

"Please. Just take a look and then I promise to leave," she said.

With obvious reluctance he took the copy of the photograph. She watched his expressive dark eyes. Recognition then confusion flashed in them. "What the hell is this?"

"It's your wife. Only her name wasn't Grace Browning. It was Starr Calhoun. That photo was taken by a surveillance camera in the bank she robbed six years ago—not long before she showed up here in Whitehorse."

"Get out," he said. "I don't know what your game is, Tex, but I'm not playing."

"Neither am I," she said as he reached for her arm. "Starr Calhoun was one of the infamous bank-robbing Calhouns from Texas," she said, dodging his grasp, her hand again clutching the can of pepper spray in her purse. "The three million dollars she and her male accomplice stole was never recovered."

"If you don't get out of here right now, you're going to be sorry," he said through gritted teeth. "What the hell do you keep reaching in that purse for?" He grabbed her arm.

As he jerked her hand out of the shoulder bag, her finger hit the trigger on the pepper spray.

* * *

On the laptop propped up in her kitchen, Arlene Evans studied the latest applicant on her Meet-A-Mate site with pride as she whipped up a batch of pancakes.

Since she'd started her rural online dating service she'd had a few good-looking men sign up but none who could match Jud Corbett, a former stuntman and actor, who liked long walks in the rain, horseback riding, dancing in the moonlight and was interested in finding a nice cowgirl to ride off into the sunset with.

Arlene had proven she was a great matchmaker when she'd gotten the Whitehorse deputy sheriff together with that Cavanaugh girl.

But that was nothing compared to who she had picked out for the handsome Jud Corbett.

Her very own daughter Charlotte. True, Charlotte wasn't a cowgirl, so to speak, but she could ride a horse. And Jud Corbett was just what her daughter needed right now.

Charlotte had seemed a little down lately. But a man like Jud Corbett could bring her out of it quick!

The two would make beautiful children together, Arlene thought with longing as she broke a couple of eggs into the batter and stirred as she admired Jud Corbett's good looks. If she were twenty years younger...

"Are the pancakes about ready?" her son, Bo, demanded. At twenty-one, Bo had gotten his looks and personality from his father, damn Floyd Evans to hell.

Floyd had up and left them a few months ago. The divorce papers were somewhere on the overflowing coffee table. The bastard had left her with their three children to finish raising.

Not that the three weren't pretty much raised since the oldest, Violet, was in her thirties, unmarried and no longer under the roof, but that was another story. Bo was of legal age, although that didn't seem to mean anything other than he drank beer in front of her now. Charlotte had just celebrated her eighteenth birthday, eating most of the cake all by herself before going out with her friends and getting high.

The phone rang before Arlene could come up with a proper retort for her son. It rang another time but neither of her offspring seemed to hear it.

"Let me get that, why don't you?" Arlene said doubting they got her sarcasm, either, since neither seemed to hear anything over the blaring television.

"Mrs. Evans?" a woman said on the other end of the line.

Arlene didn't correct her. "I'm not buying anything," she snapped and started to hang up the phone.

"I'm calling about your daughter Violet."

Arlene put the receiver back to her ear. "Yes?" she asked suspiciously. Calls about Violet were never good.

"My name is Myrna Lynch, I'm the media coordinator here at the state hospital. Your daughter Violet would like you all to come up for Family Day."

"*Family* Day?" Arlene Evans echoed into the phone. "You can't be talking about my daughter. Violet is completely out of it and the last time I came up there to see her you guys wouldn't even let me in."

Arlene was still mad about that. As if she enjoyed driving clear up to the state mental hospital to be turned away.

"No one told you?" asked the woman, whose name Arlene couldn't remember. "Your daughter Violet has made remarkable progress. She's no longer in a catatonic state."

"What are you saying? She's not nuts anymore?" How was that possible? "Did she tell you what she did to end up there?"

"Mental illness is a medical disorder that is treatable, Mrs. Evans. Your daughter is getting care that will let her be a responsible member of society again," the woman said, clearly upset at Arlene's use of the word "nuts." "In order to do that, she needs to work through any issues she has with her family. So can I tell the doctor you and your family will be here Saturday?"

"Wait a minute. Issues? She tried to kill me!" Arlene bellowed.

"Your daughter doesn't recall any of that, Mrs. Evans."

Arlene just bet she didn't.

"Violet needs the support of her family. I'm sure you want to do what is best for her."

Arlene bristled at the woman's tone. "I've always supported Violet. You have no idea what I have done for that girl and what did I get for it? Why she—"

"Mrs. Evans, if you can't attend family day Saturday then—"

"I'll be there," she said with a sigh.

"Violet has asked that her brother and sister also attend," the woman said.

Arlene glanced over at her daughter Charlotte curled up on the couch chewing on the end of her long blond hair. Bo was slouched in the recliner, a jumbo bag of corn chips open on his lap and an open can of beer at his elbow, in his own catatonic state as he stared at some reality show on the television where a woman was shrieking at one of the other contestants.

"Turn down the damned TV," Arlene yelled, covering the mouthpiece. "Can't you see I'm on the phone?"

Neither of her grown children responded.

"I have to bring Charlotte and Bo?" Arlene asked the woman, turning her back to the two. "I'm not sure it's a good idea for them to be around Violet."

"It's important for *Violet's* healing process."

"Well, whatever is important for Violet," Arlene snapped. "Never mind the rest of us. She really is better?"

"I think you will be surprised when you see her. We'll plan on your family Saturday."

Arlene hung up, wondering how Violet could surprise her more than she had. Her old-maid daughter had plotted to kill her and even gotten her brother and sister involved.

Arlene could never forgive Violet for that. She'd been so sure her daughter would never get out of the mental hospital and now this. *Family* Day.

Surely those fools at that hospital weren't really considering letting Violet out?

As she spooned the pancake batter into the smoking skillet, the scent of oil and sizzling pancake batter filled the kitchen and adjoining living room.

Behind her, Charlotte made an odd sound, then sprung up from the couch to run down the hall, her hand over her mouth. It was the fastest Arlene had seen the girl move in years. A moment later she heard Charlotte retching in the bathroom.

"What on earth is wrong with her?" Arlene demanded of her son.

He glanced away from the TV to scowl at his mother. "What do you think? She's pregnant. Haven't you noticed how big she's been getting? Where have you been?" He looked past her and swore. "Damn it, Mother, you're burning the pancakes!"

Cade Jackson swore as he wrenched the can of pepper spray from Andi.

Unfortunately the spray nozzle had been pointed in the wrong direction—her direction. Fortunately only a little had shot out. Enough that her eyes instantly watered and she began to cough uncontrollably.

He grabbed her, cursing with each step as he tried to drag her to the back of his apartment. She fought him, although it was clearly a losing battle, unaware of what he was trying to do until he shoved her out the back door and into the fresh air.

She took huge gulps, tears running down her face as she coughed and tried to get the fresh air into her lungs.

He stood for a moment shaking his head, his arms crossed over his bare chest, his dark eyes boring into her.

"I think you're going to live," he said, giving her can of pepper spray a heave. It landed in the deep snow out by the trees along the Milk River and disappeared. "Now get the hell off my porch."

He stepped back inside, not even looking chilled though still only wearing a towel, and slammed the door behind him. She heard the lock turn.

On the other side of the door, Cade Jackson took a ragged breath and looked down at the grainy photograph still clutched in his hand.

It wasn't Grace. True it looked enough like her to be her twin. Enough like her to rattle the hell out of him.

The woman in the photograph, Starr Calhoun, had robbed a bunch of banks and gotten away with three million dollars?

He wanted to laugh. Not for a minute would anyone believe that this Starr Calhoun was Grace except some wet-behind-the-ears reporter. It was beyond crazy.

He realized he was shaking. From anger. From shock. From the scare she'd given him. Earlier, for just a fleeting panicked instant, he'd thought the woman in the photo was Grace.

It was clear why the reporter had thought so as well as he took one last look at the photo. Even the poor quality print revealed a little of Grace in this woman and it shook him to his core. It was the eyes. She had Grace's eyes.

The reporter had made an honest mistake, he told himself as he balled up the photo of Starr Calhoun and tossed it in the trash can. The rumpled-up photograph landed on the note and business card the reporter had left the night before. M. W. Blake. He still wanted to break her pretty little neck for giving him such a scare. And that stunt with the pepper spray...

He shook his head as he returned to his apartment at the back of shop to get dressed. Someday he would look back on this and laugh. Let Tex wait by the phone. He wouldn't be calling her.

Still he felt shaken by the encounter. Anyone would have been rattled, though, he told himself, after being caught coming out of his shower first thing in the morning by someone like Ms. Blake. He'd foolishly left the shop's front door open after getting his newspaper this morning. Maybe he'd better start locking his apartment, as well.

When he'd first seen her standing there, he'd been a little surprised but he sure hadn't expected what was coming. Not from someone who looked like her, small, demure, sweet looking and sounding with that Texas accent of hers. And a determination that rivaled his own.

Too bad he couldn't shake off the worry that pressed on his chest like a two-ton truck. The woman wasn't foolish enough to run the story, was she?

As he started to leave, he went back into the shop to retrieve the photo, note and business card from the trash. Smoothing the photo, he felt his original jolt of surprise.

He quickly folded the paper and stuck all three items in his coat pocket as he headed for the door again.

Cade would just show the photo to Carter, have him find out who this Starr Calhoun was and put an end to this foolishness before the reporter made a fool of herself and tarnished Grace's memory. That, after all, was the benefit of having a brother who was sheriff.

Cade glanced at his watch, knowing where to find his brother this time of the morning. At the same place he was seven days a week, the Hi-Line Café.

Leaving his Closed sign in the window, Cade headed for the café just a few blocks to the west. It was one of those beautiful December days, cold and crisp, the sky a crystalline-blue, the clouds mere wisps high above him and the new snow brilliant and blinding.

It was supposed to snow again by evening, he'd heard on the radio this morning before his shower. The shower brought back the image of M. W. Blake standing in his bait shop. He remembered now that his first impression had been one of male interest—before he'd found out who she was and what she wanted.

He recalled being a little taken aback by the sharp pang of desire he'd felt. But given how long it had been, he supposed he shouldn't have been surprised. The feeling had been more than lust, though. He'd actually been interested.

Even before she'd opened her mouth, it had been clear she wasn't local. She was wearing some fancy black boots with a gray pin-striped three-piece suit and a lightweight leather coat, her long dark hair pulled up to give him a good view of her long, graceful neck.

When she'd turned, he'd been thrown off guard by how young she was. It was the freckles she'd failed to completely hide with makeup and those wide green eyes.

Wisps of dark hair curled on each side of the high cheek-bones. She was a stunner. The soft Southern drawl was just icing on the cake.

He swore under his breath. She wasn't even half as appealing when it turned out she was a damned reporter, though. And it had only gotten worse when he realized she was a reporter who didn't have her facts straight. What could he expect of someone who was obviously too young to be anything but a rookie?

As he passed the big bare-limbed cottonwoods along the Milk River etching dark against the bright day, he thought of the fall day he'd met Grace and felt a sharp jab of longing.

The woman in the photo hadn't been Grace, but even the resemblance to her made him hurt all over again. He cursed the damned reporter all the way to the café.

Sheriff Carter Jackson was sitting at the counter. Cade dropped onto the stool next to him and motioned to the waitress that he would have the same thing he always did. Coffee.

"Good mornin'," he said to his brother as the waitress slid a cup in front of him.

"Is it?" the sheriff said.

The waitress brought Cade extra sugar packets. He tore open a half dozen and poured them into his cup.

"If you don't like coffee, why drink it?" Carter asked irritably.

"Who says I don't like coffee?" He poured in most of the small pitcher of milk the waitress brought and glanced at his brother, wondering what had put Carter in such a foul mood. He suspected he knew. Eve Bailey.

Carter had been trying to get Eve back for months now. They'd dated in high school but Carter had married someone else. Now divorced, he wasn't finding Eve

Bailey very forgiving. Not that Cade could blame her, although it was clear his brother had always loved her.

"You're up early," Carter said, eyeing him. "What's goin' on with you?"

Cade had planned to show his brother the photo of Starr Calhoun and tell him about the ridiculous claim made by the new reporter in town. But something stopped him.

"Nothin'," Cade said. "Just thought I'd join you for a cup of coffee this morning."

His brother turned now to stare at him. "You sure you're all right?"

"Don't I look all right?" Cade shot back.

"You look a little peaked."

Cade concentrated on his coffee, telling himself he was a fool not to show his brother the Wanted poster and put an end to this. So what was holding him back?

"You're usually out in your ice-fishing house by now," Carter said, sounding suspicious. That also went with having a sheriff for a brother.

"I haven't got my house out yet," he said, although that had been his plan just this morning. Before his early visit from Tex. Normally as soon as Nelson Reservoir froze over he would be on the ice.

"I heard Harvey Alderson speared a nice Northern the other day," Carter said.

Cade nodded. "The photo's already on the wall at the shop." Harvey had come straight there to have his photograph taken. It was a Whitehorse tradition.

"Maybe you're starting to realize there is more to life than fishing," his brother said, sounding as if he thought that was progress.

On any other day Cade might have argued the point. "So how is Eve?"

"She's impossible as ever," Carter groused. "And I don't want to talk about her."

Cade laughed as he watched his brother wolf down his breakfast and between bites, go on and on about Eve. Some things didn't change and today Cade was damned glad of it.

Andi finished her story on the Parade of Lights and laid out the page for the next day's edition, trying to keep busy.

She'd expected Cade to call. He hadn't.

Wouldn't a man who'd been given evidence that his wife was a known criminal call? Unless he'd already known and was sitting over in his bait shop planning how to keep her from telling another living soul.

She slammed the drawer on the filing cabinet and cursed mildly under her breath. It was time to use her ace in the hole: the cassette tape.

It was dangerous, but once he heard the voice on the tape, he would confirm that the voice was Starr Calhoun's and she would have the proof she needed. She hoped that faced with even more evidence and his own innocence in all this, he would break down and tell her everything about his relationship with Starr.

Unless of course he wasn't innocent.

Andi couldn't help the rush of excitement she felt at just the thought of playing the copy of the tape she'd made for him. Maybe she should have told him about the tape when she'd shown him the photo.

No, she thought, given how angry he'd been she doubted he would have listened to the tape. He had needed time to calm down, to let it sink in, to realize he couldn't hide from the truth.

Right. But how was she going to get him to listen to

the tape if he refused to talk to her again? The man was obviously more stubborn than she had anticipated. She'd been convinced, guilty or innocent, he wouldn't be able to rest until he heard her out. So much for that thought.

She sighed as she sat down and checked her schedule. She didn't have another story to cover for several days. The newspaper would hit the stands in the morning and she would have a whole week before the next edition. She couldn't believe how laid-back weekly newspaper work was compared to broadcast news in a metropolitan city.

But it would work out well for her. She'd need time to mine this story. Time to convince Cade Jackson to talk to her.

That was the problem. To get the story she wanted, she needed Cade's side of it. She needed to know how he and Starr had met, how she'd deceived him into marrying her.

Andi felt a twinge of guilt. Cade hadn't just been furious this morning. He'd seemed stunned. Even though he denied the photo was of his wife, she'd seen his shock. He'd recognized Starr.

What would his reaction be when he heard his wife's voice on the tape, callously planning the bank robberies with her accomplice? Unless, of course, Cade *was* her accomplice.

No, the man caught on the bank surveillance cameras had pale blue eyes. Cade Jackson had dark, expressive eyes. Nor was he built like Starr's accomplice.

If Cade Jackson was involved, then it was from the sidelines. Which didn't mean he hadn't known who his wife really was—or that he didn't know what had happened to the robbery money.

A thought struck her like a bolt out of the blue. How badly *had* Starr deceived him? Hadn't the article in the newspaper about her death said that the car had rolled numerous times before catching fire? Her body had apparently burned beyond recognition.

What if Starr had faked her death just as Andi had first suspected? What if she was somewhere living off that three mil with her accomplice? Then who had been killed in the car wreck?

Mind racing, Andi realized the pieces still didn't fit. Lubbock was out of prison and missing. But whoever had sent her the job information about Whitehorse knew she had information about Lubbock's arrest in Montana. That meant the person knew about her interest in the Calhoun family. Might even know about her connection to the Calhouns.

She groaned, realizing how that was possible. A few years back, she'd driven over to the prison where Amarillo Calhoun had been sentenced. The eldest of the Calhoun children, Amarillo had followed in his parents' footsteps, his life of crime going from bank robbing to murder.

She'd seen him sitting in the glassed-in cubicle. Their eyes had met. He must have recognized her because he told the guard he didn't want to speak with her—backing out on their interview. Her face had been all over the TV news. She'd just broken a big news story. That was right before she'd gotten her newscaster job in Fort Worth.

So it was possible Lubbock knew who she was and why she would jump at digging into this story.

If her friend Bradley was right, then Lubbock was after the missing money. Or Starr *and* the money, if she'd faked her death. Or there was Houston Calhoun, who'd disappeared the same time as Starr.

Clearly if Lubbock had left her the tape and newspaper clipping, he wasn't interested in the truth coming out. And he wasn't the only one, Andi thought. Cade Jackson wouldn't want a story about his wife being Starr Calhoun, the bank robber, hitting the news, either, she thought, remembering the look on his face when he'd recognized the woman on the Wanted poster. If he'd loved his wife as much as he appeared to, what would the truth do to him?

She pushed the thought away. She'd never backed down from a story and wasn't going to now. The best stories rose out of someone's pain. This was one of those stories.

A niggling concern wormed its way into her thoughts, though. Whoever was sending her the information was playing her like a marionette until he got what he wanted. Then what?

Her phone rang, making her jump.

"Hello?"

Silence.

"Hello?" she said again, feeling suddenly spooked. Lubbock?

Then to her relief, Cade said, "It's me." He didn't sound happy about it, though.

She waited, suspecting he was sorry he'd called and might even hang up.

"I need to see you," he said gruffly.

"All right. Do you want me to—"

"I'm right outside."

Chapter 4

Cade watched Miranda Blake come out of the newspaper office. She had to be freezing. The temperature was still hovering around zero. Another snowstorm was expected before evening. And here she was dressed like she was still in Texas.

Didn't she notice that no one dressed up in Montana let alone in Whitehorse? And she had to be kidding in those high-heeled boots that certainly were never intended for walking on ice and snow.

He reached across to open the passenger-side door, shaking his head. What the hell was he thinking? He should have just told her what he had to say on the phone. At least he'd left the pickup running. He'd make this quick.

There was a regal air about her that set his teeth on edge as she climbed in and smoothed her suit skirt. She'd brought along an old-fashioned black boom box. What the hell was that about? He turned up the heat, furious with himself for doing this. Why hadn't he left well enough alone?

Because he knew M. W. Blake sure as hell wasn't going to.

"I just wanted to tell you that you're wrong," he said, looking out at the snowy day through the windshield. He'd just have his say then get on his way. "That woman in the photo isn't Grace. Admittedly it resembles her. It sure sent me for a loop." He cleared his throat. "But if you'd known her, you'd know that she wasn't some bank robber and you would have realized your mistake."

She didn't say anything and he was finally forced to look over at her.

"It was an honest mistake, I'm sure," he said. "I just didn't want you doing a story and having to retract it. Nor am I looking for an apology."

She laughed softly. "Well, that's good because I wasn't going to give you one. You're the one who's mistaken."

He jerked off his Stetson and raked a hand through his hair. This woman was impossible. "I'm telling you that photo isn't of Grace."

"No, it's of Starr Calhoun, the woman you married," she said in that sweet Southern drawl of hers.

He slapped his hat back on his head and gave the pickup a little gas as he gripped the wheel to keep from strangling the damned woman. "I don't know why I bothered to come by and try to talk sense into you, Tex."

The inside of the pickup cab was warm and smelled of the soap he'd used that morning in the shower. Andi recognized the pleasant scent. "My name is Miranda and you came by to see me because you recognized her and whether you want to admit it or not, you want to know the truth about the woman you knew as Grace Browning."

"Like hell, Tex," he snapped.

As intimidating as he was, she turned to face him. "You can't keep me from doing the story."

"Maybe I can't keep you from making a fool of yourself, but I can sure as hell keep you from involving me in it." He shifted the pickup into gear and gave her a pointed look. "You and I don't have any more to say to each other."

"You're wrong about that. You *are* involved," she said calmly as he reached across and opened her door. A blast of freezing air rushed in.

"Maybe, but you'll have to do your story without my help," he snapped.

"Then I guess you'll have to hear the truth with the rest of the town when it comes out in my article." She started to get out. "Oh, by the way, you should know I'm not the only one who knows about your wife's true identity. Someone sent me a newspaper clipping about her death along with a cassette tape of Starr Calhoun and her male accomplice planning the bank robberies. Want to make a bet it's your wife's voice on the tape?"

He swore and looked away for a moment before he said, "When were you going to tell me about the tape?" He sounded scared and she felt again that prickle of guilt that she was about to destroy this man's life.

"When I thought you could handle it."

He cut his eyes to her, his expression one of anger and fear. He let out a humorless laugh. "And you think I can handle it *now?*"

Cade told himself that the tape would prove this woman was wrong and that would be the end of it. Not that he didn't realize she was banking on the tape proving just the opposite.

"Fine, let's hear the tape," he said, and reached across her to slam her door.

"I think the sound quality would be better without your pickup truck's engine running in the background, don't you? Also the player's batteries are low. I need to plug it in."

He didn't really want to take her back to his apartment behind the bait shop, but he had little choice. He much preferred doing this on his own turf. And the newspaper office was out. Anyone could come walking in. He sure as hell didn't want an audience.

Pulling out, he flipped a U-turn in the middle of the main street and headed back toward the bait shop.

One of the benefits of living in Whitehorse was the lack of traffic. But today he would have loved a traffic jam. Anything to postpone this.

It wasn't that he feared the voice would be Grace's. All this talk of Grace had brought back the pain. He just wanted to hide as he'd done the last six holidays. He didn't need to see more photographs of women who reminded him of Grace. Or hear some woman's voice that might sound even a little like his dead wife's.

But clearly Miranda Blake wasn't going to give him any peace. Not until he proved her wrong. He glanced over at her, worried about her apparent calm. Did she know something he didn't?

"Pregnant?" Arlene Evans cried as she threw the spatula at her son.

"Why are you yelling at me? Charlotte's the one who got knocked up, not me," he said and picked up the remote to turn up the sound on the TV.

Arlene grabbed the skillet, tossing the burned pancakes in the trash and turning off the burner before she wiped off her hands and stormed down the hallway.

She wished she was Catholic because she had the strongest urge to cross herself. First Violet and that disgrace and now Charlotte? She couldn't bear it.

Tapping lightly at the bathroom door, she said, "Charlotte, precious, can I come in?"

"No!" Then more retching and the *whoosh* of the toilet as it flushed.

"Open this damned door now or I will break it down," Arlene yelled.

The door opened slowly and Charlotte's bloated face appeared.

Arlene had seen her daughter getting heavier by the day and had just assumed it was all the sweets the girl put away. Violet had always had a weight problem and Arlene hadn't known how to deal with it. She'd told herself that Charlotte, who'd always been slim, would outgrow it.

"What do you want?" Charlotte asked irritably.

Arlene pushed open the bathroom door and stepped in, closing it behind her. She spoke carefully, determined not to lose her temper. "Aren't you feeling well?"

Her daughter gave her a withering look.

"Your brother seems to think you're pregnant but how is that possible?"

Another withering look. Arlene fought the urge to smack the look off her youngest daughter's face.

"You're pregnant?" Her voice broke. One daughter in the nuthouse and one pregnant out of wedlock. She'd never be able to hold her head up in this county again.

Charlotte didn't answer, just looked down at her stomach as she smoothed her large sweatshirt over her protruding stomach.

Arlene was stunned. "Good heavens, how far along are you?"

Her daughter shrugged. "Four months, I think."

Arlene stumbled over to the toilet, dropped the lid and sat. "*Four* months? Four *months* and you don't say a word? What were you thinking?"

Charlotte was still looking down at her stomach as if admiring it.

"Who is the father? Tell me who he is and the two of you can run down to Vegas. No one has to know you didn't get married four months ago."

"I'm not getting married."

Arlene stared at her daughter. Lately Charlotte had been reminding her more and more of Violet, an unpleasant similarity at best. "Of course you're getting married."

Charlotte raised her gaze. "Not likely since he's already married," she said with a chuckle.

Arlene thought she'd have a stroke and imagined the paramedics hauling her out of the bathroom on a stretcher. As if her life wasn't already humiliating enough.

She willed herself not to have a stroke. "Who is he?" She would castrate him. Then kill him.

Charlotte shook her head. "I'm not telling you. I'm never telling you." She gave Arlene a challenging look. "And there is nothing you can do to make me tell."

The Closed sign was still in the front window of Jackson's Bait Shop and no customers out front waiting, Cade noticed with relief as he pulled around to the back and got out.

The reporter followed him, bringing along that huge shoulder bag of hers and the boom box. He opened the rear door and stepped aside, clenching his jaw as he let her pass. Now that he was here, he just wanted this over with—and as quickly as possible.

"I don't have a lot of time," he said.

She smiled at that no doubt noticing that there hadn't been a crowd of fishermen beating down his door this morning. But she walked right to his kitchen table and set down the boom box.

He wondered if she had retrieved the can of pepper spray from the snowbank out back or bought more as he watched her plug in the boom box and then produce a tape from her pocket. She dropped the cassette tape into the player and lifted a brow in his direction.

He sighed and stepped over to the table to pull out a chair. Swinging it around, he straddled it and sat down, resting his arms on the back as he gave her an impatient nod. "Let's get this over with."

She hit play.

At first all he heard was static. The sound was like scraping a fingernail down a blackboard and he flinched, his nerves on edge. He tried to find calm, to breathe. This would be over soon. And yet his heart thudded in his chest with an apprehension that scared him as much as the impossible thought he could have been wrong about Grace.

The static and whir of the tape stopped abruptly with the sound of a female voice.

His heart stopped as well, as he heard a voice from the grave. He tried to catch his breath, his pulse a bass drum in his ears and his limbs numb with a bone-aching chill that rattled through him.

The woman across from him hadn't missed his reaction. Hell, she'd been expecting it. His blood ran colder than the Milk River outside his door and he thought for a moment that he might black out.

There was no doubt about it. The voice on the tape was Grace's. Staggered, he hadn't even heard what she was saying. But slowly, the words began to register.

And just when he thought it couldn't get any worse, he heard another voice, this one male, as the two planned what banks they would rob and in what order.

There was no denying it. The woman he'd married six years ago and lost wasn't who he thought she was.

He stood, knocking over the chair as he lunged at the table to shut off the tape player.

"There's more that you might want to hear," the reporter said.

"Not now." His voice felt as rough as it sounded. "Please go. I need to be alone."

She started to collect the big black tape player.

"Leave it. I'll make sure you get it back."

Her gaze locked with his. "I made a copy of the tape."

"I was sure you had."

She seemed to hesitate, but then rose slowly, all the time watching him as if worried he might come unglued on her.

"I'm fine," he said a little sharper than he'd meant to.

She nodded but didn't look convinced. He figured he probably looked as horrible as he felt.

"Call me when you're ready to talk."

He walked over to the door, opened it and stood waiting, not looking at her. He was afraid of what he'd do if she didn't leave soon.

"Take my truck," he said, removing the keys from his pocket and holding them out to her.

"It's not far, I'll walk."

"Suit yourself."

She stepped out and he slammed the door, leaning against it as he fought to breathe. Grace. Her memory blurred in his mind and he knew even if he pretended this had never happened, Grace Browning was lost to him. More lost than she'd been even in death.

He lurched forward, slamming into the bathroom to be sick.

There was nothing Arlene Evans enjoyed more than a mission. Finding the father of Charlotte's baby was now at the top of her list.

"Take a shower, you smell," she told her daughter as she left the bathroom and walked down the hall.

The television was so loud it made the old windows in the farmhouse rattle. Arlene walked calmly over to where her son slouched in the chair. She picked up the remote and pressed off.

"What the hell?" Bo demanded, sitting up.

She shoved him back down, snatching the bag of chips off his lap and carefully folding the top down before she put the bag aside. "Who is the father of that baby?"

"You're asking *me?* Why don't you ask her?"

Arlene wet her lips. She liked to think of herself as one of those patient mothers.

"I'm asking you, Bo. Now please tell me. Who has she been with?" Arlene tried again calmly.

"Who hasn't she been with?" he said with a laugh.

Arlene hadn't meant to smack him. If she had, she would have cuffed him harder.

He recoiled, looking hurt and angry, even though she'd barely touched him.

"She said the man is *married.*"

"So?"

"I would think that would narrow the field some," Arlene snapped. "Now think. You're going to help me with this."

Bo groaned and reached for the chips.

Arlene held them out of his reach. "I'm going to make you some pancakes and when I'm done, I expect some names."

Andi walked back to her office, the frigid winter air like a slap in the face. The snowstorm moved in before she'd traveled a block. She welcomed it. She was still shaken by Cade's reaction to the voice on the tape—even though she'd known it had to be the woman he'd known as Grace Browning.

The look on his face, the shocked horror, the devastation. If Andi had wondered how he felt about his wife, she didn't anymore. His stricken face had been filled with pain and anguish. Sticking a knife in his heart might have been less painful.

She shivered from the cold, glad she had only a few blocks to go. The fact that she'd been right—Grace Browning *had* been Starr Calhoun—gave her little satisfaction. She glanced back toward the bait shop, hoping Cade was all right, wishing he wasn't alone, a little afraid of what he might do.

Not that she had any choice but to leave. She'd known better than to argue with him. He'd already thrown her out once today.

Afraid he's going to off himself before you get the rest of the story?

She bristled, hating that he'd been hurt. But he'd needed to hear the truth. It wasn't as if this all wouldn't come out even if she didn't do the story.

Not that this wasn't going to be an amazing story and it would do even more amazing things for her career. She would get national recognition.

But that really wasn't the point. She wasn't doing this

story for her career. This one was personal and she'd see it through till the end—no matter how difficult this was for Cade.

Clearly he hadn't moved on with his life since his wife had died. Once this was over, maybe he finally could.

When Andi looked at it that way, she was doing him a favor.

Nice spin, her irritating conscience noted sarcastically.

"I haven't gotten where I am today by backing down from a story," she snapped, her words lost in a gust of wind and snow.

Yeah, just look where you are.

She told herself that she refused to feel guilty for doing her job and walked a little faster, the earlier chill no longer refreshing.

By the time she reached the newspaper office her teeth were chattering. The air shimmered with snowflakes that whirled around her as if she was inside a snow globe.

She opened the door and hurriedly ducked inside. Immediately she saw that she had the office to herself. Without sitting down at her desk, she pulled out her cell phone and dialed Bradley's number.

"I've been on pins and needles waiting to hear from you," he said without preamble. "Did he hear the tape? What was his reaction?"

"He was devastated," she said, surprised how close she was to tears. "Until he heard her voice, I don't think he believed she was Starr Calhoun."

"So he really didn't know?"

"No. I just feel so badly for him."

"Let me guess. He's ruggedly handsome."

She shook her head, smiling a little. "He's good-looking, if that's what you're asking, but that has nothing to do with—"

"You feeling sorry for him. Right?"

"He loved her. From what I can gather, he hasn't even dated since she died. Everyone in town who I've mentioned his name to has told me he became a recluse after he lost her."

"So you have a great story," Bradley said.

"Yeah, I guess."

"Excuse me, that isn't you getting emotionally involved, is it? Miss Hard-Core News Reporter."

"He's a victim of the Calhouns. I can relate."

"Yes, I guess you can. I guess when the story breaks it will be a form of justice for you both then."

She smiled ruefully. She'd always suspected he knew her connection to the Calhouns. His comment confirmed it. "You always know what to say." She spotted Shirley heading back to the office. "I have to go. I'll call you." She snapped off her phone and walked to her desk.

It wasn't until she was taking off her coat that she saw the envelope on her desk. Manila, with her name neatly typed on the front. Nothing else. Just like the last one.

Chapter 5

With Charlotte still refusing to divulge the name of the baby's father and Bo, it turned out, knowing little or nothing about his sister's "friends," Arlene was forced to do her own investigating.

Four months ago her daughter had worked at the Whitehorse nursing home. Arlene realized that she'd been remiss in not visiting one of Old Town Whitehorse's leading citizens. The Cavanaughs were as close to royalty as it came in Old Town, and Pearl Cavanaugh was the queen. A few months ago she'd had a stroke and had gone into the home.

Pearl's husband, Titus, still ran Old Town and Whitehorse and half the county if the truth was known. He did everything from preach at the community church to organize every Old Town event. Arlene had heard that he spent hours at his wife's bedside.

Not prone to jealousy, Arlene still couldn't curb her irritation. How had Pearl gotten a man like that when

Arlene had gotten *Floyd?* Life wasn't fair, that was for sure, she thought as she pushed open the door to the nursing home carrying the Christmas cactus she'd bought for Pearl.

Arlene asked directions to Pearl's room. She passed Bertie Cavanaugh, who scowled at her as she slinked down the hall. The woman always looked guilty.

As she passed Nina Mae Cross's room, Arlene stopped to say hello to McKenna and Faith Bailey, who were visiting their grandmother—not that Nina Mae had a clue who they were. Alzheimer's, Arlene had heard.

"I sent you an e-mail," Arlene told McKenna. "I'm still looking for the perfect man for you."

The cactus was getting heavy so she hurried on down to Pearl's, anxious now to get this over with.

She'd checked out the staff on her way and was disappointed to find that most of the people who worked here were female. The new doctor in town was practically a baby himself—and single. And the one male orderly was anything but her daughter's type.

To Arlene's surprise, Pearl was sitting in a wheelchair by the window. When had she gotten well enough for a wheelchair? She turned as Arlene entered the room.

"Pearl," Arlene said loudly. "How are you?"

"Her hearing is fine," said a male voice behind her.

Arlene turned to find Bridger Duvall standing in the doorway. He moved to Pearl's side. "She can understand you but she's having a little trouble talking, aren't you, Pearl?" He took the elderly woman's hand in both of his and gently stroked the pale skin.

Pearl smiled, a lopsided smile but nonetheless a smile, shocking Arlene.

"I didn't realize you knew Pearl," she said. After all, Bridger Duvall was a mystery. No one really knew who he was or why he'd come here. He'd opened a restaurant in town with Laci Cavanaugh, Pearl's granddaughter.

That, Arlene realized, must explain this odd friendship.

"I brought you a cactus," Arlene said to Pearl, enunciating each word carefully.

"How thoughtful," Bridger said, taking it from Arlene to place the plant over by the window.

"She's certainly doing well." The last Arlene had heard Pearl was paralyzed and unresponsive. Now she looked alert. But then Pearl Cavanaugh had always been a sharp old broad.

"I just stopped by to say hello," Bridger said, returning to Pearl's side. "Laci and I are cooking for parties all month. Not that we're complaining. Business has been good."

Pearl smiled up at him and said something Arlene couldn't understand.

"I'll give Laci your love. She's busy baking Christmas cookies. She'll be bringing some down to the staff. You know how she is."

What could have been a chuckle arose from Pearl.

As Bridger started to leave, Arlene said, "I'll walk out with you." She waved over her shoulder at Pearl. "Glad to see you're doing so well."

Once out in the hall, Arlene said to him, "You spend a lot of time here? You might know my daughter Charlotte."

He nodded.

"I was wondering if you've seen her with anyone, you know, a man, romantically, you understand?"

From the look on his face, he understood perfectly. "I'm sorry, but I wouldn't know anything about that. Now if you'll excuse me."

As Arlene watched him hurry away, she looked back at Pearl. The old gal had a sympathetic look on her face. There was nothing Arlene Evans hated worse than pity, she thought, as she hurried down the hall and out into the cold December day.

Andi stared at the envelope on her desk for a long moment. Then she put her coat on the back of her chair and, rubbing her freezing hands together, sat down. Like her coat and boots, her gloves were a thin leather that had been perfect for winters in Fort Worth.

Gingerly she picked up the envelope, turning it in her fingers. No return address, of course. No clue as to who might have sent it.

Shirley, the newspaper receptionist/bookkeeper, had stopped outside to talk to a passerby.

The newspaper had little staff, just Shirley and several columnists who stopped by on occasion. The only time the office was busy was when the publisher and his oldest daughter put the paper together the night before it came out.

Shirley was a grandmother who only worked part-time. Most of that time she was next door at the coffee shop. Apparently everyone in town knew where to find her if they needed anything.

With a sigh, Andi took out her letter opener and sliced the envelope open. Inside was another newspaper clipping. Andi unfolded it, flattening it, then turned the clipping over, frowning.

On one side was an article about Kid Curry's last holdup in the Whitehorse area. On the other side was an ad for tractors. What could this possibly have to do with Starr Calhoun or Grace Browning?

Shirley entered with a latte and fry bread from the

shop next door. "Oh, if I'd known you were here I would have brought you something." She was tiny with white hair and small brown eyes.

"Thank you, but I'm fine," Andi said.

Shirley saw the article lying on the desk and smiled. "You like our colorful history?" she asked. "Kid Curry and his brothers hung out up here for a while. Had a place to the south."

"Really?" Andi couldn't imagine what that had to do with Starr Calhoun and the missing bank robbery money.

Shirley quickly warmed to her subject. "This area was home to many an outlaw. It was the last lawless part of the state. You might be surprised how wild this town used to be. Why, one of the outlaws' six-guns is on display at the museum. Can't think of his name right now and my fry bread is getting cold, but you should check it out."

"I'll do that," Andi promised.

As Shirley hurried to her desk in the back, Andi dug out the first envelope she'd received. She compared the type on both. Identical. Sent no doubt by the same person. Both postmarked Whitehorse.

But what was the connection to Kid Curry? Other than they were all outlaws?

A thought struck her and she wondered why she hadn't considered it before. Was it possible Houston was still in Whitehorse? He could have done what Starr did, found someone, gotten married under an alias and was still living here.

Although if Houston was behind this, she had to wonder why he'd waited six years. Lubbock had been in prison until just recently so the timing made more sense.

She told herself that she didn't care who was pulling her strings. All she cared about was the story. But even as she thought it, she knew that eventually she'd find out who was behind the information being fed to her. And what that person wanted from her.

Folding up the newspaper clipping she shoved it back into the envelope and put it with the other one in her drawer.

"Shirley?" Andi called as she reached for her coat. "If anyone wants me, I'll be at the museum learning about Whitehorse's infamous past."

Cade couldn't move, couldn't breathe. He dropped into a chair at the table and covered his face with his hands, telling himself this wasn't happening. Not after six years of grieving. Not after he was finally coming to grips with losing Grace.

Too stunned to hear or feel anything, the hammering at the front door of the shop didn't register for a while. Not that he would have opened the door even if he had heard it before the knocking abruptly stopped.

He stared at the tape player but didn't touch the play button. Not after hearing it three more times. Each time he thought the voice wouldn't be Grace's. Each time, he prayed it wouldn't.

Each time it was.

He heard the crunch of snow outside, then the rattle of the knob as someone tried the back door only to find it locked, something nearly unheard of in Whitehorse.

"Cade?"

At the concern he heard in his brother's voice, Cade rose and went to unlock the door.

One glance at Carter's expression and he knew he must look like hell.

"What's wrong? It isn't Dad, is it?"

Cade shook his head. "Everyone's fine."

His brother came in, closing the door behind him.

"Everyone's not fine. You were acting weird at breakfast. And now you look like your best friend died. What's going on?" He glanced toward the large black tape player on the table, the worry in his expression deepening.

"I need a favor," Cade said, knowing his brother. Carter would keep after him until he gave him at least a plausible explanation.

"Are you in some kind of trouble?"

He shook his head. "A *couple* of favors actually. There's a new reporter in town from Texas. Her name's Miranda Blake. She goes by M. W. Blake."

"This is about a *woman?*" Carter asked incredulously. He laughed, looking relieved.

"I hate to ask but could you see what you can find out about her?"

Carter was smiling. "You had me scared. You looked so horrible, I thought…" He quit smiling and shook his head. "I thought for sure someone had died."

"There is something else," Cade said. "It's about Grace."

His brother instantly looked worried. "Grace?" He seemed to be holding his breath.

Carter had once asked him what it was about Grace that Cade couldn't forget. "Everything," he'd said. *"Everything."*

"I want to close that chapter on my life," Cade said now, meaning it more than he thought possible.

His brother's relief was palpable. After the first couple of years when Cade couldn't seem to get over Grace's death, Carter had become concerned.

"I'm worried about you," he'd said. "I'm afraid you're never going to get over this."

Cade had smiled ruefully. "I don't think I am."

"In order to move on," Cade said now. "I need to find out if Grace's parents are still alive."

"I thought she said they were dead?" Carter asked in obvious surprise.

"That's what she told me, but I learned something recently that makes me wonder," he said. "Could you see what you can find out? I don't want to contact them, I just want to find out if what Grace told me was true."

"Grace have a middle name?" Carter asked, pulling out his notebook and pen. Cade had known his brother would do anything to get him to move on with his life.

"Eden," Cade said.

His brother looked up. "Eden? Like in Adam and Eve?"

Cade shrugged. "I guess so. Her birthday was July 4, 1974."

"Birthplace?"

"Los Angeles, California."

Carter looked up and frowned. "No kidding? I always thought she was born in the South. I wonder where she picked up the accent?"

"Accent?"

"You never noticed her accent?" Carter laughed. "It only came out when she was upset. Like that time you got thrown from the horse. When we were at the hospital waiting for the doctor to tell us how bad it was, I could really hear her Southern accent." He frowned. "Wait a minute. This new reporter..." He glanced at his notes. "She's from Texas?" He swore. "She's got a Southern accent, too?" He looked at Cade with suspicion.

"She's nothing like Grace," Cade said quickly. "And anyway, Grace didn't have a Southern accent."

Carter raised a brow. "You never noticed it?"

"No." He realized that wasn't quite true. A few times he had picked up an accent, but she'd said her father was in the military and they'd spent some time in Alabama when she was young. He'd noticed after that how she seemed to do everything she could to hide it.

Carter put away his notebook and pen and placed a hand on Cade's shoulder. "Don't worry, bro. I'll find out what I can. You didn't say what you heard that made you think Grace's parents were still alive."

Cade shook his head, hating that he was lying to his brother. But he wasn't ready to talk about this. Maybe he was still holding on to the hope that there had been a Grace Browning. Another woman bedsides Starr Calhoun who looked and sounded just like his wife.

"I saw a couple on CNN," Cade said. "Their name was Browning. They lived in Los Angeles and were about the right ages. I swear they looked enough like Grace that they could have been her parents. It just seemed like too much of a coincidence. I know it's crazy."

He saw that his brother agreed. "Heck, why not check it out? I'll let you know what I find," Carter said as he headed for the door. He stopped and glanced back at Cade. "Does it matter if her parents are still alive or not? I mean, are you sure you want to dig up the past?"

"To me Grace was perfect, you know? But the truth is I sensed that she wasn't telling me something about her past. I guess if I found out that she'd lied about her parents being dead it would make it easier to let go for good," Cade said, knowing his brother would buy this explanation.

Carter nodded. "Speaking of favors… I have one to ask of you."

Cade braced himself. He hoped this wasn't about Christmas. He wouldn't be having any happy holidays this year.

"The families are getting together Christmas Eve at

Northern Lights restaurant," Carter said. The families being the Jacksons and the Baileys.

"Yeah, about that…" Cade said quickly. "I'm probably not going to make that."

Carter looked upset. "Not good enough. Not this year. You have to come."

"Maybe I could drop by—"

"Cade, you've missed Christmas now for six years. You can't this year. It's important. The truth is I need you there."

Cade stared at his brother. "You're going to ask Eve to marry you."

Carter gave an embarrassed laugh. "Am I that transparent? Yeah, I am and I need as much of the family there as I can get. Less chance she'll say no."

"She won't say no. She loves you."

"I mean it, Cade, I need you there. You can bring the reporter if that's what you want."

Cade swore silently. "Naw, that's all right. I'll be there."

"Thanks, I really need the moral support." Carter didn't ask why Cade hadn't wanted to come originally. He'd probably just assumed that it was because of Grace. He had no idea just how true that was.

"So you've bought the ring, I assume?" Cade asked.

"Dad gave me Mother's," he said a little sheepishly.

Of course Dad would have given it to Carter, their mother's favorite. "Cool," Cade said. "That's great."

"Dad didn't think you'd mind." Carter stepped to him, surprised Cade by pulling him into a hug. "I've missed you, bro. It's good that you'll be there this Christmas."

Cade felt bad that he'd been a recluse for the past six years. He'd burrowed in with his pain, just wanting to be alone to grieve.

He'd been so much better this year. Until that damned reporter had shown up.

Carter drew back looking a little embarrassed. "Okay. I'll see what I can do about finding Grace's parents." He smiled. "And I'll also check on the new reporter for you. I've heard she's a stunner."

"She is that," Cade agreed. She sure as hell stunned him.

Chapter 6

The Whitehorse Museum was housed in a small building on the edge of town. A couple of elderly ladies were behind the desk as Andi entered.

They greeted her warmly.

"Are you doing a story on our museum?" the shorter of the two asked. "She's the new reporter at the *Examiner,*" the woman informed her coworker, who nodded.

Andi couldn't help being amused. So few newcomers moved to Whitehorse that apparently she stood out even before she opened her mouth. The way news traveled in this town, she wondered why they even bothered with a newspaper.

On the way to the museum, she'd driven by the bait shop and seen a sheriff's department patrol car parked out front. That worried her. She had no idea what Cade would do.

Had he called his brother and told him about Starr Calhoun? she wondered as she paid her admission price and wandered through exhibits that chronicled everything from the story of the hundreds of thousands of buffalo that had roamed this prairie to the coming of the railroad and the birth of present day Whitehorse.

She found the outlaw exhibit at the back. Apparently Shirley was right. This part of Montana had remained lawless late into the 1800s. Along with Kid Curry, Whitehorse had seen Butch Cassidy, the Sundance Kid and other less-known outlaws. It had been a place of murder and mayhem. Curry had been the leader of the notorious Wild Bunch, was alleged to have killed ten men, although it was said he'd grown up reading the Bible.

According to the museum exhibit, there'd been Western holdup artists, bank robbers, road agents, killers and railroad thieves.

While interesting, Andi was wondering what something that had happened so long ago had to do with Starr Calhoun when she spotted a name that leaped out at her. It was in the part of the exhibit detailing an outlaw named Long Henry Thompson.

Long Henry was credited with having belonged to the Henry Starr gang out of Texas that robbed everything they could, along with stealing livestock on the Texan-Mexican border. Long Henry, wanted in Texas for these crimes, had allegedly hired on to bring cattle to Montana along with some others from the Starr gang.

Andi had heard of Henry Starr. He was descended from the Starr criminal dynasty that began with Tom "Giant" Starr and his son Sam.

Hadn't she read somewhere that Hodge and Eden Calhoun had named their youngest daughter Starr after the famous Henry Starr criminal family that had operated in Texas during the 1800s?

And now it seemed at least one of the Starr gang had

ended up in Whitehorse, Montana, back when this part of the country was known for its outlaw hideouts.

Was this the Calhoun connection to Montana? Is this why Starr had come here—just as some of her namesake had more than a hundred years before? The Texas outlaws had changed their names, she realized, and re-invented themselves.

Just as Starr had done.

Was that why she'd been given the Kid Curry clipping? Was whoever had sent her the clippings just seeing whether or not she would follow up each lead?

That would mean, though, that she was being watched. She glanced toward the large plate-glass windows, but all she could see was the falling snow.

She turned back to the exhibit, studying the black and white photographs of robbers—not unlike the one she had of Starr, she thought as she heard the tap of boot heels behind her and turned to see Cade Jackson.

He glanced at the outlaw exhibit and she caught his surprised—and worried—expression. "We need to talk."

Cade walked out to his pickup. This woman had knocked him for a loop. And now to find her standing in front of the outlaw exhibit... Idle curiosity? Or something more?

He feared he knew exactly what that more might be. But how had she found out?

Because she was hell-bent on finding out everything there was to know about Grace. And, in turn, him.

If he'd doubted before that the woman meant business, he no longer did. His whole life was about to be opened up and every detail exposed to the media. And he didn't need Miranda Blake to tell him that a story like this would go nationwide.

He was losing his past like a shoreline being washed away by waves. He could feel a little more of it drop out from under him, swept out by the storm.

And Tex was that storm. She'd blown in and now she was causing havoc in his life. Worse, with Grace's.

"How did you know I was here?" she asked, stopping short of his truck as snow fell around her.

"I called the newspaper. Shirley said you were at the museum. Get in."

She crossed her arms over her chest and glared at him, unmoving. "What did you want to talk to me about?" Her dark hair sparkled with ice crystals as snow fell around her.

"You want to talk about this out in the middle of a snowstorm? Go right ahead, Tex. I'll be in the truck." He didn't wait for an answer.

"As I told you before, my name is Miranda. Or Andi. *Not* Tex. Remember?" she snapped as she got in and he started the engine.

Miranda sounded too old. Andi was a little too friendly and he was feeling anything but friendly.

"I saw your expression in there," she said. "What was it about the outlaw exhibit that ties in with Starr?"

He shook his head, not in answer, but in awe. The woman was like a bloodhound on his scent and she was tracking his life with an instinct that scared him.

"Don't even bother to tell me that you don't know what I'm talking about," she said, sounding angry. "You *know* something about all this. You couldn't have lived with Starr and not suspected *something*. Why do you keep fighting me?"

He looked over at her. "Because it's my life you want to destroy for a damned news story and fifteen minutes of fame."

She looked chastened. "I'm sorry. I know how hard this must be on you. But this isn't going away just because you want it to."

"*You're* not going away, you mean," he said, trying to curb the anger he felt the instant he was in her presence.

"Even if I left tomorrow, do you really think whoever fed me the information about Starr is going away, as well?"

He didn't know what to think. Or feel. Other than numb. Just not numb enough.

"There's something you should know. Lubbock Calhoun, Starr's brother, was recently released from prison. Apparently he's broken his parole. No one knows where he is."

Cade shot her a look. "You think he's the one who sent you the tape?"

"Well, if it's him, then he's already in town," she said. "The envelope was postmarked Whitehorse."

Cade swore. Just when he thought things couldn't get any worse. What a fool he'd been to think that this might all blow over. "What does he want?"

"Probably the money. Until the three million is found…" She looked up as he backed out onto the highway and turned north. "Where are we going?" She sounded worried.

"I thought we'd take a ride."

"I put the original cassette tape with a copy of all my notes in a secure place," she said, looking away. "In case I should disappear."

He laughed. "I wasn't planning to kill you, Tex."

She glanced over at him. "I guess neither of us have anything to worry about then."

He wished that were true as he drove north out of town on the wide two-lane. A few locals were trying to get the highway across what was known as the Hi-Line made into a four-lane. They had some crazy idea that it would bring more people to this isolated part of the state.

He wasn't opposed to the idea, he just knew it would never fly—not when he could go for miles and never see another car on the highway.

"Tell me about Starr Calhoun," he said after White-horse disappeared in his rearview mirror.

The question seemed to take her by surprise. "Like what?"

"Everything you know about her."

"Okay." She took a breath and let it out slowly. "She is one of six children born to Hodge and Eden Calhoun."

Eden? Grace had picked her real mother's name for a middle name. He felt sick. There was no doubt about who Grace had been.

"Her parents took all the kids with them when they robbed banks until they were captured and the children were put into foster homes."

Grace had been in a foster home? He couldn't help but feel for her, just as he couldn't help but think of her as Grace even if she really had been Starr Calhoun. "What happened to the kids?"

She shrugged. "They grew up. Some of them made the news as they followed in their parents' footsteps."

"And the parents?"

"Hodge and Eden died in prison a few years apart. Hodge was killed by another inmate. Eden killed herself."

He practically drove off the highway. He remembered how sad Grace had looked when she'd told him that both her parents were deceased. Killed in a plane crash, as he recalled. A lie. On top of the biggest lie of all.

"All of the kids dropped off the radar until one after another all but one turned up on police reports," she was saying. "Amarillo, the oldest, died in prison of hepatitis C. Dallas is doing time in California. Houston has been missing since the robberies six years ago. Worth seems to be the only one who went straight. He was the youngest of the boys so he was probably adopted and his name changed. Lubbock…well, who knows where he is?"

Cade couldn't believe what he was hearing about Starr and her family.

"For all we know, Houston could be living in Whitehorse," she was saying. "Did Starr ever mention her family, her brothers?"

"She told me she was an only child." Another lie. "You know an awful lot about the Calhouns," he said.

She looked out her side window even though there was nothing to see but snow. "I'm a reporter. I do a lot of research."

There was more to it, he thought. He couldn't wait to see what his brother found out about Andi Blake. "That's all you know about Starr?"

"I know she robbed a bunch of banks and disappeared," Andi said, bristling. "And now I know where she disappeared to—at least for a while."

"What does that mean?"

"Are you sure she's dead?"

"What?" he snapped. "I buried her. You think she walked away from that car accident?"

"Someone died in that car, but how can you be sure it was your wife?"

"She was wearing the wedding band I bought her." He wished he'd left Tex at the museum.

"Was an autopsy done? Was any DNA taken?"

"You think she faked her death?" he asked incredulously.

"She had three million good reasons to fake her death."

"She had at least one damned good reason not to," he snapped and shook his head, wondering how this could be any more painful. If it hadn't been the middle of winter he might have just dumped Tex off beside the road. Let her find her own way home.

"Grace didn't fake her death," he said, trying to keep his voice down. "I know because…" He took a breath and let it out. "Because she'd gone shopping in Billings for my Christmas present. She called on her way home to tell me she had a surprise for me and couldn't wait to tell me. An early present." He glared over at Andi. "She'd been to a doctor. She was pregnant with our baby."

He took satisfaction in the shock he witnessed on Andi Blake's face before he turned back to his driving and fought to swallow back the gutting pain of the memory. "The woman who died in that car on the way back to Whitehorse was two months pregnant with my child. And yes, I know that for a fact. I got a copy of the results from the doctor after she died."

Andi stared at his granitelike profile for a moment before turning to gaze out at the snow-covered landscape. It suddenly felt colder, definitely more isolated.

Starr had been pregnant. The story just kept getting better and better. All she had to do was keep badgering Cade, keep getting the bits and pieces he was trying so hard to keep from her.

She knew she was treading on thin ice. She'd hurt this man, angered him and feared what he might do if she pushed him too hard. She was 99 percent sure he hadn't known who Grace was. But he had to have suspected something wasn't right.

"I'm sorry," she said. Starr hadn't just married Cade Jackson, but she'd also gotten pregnant with his child? That didn't sound anything like the woman Andi had read about in the police reports. Nor the one planning the robberies on the cassette tape.

Starr Calhoun hadn't been talked into robbing banks. She'd been the ring leader. Even if she was pregnant, it didn't mean she'd died in that car six years ago. There was no way of knowing if Starr Calhoun was dead without doing an exhumation.

But Andi wasn't about to voice that. Especially right now, she thought, looking out at the desolate landscape. She couldn't even be sure where they were let alone where they were headed.

Ahead all she could see was snow. It filled the sky, drifted in the barrow pits, clung to the fence posts on each side of the road and covered the rolling hills for miles.

And it was still falling. Earlier on the radio she'd heard something about a winter storm warning alert—whatever that was.

The women at the museum had told them as they were leaving earlier to bundle up because there was a storm coming. Another foot of snow was expected and temperatures were going to drop. She couldn't imagine it getting any colder.

She saw Cade look in his rearview mirror as they topped a hill. Glancing back she saw nothing but empty highway. As she turned around she felt a little sick. The lack of contrast gave her the feeling that the earth was flat white and that if Cade kept driving, he would drive right off the edge of it.

Cade slowed the pickup and turned off the highway. She caught a glimpse of a sign that read Sleeping Buffalo.

"What was that?" she asked as they passed a manger-like structure that housed two large rocks. She hoped he was taking her somewhere public. Being alone with him was wearing on her nerves. She didn't like how upset he was.

"It's sleeping buffalo," he said. "During the Ice Age, glaciers carved this country, leaving behind a field of large boulders the Native Americans thought looked like buffalo. The buffalo had been scarce. When the Indians saw the two rocks, they thought they were buffalo and rode toward them. Just as they reached the rocks, though, they saw a huge herd of buffalo beyond them. The two buffalo-appearing rocks were then considered sacred, having led the hunters to the buffalo. The rocks are kept so the Native Americans can pay their respects by leaving tobacco on them."

She took that in as they passed a cluster of buildings that according to the sign was Sleeping Buffalo Resort. She recalled something about a shoot-out there a few months ago. If she had any doubt she was in the Wild West, all she had to do was read the old newspaper stories.

Over the next rise, she saw an expanse of ice dotted with a half dozen small fishing huts. "People really don't fish when it's this cold, do they?"

"If cold stopped 'em, nobody in Montana would fish," he said. "And I'd be out of business."

They drove in silence as the snowpacked road narrowed and a few houses gave way to nothing but rolling, snowy hills. Out here there was no hint of the fast-approaching holiday. Just as there was no Christmas tree or any decorations at her apartment. Or at Cade's. No reminder that Christmas was just days away.

"So what's your life story, Tex?" Cade asked. "Let's hear it. Seems only fair since you're so interested in mine."

She ignored the "Tex." "I don't have a story."

He let out a humorless laugh. "We all have a story. Isn't that how your profession works? You prey on our life stories for the amusement and edification of your readers? But *your* life is private?"

She didn't answer, more concerned about where he was taking her.

"Wasn't there some man you left in Texas?" he asked, glancing over at her. He must have seen the answer in her face although he misread it. "That's what I thought. And you give me a hard time for trying to run away from this?"

"You're mistaken."

"Right," he said with a laugh as he slowed to turn on an even narrower road, the deep snow scraping on the undercarriage of the pickup as he busted through drifts, snow flying.

Andi held on for dear life, afraid now of not only where he was taking her, but also what he planned to do when he got there.

"A woman who dresses like you working for a weekly newspaper in Whitehorse, Montana, and you're telling me you're not running away from something?" He had to fight to keep the pickup in the narrow tracks. "Save your breath."

Had he found out about her broadcast news job in Fort Worth through his brother the sheriff? "This isn't about *me*. But if you must know, I worked for a television station but I wanted a change of pace."

"A change of pace?" He shook his head. "Come on, Tex, you're into this up to your eyeballs. You're the one who got the newspaper clipping and cassette tape. Not me. Don't tell me you haven't wondered: Why *you*? I sure have."

She'd wondered all right. "I'm a reporter. Whoever sent me the information knew I would follow it up."

"Lubbock Calhoun, straight from prison, would know that about you?" he asked.

"Or Houston. For all you know he married someone right here in Whitehorse just like his sister did. He could be your neighbor."

Cade shook his head. "I know all my neighbors and have for many years. Any other theories?"

"I don't know who is sending me the information. I'm sure they have their reasons. If it's Lubbock, then he must have seen me on the news."

"You made the news?"

"I was a TV broadcast newswoman."

"Oh, you *read* the news," he said.

"I did more than *read* the news. I—" She stopped abruptly as she saw the trap he'd laid for her.

"Yes?" he asked smiling over at her. "What? You want your life to remain private? You just tell the news. Forget that it's my life and Grace's memory that you're trying to destroy."

"There was no Grace," she snapped.

"Like hell there wasn't," he shot back. "She was Grace when I fell in love with her, when I married her, when I buried her."

Andi heard the horrible pain in his voice and was hit with a wave of guilt that angered her. She didn't start this. The Calhouns did. She was just doing her job. She was sick of him trying to blame her because his wife was a liar and a criminal.

"You might never have known the truth if I had just ignored it," she snarled.

"Yeah, and wouldn't that have been terrible?" he said sarcastically as he glared over at her for a moment.

"You can't just stick your head in the sand and pretend none of this happened. Whoever is sending me the information about Starr, you think that person is going to keep quiet?"

Cade realized where he was headed and swore under his breath. He hadn't really planned to come out here. Hell, he hadn't planned to go anywhere with this woman. There was no place he could find peace right now, but he especially didn't want her near the home he'd shared with Grace.

So why had he come here?

He glanced over at her, wondering how she fit into all this. It was no act of fate that she'd ended up in Whitehorse—or that she was the one someone had chosen to tell their secrets to. No coincidence at all.

And Andi Blake had to know it.

Chapter 7

"Where are we?" Andi asked, squinting into the storm.

Cade had taken the back way into the cabin, circling around the north end of Nelson Reservoir, figuring he'd give her a taste of rural Montana in the winter. He took perverse satisfaction in the way she'd been forced to hang on.

As the cabin came into view and the frozen reservoir beyond it, he thought about the first time he'd laid eyes on Grace Browning.

He'd been driving northwest on Hwy 2 headed toward Saco when he'd seen her crouched beside her car just off the highway with a flat tire on the left rear.

He'd stopped, seeing that she appeared to be a woman alone, and got out to walk back to her.

She hadn't looked up, just flicked a glance at his boots before she said, "Thanks, but I've got it."

He'd smiled to himself. She was a little thing but she was tackling that flat tire as if she was a truck driver.

He'd thought about telling her not to be ridiculous, to move aside and let him change it.

But he'd stood back instead and watched her, seeing how not only capable she was, but also how determined. If he'd learned anything about women it was to give them their space when they had that particular look in their eyes.

But he wasn't about to leave her alone on this empty stretch of highway. So he stood back and watched with a mixture of amusement and awe.

Now, though, he wondered if she hadn't wanted him to help her because she had something to hide. Like a trunkful of stolen cash and a bounty on her head.

Clearly she'd been hiding everything, he thought bitterly.

But a part of him argued that if she had the robbery money, why had she married him? Why had she stayed in Whitehorse, Montana? Why had she gotten pregnant with his child?

The memory was like a stake to his heart. His foot came off the gas, the pickup's front tires sliding off into the deep snow. He fought to wrestle the truck back into the tracks.

"Are you all right?" Andi asked beside him.

"Fine," he snapped. He'd thought he'd been grieving the last six years. It was nothing compared to now. At least he'd had his memories of Grace. And now even those were tainted because didn't common sense tell him that Grace had just been hiding out here, the marriage to him having just been a cover until she divvied up the money with her accomplice and split, just as Andi suspected?

But if Starr had had the money from the bank robberies in her trunk that day, what had she done with it? She'd have had to hide it somewhere, otherwise he would have known about it. Three million dollars wouldn't have fit in her purse. Or one of her shoe boxes.

And why the hell hadn't she just kept going?

She'd finished changing the tire, then looked up for the first time at him.

He'd been startled by the same thing that had given away her identification when Tex had seen her photograph in the newspaper clipping. Her eyes.

They were pale blue and bottomless.

"You're still here," she'd said, sounding amused. "Haven't you ever seen a woman change a tire before?"

"Not with that kind of determination," he admitted.

She'd laughed.

He'd often wondered if he'd fallen in love with her the moment he'd looked into her eyes—or if it had been when she'd laughed. Either way, it had been like a jolt of electricity straight to his heart.

The day had been hot and he'd said the first thing he'd thought to say.

"Buy you a beer at the bar up the road."

She'd smiled at him, those eyes twinkling. "A beer?" She'd nodded thoughtfully. "I could use a beer."

"Cade Jackson," he'd said and held out his hand.

"Grace Browning." Was that the moment her alias and her cover had been born? There had been no hesitation when she'd said the name, no clue that this woman was anything but who she said she was.

Or had he been so enamored that he just hadn't noticed?

A part of him hadn't expected her to follow him to the bar, let alone come in and have a beer with him.

But she had.

"You're from here," she'd said.

It really hadn't been a question, but he'd answered anyway. "Born and raised south of here on a ranch."

She'd eyed him for a moment. "So you really are a cowboy."

He'd laughed. "If you mean do I ride a horse, yes. My father sold the ranch, but I bought a smaller one to the north. I raise horses more as a sideline. The rest of the time I run a bait shop here in town."

He remembered her smile, the amusement that played in her eyes.

"Horses and a bait shop." She shook her head. "Diversification, huh. Well, Cade Jackson, that's quite a combination. You make any money at it?"

He remembered being a little defensive. "I have all I need."

Her expression had changed, her features softening. "I envy you. Most people never have enough."

"Most people want too much," he'd said.

He smiled at that now as he realized that the woman he'd said that to had more than three million dollars.

So why hadn't she kept on going down that highway? Why had she hung around to have another beer and dinner? Hung around long enough that he fell more deeply in love with her? Hung around long enough to get pregnant with his child?

"Starr could have kept on going," he said as he parked in front of the cabin. "Why didn't she?"

"You tell me," Andi said as he saw her look down the plowed road that led to the cabin, her eyes narrowing. "Do you think you can scare me into not doing the story?" she demanded, clearly irate.

Is that what he thought? Or was he just angry at the messenger? He reminded himself that she hadn't just brought him the bad news. She planned to *publicize* it.

Once her story broke, the media would have a field day and he'd be right in the heart of the storm.

He knew then why he'd brought her here. He wanted her to know the woman he had. He wanted to convince Andi that Grace Browning had existed. And while a part of him knew he was wasting his time, he knew he had to try. Not so much for Andi as for himself.

"Grace could have chosen a life on the run with the money. She didn't. How do you explain that, Tex?" he asked as he cut the engine and turned his attention on her.

"I can't. So are you telling me that there weren't things she said or did that made you wonder if there wasn't more to her staying here? Things that made you worry she wasn't telling the truth?"

"Stop looking at me like I'm an idiot. I knew my wife. I'm not a fool."

And he'd known something was wrong. He'd seen her fighting a battle with herself. He just hadn't known what it was. Or how to help her. He'd hoped whatever had been haunting her would blow over. When she'd called from Billings about the baby, she'd sounded completely happy.

And he'd known then that she'd won whatever battle had been going on inside her. A battle he'd just assumed had something to do with another man.

Maybe he was a fool after all.

"Isn't it possible that Grace wanted to put her past behind her and start over?" he asked, hating the emotion he heard in his voice. "Isn't it possible that she was tired of that life, that she wanted something more, that she'd found it with me? That maybe Grace was exactly who I believed her to be?"

He knew what he was saying. That he and his love had changed Starr Calhoun into Grace Browning Jackson, a woman he would have died for.

Something caught his eye in the rearview mirror. The wind whipped the snow past and for just a moment he saw the glare off the windshield of a car on the road by the reservoir.

Earlier he'd had the strangest feeling that they were being followed. Crazy. This was Whitehorse. All this talk of outlaws was making him paranoid.

He lost sight of the vehicle in the falling snow and felt a wave of relief. But as he looked at Andi, he saw both skepticism—and pity—and felt his temper boil. Not only had she turned his life upside down, but she was also making him doubt everything—including the safety of the community he'd lived in his entire life.

"Maybe you just saw the woman she wanted you to see," Andi said.

"Were you this cynical before or does it come with being a reporter?" he demanded with no small amount of disdain.

"Now who's being contemptuous? I'm proud of my profession."

He lifted a brow.

"People have the right to know the truth." She snapped. "If there weren't individuals willing to go out on a limb to get the truth, what would that leave?"

"Peace?" he asked with a laugh.

She scoffed. "Some people just can't take the truth obviously."

Obviously. "Truth is relative. Your truth apparently isn't mine because you're wrong about my wife." He could feel her gaze on him like a weight. "Maybe she was Starr Calhoun."

"Maybe?"

"You want to know about Grace Browning? Take this down, girl reporter. Grace was as different from

Starr Calhoun as night and day." With that he opened his pickup door and climbed out.

Andi heard how desperately he wanted to believe that Starr had changed before she died. That she'd become Grace Browning, the woman he'd fallen in love with. That Starr had wanted to put that other life behind her.

Who knows what Starr had been thinking when she hit Whitehorse? But Andi could see that Cade needed to believe that the woman had stayed because she'd fallen in love with him instead of merely using him and this place as a hideout like the outlaw she was.

As she watched Cade stride away from the pickup through the snow, she wondered. Had he grieved six years because he'd loved his wife that much? Or had his pain been one of disillusionment and denial?

"You knew her best," Andi said diplomatically as she caught up with him.

"I *did* know her," he said, stopping to turn to face her.

That was why she needed his part of the story. Not that she believed for a minute that Starr Calhoun had changed. How could someone go from being the cold-hearted, calculating criminal on the audio tape to becoming an upstanding citizen and a wife to this man in a matter of months?

But if true, it would make a great story.

Not that anyone would believe the transformation except Cade. Look at the woman's genes. Had anyone in the family stayed out of prison? Maybe Worth. Unfortunately that was hard to verify since he could be breaking the law at this moment just under another name.

Starr and a change of heart? No way. Not even for this good-looking cowboy, Andi thought.

As she followed him toward the small cabin, she wondered how Starr could have stayed as long as she did here. A woman used to big cities and everything stolen money could buy would have gone crazy here, wouldn't she have?

All Andi could figure is that Starr had been waiting for something. The money? Or for her brother Houston to meet up with her? Then where did Lubbock come in?

She doubted Starr would trust Houston to bring the money. Rightly so apparently since Houston hadn't shown up. Or had he?

Andi's suspicious nature couldn't help but come back to Starr's death. Just as she worried about the person who had wanted her to know that Grace Jackson was really Starr Calhoun.

She was still going with the theory that Starr had staged her death and taken off with the money and that someone possibly in Starr's own family might be looking for her and using Andi to do it.

Cade had stopped at the edge of the porch and was looking back at her. He didn't seem like anybody's fool, she thought. So how had Starr tricked him into not only buying her act, but also falling madly in love with her and now defending her even when he knew who she really had been?

Andi saw him frown as he looked past her back up the road from the way they'd come.

"Is something wrong?" she asked, turning to follow his gaze. Through the falling snow she caught the glint of the dull gray light off a vehicle just before it disappeared over a hill.

"I think we might have been followed," he said distractedly but she could tell he was worried. She recalled how he'd been watching his rearview mirror earlier. Or maybe he was just trying to scare her.

"I didn't see anyone." She was still irritated that he'd taken some back road through the deep snow, no doubt just to frighten her. But she felt a stab of apprehension as she realized they could have been followed.

The cabin couldn't have been in a more deserted place. She shivered as she stared through the falling snow at the reservoir and saw an ice-fishing shack not far off shore. She realized it must be Cade's since there was no sign of anyone else around.

What an isolated place, she thought as she clutched her shoulder bag to her side, slipping her hand in to make sure she had her new can of pepper spray.

Cade waited to see if the vehicle he'd spotted earlier drove by again. Could just be someone lost since no one used this road this time of year. From this side of the reservoir, there was no way to drive out onto the ice.

Other than ice fishing, there wasn't any other reason to come down this road since it ended at the bottom of a rocky outcropping.

If not someone lost, then they had been followed. Which would mean Andi Blake might actually know what she was talking about. In which case, there just might be cause for concern.

"You realize you're being used," he said. She didn't answer. "Aren't you worried as hell what this person wants and what he'll do when he doesn't get it?"

"What do you suggest I do?"

He ignored the sarcasm in her tone. "Go back to Texas. Forget you ever saw that clipping or heard that tape."

She raised a brow. "And what will you do? Can you just forget it? I didn't think so."

"I'll turn it over to my brother because frankly, I don't give a damn what happened to the money." His gaze fell on her. "But you're in it for the story to the bitter end, aren't you? Whoever is feeding you the information knows that. They know you won't back down."

"And they're right."

He shook his head.

"Do you really think they are just going to let me stop now?" she asked.

"You're in *danger*."

"Not as long as I keep digging until I find what that person wants."

"You think you're going to find the money." He let out a laugh. "That's the topping on your story, isn't it?"

What had he been thinking bringing her to the cabin he and Grace had shared. It felt like a betrayal. The thought made him want to laugh. Grace had *betrayed* him.

He scowled over at Andi. What did any of us know about each other really? All his instincts told him that Andi Blake had her own secrets—but not for long. At this very moment, his brother was working on finding out everything there was to know about her.

And Cade was anxious to know. He knew he was looking for some kind of leverage. So far Andi Blake had been holding all the cards.

"What are we doing here?" she asked impatiently.

What were they doing here? He'd thought maybe here, in the home that he and Grace had shared, would be proof that Grace Browning had existed. But the only proof was what he felt in his heart and even he was starting to question whether it had been real.

As Andi had pointed out, the three million dollars was still missing. Apparently someone was looking for it. And Andi Blake wasn't the only one who knew about Grace being Starr.

Something had happened in Texas to catapult her to Montana. He'd bet the ranch on it. He had a bad feeling whatever it was would end up being connected to Starr and the Calhoun family.

He thought about turning around and going back to town. But he'd come this far...

"Come on," he said. "You want to know about Grace..." He headed toward the arena, not ready to take Andi inside the cabin, if ever.

"Where are the horses?" she asked once inside. He'd taken his time showing her around, stalling.

"I board them during the winter," he said. The truth was he had boarded them in town ever since Grace died, avoiding the cabin and thoughts of the future they had planned here.

It was cold in the arena. He could see his breath and Andi wasn't dressed for winter in Montana. The fool woman was still wearing that lightweight leather coat and high-heeled boots. She was shivering, her teeth practically chattering. She had her arms wrapped tightly around herself and looked as if she was close to hypothermia.

He swore silently. Whatever animosity he felt toward her for coming into his life and blowing it all to hell, he hadn't meant to let her freeze.

"You look cold," he said.

"I'm fine."

Her teeth were chattering now.

"Right," he said. "Come on." There would be no getting out of it. He'd have to take her into the cabin and get her warmed up before they headed back to town.

For just an instant it crossed his mind how alike Grace and Andi had been when it came to stubborn determination.

He quickly pushed that thought away with distaste. Andi was nothing like Grace. At least the Grace he'd thought he'd married.

"What is that?" Andi asked, trying to keep her mind off the freezing cold as they walked toward the cabin. The snow was deep and the ice under it slick. She couldn't feel her fingers in her leather gloves. Nor her toes in her boots.

"What?" He stopped to look back at her.

She pointed in the distance to what appeared to be the skeleton of a house someone had started and abandoned. The wood was weathered gray against a backdrop of rocky bluffs.

"I was building a bigger place for us when Grace was killed," he said, following her gaze.

"You plan to finish it?"

"No."

"So you're just going to leave it like that? I would think it would only act as a constant reminder of what you'd lost."

He turned to glare at her. "I don't know what I'm going to do with it, all right? What's it to you anyway?"

"Nothing. I was just curious," she said.

"Maybe one of these days I'll raze it. Happy?" With that he turned and strode off toward the cabin.

She stared at his strong back, the determined set of his shoulders and shook her head. Would she ever understand this man?

Reminding herself that she didn't need to understand him, she tucked the information away, already weaving it along with this place into her story as she trailed after Cade, colder than she'd ever been in her life.

A gust of wind whirled snow into her face as she

neared the house. She felt her boot heel slip on the ice and would have gone down if Cade hadn't grabbed her.

He shook his head in apparent amused disgust as he took her leather gloved hand and led her up the steps to the cabin.

She drew her hand back once they were on the porch, angry with herself and with him. She was out of her realm—just as he would be in Fort Worth. So she hadn't walked on anything but sidewalk most of her life. So she was cold and not as surefooted on the ice as he was. She didn't need his condescending attitude.

As he unlocked the front door of the cabin, she realized she could no longer feel her feet. And she couldn't stop shaking.

Cade ushered her inside where the interior of the cabin was only a little warmer than the arena.

Andi stood just inside the door looking around. She hadn't been sure what to expect. The outside of the cabin was rustic, appearing to have been built back in the 1930s. It was log-framed with chinking between the logs and a weathered rail porch, all grayed with age.

So it was a surprise to see that the inside of the cabin was quite homey. She instantly recognized a woman's touch—this cabin was so different from the apartment where Cade stayed in town behind the bait shop.

Cade must have noticed her startled expression. "It was all Grace's doing."

The decor was warm and inviting with comfortable furniture and welcoming colors. Also the place was more spacious than she would have guessed from the outside.

There was a rock fireplace against one wall with bookshelves on both sides to the ceiling. She walked over to glance at the books. They all looked as if they'd been read, and more than once. The variety of topics surprised her given that a cowboy and a bank robber had lived here. She looked up to find Cade's dark gaze on her.

"Most of the books are mine." He sounded defensive. "Or didn't you think I could read?"

She ignored that as she moved around, trying to warm up her hands and feet. What had she been thinking, moving to Montana in the middle of winter? It was literally freezing up here.

She pulled several books from the shelves, then put them back.

"I'll make us some coffee," he said, then seemed to hesitate. "Maybe I'd better make a fire."

She glanced around as he got a blaze going in the fireplace. All of the walls had interesting black-and-white photographs of what she assumed was the area. They had such a Western feel to them that Andi was reminded of old movies she'd watched as a child with her father. He loved Roy Rogers and Gene Autry films.

"Grace took those," Cade said behind her.

It surprised her that Starr was such a good photographer. "I had no idea Starr was this talented."

Cade met her gaze. "There's a lot you didn't know about my wife."

Apparently so. But a lot he didn't know, either.

"She was going to have a show in Great Falls in the spring. She was shy about her work, but I talked her into it." He stopped as if he realized another reason Starr might not have wanted to go public with her work.

"Wrap up in that quilt on the couch. You need to warm your fingers and toes slowly otherwise they'll hurt," he said as he turned and went into the kitchen.

Her fingers and toes already ached from the cold. She couldn't imagine them hurting any worse as she went to stand by the blaze he'd gotten going in the fireplace.

Within moments, she felt a painful tingling in her fingers. Her toes were starting to tingle, as well. She could hear him banging around in the kitchen. She sat down on the couch, her eyes tearing with the pain.

Why had he brought her here? She pulled her shoulder bag with the pepper spray in it closer—just in case she might need it, then wrapped the quilt around her, wondering if Starr had made it as she stared into the flames.

Cade came out of the kitchen and handed her a mug of steaming instant coffee.

Her hands and feet hurt, just as he said they would. She grimaced as she wrapped her fingers around the hot mug.

"Here," he said. "We need to get those wet boots off." Before she could protest he knelt in front of her and taking one of her boots in both hands began to unzip them. "If you're going to live here, you've got to dress for the weather."

"I'm fine," she lied and attempted to pull her foot back.

He gave her an impatient look, pulled off her boot, then reached for the other one. He removed the second boot, put both boots to warm near the fire and began to gently rub her feet.

"They're hurtin', aren't they?" he said, nodding before she could answer. "They'll be better in a minute."

She'd have to take his word for it. She sipped her coffee, trying to ignore the feel of his strong but gentle fingers rubbing her feet.

The cabin felt much smaller. Cade Jackson seemed to fill the entire space with his very male presence. She knew how much this was hurting him, being here in his cabin he'd shared with his wife. Clearly he didn't spend much time here since her death. Andi could tell that he'd been reluctant to bring her here. So why had he? As hard as he tried not to show it, she could see that this was killing him.

"Better?" he asked after a few minutes.

She nodded. "Thank you." The moment he stood again, she tucked her feet under her. Not that she didn't appreciate his kindness. As she sipped her coffee she watched him. He stood next to the fireplace, the flames playing on his strong features.

Had Starr fallen so deeply in love with this man that she really had wanted to change? As Andi studied him, she thought it actually possible. There was something so comforting about this man, a strength, and yet an aliveness that drew even her.

"What now?" Cade asked quietly.

She shook her head, not understanding since only moments before her thoughts had been on anything but Starr and the news article she would write.

"I've shown you my life with Grace," he said. "You can do your story. What else do you want from me?"

There was one thing she needed before she broke the story, but she knew it would be over Cade Jackson's dead body.

However, none of this felt as if it was in her hands anymore—if it ever had been. She was being led by whoever was providing her with the information. That person knew her, knew that this was personal for her, knew she wouldn't quit until she got to the truth.

"It isn't about what I want," she said, believing that to be true. "Whoever is supplying me with the information, wants something."

He nodded solemnly. "The money." He said it with such distaste she didn't doubt he'd never seen it let alone spent it.

"That would be my guess," she said.

"We already know that." Cade rubbed a hand over his face in frustration. "But I don't know where the money is. If Starr had it, I was never aware of it."

She nodded. "I believe that. The question is, does Starr still have it?"

"You're not back to your theory that Starr walked away from that wreck, are you?"

Her gaze locked with his. "What if she isn't dead? What if you didn't bury your wife? Then she is alive somewhere with your child. We need to know if that body you buried is actually Starr's. You're the only one who can have her body exhumed."

Cade froze, his mug partway to his mouth, his eyes suddenly hard as stones.

Andi rushed on, "If her DNA matches that of one of her brothers in prison—"

He threw the mug with enough force that it shattered when it hit the wall. Coffee made a dark stain across the woodwork and floor.

Without a word, he stormed out of the cabin.

Chapter 8

"You can go visit my cousin in Minnesota until the baby is born and then come back," Arlene said.

Charlotte looked up at her from the couch, where she was eating cold leftover pancakes dripping with syrup. "I'm not going anywhere. It's not like everyone doesn't already know I'm pregnant."

"What about the father?" Arlene asked, wiping up crumbs from the plastic on the couch beside her daughter.

"What about him?" Charlotte asked, licking her fingers.

"Have you told him the baby's his?"

Charlotte turned her attention to the last pancake on the plate. She dredged it through a lake of syrup but didn't lift it to her mouth. "He doesn't believe me that it's his."

"And you're *protecting* this man?" Arlene demanded. "What is wrong with you?"

"Nothing. It's my baby. I *want* it."

Arlene raised a brow. "Want it? What do you intend to *do* with it?"

"Raise it," Charlotte snapped.

"You? Raise a baby?"

"I figure I can do a hell of a lot better than you have," her daughter said, shoving away her plate. The pancake spilled to the floor in a pool of syrup as Charlotte stormed off to her bedroom, slamming the door solidly behind her.

Arlene stared down at the pancake and syrup soaking into the rug for a moment, then dropped to her knees to hurriedly clean up the mess. She'd always kept a clean house, prided herself in her neatness. Floyd had hated the way she fussed around the house.

"Sit down, for cripe's sake, Arlene," he'd bark. "You're driving me crazy with your cleaning."

Nervous energy. She'd always had more than her share.

She scrubbed at the rug, frantic to get the syrup up before it stained the rug, wondering why she'd tried so hard. She'd wanted to be a good wife and mother. Her own mother had been cold and uncaring. Arlene had never been able to do anything right according to her.

She quit scrubbing at the rug. The dishrag felt sticky in her hands. Her eyes burned hot. She couldn't remember the last time she'd cried and was surprised when scalding tears began to run down her face.

Her body shook with chest-rattling sobs. Through blinding tears, she saw herself on the floor crying as a child, her mother standing over her.

Her mother had always said Arlene wouldn't amount to anything. Even when Arlene had kept her house and her kids spotless, her mother had found fault until the day she died.

But that day, on the floor, her mother standing over her with the leather strap, Arlene had prayed that she could prove her mother wrong as she cried for the father she'd never known to save her.

He hadn't and her mother's prophecy had now come true. Arlene Evans was a disgrace, a failed wife, a failed mother. How could she allow another generation to be born into this mess?

Andi stared after Cade as a gust of cold air blew in with the slamming of the door.

She'd known he wasn't going to take the idea of the exhumation well. Not that she blamed him. She found she was shaking and wondered if it was from his reaction—or her own. She'd just asked a man to dig up his dead wife, a woman he had clearly loved almost more than life itself.

She felt sick. Had she no compassion anymore? Not for the Calhouns. And even less for Starr, who had obviously broken Cade Jackson's heart—and Andi feared would completely destroy it by the time this was finished.

She hated being a part of it. But she was and had been for more years than she wanted to admit.

Not that she thought the person who sent her the clippings and tape would let her stop now anyway. How far was he willing to go to get what he wanted? And what exactly did he want besides the money?

She rose from her chair in front of the fire to retrieve her boots. They felt warm as she slipped her feet into them. As she did, she noticed a row of books—all about the outlaws of the Old West.

Andi pulled down one with a well-used paperback cover and thumbed through it, stopping on the title page. It was signed: "Grace, I know how much you like these stories. Love, Cade."

She heard a sound outside the cabin and put the book

back. Now she understood Cade's expression when he'd found her in the outlaw section at the museum. He'd known about Grace's interest in the outlaws of the Old West.

So what did that have to do with anything?

And where was Cade? she wondered as she took her mug to the kitchen. She rinsed it out and set it on the counter, admiring what Starr had done with the house.

Why had Starr bothered fixing up this place if she was planning to take off? Or had the decorating just been something to do until she could take the money and leave?

Andi cleaned up the broken mug and spilled coffee. Past the kitchen was an open door. Through it she could see the bedroom. The colors alone drew her toward the room. An antique high bed with an iron frame sat in the middle of the room. The iron bed had been painted white, stark next to the color-crazy quilt on the bed.

But it was the photograph over the bed that drew her. She moved closer. The shot was of Cade. Starr had captured the man so perfectly, both his strength and his stubbornness as well as a vulnerability that pulled at Andi's heart. This was the man Starr had fallen in love with. The man who had changed her into Grace Browning.

"Are you ready?"

Andi jumped at the sound of Cade's voice directly behind her. She'd been so taken with the photograph and what it said about Cade—and Starr—that she hadn't heard him come back. "It's a wonderful photo of you."

He said nothing as he waited for her to leave the room before he firmly closed the door behind them.

"I should get you back to town," he said, taking her coat from where he'd hung it earlier to dry.

She wanted to tell him she was sorry. Sorry for suggesting the exhumation. Sorry that she was the one who'd brought this to him. But what she was really sorry for was that she hadn't believed him that Starr had become the woman, Grace Browning, whom he'd loved.

She understood his pain more acutely. It was another reason she said nothing as he drove her back to Whitehorse in a fierce silence that brooked no arguments or discussions.

Cade mentally kicked himself all the way back to town. What in the hell had he been thinking? All Tex cared about was her damned news story. Seeing the home Grace had made for him had only given the reporter something more to write about.

But now she wanted him to exhume Grace's body?

It had been all he could do not to dump her in a snow-bank on the way back to town.

Fortunately she'd had the good sense not to say a word all the way back, otherwise he couldn't be responsible for what he would have done.

He dropped her off without a word at the newspaper office and drove toward the bait shop, still kicking himself.

As he drove home, Christmas music played from somewhere down the street. Everywhere he looked there were twinkling Christmas lights.

Grace had been so excited about their first Christmas together. She'd decorated the cabin and made sugar cookies and eggnog.

It had started snowing the week before Christmas that year. Grace had been like a little kid, catching snowflakes in her mouth, making snow angels out in the yard. She'd said she'd never seen that much snow before. He promised they would make a snowman when she got back from her shopping trip to Billings.

He had wanted to go with her, but she'd been insistent that she had to go alone.

"It's a surprise and you're not going to ruin it," she'd said. "The roads are plowed and sanded. I'll be careful." She'd kissed him, holding his face between her warm palms, those blue eyes of hers filling with tears.

"You make me happier than I ever dreamed possible," she'd said.

He shoved the memory away, no longer sure what had been a lie, and looked in his rearview mirror.

His mood didn't improve at the sight of his brother's patrol car behind him. With a curse, Cade pulled into the bait shop, his brother pulling in behind him.

"Where you been?" the sheriff asked after motioning for Cade to get into the patrol car.

Cade cringed under his brother's intent gaze as he slid into the passenger seat. "Out to the cabin. Fishing." Why was he lying? Why didn't he just tell Carter he'd been with the reporter? "Why? What's going on?"

Carter had his bad news look on.

"Just tell me." Cade hadn't meant to sound so abrupt. "Is it about Grace. Or Andi?"

"Andi?"

"Miranda Blake," Cade snapped, knowing he'd given himself away. He already knew about Grace. What he didn't want, he realized with surprise, was bad news about Tex.

Cade wanted the news, short and sweet. He didn't want sympathy. Nor did he want to have to explain himself.

"I can't find any record of Grace Eden Browning," his brother said. Carter looked more than a little uncomfortable. "No record of any kind. All I can figure is that she must have been born under another name. Do you happen to have her social security number?"

Cade shook his head. This wasn't news but hearing it from the sheriff definitely made it all the more real. "I'll see if I can find it. I'm sure there's an explanation."

"Yeah." Carter didn't sound convinced. "You don't seem surprised by this."

Cade knew it was just a matter of time before he was going to have to tell his brother the truth. But not yet. "What did you come up with on Miranda Blake?"

Carter seemed a little taken aback that Cade appeared more interested in Ms. Blake than this news about his former wife, but opened his notebook and said, "As for Miranda Blake…"

Cade listened, not surprised that Andi had been a top news anchorwoman in Fort Worth, working her way up as an investigative reporter and making quite a name for herself.

But her reason for leaving Fort Worth did surprise him.

"She took the job up here to get away from a stalker. Apparently one of her viewers had a crush on her," Carter said. "At first he sent her flowers, candy, love letters all anonymously. But when she asked him on the air to please stop, he felt rejected and started threatening her."

"Didn't she contact the police?" Cade asked.

The sheriff nodded. "But it's hard to catch these kinds of secret admirers. The threats escalated and she left the station. Not even her former boss knew where she'd gone."

"You didn't tell him where she was," Cade said, unable to hide his fear for Andi.

His brother looked even more surprised. "He knew

I was with the Phillips County Sheriff's Department in Montana, but I doubt he was her secret admirer."

Still, Cade couldn't help being concerned.

"Her boss said they are holding her job for her for six months," his brother was saying. "That's why I would hate to see you get involved with this woman since you know she won't be staying for probably even that long."

Cade wanted to laugh out loud, but he had to go on letting his brother think his interest in Andi was romantic for a while longer.

"Don't worry," he told Carter. "I've already figured that out. I just thought it would be smart to know what I was dealing with."

His brother eyed him. "Dealing with?"

Cade shrugged and looked away, realizing he'd been too truthful. "Well, it has been a while since I've... dated."

"Yeah," Carter agreed quickly. "You'll want to take it slow." But he sounded pleased that Cade might even be thinking of dating again.

He felt a little guilty for leading his brother on like that. But in time, he would have to confide in Carter on a professional basis.

Cade didn't want to spoil the holidays. This could wait until after then. Until after his brother popped the question to Eve Bailey. Cade just hoped to hell she accepted Carter's proposal. There was enough heartbreak as it was.

"I'm glad you're doing better. I really am," his brother said. "I've been worried about you."

Cade knew he'd put his family through a lot. "I'm sorry I haven't been around much for you."

"Hey, I'm not complaining," Carter said. "I know you've been through hell." He smiled. "Just don't forget Christmas Eve. Unless I lose my nerve."

"You won't," Cade assured him. "You and Eve are made for each other."

"You care about this Andi Blake," Carter said.

He nodded. He could have argued the point, but didn't.

"Just be careful, okay?" his brother said. "I don't want to see you get hurt."

Carter had no idea just how he'd been hurt by the woman. "Don't worry. I know what I'm doing."

Carter didn't look as if he believed him.

"I have another favor," Cade said, quickly changing the subject. "I was hoping you could find out about a woman named Starr Calhoun for me."

His brother's expression didn't change. "Starr Calhoun?"

"She was originally from Texas."

"Texas? Like Miranda Blake," Carter said.

"Yeah. Thanks for doing this." Cade reached for the door and opened it.

Carter reached past him and closed it. "When are you going to be honest with me and tell me what's really going on?"

Cade felt the full weight of his brother's gaze. He squirmed. "Soon. Just trust me a little longer?"

Carter met his gaze and held it. "I'll trust you. But I have to know. Are you involved in anything illegal?"

"No." Not unless you considered withholding evidence illegal.

A winter storm warning alert had been put out for Whitehorse and all counties east of the Rockies. With the blowing and drifting snow, the road south of Whitehorse was closed to all but emergency traffic.

Andi did what she had to at the newspaper, then

headed back to her apartment. In this part of the county during winter, it got dark shortly after 4:30 p.m.

Once home, she got out of her cold car since the drive hadn't been far enough for the engine to even warm up a little. Snow fell silently around her. She didn't want to go up to her apartment, but she had nowhere else to go.

And while she was too upset to sit still, she didn't feel like unpacking any boxes. She wasn't even sure why she'd brought so much stuff. She wouldn't be staying. Especially the way she was feeling right now.

She was cold and tired and sick at heart as she climbed the stairs to her second-story apartment. Her thoughts kept coming back to Cade Jackson. He was a victim in all this. And the woman who'd involved him was allegedly dead and buried. Andi could understand how Cade didn't want to exhume the body of the woman he'd loved.

But how could he still love a woman who had deceived him the way Starr had? And wouldn't he need to know if she'd pulled a disappearing act, possibly with his baby?

The moment she flipped the lightswitch and nothing happened Andi knew someone was there in the dark waiting for her just as the man had been in Texas.

He came out of the blackness. She felt the air around her move an instant before he was on her. She caught his scent, a mix of body odor and cheap aftershave.

He slammed her back into the wall, knocking the air out of her, his fingers closing around her throat.

She tried to call out, but she had no breath and the pressure on her throat choked off any sound. She scratched at his face, only to get a handful of thick mask.

He let go of her throat with one hand and slapped her hand away, wrestling her arms behind her as he pinned her body to the wall, his fingers digging into her throat.

She'd been wrong. It wasn't her attacker from Texas. This man was larger, stronger. She couldn't breathe.

"Listen, bitch. Hurry up and find the money like you're supposed to. Run and I'll track you down and kill you. Don't even think about telling your friend's cop brother."

At the sound of pounding footsteps on the stairs to her apartment, he loosened his hold, then slammed her hard against the wall before letting her go. "I'll be in touch."

She saw stars. She gasped for breath, her throat on fire. Her legs gave out. As she slid down the wall to the floor someone burst into the apartment. She caught the glint of a star—and a weapon.

"Help." The word came out in a whisper. But even as she said it, she knew that her attacker was gone. She could feel the cold breeze blowing across the floor and knew the back door was open.

"Stay with her," the man with the badge ordered as he turned on a flashlight and swept the beam across her small apartment. She looked away, blinded by the sudden light.

"Are you all right?" The voice surprised her. Just as Cade did as he knelt down next to her.

She looked up into his face and began to shake. He gently pulled her toward him.

"It's okay," he said as he rubbed her back.

His kindness brought the tears. She hated this feeling of weakness, and worse letting him see her like this. She'd always had to be strong. For her mother. For herself because there was no one else.

"You're okay," he said, as if he knew how hard it was for her to be vulnerable in front of him.

She leaned into his strength, no longer able to fight back her emotions as she remembered the man's threat—

and the sensation of knowing she was going to die if she didn't get air.

The lights flickered on. She pulled herself together and Cade handed her a tissue from the end table nearby.

"How is she?" the sheriff asked standing over them.

Cade got to his feet, gently pulling her up and easing her over to the couch. "Give her a minute."

"I'm all right." Her voice came out in a whisper. She was far from all right.

The sheriff took out his notebook. "I'm going to need to ask you some questions. I'm Sheriff Carter Jackson, Cade's brother."

She nodded and told him about reaching for the light. When it hadn't gone on, she'd known someone was in her apartment.

"How did you make the call?"

She shook her head. "I didn't." She'd wondered how they'd gotten to her so quickly. She saw the sheriff exchange a look with his brother.

"I was with my brother when he got the call about the break-in," Cade said, as if seeing her confusion.

"Someone must have seen him break in." It hurt to talk. She swallowed, her eyes tearing from the pain.

The sheriff looked up from his notebook. "Is your apartment number 555-0044?" he asked.

She nodded numbly, knowing what was coming.

"According to the dispatcher, the call came from that number. From inside your apartment."

She felt her eyes widen in alarm. "I don't understand."

"Neither do I," the sheriff said as he walked into her kitchen and picked up the phone near the back door and hit redial.

She watched his face, knew the emergency operator had answered.

"This is Sheriff Jackson. I was just testing the line." He hung up and looked at Andi. "The last call made was to the 911 operator. If you didn't make the call from here, then who did?"

Chapter 9

"What the hell was that about in there?" Cade demanded the moment he and his brother were outside again. "Did you see her throat? She was *attacked*. You're acting as if she staged the whole thing."

Carter said nothing as he opened the door of his patrol car. "You want a ride home?"

"No, I want you to tell me what the hell is going on."

"I don't know," his brother said calmly. "I just know that the 911 call originated inside that apartment. Either she made the call, or her attacker did."

"That's crazy. Did the dispatcher say whether it was a man or a woman on the phone?"

"The voice was muffled."

Cade swore. "You should be out looking for her attacker."

Carter was studying him. "This has something to do with why you wanted me to check on her, doesn't it?"

"Forget it," Cade said, holding up his hands in surrender as he backed away from the patrol car. "There's no talking to you."

"Try telling me what's going on with you and that woman in there. She's trouble. Can't you see that?"

Carter called after him as he headed down the street. "Come on, I'll give you a ride."

Cade didn't answer as he kept walking toward home and his truck. He didn't know what to think, but he wasn't leaving her alone tonight.

Andi bolted the door behind the sheriff and Cade. She was still shaken but the sheriff had checked the apartment and assured her there was no one in it. He'd found a window that had been ajar and shut it for her.

The sheriff had offered to take her to the emergency room to have her throat checked, but she'd declined. It was feeling better and she didn't want to be seen with the sheriff after the threat her attacker had made.

Lubbock Calhoun. That's who it had to have been. Hadn't she suspected once she'd learned he was out of prison and on the loose that he was the one sending her the information?

She shuddered at the memory of his hands on her throat. Why did he think *she* could find the money? This was crazy, but no crazier than her coming to Montana because of the Calhouns. This is where her obsession had gotten her—in worse trouble than she could imagine. Bradley was right. She should never have come up here.

She had to get out of Montana. But even as she thought it, she reminded herself that she'd already run from trouble in Texas. She'd thought she was safe here in Whitehorse, Montana. But Lubbock had found her.

She remembered what he'd said and began to shake.

Hurry up and find the money like you're supposed to.
Like you're supposed to?

Was it possible someone had tricked her into coming
here? Feeding on her obsession with the Calhoun family?

Her heart began to beat harder. The stalker in Texas.
"Oh, no." She put her hand over her mouth, tears burning her eyes. She'd been set up from the beginning. First
the stalker to scare her out of Texas, then the job ad that
had been sent to her.

Whoever had done it had known that she'd been running scared and had wanted to get away from Texas. She
would never have come to Montana if Lubbock hadn't
been arrested just miles from here.

She shook her head. She'd been set up. By Lubbock?
It was too preposterous that a man like Lubbock Calhoun had planned this, manipulating her through each
step to the point where he would physically threaten her
into finding the money? As if she could.

She tried to imagine the man who'd almost strangled
her to death having the patience to lay the groundwork to
get her here and couldn't. It would have had to have been
someone in Texas. Someone who knew her. Someone...

Fear curdled her stomach as she dug out her cell phone.

Bradley answered on the first ring. "I'm so glad you
called. I have news."

She said nothing, all her fears growing inside her.
Bradley knew her better than anyone. He was the one
person who knew about her obsession with the Calhouns
and how she would jump at a chance at retribution. But
he'd also fanned the fires of her terror when her secret
admirer had become a stalker. He'd encouraged her to
leave Texas, for her own safety. If Bradley had hired
someone to stalk her...

"Are you all right? You sound funny," he asked as if hearing the change in her.

"News?" she said, her voice breaking. How could she be thinking these things about her friend? Her closest friend?

"Great news," Bradley said with a flourish. "There's been an arrest. The police found your stalker."

"What?" It was the last thing she'd expected. She dropped into a chair.

"And wait until you hear who it is." He did a drumroll. So like Bradley to play the moment to the hilt. "Rachel, your nemesis. That's right, sweetie. The police found evidence in her locker—and in her boyfriend's car. She got her boyfriend to do the dirty deed."

"Rachel?" Andi was still in shock. "Why would she—"

"Isn't it obvious? She wanted your job—and it worked like a charm, didn't it? She continued sending the threats hoping you wouldn't return and the newscaster job would become permanent."

Andi didn't know what to say. Her whole theory that there had been an elaborate plot to get her to Montana came unraveled. Just moments before she'd been suspecting Bradley… She began to cry.

"Sweetie, I thought you'd be *happy* to hear this."

"I am," she managed to say. "I'm just so relieved." So relieved that her stupid suspicions were unfounded and feeling guilty for even having them. "Rachel confessed?"

"*Right,* sweetie. She's denying everything and so is her boyfriend but the police found enough evidence between the two of them so it's a slam dunk and truthfully, no one at the station is surprised in the least. So now you can come back to Texas. Your old job is waiting for you— and you have one fantastic story to break."

She didn't know how to tell him. "There's news up here as well."

"You sound funny. Are you all right?"

She told him about the attack.

"That's it," he said. "You're getting out of there."

"If I thought there was someplace I could run and get away from him, I would."

"You're that convinced it was Lubbock Calhoun?"

"Yes." Her throat was sore and painful again. "I shouldn't talk anymore."

"Then just listen," Bradley said. "I have some more news although I was hoping you'd forget about the Calhouns and just come home. But the robbery money? It's never turned up. At least none of the 'bait' money. I'm betting one of them hid it and for one reason or another couldn't get back to it. Which could explain why Lubbock, if that's who it is, put you on Starr's trail."

What he said made sense. "Bradley, I feel as if I've been set up. I knew someone was pulling my strings once I got here, but I think it goes deeper than that." She told him what Lubbock—if that's who it had been—had said to her.

"I didn't want to say anything, but I think you're dead-on," Bradley said. "It seemed pretty obvious why. They have to know who you are, your connection to their family, and given the amount of exposure you've gotten in Texas…"

"But why would they think I could find the money? That's just crazy."

"Are you serious? Look, I've given this some thought. What else do I have to do at work all day?" he joked. "Number one, Lubbock sure as the devil couldn't get close to Cade Jackson, but you can. Two, you're trained to get information. Look at the stories you broke, including that famous murder case that you practically solved single-handedly."

She groaned, realizing that there were viewers out there who thought they knew her.

"The good news is that it must mean that there is information to be found," he was saying. "Whoever is after the money, Lubbock or Houston or even Starr possibly if you're right and she faked her death, know who you are. They're using you, kiddo. Maybe even one of them got to Rachel for all we know."

She felt sick. "How am I going to find the money?"

"The same way you go after news stories," Bradley said. "If anyone can do this, it's you."

"You haven't seen this country. It's vast and right now it's covered in snow. A lot of it looks the same. It would be so easy to get lost in."

"Exactly," he said, sounding excited. "You've just hit the nail on the head. The Calhouns would have had the same problems when they hid that money."

Even as exhausted and scared as she was, she saw where he was going with this. "You think they would have made a map back to the money."

Bradley laughed. "Isn't that what you would have done? So now all you have to do is find the map. Don't thank me yet," he joked.

"It seems like a lot of trouble to go to," she said. "Why didn't Starr just split the money with Houston and skip the country?"

"Don't forget Lubbock. He would have wanted a taste and I have a feeling him being arrested on that old warrant near Whitehorse was no coincidence. I'm betting the cops got an anonymous tip."

"*Starr?*"

"That would take care of one brother for six years,"

Bradley said. "Now all she had to do was contend with Houston. So she hid the money where she's the only one who knows how to find it. Gives her leverage."

Especially if Cade was right and she wanted to start her life over. But then why not give up all the money?

"I'm not so sure about the map, sorry," she said. "Wouldn't Cade have found it by now if there'd been one?"

"It wouldn't have been something obvious," Bradley said. "It would have to be disguised as something else."

Andi laughed. It felt good to talk to him even if it did hurt her throat a little. "You're really getting into this, aren't you?"

"I can't help it. I'm down here where it's safe and I can live vicariously through you," he said. "Aren't you scared?"

"Terrified. I'm afraid the Calhouns think I'm a lot smarter than I actually am."

"I'd argue that. But you can quit, go to the cops, get out of there. Just tell me what time I should pick you up at the airport."

"You know I'm no quitter and quite frankly I'm afraid to go to the cops. The ones in Fort Worth certainly didn't do much to find my stalker when I was down there." She didn't mention that the sheriff up here was more suspicious of her than her attacker because of a phone call she couldn't explain.

If she told Sheriff Jackson what she was really thinking about this whole mess, she knew he'd be as disbelieving as she was.

"You are so much braver than I would be," Bradley said.

"Goes without saying," she joked, so glad her fears about him were baseless. Talking to Bradley, it was easy to forget the trouble she was in. At least for a while. "I do miss you."

"Good. So keep in touch, okay? Call me every day. I need to know that you're all right. And be careful of this Cade Jackson character. I think he knows more than he's telling you. I'd hate to see you get taken in by a pretty face."

She thought of Cade, remembering his expression when he'd seen her looking at the outlaw exhibit. There was no doubt that he knew more than he was telling her.

"You're probably right," she said noncommittally as she thought of the way he'd rubbed her feet, the way he'd thrown the mug of coffee and stomped out at even the suggestion of digging up his wife's grave and how he'd held her earlier after the attack.

"I do love a treasure hunt. Except for the fact that it's a killer sending you the clues."

She groaned. "I thought gay men are supposed to be so sensitive?"

He laughed. "Sleep tight. And by all means, be careful."

After she hung up, she wished for a moment that she'd taken the sheriff's advice. "You might consider staying at a motel tonight if you don't feel safe here," he'd said before he left.

She'd seen his suspicion. He didn't believe that she hadn't made the call. She couldn't blame him. It made no sense to her, either. Why would Lubbock make the call? Unless someone else had been in her apartment.

With the blinds closed and the doors locked, she had to check the apartment again for herself. She didn't expect her attacker to return. He wanted the money. His threat had been strong enough that he didn't need to come back tonight to make sure she got the message.

She knew she should have told the sheriff everything. But then she would have to tell him the rest of it and she didn't doubt that Lubbock's threat was more of a promise. A man like Lubbock Calhoun could and would carry out that promise.

Look what had happened in Texas with her stalker. The police hadn't been able to protect her. Nor had they caught the people behind it until after she left—and as Bradley said, it was so obvious who had the most to gain with her gone. If the police hadn't been able to catch Rachel until now, then Andi had even less faith that the local sheriff could stop someone like Lubbock Calhoun.

At least the stalker had been caught. She still felt guilty about her suspicions about Bradley. Thank goodness she hadn't voiced them.

She turned on the television, found an old Western, Bradley's favorite, and curled up to watch it, knowing she would never be able to sleep.

She was still shocked about Rachel even though she'd known how ambitious and competitive the woman had always been.

A little after midnight, though, Andi's apartment windows began to rattle from the wind. Snow pelted the glass that had already frosted over. She scraped at the frost on the inside of the glass, trying to see out. But she couldn't even see across the street because of the falling and drifting snow.

She realized she couldn't tell if Lubbock Calhoun or anyone else was out there watching her apartment. But as a gust of wind whirled snow down the street, she saw a familiar pickup parked directly below her window. Cade?

Andi told herself it couldn't be, but secretly she hoped it was him keeping a vigil over her.

She finally fell asleep in the wee hours of the morning, after she'd talked herself out of going down and seeing if Cade was in that pickup. What would she do if he was? Invite him up?

Cade spent the night in his pickup parked outside Andi's apartment. He was angry at his brother but after he'd cooled down, he had to admit he had a lot of questions himself.

If this was the stalker from Texas, then why hadn't Andi mentioned it to his brother? Instead she'd acted like she didn't know who had attacked her.

He'd seen how scared she'd been. Wasn't it time to tell Carter everything? And yet, he hadn't spoken up either, he reminded himself.

His sleeping bag was good to fifty below zero and he was damned glad of it. Snow swirled around the truck, burying it by morning.

Her light was on late into the night. He could see the flicker of her television screen. He took comfort in the fact that she couldn't sleep, either.

Several times he thought about going up to her apartment. He had a lot he wanted to talk to her about, including the attack and what she was keeping from him. His biggest fear was that the attack had something to do with Grace. And that damned money.

But he talked himself out of going upstairs. At this late hour and feeling the way he was toward her, going up to her apartment wasn't a good idea.

At one point, his brother had cruised by in his patrol car. Cade had slid down in his seat, but he was sure his brother had seen him—and thought him a fool.

The next morning Andi heard on the radio that because of the chill factor with the wind the temperature was twenty-four degrees below zero. She'd never been anywhere that cold and when she looked out the icy window she was startled to see that the snow had blown into huge sculpted drifts.

Cade's pickup was gone, she noted with a disappointment she had no business feeling. Her own car was buried in the snow, a huge drift completely hiding the rear of the car.

What was she doing here? All her life she'd felt more than able to handle anything that came her way. But she was completely out of her league. Not just that a hardened criminal was threatening her life. She wasn't prepared for this kind of weather.

This morning, her throat bruised and raw, she didn't feel strong enough to do this. She hated what she was doing to Cade Jackson. She was completely inept in this wild and dangerous country. And common sense told her she was so far in over her head that it was doubtful she'd get out of this alive.

Feeling the chill of the apartment, she turned up the heat and went to shower, angry with herself for bailing out of Texas. She'd jumped out of the frying pan and into the fire. If she hadn't run, none of this would be happening. But even as she thought it, she knew it wasn't true.

Come hell or high water, someone had been determined to get her here—and now she knew why. And she wasn't about to leave without the story.

When she came out of the shower after drying her hair and dressing for work, she put on her warmest coat, hat, boots and gloves—which she knew would be sorely inadequate for this weather. Unfortunately she would have to wade through the drift to get to the hardware store to buy a snow shovel.

But when she opened the door she was shocked to

see that a walkway had been carved through the drifted snow to her car.

The snow was piled deep on each side and as she neared the street and her car she saw snow flying through the air.

Closer she saw that someone with a shovel was on the other side of her car making that cloud of snow as they dug out her car. Some Good Samaritan. She only caught a glimpse of a stocking-capped head coming out of the cloud with each shovelful, but she was more than grateful for the help.

She'd reached the end of her car and had to yell to be heard over the howling wind and the scrape of the shovel.

The man stopped shoveling to turn around to look at her.

Cade Jackson. And he didn't look happy.

She couldn't have been more surprised. "What are you doing?"

"What does it look like?" he snapped and went back to shoveling.

"I could have done that myself," she hollered at him, wondering why he was angry with her. Because he'd had to sleep in his pickup last night in the cold? Whose idea had that been? Not hers.

"You have a snow shovel?" he asked as he stopped to lean on his. "I didn't think so." He held out his hand. "Give me your keys. I doubt your car will start since you forgot to plug it in last night, but I'll try it for you."

Plug in her car? Was he joking?

He seemed to see her confusion.

"When it's this cold you have to get a head-bolt heater and plug your car in every night. Welcome to Montana."

She dropped her keys into his outstretched palm. "Thank you," she said meekly.

He grunted something she couldn't hear and handed her the snow shovel as he went to her car and tried to start the engine. The engine growled a few times.

"Come on," Cade said, getting back out of the car and slamming the door. "I'll give you a ride to work." Without waiting, he turned and started toward his pickup parked down the block, leaving her holding the snow shovel. "Keep the shovel, you're going to need it," he said over his shoulder.

Chilled to the bone, she wasn't about to argue as she stood the shovel against the wall of snow next to her apartment and hurried after Cade.

He'd left his pickup running. The inside of the truck was warm when she climbed in. She wanted to kiss him she was so glad to be inside somewhere warm. Just that few minutes outside had chilled her to the bone.

He glanced over at her as he put the truck in gear. "How ya like Montana now, Tex?"

"Just fine," she managed to say through her chattering teeth. "It's beautiful."

He smiled at that. "It's a lot prettier if you're properly dressed. Stop by the department store. They'll get you outfitted. Unless of course you're having second thoughts about staying after what happened."

He'd stopped in front of the *Milk River Examiner* office. He glanced over at her. "Anything you want to tell me?"

"Thank you for the ride and the snow shovel," she said as she opened her door. She had to hang on to the handle to keep the door from blowing away. The cold took her breath away. "I'm not going anywhere."

"You might change your mind about that sooner than you think," he said and revved the engine.

She was already halfway out of the pickup or she

would have demanded to know what that was about. As she hurried into the office and Cade Jackson sped away, she saw Sheriff Carter Jackson waiting for her inside.

Cade went back to the bait shop to find Harvey Alderson waiting in his pickup.

"'Bout time," Harvey said irritably and glanced at his watch.

"Kind of cold for ice fishing, isn't it, Harvey?" Cade said, opening the shop.

"It's warm in the icehouse," Harvey said and began going through the fish decoys before he began to inspect one of the spears.

It was clear to Cade that Harvey was just killing time and had no intention of buying anything let alone going spearfishing out on the reservoir even though the ice was plenty thick.

The moment Harvey left without buying anything, Cade put up the Closed sign. He'd been mulling over everything his brother had told him, especially the part about Andi Blake.

Could he believe that a stalker had run her out of Texas and that she just happened to end up in Whitehorse, Montana?

He wondered if he was just a fool when it came to women. He'd believed Grace Browning was the woman she appeared to be. Look how wrong he'd been.

And now he'd bought into Andi Blake's story when clearly it was no coincidence the woman was here.

His head hurt from trying to sort it all out. Part of him wanted to go over to the newspaper office and get the truth out of her. But his good sense told him he needed to calm down, to figure a few things out before he talked to her again.

What he needed more than ever was to do the one thing that had kept him sane the last six years—fish. He'd always thought better out fishing.

"Ms. Blake," Sheriff Carter Jackson said, his hat in his hand. "I need to have a few words with you."

Andi glanced toward the back of the newspaper office. Empty. "Please have a seat," she said and turned back to lock the front door. "This won't take long, will it?"

He shook his head.

She felt his eyes on her as she walked over to her desk and sat down behind it. He pulled up a chair next to it.

"I would imagine you know why I'm here," the sheriff said.

She waited. It was a technique she'd learned quickly as a reporter. Let them do the talking.

"I know about the problems you had in Fort Worth," he said. "Why didn't you mention that you'd had a stalker after you in Texas yesterday when you were attacked?"

"I had no reason to connect the two," she said carefully.

He frowned. "Two different men are after you?"

"Actually I just learned last night that my stalker in Texas has been caught so there is no way it was the same man. It turned out to be the boyfriend of a coworker who apparently wanted my job."

"That's good news about the stalker being caught," the sheriff said. "May I see your throat?"

It was so badly bruised that she'd worn a turtleneck, not wanting to have to tell anyone about the attack. She pulled down the top of her turtleneck.

He whistled and shook his head. "That's some bruising you got there. It must hurt to talk. I'll try to make this quick. Did he say anything, make any kind of threat, demand your money?"

"You got there so quickly and scared him off, he really didn't have time to tell me what he had planned for me."

"Yeah," Carter said and scratched his jaw. "That phone call still bothers me."

"Me, as well." She made a point of looking at her watch.

"Am I keeping you from something?" he asked.

"I have an interview. If there isn't anything else…"

He studied her for a moment. His eyes weren't as dark as his brother's and while he was probably the better looking of the two men, he didn't have the raw maleness that Cade had.

He slowly rose from the chair across from her desk. "What are your plans now?"

"My plans?"

He seemed to hesitate. "Now that it's safe for you to return to Texas."

She shook her head. "I have no plans to leave Whitehorse. At least not yet."

"You do know you can come to me if you need help." He said the words quietly. His gaze met hers.

"Thank you. I appreciate that."

Andi watched him drive away before she put on her coat again and left the office, locking the door behind her. The wind whipped at her Texas-climate clothing and she knew it was time she took Cade's advice.

Chapter 10

Just as Cade was loading a few fishing supplies into his pickup, his brother pulled up in the patrol car.

Cade swore under his breath as Carter got out and walked toward him. A few more minutes and Carter would have missed him.

"I need to talk to you," Carter said in his cop voice.

Cade nodded and reached for his keys to open his apartment door. "What's up?" he asked, surprised how the snow had drifted around his back porch just in the time he was getting packed to go.

"When did you start locking your door?" Carter asked.

Cade didn't answer as he unlocked the door and stepped inside to flip on the light. It was one of those dark snowy days when the only good place to be was sitting in a fishing shack on the ice.

Opening the refrigerator, he took out two beers. He shot a look at Carter. "Isn't it your day off?" Carter grunted in response and Cade handed his brother a bottle. Carter took it reluctantly but didn't open it as Cade screwed off the top of his and took a drink. He knew he was going to need it.

"What the hell, Cade?" Carter said, shaking his head at him.

Cade tilted his beer toward a chair in the small living room, dropping into one. He couldn't remember ever seeing his brother this angry and was betting Carter had run Starr Calhoun's name through the system as he'd requested. Once Carter saw a picture of Starr...

"I feel like running you in," Carter said.

Cade took a drink of his beer, watching his brother over the bottle.

With a curse, his brother twisted off the cap on his beer and sat down, tossing the cap onto the end table.

"First you say you want to know about Grace's parents," Carter said, biting off each word. "Which we both know was bull. You wanted to know if Grace Eden Browning existed, but I suspect you wouldn't have asked me to find out if you hadn't already known that no one by that name did."

Cade said nothing as his brother rushed on.

"Then you ask me to check out Miranda Blake, leading me to believe your interest in her was romantic." He hesitated but seeing that Cade wasn't going to comment continued. "Then you want to know about Starr Calhoun. When I ran the names I also requested photos. Why the hell didn't you tell me?"

Cade shook his head. "I was still trying to assimilate it myself."

"Grace was Starr Calhoun."

"So it appears," Cade said. "I couldn't come to you with this until I figured out some things for myself."

"The Lone Ranger," Carter said under his breath. "You've always been like this. Can't stand to ask for help. You're just like the old man."

Cade couldn't argue that.

"So what have you figured out?" Carter asked sarcastically.

Cade shook his head.

Carter glared at him for a long moment, then took a pull on his beer. He swallowed and put the bottle down on the table beside him. He pulled a thick file from inside his jacket and tossed it on the small coffee table between them.

"Starr Calhoun and her family of criminals."

Cade looked down at the file, but didn't pick it up.

"Why do I have the feeling that nothing in there is going to come as a surprise to you?" his brother asked.

Cade said nothing, waiting for Carter to run out of steam. He knew his brother. Carter needed to get everything off his chest, then they could talk.

Carter took another drink of his beer. "How long have you known that Grace was Starr Calhoun?" he asked more calmly.

"Not long." He'd been two steps behind on all of this from the time he'd seen Grace on the highway that summer day more than six years ago.

He wasn't equipped to handle any of it given the way he'd felt about her. Worse, his brother was right about him. He wasn't good at asking for help. But right now he wanted nothing more than to turn this all over to him. Carter was the sheriff. He would know what to do when Cade didn't. Mostly it would take it out of his hands.

"I've been behind the eight ball on this from the moment I met Grace... Starr," he corrected.

"Then you had no clue she wasn't who she said she was?"

"I knew something in her past was bothering her. I thought she was still in love with some man." He chuckled at his own foolishness.

Carter shook his head and took another drink of his beer as Cade told him about Miranda Blake showing up at his door with the photograph of Starr Calhoun. "I still have trouble believing it, let alone accepting it."

"I assume you know about the bank robberies."

Cade nodded. "And before you ask, I don't know anything about the money."

"Three million dollars," Carter said. "Never found. On top of that, one of Starr's brothers was released from prison about three weeks ago. He's broken his parole and no one knows where he is. He's considered dangerous. Name's Lubbock Calhoun."

His brother must have seen his expression. "So you know about that, too." Carter swore. "Then you know the connection between the Calhouns and Miranda Blake."

Cade frowned. Connection?

"Other than the fact that they were both from Texas, it turns out that Ms. Blake's father was killed in a bank robbery. He was gunned down by Amarillo Calhoun, the eldest son of the Calhouns. It's all in the file, including the fact Miranda Blake was there that day at the bank." He nodded at Cade's no doubt shocked expression. "It gets better. Both she and Starr Calhoun were there. They were both about five at the time."

Cade couldn't have spoken even if he'd wanted to. Andi and Starr. Hadn't he known there was more to the story?

"What does Miranda Blake want out of this?" Carter asked.

"The story," Cade said slowly, still stunned by the import of what his brother had told him.

"You don't think she might be looking for a little revenge?" Carter asked.

"For her father's death? I would imagine there's some of that, too."

"You don't really believe it's a coincidence that both Starr and Miranda ended up here, do you?" Carter asked.

Cade smiled ruefully. "Someone wanted her to uncover this story. They've been giving her information anonymously."

"And that doesn't worry you?" Carter snapped.

"Yeah, it worries me. Especially after what you just told me."

"Especially after whoever was at her apartment last night," Carter said. "Three million dollars. Men have killed for a lot less. And so have women."

"Andi isn't after the money," Cade said.

His brother raised a brow. "And you know that how?"

Cade glanced at the file on the coffee table, no longer sure of anything.

"There's something else in that file," Carter said. "It's about Houston Calhoun, the brother Starr allegedly robbed the banks with."

"I know he's been missing—"

"Not anymore," the sheriff said. "That body we found in the abandoned Cherry House down in Old Town a while back? Well, I finally got an ID on it. It was Houston Calhoun."

Cade took the news like a blow.

"We were able to identify the remains through DNA. He'd had his DNA taken the last time he did prison time."

Cade swore, knowing what was coming next.

"You still have that .45 Colt Dad gave you?" Carter asked.

"I haven't seen it for a while," Cade said, surprised how calm he sounded when his whole life was about to blow sky-high. "Why?"

"Because Houston Calhoun had a .45 slug embedded in his skull. That's right, big brother. Houston was murdered and you better hope to hell you can find that gun and it doesn't match the slug taken out of the back of your former wife's brother's skull."

"Stop looking at me like I'm a suspect," he said, more angry with himself than his brother. He'd gotten himself involved in this when he'd fallen for Starr Calhoun. Not just fallen for her, but married her and fathered their child. A woman he'd never really known.

"Did you ever meet her brother?" Carter asked, sounding more like the sheriff than his brother.

"No. I didn't even know she had a brother. She told me she was an only child."

"He would have been a threat to your life with her," Carter said. "Based on the way the body decomposed, the anthropologist at the crime lab says Houston Calhoun died before winter set in approximately six years ago."

Cade swore. "I didn't know who Starr was or that Houston Calhoun even existed. And I sure as hell didn't kill him."

"Someone did. Knowing what we do now, he probably came to get his share of the money."

Cade watched another chunk of his life with Grace wash away. Soon there wouldn't be anything left but the lies. He had to face the fact that she might have killed her brother—and possibly with Cade's own gun.

He told himself if she'd done it, she did it because Houston was threatening to expose her. She would have wanted to stay and have Cade's baby, to put that old life behind her, to protect him from her past.

"If Grace killed him, she'd only been defending herself." Cade just didn't want to believe it had been about the money.

"No way to ever prove that now," Carter said. "You should be more concerned about keeping yourself out of prison."

"Damn, Carter, I'm your brother. You really think I shot that man and hid his body in the old Cherry House?"

"No. But you have to admit given all the facts, including that the body was hidden in an old house that you and I used to play in when we were kids, makes you look damned suspicious."

Cade knew what his brother was saying. How had the killer known that the house was abandoned, boarded-up and marked with No Trespassing signs? Or that the house was considered haunted by most everyone in Old Town Whitehorse?

"You ever mention the place to Grace? Maybe even show it to her on your way out to see our old ranch?" Carter asked, then read his expression and swore. "Damn, Cade, this is one hell of a mess."

Andi had been right. He was up to his neck in this whether he liked it or not with little way out unless he could prove he didn't know Grace was Starr Calhoun.

And there was little chance of that.

At the mercantile store, Andi told the clerk that she needed some Montana winter clothing.

The clerk laughed. "Did you have something in mind?"

"Whatever it takes for me to be warm."

Forty minutes later, Andi left the store carrying her business suit, leather coat and stylish boots in a large bag.

She wore flannel-lined canvas pants, a cotton turtleneck, a wool sweater, a sheepskin-lined coat, heavy snowpacks on her feet and a thick knitted wool hat, leather mittens with wool liners and a knitted scarf.

She felt like a sumo wrestler, but she *was* finally warm. She smiled as she called the local automotive shop to see about getting a head-bolt heater for her car and whatever it would take to get it running.

Once she had her car, she went looking for Cade. She had to tell him the truth about last night. He was in this almost as deep as she was. He had to be careful.

At his bait and tackle shop, she found a note on his door: Gone Fishing!

Great. At the convenience store, she filled up with gas and asked where everyone fished.

"This time of year?" the clerk said. "The reservoir. Drive north. You can't miss it."

The clerk was right. About fifteen minutes out of town, Andi spotted the white, smooth surface of the reservoir wedged between the low hills, and realized this was where Cade had brought her, only she didn't recall how to get to his cabin.

She parked on the edge of the ice, debating what to do. She could see four-wheelers and pickups parked out on the ice beside a dozen or more fishing shacks spread along the reservoir, but she wasn't about to drive her car out there because she could also see places where the ice looked thin or had a break in it. One of those shacks was Cade's.

At the sound of a four-wheeler coming across the ice, she got out of her car and waved down the man driving.

"You can drive out on the ice, it's plenty solid," the fishermen said over the thump of the four-wheeler's engine.

Andi stared out at the frozen expanse. She could see

places where the ice had buckled. There wasn't a chance she was going to drive out there. It had been frightening enough just driving out from town on the snow-packed highway even with the new tires the automotive shop had put on for her when they'd added the head-bolt heater for the engine to keep it warm.

As if seeing her hesitation, the fisherman added, "Or I could give you a ride." He motioned to the seat behind him on the four-wheeler.

At least a four-wheeler would be lighter than a car, and the man obviously knew where to go to avoid any thin ice. At least she hoped so.

"Thank you. I will take you up on your kind offer," she said.

"Best get your warmest clothing out of the car," he suggested.

She grabbed her hat, mittens and scarf from the car and waddled over to the four-wheeler to awkwardly climb on behind him. She would never get used to all this clothing.

He gave the four-wheeler gas and they sped off down the rocky shore, bouncing along until they hit the ice of the reservoir.

They raced across the frozen expanse, the cold air making her eyes tear. She hung on for dear life expecting to hear the crack of the ice followed by the deadly cold splash of the frigid water.

After what seemed like forever, her driver slowed the four-wheeler, coming to a stop next to what looked like a large outhouse. To her surprise, she could see that it had a stovepipe and smoke was blowing horizontally across the gray sky the moment the wind caught it. Snow had been packed around the bottom of the shack except in front of the door.

"Cade," the man called. "You've got a visitor."

* * *

Cade was half-afraid it would be his brother with an arrest warrant.

The first thing Cade had done after talking to Carter back in town was head out to the cabin. He owned half a dozen guns that he kept in a safe in the back room of the cabin. He used to hunt with his father and he kept a .357 Magnum out for protection although he'd never had to use it for that.

Once inside the cabin, he'd gone right to the back bedroom, opened the closet and turned on the light so he could open the safe. It held twelve rifles. He had only three in it and a couple of shotguns along with the .45 his father had given him.

As he turned the dial, his fingers trembling as he tried to remember the combination, he recalled the day Grace had asked him what was in the safe.

"Guns."

She'd raised a brow and he'd laughed.

"You're in Montana. Practically everyone owns at least one, most a whole lot more than that. We still hunt in this state."

"Can I see them?" she'd asked.

"Sure. Have you ever shot a pistol?"

She'd shaken her head. "Could I?"

He recalled her excitement, his mouth going dry, his stomach roiling. Right away, she'd taken to shooting the .45 his father had given him.

"It looks like something one of the Old West outlaws would have used," she'd said.

He hadn't told Andi, but he was more than aware of Grace's interest in outlaws. He'd thought of it more as an interest in the history of the area and he'd encouraged it, wanting her to feel about this place as he did.

He heard a click and reached for the safe's handle, half praying the .45 would be there and half hoping it wouldn't. Without the gun, Carter couldn't prove that the bullet that killed Houston Calhoun had come from Cade's pistol.

But the gun might also clear him—and Grace as well. He'd been praying that would be the case as he'd opened the safe door.

He'd had a bad feeling even before he opened the safe door that the .45 wouldn't be there.

If Grace shot her brother with it, then she would have gotten rid of the gun, right?

Or put the gun back where it would be found long after she was gone to incriminate Cade.

The gun wasn't where he usually kept it.

Panicked, he'd begun to search the other drawers, knowing he wasn't going to find it. He had sat down on the hardwood floor, sick at heart with what this meant. The only person who could have taken the gun was Grace. Starr, he reminded himself. There had been no Grace.

His heart had sunk with the realization that he hadn't known his wife at all. He'd trusted her. When he'd opened the safe that day to teach her how to use a gun, he'd let her see the combination—no doubt exactly why she'd asked him to teach her to shoot. He would bet Starr Calhoun and guns were no strangers to each other.

He'd gotten up from the floor, closed the safe door and called his brother with the bad news.

All Carter had done was swear. The loss of the .45 was a double-edged sword. Without the gun, Cade couldn't prove he was innocent of Houston Calhoun's murder. But with it, the gun might have seen him straight to prison.

As he'd left the cabin to go down to his fishing shack

he was thankful at least that Starr hadn't put the gun back into the safe to frame him for murder.

Maybe there was a little Grace in her after all.

He'd gone fishing, just wanting to be left alone. And he had been until now.

Andi watched as a plywood door scraped open and Cade Jackson looked out. He appeared anything but pleased to see her as she swung off the four-wheeler, thanked the fisherman for the lift and waited for him to speed off again before she looked at Cade.

"Aren't you going to invite me in?" she asked when he said nothing.

Without answering he disappeared back inside, but left the door ajar. She moved across the glare of wind-scoured ice and stepped inside.

Being from Texas she'd never seen an ice-fishing house except on the movie *Grumpy Old Men*. This one was a lot like Cade's apartment—small and light on amenities.

"Watch your step," he said, moving around a large square hole in the ice to close the door behind her.

They were instantly pitched into darkness. The only light came from below her feet. The ice seemed to glow, the large hole cut into it like a wide-screen television.

She let out a cry of surprise as several fish crossed the open water in the hole and heard Cade's amused chuckle.

He pointed to a small folding stool. "Since you're here you might as well sit down."

He picked up what looked like a metal pitchfork and stood over the hole in the ice as fish passed beneath them.

"You don't use a fishing pole?" she asked.

He shook his head and motioned for her to be quiet.

Suddenly a large fish appeared. Cade moved so fast she almost missed it.

An instant later he drew the speared fish out of the water and grinned at her. "Hungry?"

"I need to tell you something," she said. "It's about the man who attacked me yesterday."

"Not on an empty stomach, okay?" He gave her a pleading grin.

She nodded, but as they left the fishing house she couldn't help but feel they were being watched.

Chapter 11

Arlene Evans was at the end of her rope by the time she reached the mental hospital. For days she'd done everything possible to discover the identity of the man who'd fathered Charlotte's baby.

Her daughter had observed her efforts with sly amusement. "You'll never find out because you wouldn't be able to guess in a million years."

And now Arlene had just spent hours in the car with her pregnant, obstinate daughter and her reticent son.

"Why do we have to go in?" Charlotte whined as Arlene Evans came around to the passenger side of the car, opened the door and ordered her adult children to get out.

"Your sister has asked for the three of us to come to Family Day and we didn't drive all this way for you not to go in," Arlene snapped. "Now get out and shut up."

Charlotte shot her a deadly look but climbed out of the car, making Arlene wonder how she could have missed the fact that her daughter was pregnant.

She flushed with shame as she watched her son slowly climb out of the backseat. He wore black combat boots, a tattered pair of jeans with huge holes in them, a T-shirt with obscenities scrawled across the front and a gray knitted-wool stocking cap, his dirty hair sticking out.

"Do you have to wear that hat?" she demanded.

He grunted and walked toward the gate into the mental hospital.

Arlene followed Bo and Charlotte, afraid there was even worse waiting inside for her.

The eldest daughter of Arlene Evans watched from the third floor window, smiling to herself. The family had arrived. Bile rose in her throat. Violet Evans had looked forward to this day almost from the first.

Soon it would be all worth it. Soon she would walk out those doors and be a free woman. Excitement rippled through her, but she quickly squelched it.

She had to be very careful now and not overplay her hand. It would be difficult to be in the same room as her mother and not go for her throat. Not to mention let on her feelings toward her siblings.

But she had come this far using her brains and the drugs her brother had been able to sneak in for her.

She knew the picture she had to portray during Family Day. As long as she kept her true feelings hidden…

She laughed to herself. She'd been hiding her feelings since she was old enough to realize what a disappointment she was to her mother.

Violet hadn't known why her mother found her lacking until she got older and heard some of the girls at school saying she was ugly.

She had looked into the mirror and seen a version of her own mother's face.

That's when she'd known the reason her mother hated her: her mother saw herself in her oldest daughter.

"Violet?"

She turned to see the nurse coming down the hall.

"It's time. Your family has arrived and they're anxiously waiting downstairs to see you."

Sure they were. Violet put on her timid, withdrawn look as she nodded and let the nurse lead her down to Family Day.

After a short walk to his cabin, Cade filleted the fish, seasoned it and put the Northern Pike on the grill while Andi made a salad. He watched her out of the corner of his eye, her movements precise. He liked her hands. They were small, the fingers tapered, the nails a pale pink, the skin smooth as porcelain.

"What?" she asked and he realized she'd caught him staring at her.

"You make a nice salad."

She seemed to relax. She'd probably been as surprised as he was when he suggested they take the fish back to his cabin for lunch. He'd never thought he'd bring her back here.

"Mind setting the table?" he asked, getting down two plates, knowing she wouldn't.

He watched her for a moment, warmed by the heat of the kitchen—and the closeness of another human being—before going back outside to the grill.

Lifting the lid on the charcoal grill, he turned the fish. Grace had suggested they get a stove with a grill so he wouldn't have to cook outside in the winter.

But he liked grilling when it was cold. Even when it was snowing as it was now. He liked seeing his breath mingle with the scent of the Northern Pike filets grilling just under the metal hood.

He felt his stomach rumble and tried to remember the last time he'd been this hungry. Most of the time he forgot to eat and then just cooked up something to keep himself going.

When the fish was ready, he went inside for a serving platter. Andi had set the table in front of the fire. The flames played off her face as she looked up at him. Her features softened and she smiled.

"How is it out there?" she asked. She'd been shocked that he planned to grill the fish outside in this kind of weather.

"It's ready. I hope you're hungry."

She nodded. "Starved."

He went back outside in the falling snow and cold and shut down the grill. With the fish filets on the serving plate he returned to the cabin to find her waiting by the door.

She took the plate from him. "Oh, it smells wonderful," she said as she carried it over to the table.

Cade knocked the snow from his coat and hat and slipped off his boots before joining her.

She had turned on the stereo. One of his Country and Western CDs was playing softly.

"I hope you don't mind," she said, obviously seeing his surprise. "This CD is one of my favorites."

He shook his head. It was also one of his favorites.

They ate listening to the music, neither saying much other than to compliment the food.

"Your first Northern Pike?" he asked.

She nodded. "It's good."

"So's the salad." They were being so polite to each other it was making him nervous. "Look," he said, putting down his fork. "There must be something you and I can talk about other than criminals, isn't there?"

She smiled. "Who knows? We've never tried."

He returned her smile and picked up his fork. "So let me guess, your favorite food is Tex-Mex."

She laughed. "How did you know?"

They spent the rest of the meal talking about food, music, television and books that they liked, bands they'd heard, places they wanted to visit.

After they finished eating, they cleared the dishes together. As he washed and she dried, she told him about what the attacker had said to her.

"I have some news, too," he said and told her about the talk he'd had with his brother—and about the missing .45.

Arlene squirmed in her chair as she heard footfalls coming down the hall. It had been months since she'd seen her daughter Violet. Not since the night her eldest daughter had tried to smother her with a pillow.

She didn't like to recall the events of last summer. All her near-death "accidents." Sometimes late at night when she couldn't sleep she would know that she had done a horrible disservice to Violet.

She hadn't wanted the child, hadn't wanted to be pregnant, certainly hadn't enjoyed lovemaking with Floyd. But as her mother said, beggars can't be choosers.

And that was how Arlene had gotten pregnant. In the backseat of a beat-up old sedan. Floyd had only agreed to marry her after her father had threatened him. They'd gone before a justice of the peace over in Choteau and come back to Whitehorse married.

While she was tied down with a squalling baby, Floyd escaped to the barn or the tractor out in a field or town for fertilizer.

Arlene had hated marriage, motherhood and the baby. She'd just been thankful that the day would come that she could marry Violet off.

And then along had come Bo almost ten years later and then Charlotte shortly after that. Both times only because Floyd had forced himself on her.

After that, she saw even less of Floyd, which suited them both fine. Until last summer when he'd left her for good.

Arlene watched the doorway for Violet, telling herself that it wasn't too late to make it up to her.

But then her daughter appeared in the doorway, stooped, lanky, dull brown hair, hollow eyed, resembling a kicked puppy, and Arlene knew that coming here had been a huge mistake.

Andi couldn't believe Houston was dead. Murdered. "Your brother doesn't think you killed him."

"No. But I have to admit, I look guilty as hell," Cade said. "Not only was it my gun, but everyone knows how I felt about Grace. For the last six years I've mourned the loss of her and our baby. I would have done anything to protect Grace and our baby."

"Even kill?"

Cade looked away for a moment. "I didn't kill Houston in case you're wondering."

"I wasn't. I know you didn't kill anyone."

He turned back to look at her again. "You could be wrong about me."

She shook her head. "I'm a pretty good judge of character since I make a living telling other people's stories." She said nothing for a moment, then, "You don't seem all that surprised that Lubbock's after the money."

"I'm not. I've thought this was about the money since

I found out about it. I just wasn't sure how *you* fit into it." He met her gaze. "Did you call 911 from your apartment?"

"No, just as I told your brother. I can't explain it. Unless Lubbock called right before he grabbed me. Maybe it was a test to see if I would tell your brother what he said."

"Unless there was someone else in your apartment and the whole thing was a setup," Cade said.

"You don't think I—"

He cut her off. "No. I was thinking more of Starr. If you're right and she's alive."

"Then that would mean that Houston hid the money and she and Lubbock don't know where."

He shrugged as he finished the dishes and drained the water in the sink, reaching for the end of her dish towel to dry his hands.

"Have you ever caught a fish through a hole in the ice?" he asked with an obvious change of subject.

"Do I have to spear it?"

He laughed. "No, you can use a hook and a line if you're squeamish."

"I'm not squeamish," she said.

He'd cocked a brow at her. "It's still light out if you'd like to go back down and fish for a while."

Neither Arlene nor Bo nor Charlotte moved as Violet stepped tentatively into the room.

"What do you have to say to your daughter, Mrs. Evans?" the doctor said, an edge to his voice.

Arlene found her feet and, opening her arms, moved toward Violet. "How are you, dear?"

Violet cringed as her mother touched her.

"It's all right, Violet," the doctor said. "Please come in and join us." He got up to close the door.

Arlene felt his gaze as it swept from her to Charlotte to Bo. He was looking at the three of them as if they were the ones who needed psychiatric counseling.

Violet, her head down, her fingers picking nervously at the sacklike dress she wore, took a chair near the doctor. Arlene sat down again although what she really wanted was to flee. She should never have come here let alone brought Bo and Charlotte. This was all about blaming the family, making them feel bad.

"Violet, what is it like having your family here?" the doctor asked.

"Good."

"Isn't there something you want to say to them?" he asked.

Violet slowly raised her gaze to her mother. "Where's Daddy?"

Arlene winced. Daddy? Violet and her father had never been close. He'd avoided the child just as he had them all.

"Floyd left after what you did, Violet. I have no idea where he is," Arlene said, getting angrier by the moment.

"Oh," Violet said and dropped her gaze again.

"Is there something you'd like to say to your daughter, Mrs. Evans?" the doctor asked pointedly.

Violet raised her head. What could have been a smile played at her lips. Arlene looked into her daughter's eyes and winced at the carefully hidden hatred she saw there.

"No," she said. "There isn't."

The doctor looked shocked. He blinked then turned to Charlotte. She was playing with her hair and looking bored. "Perhaps you'd like to say something to your sister?"

"Do they make you wear those awful clothes?" Charlotte asked.

Violet let her gaze slide to her sister. She looked sad and embarrassed as she touched the worn fabric. "I didn't have any of my own clothes."

The doctor looked down at the notebook on his lap. Arlene hadn't seen him take any notes. He seemed stunned by the lack of interaction between them.

"What about you?" he asked Bo. "Isn't there something you'd like to say to your sister?"

Bo also had a bored expression. Slouched in his chair, he scratched his neck for a moment and considered Violet.

"When are you getting out of here?" he asked.

Violet gave him a cheerless smile. "I don't know. When I'm well."

"You look…" Arlene couldn't finish. There was a lump in her throat. "Your sister is pregnant." The words just came out. She felt shame that they sounded like an accusation. But then everything had always been Violet's fault in one way or another.

Violet looked at Charlotte. "A baby? Oh, I'd love to see it when it's born." She looked hopefully at the doctor. "Do you think there's any chance…"

"We'll have to see," he said noncommittally. "You keep making improvements like you have…"

Arlene rose. "I'm glad you're getting well, Violet."

"Thank you, Mother," Violet said, lowering her head again.

"We should go," Arlene said.

"Violet, was there anything else you wanted to say?" the doctor prodded.

She nodded. "The doctors told me what I did." She raised her head. Huge tears welled in her eyes and slowly rolled down her cheeks as she looked at her mother. "I can't believe I would do such a thing. I'm so sorry. I just hope you can forgive me someday." Violet began to cry softly.

Arlene nodded and turned to give her two youngest an impatient look. They finally rose to leave.

"It was good seeing you, Violet," Charlotte said. "If my baby is a girl maybe I'll name her after you."

As Bo walked by Violet, he knelt down and took both her hands in his. "Take care, Vi." He rose again and walked out the door.

Arlene saw Violet palm something in her hand, then secretly slip it into her pocket.

Bo had given his sister something. A note? What?

Violet rose as Arlene started to move past her. Standing, she and her mother were about the same height. "Thank you for coming, Mother."

Arlene was still shocked by the hatred she'd seen in Violet's eyes earlier. Now that hatred was watered down with tears, but still shining brightly, leaving little doubt what Violet would do if she was ever released from here.

"My daughter isn't well," Arlene said to the doctor suddenly. "She has no business leaving here. Ever."

Violet seemed to crumble as she dropped into her chair and put her face in her hands.

"Really, Mrs. Evans," the doctor chided. "Violet was sick but now she is trying so hard to get well."

"You don't know her like I do," Arlene argued over the quietly weeping Violet curled up in her chair like a child. "All this is for show. She wants you to believe that *we're* the problem—not her, but it's not true. You can't let her out."

"That decision isn't up to you, Mrs. Evans," the doctor said sharply. "Violet is an adult. When she's well, she has a right to make a life for herself outside these walls."

"She's fooled you, but she hasn't me," Arlene said.

"Look in her pocket. I saw her take something from her brother and put it in her pocket."

The doctor started to refuse but Arlene insisted.

"I'll show you how deceptive my daughter is, Doctor."

With apologies to Violet, he checked one pocket of her loose jumper, then the other.

"Her pockets are empty, Mrs. Evans," he said angrily. "Are there any more allegations you'd like to make before you leave?"

Violet raised her head just enough that Arlene could see the triumph in her eyes.

What had Violet done with whatever it was her brother had given her?

"I'm going to have to ask you to leave now, Mrs. Evans," the doctor said. "I won't have you upsetting my patient further. You will not be welcome here again."

"Don't worry," Arlene said. "I won't be back and I'll fight to keep Violet in here where she belongs. You can't let her come back to Whitehorse. Ever."

"Goodbye, Mother," Violet said, teary voice cracking.

Arlene stopped at the door but she didn't look back. "Goodbye, Violet." As she left, she prayed she'd never set eyes on her oldest daughter again.

Chapter 12

Andi couldn't remember a time she'd enjoyed more. For a while she forgot about everything and just enjoyed herself. This Cade Jackson was fun. They'd laughed a lot, spending most of their time in the ice-fishing house talking until it was too dark to see the fish any longer.

They walked back up to the cabin and she was surprised to see that Cade was armed. She hadn't seen him get the pistol before they'd gone down to the fishing shack. He must have had it hidden under his coat.

It reassured her. She'd thought he hadn't been taking any of this seriously. But the gun proved that he had. The man continued to surprise her.

A sliver of moon peeked out of the clouds and for once it wasn't snowing. The air was cold but walking next to Cade she felt more than toasty, the snow crunching under their feet. The night was bright enough that they could see for a great distance in this open country.

Andi realized she wasn't afraid with Cade. There was

a strength about him, a determination that might even match her own. He understood the danger they were in, and she felt safe here with him.

Without looking at her, he said, "You've been through a lot with what happened to your father, the stalker in Texas and now this."

"I was in the public eye," she said, thinking about what Bradley had said. "Sometimes viewers think they know you. They would send presents or cards and letters. One time on the air I mentioned that my favorite flower was the daisy. I got dozens of daisies over the next few weeks. It's amazing also how much there was about me on the internet."

"But you said the stalker turned out to be someone you worked with?"

She nodded. "A woman who wanted my job, I guess. She got her boyfriend to help her."

"The police didn't suspect her right away?" he asked.

"Apparently not." Andi frowned. "I still have a hard time believing it. I met her boyfriend once when she brought him down to the station to show him around. He seemed nice."

"She must have wanted your job awfully bad," he said. "It doesn't surprise me that she could talk her boyfriend into helping her. He probably loves her."

"Or did. They both deny it, but apparently the police found evidence that ties them both into the stalking." She sighed. "Anyway, it's over. Now I feel as if I panicked unnecessarily, leaping, as it is, from the skillet into the fire."

"And you're angry with yourself, right?"

She looked over. "Yes, how did you—"

"I've been doing a little running myself so I know the feeling." There was a smile in his voice.

"At least you were grieving for the death of the woman you loved," she said.

He chuckled softly, stopping at the top of the rise to turn to look back at the frozen reservoir. "That's what I told myself. But I think you and I know it was a little more complicated than that." He grew silent for a moment. She could hear the sound of the wind in the trees behind the dark outline of the cabin.

"You asked me the other day if I hadn't seen something that made me question my relationship with Grace," he said quietly.

She held her breath.

"They were such little things. Little doubts that nagged at me all these years even after she was gone." He looked over at her. "A part of me knew something was wrong. I could see her struggling sometimes." He chuckled. "I thought it was a man. The day I met her beside the highway changing her flat tire, I knew she had some past she was escaping from. I just assumed it was from a relationship. When I caught her looking anxious or worried, I told myself she was thinking about him."

Her heart went out to Cade. "I'm sorry it was so painful. I guess the truth wouldn't have been any easier, though."

He laughed and they started walking again toward the cabin. "No, the truth I'm afraid is going to get us both killed."

Cade didn't add that being with a desirable woman again was also helping. He felt as if they were in the same boat. Both of their lives on the line. Both of them fighting the ghosts of their pasts.

It surprised him that he could feel that way about Andi

Blake. Oh, desire, that was a given. Same with compassion for what she'd been through.

But at some point, he'd actually started liking her. A reporter. He never would have expected that in a million years.

"My car's on the other side of the lake," she said when they reached his front porch.

He nodded and looked back toward the reservoir. He could barely make out the shape of the fishing shack in the blackness of the winter night.

Across the lake, he could see multicolored Christmas lights glittering. He'd forgotten about Christmas, but in a few days he was expected at a party where his brother would be asking the woman he loved to marry him.

The clouds parted and a sliver of silver moon appeared, then dozens of tiny sparkling stars. Suddenly Cade felt very small in this huge universe. He looked up. A few more stars popped out of the clouds while tiny ice crystals sifted down from the cold blue of the sky.

The way he was feeling, he knew the smart thing was not to invite her in but to give her a ride to her car and go on back to his apartment tonight.

But he'd seldom, if ever, done the smart thing. He'd proved that by falling in love with Grace Browning.

Earlier he'd been glad to see that Andi had taken his advice and gotten some warm Montana clothing. She was bundled up, a thick knitted cap pulled down over her dark hair. In the faint moonlight, he could see that her cheeks were flushed from the cold, her eyes sparking.

He reached over and grabbed a handful of the front of her coat and pulled her to him.

She stumbled into him, her eyes widening.

"There's something I've wanted to do since the first time I laid eyes on you," he said.

He cupped Andi's face in his gloved hands and pulled her into a kiss.

He felt her resist for an instant, tears welling in her eyes and then his lips touched hers. He felt a hot tear, tasted the salt. He pulled her into his arms, holding her tightly, telling himself he was in over his head.

But this felt right and for the first time in years, he wasn't afraid to feel. Her lips parted, her breath warm and sweet. He drew her closer, deepening the kiss.

Desire shot through him, heating his blood. He encircled her in his arms, pulling her as close as possible through all their winter clothing.

It wasn't close enough. He drew back from the kiss and realized he'd never wanted a woman the way he wanted this one. Not even Grace. He heard the soft intake of her breath as he pulled her toward him again, dropping his mouth to hers.

She answered in kind as he reached behind him and opened the door to the cabin.

In a flurry of clothing and kisses, they stripped off their coats and boots, hats and mittens, peeling off pants and sweaters as they stumbled locked together toward the couch.

The fire he'd made earlier before dinner had burned down to a few glowing embers, but they didn't need the heat. They were making their own.

Her skin felt on fire as he brushed his lips along her throat. He could feel her pulse quicken as he slipped his fingers beneath the thin fabric of her bra. Her nipples were hard and erect. She moaned as his fingers brushed over one then the other. He dropped his mouth to her warm breast, making her moan, and ran his hand over her flat, smooth, warm belly to slip into her panties.

She was hot and wet and pressing into him with a

fierceness that matched his own. He looked into her eyes and saw that there would be no turning back for either of them as his fingers found her center.

Andi arched against him. From the moment Cade had pulled her to him on the porch, she knew she was a goner. She'd wanted him on a primal level that terrified and excited her. There was no thought, only the feel of him and the fire that shot through her straight to her core.

His fingers filled her as his mouth came back to hers. She could feel herself rising higher and higher, the pleasure building in intensity until she thought she couldn't take another instant. His skin was like a flame against hers, stoking the fire inside her. She could feel it building and building and suddenly she was bursting beneath him.

She gasped and cried out, her head thrown back, pleasure coursing through her veins. She barely felt him remove her bra, then slip her panties down her legs. She lay naked on the leather couch, him above her.

In his dark eyes, she saw raw need flash like a hot spark ready to catch fire. It fanned her own longing as he stood and took off his pants and dropped his boxers to the floor.

With an abandon she never knew she possessed, she surrendered to him completely as inside the cabin, they made love through the night completely unaware that outside it had begun to snow again.

The next morning, Cade left Andi sleeping in the cabin and went outside.

From the cabin he had a good view of the area. He checked the trees behind the cabin and the arena first, looking for fresh tracks in the snow. There were none.

As far as he could tell no one had been around during the night. The news flooded him with relief.

Yesterday he'd thrown caution to the wind, feeling as if he'd been playing Russian roulette. He'd gone fishing when he should have been worrying about the Calhouns and his future. And even crazier, he'd curled up with Andi, making love all night, when they both were in danger.

Not that he regretted either. The memory of their lovemaking warmed him on the cold, snowy morning.

This morning, though, he couldn't keep pretending this mess was going to just go away. He knew what he had to do to save himself and Andi. They were in it together now and no matter what she said, he'd gotten her into it. He was the one who'd married Starr Calhoun.

As he walked down to the ice-fishing shack watching for tracks coming up from the reservoir, he thought of the outlaw books Grace had loved. She'd reveled in this part of Montana's past. The Curry brothers, Butch Cassidy and the Sundance Kid and many more had made this area home for a while.

Some of them were so much a part of the community that area ranchers would hide them from posses and even lie on the stand for them. Not that some didn't fear them and the repercussions if they hadn't.

As he walked, the fresh snow crunched under his boots and his breath in the cold morning air came out in frosty white puffs. It was early enough that he didn't see any other fishermen down by the lake. He liked the utter silence of winter mornings. It was his favorite time.

And this morning he really needed the time to get himself together before he saw Andi. They needed a plan. There were decisions to me made. Lubbock, or whoever had attacked her, would be back. Cade didn't doubt that for a moment.

How the hell they were going to find the missing money, he had no idea. But they had to at least make the attempt because if he was right, someone had been watching them for several days now.

He could hear the ice cracking closer to shore, but he wasn't worried. The ice was thick and would be for months.

He couldn't help but think about yesterday with Andi. He'd had fun. That surprised him. She'd let down her defenses and he had, too. Maybe that's why their love-making had been like none he'd ever experienced. He got the impression that she'd been so busy building her career that she hadn't dated much—let alone gotten close to a man.

As he neared his ice fishing shack, he slowed. The wind had blown long into the night, but he could still make out the slight indentations in the snow on the lea side of the shack that had once been footprints.

The house was covered with frost. The wind had drifted the new snow up one side of the wall and left the surface of the reservoir perfectly smooth and untracked except where someone had stood.

He pulled the .357 Magnum from under his coat and stepped as quietly as possible to the door. As he cautiously pulled it open, the breeze caught the door and threw it back. He jumped back and the door banged against the side of the shack and stayed there. Then everything was deathly silent again.

No sound came from inside. Cade waited a few more seconds before he carefully peered around the edge of the door.

The first thing that hit him was the scent. The ice was

an aquamarine-green—except where he'd cut the large rectangular hole. Yesterday there had been open water in the hole but during the night it had iced over.

There was something dark smeared along the edge of the thicker ice next to the iced-over hole that made his mouth go dry. He'd smelled enough dead animals as a ranch boy to recognize it as blood.

His pulse drummed in his ears so loudly he almost didn't hear the approaching crunch of boot soles on the new snow. The steps were slow, tentative.

He flattened himself to the side of the shack, the gun ready, but not knowing which side of the shack the person would come around.

"Cade?" Andi said as she appeared to his right by the open door of the fishing shack. She looked from his face to the gun in his hand.

"Stay back," he snapped as he stepped to the doorway to shield her.

But she'd already looked in and no doubt seen the smear of blood on the ice. Her eyes widened and a gasp escaped her lips. As she stumbled back, one gloved hand over her mouth, he turned to see movement beneath the ice.

Only this time it wasn't fish.

A face appeared beneath the ice. The skin was drawn and blue, the mouth open as if gulping for breath, the pale blue eyes staring blankly up from the freezing water.

Andi couldn't get warm. She stood in front of the fire Cade had built before his brother had asked him to wait outside in the patrol car.

She rubbed her hands together and looked down into the flames. The sheriff had taken her statement and now stood next to her, making notations in his notebook.

"Where were you last night?" he asked.

"Here. All night."

He looked up from his notebook. "Can anyone verify that?"

"Cade."

He studied her for a long moment then wrote something down in the notebook. He'd already made it perfectly clear that he didn't approve of her—especially her and Cade. She wanted to assure him that she would never hurt his brother, but the truth was, she already had and she had no way of knowing what the future held any more than Cade or the sheriff did.

"Have you ever seen the deceased before?"

"No." Although she suspected she knew who he was.

"You have any idea why he was killed?"

"No."

"You don't think it might have something to do with why you're in Whitehorse?"

"I came here for a job."

"Right. You just happened to stumble across the fact that Grace Jackson was really Starr Calhoun."

"I didn't bring the Calhouns to Montana."

He nodded solemnly. "But you're up to your neck in this."

"I'm a reporter. I go after stories. I don't expect you to believe this, but someone got me involved in this—not the other way around."

He looked skeptical, just as she'd known he would. "I don't want to see my brother hurt."

"It's a little too late for that."

"I wasn't talking about Starr Calhoun," he said, glancing toward the front window. "He's vulnerable. You're the first woman since Starr. Add to that he feels responsible for what's happening."

She wanted to argue that none of this was her fault, but she knew that wasn't necessarily true.

"When this is over, you'll make headlines again," the sheriff said. "You'll go back to your old job or get offered an even better television job in some big city. Cade won't ever leave Montana. If you think he will, then you don't know him. And even if you were able to get him to leave, well, a big city would kill him. He's a cowboy. He has to have room. This is his home."

She said nothing as he rose from his chair.

He looked as if there was more he wanted to say, but after a moment he turned and left.

When she heard the door close, she walked to the window and peeked out from behind the curtains. Cade was standing by the patrol car. He got in as Carter went around to the driver's side.

Andi turned from the window and stepped over to the fire again, chilled. She knew that Cade had recognized the resemblance between his deceased wife and the man under the ice. It was a Calhoun. It had to be Lubbock since Cade had told her that some remains found down in Old Town had turned out to be those of Houston Calhoun—and according to the crime lab, he'd been there about six years.

If the body was Lubbock Calhoun's, which she suspected, then she had to ask herself: Who killed him?

She felt another chill.

What if Starr really had faked her death and was not only alive, but back in Whitehorse?

Cade watched a herd of antelope race across a windscoured snowy hillside just beyond the cabin as his brother started the patrol car and turned on the heater. The heater blew cold air, but not nearly as cold as Cade felt.

His brother was too calm, too much a cop on a case, and Cade knew he was in bad trouble.

"Any idea what a dead man was doing in your fishing shack?" Carter asked after a moment, pulling out his notebook and pen.

"I wish I knew."

"Where were you last night?"

Cade looked over at his brother. "In the cabin with Andi."

Carter swore. "We have an ID on the dead man from some jailhouse tattoos that we knew of from the APB out on him. His name is Lubbock Calhoun."

Cade nodded. No surprise there. He'd known the man was a Calhoun from his resemblance to his sister. Lubbock would have been his first guess since they'd known he had broken parole after getting out of prison.

"Had you ever seen him before?" Carter asked, writing down his responses.

"No."

"You have any idea who might have killed him?"

"None."

"When was the last time you used your fishing spear?"

"Yesterday."

"It appears he was killed with your spear," Carter said. "What are the chances the only prints on it will be yours?"

"I'd say pretty darned good."

His brother shook his head. "This all started with that damned reporter."

"Don't blame her. It actually started with Starr."

Carter put his notebook and pen away. "You're sure Ms. Blake didn't slip out last night while you were sleeping?"

He met his brother's gaze. "I didn't get much sleep last night so yes, I'm sure."

Carter swore. "Glad to see you took my advice and haven't gotten involved with her."

"I know you think I have lousy luck with women," Cade said. "But I loved Grace. Starr *was* Grace, a woman who wanted our baby, wanted this life with me and wanted to put all the rest behind her. I believe that with all my heart. Who knows how this would have ended if she hadn't died?"

Carter shook his head. "You're kiddin' yourself, bro. As long as that robbery money was missing, you and Starr, Grace, whatever, wouldn't have had a chance in hell. The only reason you haven't heard anything from this family is that Lubbock was locked up and Houston was dead. Now you've got a dead man in your fishing shack and I'm willing to bet he didn't break parole to come up here to ice fish."

"No, I think he was looking for the money. But apparently he's not the only one." Cade thought of Andi's theory about Starr. "What if Starr killed him?"

Carter shot him a look. "Starr's dead."

Cade realized it had always been coming to this. He had to know if that was her he'd buried. Or if everything he'd believed about his wife had been a lie. Otherwise, he knew he would never be able to put her to rest. "What would it take to have her body exhumed?"

"What?" Carter demanded. "You think she's *alive?*"

"I need proof that the woman who died in that car wreck was my wife. Andi thinks Starr might have faked her death and taken off with the money. Under the circumstances, I think we should know who all the players are, don't you?"

His brother looked at him. "You knew her. You can't

really believe that your wife could kill someone in cold blood with a fishing spear?"

"Not the woman I married, no," Cade said. "But I think Starr Calhoun might have been more than capable of murder. My .45 is missing and Houston Calhoun is dead. Not to mention the body found in her car—if she faked her death."

Carter shook his head. "Well, at least now we have two of her brothers' DNA to compare hers to. If it's not Starr, we'll know soon enough."

Chapter 13

"It was Lubbock, wasn't it?" Andi said as Cade entered the cabin.

He nodded. "Carter ID'd him from some prison tattoos." He stepped to her, taking her in his arms. "Are you all right?"

She nodded against his shoulder, burrowing into him. The fabric of his coat smelled of the outdoors and the cold but the feel of his arms around her warmed her to her toes.

"My brother upset you." He swore as he stepped back to look into her face, holding her at arm's length. "I should never have let him talk to you alone."

She smiled at that. "Like you could have stopped him. This is a murder investigation. He's worried about you."

Cade let out a laugh. "I'm worried about me."

"If it wasn't Lubbock who got me here, then who?" she asked.

He shook his head. "We've known all along that whoever was behind this wanted the money. Someone must think I know where it's hidden."

"But who? If Lubbock was the one who was sending me the information and attacked me, then who killed him?"

Cade looked into her eyes. "I've asked my brother to see about getting Starr's body exhumed."

She stared at him. "Are you sure?"

"We have to know. If she's alive, then…" He couldn't finish at just the thought that the woman he'd loved and married was a killer.

Andi shuddered at the thought that Starr Calhoun was alive—and killing off the competition. "If she hid the money, then why wouldn't she just take it and leave?"

He shrugged. "Maybe there's more to it than money. Or maybe she can't find the spot where she hid it. Everything looks different in the winter. There's also the possibility that Houston hid it."

Andi thought about what Bradley had said. "Wouldn't whoever hid it have made some sort of map? Or at least written down the directions?"

Cade moved to the bookshelves with the outlaw books. "Grace did some drawings… I think they were in the back of one of these books. She was always sketching. She had talent as an artist."

"I can see that in her photographs," Andi said.

He glanced back at her with a grateful look that did more than warm her toes. "I still believe she wanted to be Grace."

"I think you're right." She stepped to him and put a hand on his arm. "That photograph of you in your bedroom… She loved you."

He looked away. "Here," he said, handing her a few books. "Let's see if there is some sort of map in here."

They spent the next few hours going through Grace's books. Many of them were inscribed to her from Cade with love. While there were small drawings often in the margins or notes, none of them appeared to be a map or diagram or clue to the missing money.

When they'd gone through her last book, Cade got up from the floor. "Well, that was a dead end."

Andi was just as discouraged. Why had she been given the article about Kid Curry? There had to be some connection. "I need to go to the newspaper. There might be another manila envelope waiting for me."

"I'm worried about you," Cade said. "It's not safe."

She smiled and leaned in to brush a kiss over his lips. "I'll be all right. It's Whitehorse. No one will grab me in the middle of Central Avenue. And anyway, whoever is behind this wants us to find the money. Until we do, I'm pretty sure we'll be safe."

"I hope you're right about that. I'll drive you to your car. I want to do some looking around the apartment. I'll call you if I find anything." He stepped to her, cupping her face in his hands. "Be careful. And please don't go back to your place. Stay with me at the apartment in town."

She nodded. There was no place she wanted to be other than with him right now.

He followed her into town, driving on past as she pulled into the diagonal parking in front of the newspaper building.

Getting out she fought that feeling again that she was being watched as she entered the building.

Her desk had numerous envelopes on it. She dug through, hoping for another manila envelope. At this point, she had no idea what to do next and could use all the help she could get.

But there was no manila envelope.

She did what she had to do at the paper, all the time thinking that she'd missed something at the museum.

Glancing at her watch she saw that it was still open if she hurried.

She went straight to the outlaw exhibit and, starting at the top left, studied each photo, each story. She had to have missed something.

She hadn't heard the elderly volunteer until the woman spoke. "We're closing in fifteen minutes, but you're welcome to stay until then."

"Thank you," Andi said, then noticed something she hadn't seen before. "What is that?" She pointed to a series of numbers and letters at the bottom of one of the exhibit cards, wondering if it referred to another exhibit.

"That's a geocaching site," the woman said.

"Oh, the game you play with a GPS."

"Don't let a hard-core geocacher hear you say that. They take it very seriously. There are two sites in our area. When you find the spot, you look for a container of some kind. Inside can be anything from a coin to a toy or a book to a map."

A map? Her heart began to pound. Bradley had said Starr would have had to have some way to find the money again. Like a global positioning system coordinate?

All she needed to find out was whether or not Cade had a GPS. It was too much to hope for.

But even if Cade had a GPS device, Starr wouldn't have been foolish enough to leave the site on it. She would have hidden the coordinates.

As the volunteers locked up the museum behind her, Andi glanced at her watch. It wasn't even four-thirty and it was already almost dark. She could feel the chill in the air as she called Cade's cell, too excited to wait until she got back to his apartment at the bait shop.

Starr Calhoun probably wouldn't have known about geocaching since it wasn't even started until 2000—just a year before she died.

But she could definitely have known how to use a GPS, especially if Cade had one. A lot of hunters and fishermen used them.

The phone rang four times before voice mail picked up. Disappointed, she started to hang up, then changed her mind and left a message telling him what she'd learned at the museum.

"If Starr had access to a GPS, then she might have left behind the coordinates to find the money, but for some reason hasn't been able to get to them. Call me." She snapped shut her phone, wondering where he was.

It was full dark now, the temperature dropping rapidly. Christmas lights tinkled on the houses around the museum and carols played on her car radio. She turned up the radio as she drove, surprised that the songs made her teary-eyed. She'd missed Christmas.

Up here in this part of Montana Christmas seemed so much more real than it had in Fort Worth. The snow helped considerably. But it was more than that.

It was Cade, she thought. She was falling for him. The thought sent a jolt of panic through her. She'd worked too hard at her career to fall for any man, especially one who lived in Whitehorse, Montana.

His brother was right. How could she stay here and continue her career? And she couldn't imagine Cade Jackson anywhere but here.

A part of her wanted to just keep going. Get on Highway 191 and head south until she hit Texas. But the rest of her couldn't wait to see Cade, couldn't wait to be wrapped in his arms, as she turned into the bait shop.

Her headlights flashed across the empty spot where he parked his pickup and she was filled with disappointment. She climbed out of her car and walked to the back of the building, her spirits buoying a little when she saw that there was a note on the back door.

The back door was unlocked. She reached inside to snap on the light, stepping in to read the note. A key fell out of the envelope. She picked it up and saw that it appeared to be a key to the apartment.

Andi,
I thought of a place Starr might have hidden the money. I'm driving up there. Stay here. There's a frozen pizza in the freezer. I'll be back as soon as possible.
Cade

She smiled at this thoughtfulness as she closed and locked the back door. The apartment felt cold. She kicked up the heat as she moved through it, taking off her coat. It felt strange being here without Cade.

As she neared the door to the bait and tackle shop, she noticed the thin line of light under the door.

Had a light been left on?

Even stranger, she thought, was that she felt a breeze. Almost as if the front door had been left open.

She hung up her coat and opened the door into the shop. She was hit with a wall of cold air. As she listened, she could hear the front door of the shop banging in the wind.

A faint light glowed near the front. She hurried down

the narrow aisle, fishing items stacked almost to the ceiling, anxious to get the door closed.

The temperature was supposed to drop to more than twenty below zero tonight. She hoped nothing in the shop had been ruined because of the door being left open.

At the front door, she reached out and grabbed the achingly cold handle. She had to pull with all her strength to get it closed, the wind was so strong, and snow had drifted in, making it even more difficult.

The door finally slammed with a thunderous bang. She locked it and used the dead bolt as well, wondering how it could have gotten left open. Cade, no doubt, had other things on his mind.

She was halfway back down the aisle, when she noticed that the door to the apartment was closed. Strange, since she was sure she'd left it open. She'd almost convinced herself it had been the wind, when the small light at the front of the shop went out, pitching her into blackness.

Cade Jackson had driven up into the Bear Paw mountains to the west of Whitehorse. He and Grace had picnicked there early in the fall among the ponderosa pines along a small creek.

She had been so happy that day. They'd eaten fried chicken, potato salad and fried apple pies that she'd made early that morning.

He'd been surprised how good a cook she was. They'd made love in the shade and fallen asleep.

He'd awoken to find the sun behind the trees and Grace gone.

She'd come hiking up thirty minutes later, after he called for her and hadn't gotten an answer. He had been getting worried something had happened to her.

She'd been apologetic, saying she'd just wanted to take a little walk and had been so taken with the country she'd lost track of how far she'd gone.

He'd thought it a wonder she hadn't gotten lost and said as much.

She'd told him she had a great sense of direction.

The Bear Paws were iced with snow this time of year. The picnic spot looked nothing as it had with ice covering the creek and the boughs of the pines heavy and white with the new snowfall.

He hiked in the way Grace had come out but he'd found no spot that looked like a great hiding place for three million dollars.

It was dark by the time he headed back to Whitehorse. As soon as he could get cell service, he called Andi. The call went straight to voice mail. She must have her phone turned off.

That was odd. He glanced at his watch. She should have been to the apartment by now.

That's when he noticed that he had a message. With relief he saw that it was from Andi.

He listened to it as he drove toward home, anxious to see her. Returning to the picnic spot had brought back a lot of memories—as well as doubts about Grace. How could he not have seen how secretive she was back then?

He knew he hadn't seen it for the very reason he hadn't wanted to. He'd wanted to believe she was exactly who she pretended to be.

"Geocaching?" he said and played the message a second time, realizing he'd missed something.

He listened again, then snapped the phone shut. "Sorry, Andi, it was a great idea, but I don't have a GPS," he said to the empty pickup.

But maybe Grace had one. No, not Grace, Starr. There

was no Grace. The only way she could be more dead to him was if Starr was alive and he found himself coming face-to-face with her.

He turned on the radio, trying to exorcise the memories and not worry about Andi. Christmas carols. It was only a few days until Christmas and he hadn't even shopped.

Not that he'd shopped the last six years, but this year he'd been starting to look forward to it.

As he saw the lights of Whitehorse appear on the dark horizon, he felt his excitement growing. He couldn't wait to see Andi. He just hoped her car would be parked behind the shop and the lights on in the apartment. Hopefully, too, she'd cooked the pizza because he was starved.

But as he pulled in, he saw that the parking space at the back was empty. No light on in the shop. No Andi.

He felt a sliver of worry burrow under his skin as he parked and got out. The note was gone off the back door. That made him feel better.

She'd at least been here. He turned on the light. There was no smell of store-bought pizza. He closed the door behind him, sensing something wrong.

The door to the shop was standing open. The light he always left on was out and there seemed to be a cold draft coming from the darkness.

Without taking off his coat, he moved toward the shop. The moment he was out of the light of his apartment, he drew the .357 and slipped into the darkness just inside the door to let his eyes adjust before he reached for the overhead light switch.

The florescent lights came on in a blink, illuminating the whole place. He moved swiftly to the farthest aisle, where he could see the front door.

It was open. He remembered locking that door. It wasn't something he would forget.

Quickly he moved to the next aisle. Empty. Then the next. His heart dropped at the sight of the pile of spilled lures, the packages spread across the floor as if there'd been a struggle.

He rushed up the aisle and around the end to the counter. Nothing looked out of place—just as he'd feared. He hadn't been robbed. He'd known that the moment he'd seen that the big ticket items hadn't been taken—nor the cash register broken into.

At the front door, he peered out into the darkness. There were tracks in the snow, but the wind had filled them in except for slight hollows. He had no way of gauging how long ago the tracks had been made or by whom.

He slammed the door and bolted it, his heart in his throat. Where was Andi?

The phone rang, making him jump. He stared at the landline on the counter for a moment as he tried to calm down. It could just be a call asking if he had any minnows or if the fish were biting on Nelson.

But as he picked it up, he knew better.

Never in this world, though, did he expect to hear the voice he heard on the line.

His dead wife said, "Okay, now listen. You do as I say and we're all going to come out of this just fine."

"Grace?"

She didn't seem to hear, her voice clipped. "Do not go to the police. I've left my demands."

"Grace!" But she'd already hung up.

His hands were shaking so hard he had trouble putting the phone back into the cradle. He dropped to the stool behind the counter and tried to pull himself together.

Grace was alive. What about their baby? The child would be five years old.

He let out a sound, half sob, half choked-off howl.

This wasn't happening. It wasn't possible and yet he'd heard her voice. At first she'd sounded like her old self, then her words had become so unemotional. But it had been her.

Not Grace, he reminded himself. *Starr Calhoun* was alive.

And she had Andi.

He reached for the phone and checked caller ID. Blocked. He dialed *69. The phone rang and rang. No voice mail. Probably a cell phone that couldn't be traced.

He started to dial the sheriff's department, but stopped himself. Hanging up the phone, he remembered what she'd said. *I've left my demands.* He hurried through the shop back to the apartment and looked around, not seeing the manila envelope at first.

The envelope was propped against something in the corner of the counter. As he reached for it, he saw what had been behind the paper. Andi's shoulder bag with her new can of pepper spray. He'd seen it last night at the cabin and been thankful she had replaced the other can.

He'd known Andi had been taken when he'd seen the lures and realized there'd been a struggle. But seeing her shoulder bag brought it all home. Her car, though, hadn't been parked outside. He glanced in the purse, knowing her car keys would be gone. They were.

All his instincts told him to call Carter. As sheriff, Carter could put an APB out on Andi's car. Starr could be apprehended quickly—before she could do anything to Andi. But what if he jeopardized Andi's life? And what if Starr had kept the child, had the child with her?

He looked down at the large manila envelope still

clutched in his left hand. *Do not go to the police.* Starr hadn't said anything about the sheriff. She knew his brother was the sheriff. Did it mean anything that she'd said police?

Semantics. He understood what she'd meant. He couldn't risk Andi's life. Houston was dead. Murdered. Lubbock was dead. Also murdered. Starr wasn't bluffing. She had nothing to lose. What was another murder?

Carefully he opened the envelope.

The words had been cut from a magazine so it resembled a kidnapping demand. Which was exactly what it was, he realized.

You have twenty-four hours.
Or your precious reporter dies.
Find the money.
I will contact you this time tomorrow.
Don't let me down.

His mind raced. Starr. But if she'd hidden the money, then she would know where it was. And if Houston had hidden it…

This didn't make any sense. Why would Starr think he knew where the money was? He remembered Andi asking the same question. Only then they'd believed it had been Lubbock who thought Andi could find it.

He began to pace the floor, trying to put it together. Lubbock hadn't known where the money was. Houston was dead. And now Starr didn't seem to know where the money was, either? Who the hell had hidden it then?

Geocaching. He thought back to Andi's message. But he hadn't had a GPS. He'd since purchased one, but he wasn't very good at using it. Had Starr had a GPS he didn't know about and used it to hide the money and now lost the coordinates?

Twenty-four hours. He swore. How was he going to find the money in that length of time when apparently the Calhouns couldn't find it?

Calm down. Starr thinks you know something, remember something. He jumped as his cell phone rang.

With trembling fingers he dug it out. "Hello?"

"Cade?" It was his brother.

"Carter, hey."

"Did I catch you in the middle of something? You sound…odd."

"As a matter of fact…" Cade said.

"Then I'll make this short and sweet. I got the judge to approve an emergency exhumation. I had to go out on a limb to get this. I've also got the crime lab standing by to run the DNA. Everyone is grousing about the added expense since the ground had to be heated. You do realize it's almost Christmas and colder than hell. But by tomorrow, we'll have our answer."

Cade wanted to tell him not to bother. He already had *his* answer. But he couldn't do that without risking everything. He cleared his throat. "Thanks."

"This is going to be over soon," Carter said.

That's what Cade feared.

Chapter 14

In the wee hours of the morning, Cade sat bolt upright in his chair in the small apartment living room where he'd spent the night.

Daylight bled through the blinds. He hadn't slept more than a few minutes at a time, waking up with a start, everything coming back in a nauseating rush.

His head hurt, mind still reeling. But as he got up, he hung on to his waking thought.

Houston's body had been found down in Old Town, the original Whitehorse. The town had moved five miles north when the railroad came through to be closer to the line.

Assuming Starr had killed Houston, what was she doing in Old Town? There was little left in the old homestead town. A community center that served as the church and the home of the Whitehorse Sewing Circle famous for its quilts.

There were a half dozen houses, even more old foundations filled with weeds. Most of the population lived on ranches in the miles around Old Town.

The house where Houston's body had been found was known as the old Cherry House. Every kid in the county knew the place was haunted. Hell, Old Town had every reason to be haunted given everything that had happened out there over the years.

Most residents had seen lights not only in the abandoned, boarded-up Cherry House, but also in the old Whitehorse Cemetery. Along with lights, there'd been rumors handed down over the years of the eerie sound of babies crying late into the night.

Cade and his brother had played in the old Cherry House when they were kids even though every kid was told the house was dangerous and to stay out of it. Which only made him and Carter more anxious to go into the house.

He'd taken Starr to Old Town, past it to the ranch his family used to own, and he'd probably mentioned the place.

But still, how would she have gotten Houston into that house to kill him? There wasn't any way she could have carried his body down to the root cellar where his remains were found.

Unless he'd been alive when he'd gone down there. Unless she'd told him that's where she'd hidden the money.

Cade put call forwarding from the landline in the shop to his cell phone just in case Starr called again, then grabbed his coat and headed for the door. The sun on the new snow was blinding as he drove south. This time of the morning there was not another pickup on the road. He passed a couple of ranch houses, then there was nothing but the land, rolling hills that flattened as it fell toward the Missouri River Breaks.

He knew he was on a fool's errand. His brother and the rest of the sheriff's department had searched the entire house after getting an anonymous tip that there was a body buried in the house. The tip said the body was that of a woman who'd been missing for over thirty years.

As it turned out, the human remains were male and had only been in the ground not nearly as long.

Old Town looked like a ghost town as Cade drove past the community center, the cemetery up on the hill above town and turned down by the few houses still occupied to pull behind the Cherry House. He parked his pickup, hoping it wouldn't be noticed. The last thing he needed was to have some well-meaning resident call the sheriff.

Carter's men had boarded up the house again and put up No Trespassing signs. There'd been talk of burning the old place down since the county had taken it over for taxes and had had no luck selling it.

With a crowbar from his toolbox in the back of the truck, he pried up the plywood covering the back entrance enough that he could squeeze through. The job had gone much easier than he'd expected. Apparently he wasn't the first to enter the house since it had been reboarded up.

He was glad he'd brought the .357 under his coat since he wasn't sure who'd been here before him. Starr? Had she come back to the scene of the crime? It still bothered him. If she'd hidden the money, then why would she want him to find it? He had a hard time believing she couldn't find it again. She'd been nothing if not meticulous.

The house was cold, dark and dank inside. It smelled like rotting dead animals. He breathed through his mouth, waiting for his eyes to adjust to the darkness. The floor was littered with old clothing and newspapers.

Houston Calhoun wasn't the first person to die in this house. As the story went, one night more than thirty years ago, old man Cherry took his wife down to the root cellar, a dirt part of the basement where they kept canned goods, and shot her to death before blowing out his own brains.

To this day, no one knew why. The Cherrys left a son who died only weeks later in a car accident between Old Town and Whitehorse. The son left behind a wife, Geneva Cavanaugh Cherry, and two small children, Laney and Laci.

It was said that Geneva couldn't live with the death of her husband and took off never to be seen again.

Laney and Laci had been adopted by their grandparents, Titus and Pearl Cavanaugh, and both had recently returned to Old Town after years away.

So it was no wonder that people believed the house was haunted, Cade thought as he snapped on his flashlight. He had no idea what he was looking for. Something. Anything that would give him a way to save Andi.

For years he'd believed he would never get over Grace—let alone ever fall in love again.

But the first time he'd laid eyes on Andi Blake he'd felt more than desire. He'd felt a strange pull.

It had been push-pull ever since. He'd fought it with all the strength he could muster. But he'd finally given up.

He knew he would be a fool to fall in love with her for a half dozen good reasons.

But he also knew reason flew out the window when it came to love. Grace had certainly proved that. He'd known she was running from something—just as he'd known Andi Blake was. But we were all running from something, haunted by our own personal demons, he thought as he searched the ground floor before climbing the rickety stairs to the floor above.

There was less debris up here. A couple of old bed frames and mattresses that the mice had made nests in. A few old clothes that had faded into rotten rags.

He shined his flashlight on the walls. Someone had used spray paint to write obscenities on several of the walls. He moved through, stopping at a small bedroom off the back. It was painted a pale yellow. Grace's favorite color.

With the flashlight, he swept the beam across the room. His hand stopped as something registered. He sent the beam back until he saw where someone had written some words in a neat black script.

Like a sleepwalker, he stepped into the room, the beam illuminating on a couple of the words. His heart began to beat harder, his breath coming in painful puffs, the room suddenly chilling.

Only you know my heart.
Only you know my soul.
Find me for I am lost.

He shuddered as if an icy hand had dropped to his shoulder. The cold seemed to permeate the room.

Grace's meticulous handwriting. He would know it anywhere.

He closed his eyes. How long had this been there? This cry for help? He backed into a wall and leaned there, wanting to howl, his pain was so great.

He *had* known her.

But the fact that she'd been here, written this, told him how her struggle against her past had ended in this house six years ago. She had killed her brother. And more than likely with Cade's .45.

Had it been self-defense? Had they struggled?

His cell rang, startling him. He fumbled the phone out of his coat pocket and snapped it open. "Yeah?" He braced himself, ready to hear Starr's voice on the other end of the line.

Years before, he'd reached the woman who called herself Grace. He prayed now that he could reach her again in Starr. That woman had loved him enough to want to have his child. That woman hadn't been a cold-blooded killer. That woman, if he could reach her, would spare Andi.

"Cade? It's Carter. I have news."

Andi didn't know how long she'd been out. She woke sick, her mouth cottony and her stomach queasy. As she opened her eyes and sat up, she took in her surroundings in a kind of dazed, confused state.

The room was small, windowless, the floor bare except for the rug and sleeping bag beneath her. Off the room was a small doorless alcove that held nothing but a stained toilet and sink. Clearly no one lived here and hadn't for some time.

As she slipped from the sleeping bag and tried to stand, she noted that she was still fully dressed in the same clothing she'd had on yesterday. That alone she took as good news.

She could recall little except entering the bait and tackle shop to close the front door and the light going out. After that, nothing until a few moments ago when she'd come to, but she was sure she'd been drugged. Her limbs felt rubbery and useless. Her legs barely wanted to hold her up.

She heard a sound behind her and turned too quickly. Everything dimmed to black and she sat down hard on the floor. She could hear the steady, heavy tread of someone coming up what sounded like stairs. The footfalls grew louder.

As her vision cleared, she stared at the only door out of this room and saw where someone had cut a narrow slot under the door. The footfalls stopped. In the silence, she heard something metallic connect with the floor just an instant before a metal tray came sliding under the door and into her room.

"Wait!" she cried as she heard the footfalls begin to retreat. "Wait!" But whoever it was didn't wait and soon she heard nothing at all.

Her stomach rumbled as she crawled over to the tray, half afraid the food had been poisoned. But if the person had wanted to kill her, he or she certainly could have at the tackle shop.

The tray held a carton of milk, a small tub of butterscotch pudding and a heated frozen dinner of turkey, dressing, mashed potatoes, gravy and green beans. Beside it was a plastic spoon.

The food smelled wonderful, which told her she must not have eaten for a while. She had no idea how much time had passed or even if it was day or night.

She picked up the spoon, telling herself that she needed to regain her strength. As she ate, she watched the door, wondering who her captor was and why that person didn't want her to see them.

Cade braced himself, afraid just how bad the news would be. *Just don't let it be about Andi.*

"I'm at your apartment," Carter said. "Where are you?"

"At the cabin," he lied. "Why? What's up?"

"Maybe I should drive out. I'd prefer to tell you this in person."

"Just tell me, please," Cade said. He knew he sounded dog-tired, emotionally drained and scared. He was.

"Okay," Carter said hesitantly. "The exhumation took place this morning at daybreak. We wanted to get it done at a time that caused the least amount of interest."

Cade walked over to a straight-back chair that was missing most of the back. He righted the chair and sat down, leaning it against the wall for stability since he wasn't sure his legs would hold him.

"According to preliminary DNA tests done locally, the body in the grave, Cade, is Starr Calhoun."

"What?" How was that possible? He'd heard from Starr just last night at the shop. It had definitely been her voice. "That can't be right."

"It's her, Cade, and there's more. The coroner was examining the body while we were waiting for the DNA results. She was murdered. Like her brother, the slug was lodged in the skull. The wounds are almost identical. Whoever killed her covered it up with the fire, making it look as if she'd lost control and ended up down in that ravine. They must have cut the gas line to make sure the car burned."

The room began to swim. He could feel the sweat break out even though it had to be below zero in the boarded-up room of the old house.

"The slug was a .45 caliber—just like the one taken from her brother's body," Carter said. "We'll have to send the bullet to the crime lab to be positive that they came from the same gun, but I think it's a pretty good bet they did."

Cade couldn't speak. Starr murdered. Starr and his baby. Not Starr. Grace. He remembered the call from

Billings, her news, her excitement. She'd sounded so happy. She'd thought she'd put her past behind her, but it had caught up with her on the highway.

"Are you all right?" Carter asked.

"Yeah." He'd never been less all right. Except maybe the day he'd gotten the news of Grace's car accident. Both Grace and the baby gone.

"Maybe I should come out to the cabin," Carter said. "You shouldn't be alone now. Or I guess, you aren't alone. You have Andi."

You have Andi. "Yeah. I'll be okay. It just comes as such a shock."

"You realize there will be a double murder investigation," Carter was saying. "The state bureau will be involved. I've got to tell you, it doesn't look good. I know you didn't kill them. But—"

"Yeah," he said. "A judge might think I'd found out who Starr really was and did something crazy."

"Anyone who knows you knows that isn't like you," Carter said. "But with the money still missing…"

Yeah, Cade Jackson, the stable one of the family, doing something crazy. Not a chance.

"I gotta go," Cade said. "Thanks for doing this and letting me know." He hung up and sat for a moment, too stunned to stand.

Starr was dead. Murdered. And he was a suspect. It would have been funny if someone didn't have Andi.

Not Starr, anyway. But who?

He got to his feet, but stumbled and sank back down. The chair cracked, one leg barely holding as he held on for dear life. He felt as if he would explode. Turning his face up to the high pale-yellow ceiling, he felt the anguish rising in him, choking him as all his pain and anger and fear came out in a howl.

Grace and the baby. He cried for what could have been. The child he never got to know. The life he and a woman named Grace had shared. A life they never could have had even if she'd made it home that night. Grace could never have outrun her past. It would have caught up with her. If not that Christmas six years go, then this one. Blindsiding him, destroying anything they might have built.

Damn her. How could she have done this to him? And now someone had Andi, all because of Starr and her family.

Spent, he stumbled to his feet and tried to clear his head. He couldn't save Starr or the baby, but he had to save Andi. He had to find these people who had killed Grace and the baby before they killed the woman he was falling in love with.

He didn't look at the words Grace had left on the wall. Grace was his past. Her memory was fading like the walls of the old Cherry House.

The voice on the phone last night had been Starr's. That's why Carter's news had floored him. But the more Cade thought about it as he hurried down the stairs to his pickup, the more he realized why the call last night had bothered him.

The first few sentences sounded exactly like Grace, but the rest was stilted, oddly disjointed.

He drove the five miles north, going under the railroad underpass as he went through town to get to his shop.

The tape recorder and tape that Andi had left with him just days ago was right where he'd hidden it. He pulled it out and listened to the tape. He'd been right. The first two sentences were Starr talking to her brother about plans for the bank robberies. The other words had been taken from the tape, spliced together and no doubt put on another tape that was played when he answered the phone.

That meant that the person who had Andi also had a copy of the tape.

He took the message that had been left for him and read it again. All he could think about was Andi. Another storm was coming in bringing both snow and cold. Andi wasn't used to this weather. He prayed she was somewhere warm if not safe.

He told himself that he'd known Grace. He should know where she would hide the money.

Bull, he thought. If he'd really known his wife, then he would have known she wasn't who she said she was, that she was lying through her teeth, that she had three million dollars hidden somewhere.

Why hadn't she just given it to her brothers?

But he knew the answer. She would have kept it. Her ace in the hole in case the day came that someone found out who she was and she had to run.

He read the note again, then balled it up and threw it across the room. The paper rolled under an end table. He started to get up to retrieve it, when his gaze fell on a framed photograph on the wall.

When had Grace put that there? It was in such an odd place that he'd never noticed it before. His heart began to pound. She must have put it there shortly before she died. He'd been in such a fog the last six years, he'd never even noticed since they had lived out at the cabin and never spent any time in the apartment.

He reached to take it down, his fingers trembling. The frame slipped from his fingers, fell, hitting the floor, the glass shattering. He swore as he carefully picked it up and carried the frame into the kitchen to dump the broken glass into the wastebasket.

It was one of Grace's photographs. As he shook off the rest of the shards of glass, he frowned and walked back into the living area. Just as he'd suspected, this was the only photograph that Grace had put up in here.

He felt a strange chill as he stared down at the photo and recognized where it had been shot from—the property where he'd started the house they were to live in as a family.

Heart racing, he pried at the frame. Grace had always dated her photos and written down the locations on the back.

You know my heart, she'd written on the pale-yellow wall.

If he'd known her, really known her, then she'd left him this photo because she knew…

He carefully removed the back of the frame to expose the back of Grace's photograph.

There it was. Written in her meticulous hand. The date, the place and under it, taped to the back, was a small white envelope with his name on it.

Chapter 15

Cade plucked the envelope from the back of the photograph and dropped into a chair.

> Cade,
> I hope you will never see this. I plan to come back and destroy it if everything goes well. But if you are reading it, then I never got the chance. Which also means I am no longer with you.
>
> I understand if you can never forgive me for not telling you the truth. Just know that I loved you with all my heart. I was never happier than in the time I spent with you.
>
> I hope you will never have to use this because if you do, then I have failed you, failed us.
> I am so sorry,
> Grace

Printed in small letters under it were a series of numbers and letters. Latitude and longitude coordinates?

He glanced at the clock. The person who had taken Andi had given him twenty-four hours. It was only a little past noon. He had time if he hurried.

Andi felt better after she ate. She hadn't heard another sound from her captor, but she had found a note under the pudding cup telling her to slide her tray back under the door to get more food in the future.

She tested her legs and found herself much stronger. As her mind cleared, she looked for a way out. There was just the one door out. No windows.

The old door was made of thick wood. She realized the lock was also old and required a skeleton key. With growing excitement, she saw that the key was in the lock on the other side.

She looked around for something to use to push the key out. The plastic spoon was too large.

She hurried into the bathroom and removed the top on the tank. The mechanism that made the toilet flush included a long piece of small-diameter metal. Hurriedly she took it apart and armed with the piece of thin metal, went back into the other room to listen.

No sign of her captor.

She dumped everything off the tray but the napkin and carefully slid the tray through the slot under the door. Her fingers were shaking. She knew she would get only one chance.

She poked the metal rod into the keyhole, heard it hit the tip of the key. She pushed slowly and gently and felt the key start to move. *Easy. Not too fast.* Her fear was that the key would fall out of the lock, but then bounce out of the tray and out of her reach.

She felt the key give, and with her heart in her throat, heard it drop. It made a slight thump as it hit. Praying it had worked, she pulled the tray back into the room.

At first she didn't see the key. Her heart fell. But there it was, partly hidden under the napkin where it had landed. She snatched the key up and, holding her breath, listened.

No sound from outside the door.

She started to discard the thin rod from the inside of the tank, but it was the only thing she had for a weapon, although not a great one.

Then carefully, she fit the key into the lock, took a breath and let it out slowly, and turned the key, praying it would open the door.

It did. The door creaked as she opened it a crack and listened. Still no sound. She eased out into the narrow hallway and saw that she was being kept in an old, abandoned house.

At the top of the staircase, she glanced down. The house was empty except for a thick layer of dust. Her room had been cleaned. She knew she should be thankful for that.

It seemed odd that her captor had gone to the trouble as she began the slow, painful descent down the stairs, working to keep each step from groaning under her weight.

Where was her captor? Was it possible the person wasn't even in the house?

She reached the bottom step. The front door was just across the room. With the windows boarded up, she had no idea where she was or if it was even day or night.

It didn't matter. If she could get through that door and out of here...

She inched across the floor, noticing where the dust

had been scuffed with footprints. Holding her breath, she grabbed the doorknob and turned, praying it wouldn't be locked.

It wasn't.

She flung the door open, ready to run and stopped short at the sight of the person standing on the other side.

"Hello, Andi."

Cade had a friend who was into geocaching and not only owned a GPS, but also knew how to use it.

"You're sure it's easy?" he said after Franklin showed him the basics.

"Nothing to it. If you have any problems, just give me a call."

Franklin had written down basic directions on how to find a certain longitude and latitude.

"Hell, Cade, the next thing you'll do is computerize that shop of yours," Franklin had joked.

As Cade left, the promised winter storm blew in. The wind took his breath away as he ducked his head and made his way to his truck.

Once on the highway north, the wind blew the falling snow horizontally across the highway. He couldn't see his hand in front of his face. The going was slow, but nothing like it would be once he reached the rocky point by the house site. He'd have a hell of a time finding anything in this storm.

It wasn't the cold that chilled him, though, as he drove. It was the thought of Andi and the fear that she was out in this weather. He wouldn't let himself consider that even if he found the money, it might not save Andi.

Snow blew across the highway, the whiteout hypnotic. He kept his eye on the reflectors along the edge of the pavement. Otherwise he wouldn't have known where the road was.

Occasionally he would see lights suddenly come out of the storm as another car crept past. But travelers were few and far between.

Once off the main highway, the going wasn't much better. He plowed through the drifting snow, the GPS on the seat next to him. A gust of wind rocked the pickup and sent a shower of fresh snow over the hood.

He was almost on top of the bare bones of the house before he saw it and got the pickup stopped. Through the blowing and drifting snow, he stared at the weathered wood that his brother and some friends had helped him build. Why had he left it like this?

But he knew the answer. Inertia. He'd been paralyzed by his loss. Until Andi had come into his life. He wouldn't lose another woman he'd fallen in love with. This time he knew what was at stake. This time he would fight.

He picked up the GPS from the seat and turned it on, watching the screen as it searched for a satellite.

"Come on," he said and glanced at his watch.

Andi froze, so startled that the last thing she could have done was run. She was momentarily so stunned that she forgot about the weapon she had hidden in the back waistband of her jeans. *"Bradley?"*

He smiled and she might have misunderstood and run into his arms, thinking he'd come to Montana to save her. But the gun he pointed at her cleared that up at once.

"What…?"

He motioned her back and she stumbled into the house, not even aware that her teeth were chattering from the cold coming through the open doorway.

Bradley's heavy coat was covered in snow. So was

his blond hair. She stared at him, realizing that his eyes were no longer brown—but a pale blue.

She felt off balance and wondered if it was the drugs. This couldn't be real. She had to be tripping. Or asleep and all of this, including her almost escape, was just a dream with a nightmare ending.

"I don't understand," she managed to say.

"Don't you, sweetie?" he asked, sounding like his old self. "Why don't we go back upstairs and I'll explain it."

She didn't move.

"Please, Andi, I really don't want to have to hurt you."

She stared at him. "I thought you were my *friend?*"

"That was the idea," he said with a chuckle. "I'm surprised how well you've taken to Montana and Cade Jackson. Ice fishing, Andi? Really?"

He knew she'd gone ice fishing? "You've been in Montana all this time? But when I called you…"

"The joy of a cell phone, sweetie," he said.

"The TV station gossip?"

"Please, you weren't the only person I befriended at the station. I have my sources."

"You did befriend me, didn't you?" she said, remembering the times he'd gone out of his way to talk to her.

He nodded smugly. "It wasn't easy, either."

She couldn't believe she'd been so stupid. "I told you *everything.*"

"And I greatly appreciated that."

"You took the research job to get close to me."

He laughed. "Sweetie, that sounds so egotistical."

She was shaking her head, backing up until she stumbled into the wall.

"Andi. You should be flattered. I'd seen you on TV. It was that big story you broke about a woman who killed her husband. Hell, you did all the footwork for the police and solved the damned murder. I was so impressed. I said to myself that woman is really something. And, truthfully, that's when I got the idea. I knew I didn't have a lot of time with Lubbock getting out soon."

She stared at him, realizing something else about him that was different. "You aren't gay."

"No, I'm not."

"Why would you..."

He laughed, a sound that was so familiar and yet alien, that it sent chills racing down her spine.

"As male-female relationship-phobic as you were it was the only way I could get close to you," he said. "You wanted a pal, someone whose shoulder you could cry on, someone you could open up to." His expression soured. "But you certainly didn't have that problem with Cade Jackson, now did you?"

"I trusted you."

"Yes, you did. Now start climbing, sweetie, before I have to get angry with you."

She turned toward the stairs. "Why are you doing this?"

"Can't you guess?"

She stumbled on one of the steps.

"Careful," he said behind her.

"Tell me all this isn't just about the money."

"Don't turn up your nose at three million dollars. Like you said, I'm the best researcher you've ever known. I researched you, found out who you were. Imagine my shock when I discovered that nasty news about your father."

"You used that to manipulate me." She felt anger well inside her. It was all she could do not to go for the rod in hopes of catching him off guard.

"And it was so easy. This obsession you have with the Calhouns..." He *tsk-tsked.* "I just did what was necessary to get a job at your station and get close to you. I had faith in you from the beginning that you would come through for me."

She'd reached the top of the stairs and turned in shock to stare down at him as his words registered. "The researcher position… Alfred's accident—" Alfred Fisher, the station's former researcher, had been killed after a fall down his basement stairs.

"Wasn't really an accident. I just had to open up the job. And Alfred did give me a glowing recommendation before he died, which really cinched it, don't you think?"

She felt sick. Bradley was insane. He'd killed Alfred—after forcing the poor man to write him a recommendation and all so he could get to her? She could feel the metal rod digging into her back. But the barrel of the gun was pointed at her heart.

Bradley shook his head as if reading her expression. "Please don't make me shoot you, but I will since your part is really over. Now it's all up to Cade Jackson," he said calmly as he motioned her toward the room she'd just escaped from. "And you did an excellent job of motivating him, though I was a little surprised when you slept with him."

She clamped down on her anger. He was looking for an excuse to kill her. As he'd said, her part was over. She turned and walked slowly toward the room, mind racing, the pieces starting to finally fall into place.

"My stalker in Texas?" she asked.

"Me," he said with a chuckle. "I was afraid you were starting to get suspicious, though, after all what is the chance of you stumbling across a story like the Starr Calhoun disappearance? So I framed Rachel and her boyfriend. You never liked her anyway."

"And the job in Whitehorse?"

"That was just a lucky coincidence," he said. "I happened to see it. I've been following the Whitehorse paper for years. I kept thinking someone would find the money."

She had reached the doorway to the room and turned abruptly to face him. "You've known about the money for *years?*"

"You disappoint me, Andi. I really thought, as super an investigative reporter as you are, that you would have figured it out by now." He made a sad face. "I think it was getting involved with Cade Jackson. It took the edge off your instincts."

Her head still felt filled with fog from whatever drug he'd given her not to mention the shock. She shook her head, trying to take this all in and make sense of it. "You're the one who's been giving me the information. Not Lubbock."

He smiled. "Truthfully, Andi, I had my doubts that you could find the money. But I thought it was worth a shot. I knew I didn't have a lot of time with Lubbock getting out soon. After neither Houston nor Lubbock had managed to find out where Starr hid the money, I knew I wouldn't stand a chance, a stranger in town. And Lubbock was bound to head for Montana and screw everything up like he did the last time."

"The last time?" she echoed, although she knew what was coming.

"He killed Houston, then lost his temper and killed Starr when she wouldn't tell him where the money was. If he hadn't gotten arrested when he did, who knows what fool thing he would have done?"

Her breath caught in her throat. She remembered what Bradley had said about suspecting someone had dropped a dime on Lubbock and that's why he'd been picked up in Glasgow just northeast of Whitehorse.

"Lubbock, as you know, leaned toward brute force," Bradley said, eyeing her neck. "You should thank me for saving your life. If I hadn't made that call from your apartment and taken care of Lubbock…"

She stared at him, wondering why it had taken her so long to put the pieces together and suspected Bradley was right. Cade Jackson had clouded more than her judgment.

"You know what's always bothered me?" she said. "Is who taped Starr and Houston planning the robberies without them knowing it. It would have had to be someone close to them, someone really close."

He grinned at her. "Like one of them?"

With a wave of relief, the GPS picked up a satellite and Cade pressed the page button to get a list that included waypoints, as Franklin had instructed him.

He scrolled down to waypoints, pressed enter and scrolled down to new, pressed enter, and eventually scrolled down to the coordinates.

After pressing enter, he put in the letters and numbers Grace had left for him.

He followed the rest of the steps, climbing out of the pickup, shielding the screen on the GPS unit as he grabbed his shovel out of the back of the truck, and moved toward the outcropping of rocks that had been in Grace's photo.

On the screen was a compass ring and arrow, just as Franklin had said he would eventually get.

He walked in the direction the arrow pointed. At first he moved too fast, not giving the compass time to move. Numbers came up on the screen telling him what direction the spot was from him and how far so he'd know which direction to walk in.

He hadn't gone far when he spotted the cavelike hole back in the rocks. Pocketing the GPS, he stepped in out of the falling snow, imagining Grace doing the same. She would have hidden the money in the fall.

With the shovel, he pried up several rocks that obviously had been moved to the side of the opening, knowing on a warm fall day he would be able to see the cabin from here, as well as the reservoir.

The money had been stored in large plastic garbage bags and covered with rocks, too many packages for him to take them all. Taking the GPS out of his pocket, he deleted the coordinates he'd put in and put it back in his pocket.

He covered all but two bags, which he lugged back down to his pickup. There was no way anyone could have followed him. Or now be watching. Not in this storm.

Now that he had some of the money, all he had to do was wait for the call. He'd never been good at waiting. All he could think about was Andi. His fear for her had grown during the past twenty-four hours.

From the beginning, he'd known she was up to her neck in this mess. A more suspicious person might think she was involved the way she'd found out about Grace being Starr.

He drove down to the cabin, deciding to wait there rather than drive back to town in this storm. He checked his cell phone to make sure his battery hadn't gone dead before he went inside to wait.

Andi looked into Bradley's pale blue eyes. She'd known he wore contacts. She just hadn't known he'd worn brown ones to cover up his blue eyes. Just as she hadn't known that he had put a dark rinse in his hair. Or that he wasn't gay. Or that he was a liar, a master manipulator, a Calhoun.

"You're the missing brother, Worth Calhoun."

"Or Worthless, as my siblings used to call me," Bradley said with a laugh. "Being the youngest boy, I was adopted by a nice, normal family. But after college, Starr found me. She and the rest of them were always trying to involve me in their crimes. They really lacked imagination."

He had backed her to the doorway of the room. She put her hands behind her, leaning into the doorjamb, waiting for the right moment.

One thing she knew. She wasn't going back in that room. Not if she could help it.

"Why didn't Starr just give Lubbock the money?" she asked, hoping to keep him talking. Clearly he was proud of what he'd managed to pull off and wanted her to know all of the details.

"Don't get me wrong," he said, "Starr was crazy about Cade, but I guess she thought she could have it all, the money and the man."

"Or maybe she knew that if her brother got caught with even one of those baited bills, he would rat her out," Andi said. "Three million wouldn't have done it anyway. She had to know that the minute the bunch of you went through the money, you'd show up on her doorstep to blackmail whatever else you could out of her."

"I've got to hand it to you, sweetie, you do have a feel for the Calhoun clan," he said with an edge to his voice. "But in the end, I will be leaving here with enough money to take care of me for some time to come."

"You're that sure Cade will find the robbery money?"

It was the only flawed part of his plan and he had to know that.

"Actually," Bradley said with a smile, "I doubt he will ever find the money. But after the way you charmed him, he'll do whatever he has to do to save you—including digging into his own pockets."

"Cade doesn't have any—"

"You don't really think he makes a living off that bait and tackle shop?" Bradley laughed. "Cade Jackson invested his share of the money his father gave him from the sale of the family ranch south of Old Town. He's loaded. So see, either way, I knew you would come through for me."

"You really do resent me, don't you? All those jabs about you being a lowly researcher while I got to be center stage in the spotlight."

"No," he cried, mimicking the voice he'd used in Texas. "Although it did help when it came to the stalking part of the plan. Me? I shun the limelight for obvious reasons. If you were willing, I'd take you with me." He reached out to touch her face with the tips of his fingers.

She swung her head to the side, away from his touch, and reached under her shirt to pull the thin rod from the back waistband of her jeans, but made no move to use it yet.

"Come on," he was saying, "We'd be great together. I've often thought about what it would be like to make love to you."

She braced herself, ready to strike. "Over my dead body."

He laughed. "That would be all right, too."

"After you get the money, what then?" she asked, already knowing. He couldn't let them go. So far, he was the one Calhoun without a record. Like he said, he shunned the limelight.

He didn't answer as he glanced at his watch. "Time to call your boyfriend."

He held the phone to his ear, listened, then shoved the cell at her. "Find out if he has the money. Otherwise, make it perfectly clear that he'd better get it or you are going to die."

She took the phone with her free hand, but the moment she touched it, Bradley jammed the gun into her side, making her cry out as Cade answered.

He snatched the phone from her, catching her off guard as he shoved her into the room so hard that she fell. She scrambled to her feet, the rod in her hand, but he'd already grabbed the key and slammed the door and locked it.

Cade didn't answer on the first ring. He let it ring twice more, picking up only before it went to voice mail. He checked the calling number. Blocked. "Yeah?"

He'd expected to hear Starr's taped voice again. What he wasn't ready for was Andi's cry of pain. *"Andi?"* Another cry of pain, then a male voice he'd never heard before.

"Mr. Jackson, do you have my money?"

Cade had to bite down on his fury. "As a matter of fact, I do, but I will burn every last bill if you touch her again."

The man laughed. "I don't think you're in a position to make the rules." The man had a Southern accent. He wasn't sure why that surprised him.

"I have three million that says I am."

Silence, then, "I see why Ms. Blake has taken a liking to you. So you found the money. Congratulations. You and Ms. Blake have more than met my expectations."

"I want to speak to Andi."

"She's fine."

"Not good enough. I talk to her or we're done here," Cade said, half scared the caller would hang up.

"Maybe we're done here."

Cade held his breath, terrified that the next sound he heard would be the click as the connection was broken. But then again, there were those three million reasons for the man to work with him.

He heard a key turn in a lock, the creak of a door and then Andi's voice.

"Cade?"

He closed his eyes, squeezing the phone in his hand as he dropped onto the arm of the couch and put his head down. He cleared his voice, not wanting her to hear his fear.

"Andi. Are you all right?"

"I'm—"

A door slammed. Andi let out a cry, this one sounding more like frustration than pain.

"Okay, you heard her," the man said. "She's alive, but if you want her to stay that way, then you'd better get me the money."

Cade had had plenty of time to think while he was waiting for the call. "Here's the deal. You come to me. You bring Andi. Once I see that she's all right, I give you the money. I'll be waiting for you at my ice-fishing shack. I have a feeling you know where it is. You've got thirty minutes before I start burning the money."

"I'll kill her," the man snapped.

"I lost my wife and baby because of this damned money," Cade shot back. "Thirty minutes or it all goes up in smoke, every last damn dollar." He snapped off his phone, his hands shaking so hard he dropped it.

When the cell phone rang a few seconds later, he kicked it away, afraid he'd break down and answer it.

Andi. Oh God, Andi.

He prayed his bluff would work and that it wouldn't cost him not only his life, but also Andi's.

As he stepped to the front door of his cabin, he picked up the two bags full of money and headed for his fishing shack.

Chapter 16

Andi heard Bradley go berserk on the other side of the door, yelling and cursing and hitting the walls.

She'd heard at least Bradley's side of the conversation through the door including the last part. *I'll kill her.*

Fear rose in her as she heard the scratch of the key in the lock. She backed up to the far wall as the door swung open.

She knew that Bradley's fury could mean only one thing. Cade *had* found the robbery money. But apparently, he must have refused to pay Bradley to get her back.

Bradley's plan hadn't worked. She didn't need to ask what would happen now. A part of her was glad Bradley wouldn't get a dime. But she was now more than dispensable.

Bradley would have to get rid of her. She was the only person who knew of his involvement.

He stepped into the room, the gun dangling from the

fingers of his right hand, his head bowed. He let out an exasperated sigh.

"I can't imagine what my sister ever saw in that man," he said and raised his gaze to her, "let alone what you see in him."

She heard the jealousy in his voice. She said nothing as she swallowed the lump in her throat and waited.

Bradley seemed to brighten. "But the son of a bitch did find the robbery money—at least he says he did." He shook his head. "God help him if he didn't."

Andi wondered what Bradley had been so furious about if Cade had the money and was willing to give it to him.

"Get your coat," he said. "Your boyfriend is meeting us at his *fishing* shack."

He picked up his cell phone from the hall floor where he'd thrown it but she knew he was watching her, probably expecting her to try to get away. She got the impression he wanted her to try. Not that he would kill her. Just hurt her.

If he was going to kill her, he would have already done it. No, he needed her. Cade must have demanded her in exchange for the money. She felt her heart soar.

Also she could tell, by the way Bradley said it, that the fishing shack hadn't been his idea.

"I need to go to the bathroom," she said, sounding as defeated as she could.

"Well, hurry it up then," he snapped and checked something on his phone.

She stepped into the bathroom, making a show of turning her back to him. As she slipped behind the short wall, she hurriedly slid the thin metal rod into the top of her boot and pulled her jeans pant leg down over it. While it would be harder to get quickly, she knew there was less chance of it being discovered before she needed it.

She flushed, washed and came out to find him waiting for her. The look in his eyes told her as she pulled on her coat, hat and mittens that Bradley's original plan had been that she would never leave this house alive.

As Cade prepared for the worst possible outcome, he told himself he'd done the right thing.

He turned on the lantern, illuminating the inside of the fishing shack. With the door closed, though, whoever had Andi wouldn't know for sure if he was inside or not.

He was counting on that. Otherwise it would be like shooting fish in a barrel.

As he looked around the inside of the fishing shack, he couldn't help but think about the day Andi sat in the folding chair laughing as she caught fish and he unhooked them and threw them back until long after dark.

All he wanted was to save her. He told himself that made everything he'd done right. As long as Andi was spared.

Unfortunately he had too much time to think, to speculate on who had Andi. He remembered what she'd told him about the Calhouns. All were now accounted for. Except one. A male who would be just a little older than Starr.

The voice on the phone just now had been a male's. Cade had detected the Southern accent. He was betting the man was the missing Worth Calhoun.

Cade heard the sound of a vehicle's engine. He checked his gun, then set it just inside the door. When he heard the vehicle stop, the engine die, he opened the door of the fishing shack.

Bradley seemed nervous as he cut the engine on the SUV and looked over at her. He'd duct-taped her mouth and used plastic cuffs on both her ankles and wrists, pushing her into the floorboard of the passenger side of the SUV and ordering her to stay down.

She'd sneaked a peek as they'd left where he'd been keeping her, but she hadn't recognized the old house. It was an abandoned farmhouse and there were hundreds of them across Montana.

With her wrists bound, her door locked and the gun within Bradley's reach, there was little she could do to escape. She had to hope she'd get an opportunity once they reached their destination. Once they reached Cade.

She'd hold her fear at bay. She knew Bradley would have found another way if he hadn't used her, but still she felt responsible for jeopardizing Cade's life.

Now she looked out to see that he'd brought her to the cabin. Cade's pickup was parked out front.

It was twilight. The fallen snow seemed to glow. Earlier the snow and wind had stopped just as quickly as it had begun. Now a couple of stars popped out in the cold, dark blue canvas of the sky overhead.

Bradley reached over and with a knife from his pocket, cut the cuffs on her ankles before quickly picking up the gun. "Take it slow. Do anything stupid like run and I shoot you, understand?"

She nodded, more worried about where Cade was and what would happen next.

Bradley released the lock on the passenger side door, slid across the bench seat and opened the door. With the gun in one hand pointed at her head, he grabbed a handful of her hair with the other and pushed her out.

She stumbled in the deep snow and almost fell. He jerked her close to him, making a show of the gun pressed into her temple, as he pushed her toward the slight incline to the reservoir.

The door was open on Cade's fishing shack. A wedge of lantern light spilled across the snow and ice.

She could feel Bradley nervously looking around as if he thought he was walking into a trap. Other than the cabin, there were no other structures nearby—not even other fishing shacks. And what fishing shacks there were on the lake were apparently empty, no rigs parked outside them.

Where was Cade? Inside the fishing shack?

The land around the reservoir was rolling hills. Other than a few outcroppings of rocks and several single trees, there was little place for anyone to hide.

Fifteen yards from the shack, Bradley brought her up short. "Show yourself!" he called out to Cade.

Andi's heart raced at the sight of Cade as he stepped into the light. He wore no coat, just jeans and a flannel shirt. He held up his hands and turned slowly around to show that he had no weapon.

"Let's see the money," Bradley called.

Cade stepped back into the shack and returned with a large garbage bag. He dumped the money into the snow.

Bradley let out a curse. "Where's the rest of it?"

"Inside. Let her go and it's all yours."

Bradley voiced his reservations. "I want to see it all first," he said.

Cade didn't move. "Let her go."

Bradley tightened his hold on Andi's hair, the barrel of the gun pressed hard against her temple. She knew he had no intention of letting either her or Cade walk away. Cade had to know that.

"Either I see the money or I shoot her right now," Bradley called.

Cade didn't move for a long moment. She could feel Bradley shaking with anger.

Cade stepped back into the fishing shack. A few seconds later he came out with another bag of money, which he also dumped in the snow.

Bradley swore under his breath. "I'm going to kill that son of a bitch."

"That's all you're going to see, now let her go," Cade said, his voice dangerously calm.

Bradley pushed her on ahead of him, his hand still tangled in her hair, the gun still to her head. "Move away from the shack," Bradley ordered as he got near enough that he would be able to see inside.

Andi feared the moment Cade was out of the way, Bradley would shoot him. She tried to warn Cade, but the tape muffled her words.

"Shut up," Bradley whispered. "Move away from the shack!" he yelled at Cade.

She had to get to the metal rod in her boot, but with Bradley holding her hair... She saw Cade start to move aside. She kicked as hard as she could at Bradley's ankle then let her body go slack.

He let out a cry of pain, his fingers digging into her hair as he tried to hold her upright. But the weight of her body had pulled him forward. He stumbled into her and almost went down with her, forcing him to let go of her hair.

As she fell toward the snow, she reached down, pulling up her pant leg to retrieve the rod from her boot. Her wrists were still cuffed but she was able to grasp the rod in one palm, her hand closing over it.

Instinctively Bradley reached for her. She swung to one side and rammed the rod into his outstretched arm.

She heard a howl of pain an instant before the air exploded in gunfire. As she looked up in confusion, she saw the front of Bradley's coat bloom bright red, once, twice.

He staggered, the gun still in his hand, as he pointed the barrel at her head. Their eyes met in the dim, cold light and she saw an even colder light in his pale blue eyes.

Andi rolled to the side. Gunshots exploded. When she looked up, she saw Bradley. He had dropped the gun at his feet. The snow was painted red in front of him. He was looking toward the fishing shack.

Andi rolled up to a sitting position and saw Cade standing in the doorway, the .357 in his hands. Bradley said something she didn't understand and collapsed into the snow next to her.

It had all happened in a matter of seconds.

Over the pounding of her heart, she heard voices, one in particular, ordering Cade to stay back.

Men appeared out of the snow, cloaked all in white. In the lead was Sheriff Carter Jackson.

But before he could reach her, suddenly Cade was there, falling into the snow beside her, drawing her to him.

"Are you hit?" he was shouting as he ripped the tape from her mouth. "Are you hit?"

All she could do was shake her head.

And then he was cutting the plastic cuffs from her wrists and carrying her toward the cabin.

Behind them, more men appeared out of the snow to surround the man she'd known as Bradley Harris. She heard the sheriff say he was dead and then she was inside the cabin and in Cade's arms.

Epilogue

Andi Blake looked up from her computer as a sleigh pulled by two huge horses trotted down the main street of Whitehorse. Snowflakes danced in the air to the sound of laughter and Christmas carols.

Her eyes burned with tears as she finished typing and hit Print. The printer whirred. She hurriedly addressed an envelope with the publisher's name on it, signed and folded the one page resignation letter, put it in the envelope and sealed it.

She'd already called Mark Sanders to let him know she was quitting and would leave the letter on his desk. It had been the hardest thing she'd ever done. But her job was waiting for her in Texas. Her old boss had promised her a huge raise and a prime-time spot.

Her story about the last of the Calhouns had made all the networks. Her boss had even sent a special film crew to Montana to shoot her account.

The Calhouns were all gone now. All of the missing robbery money had been returned. Cade had been completely cleared and Andi had done what she could to give her father justice—and peace. There was nothing keeping her in Whitehorse.

Except for the way she felt about Cade Jackson.

She hadn't seen him since the shootout at the fishing shack. They'd both been taken to the sheriff's department for questioning. She'd been sent to the emergency room to be checked out. When it was all over, it was morning and the sheriff had given her a ride to her apartment.

She hadn't asked where Cade was because she knew the sheriff was right. She couldn't ask Cade to leave here. And how could she stay? She would have to give up her television career that she'd worked so hard for.

But Cade had definitely changed the way she felt about him, about her career, about herself. He'd shown her a life completely alien to the one she'd lived in Texas. She knew she would never see her old life the same after Whitehorse and Cade, let alone after what had happened here.

Not that Cade had offered her an alternative. He'd called shortly after she'd gotten back to her apartment and asked how she was doing.

"Fine," she'd said.

"You must be packing."

"I guess so." And that's where they'd left it.

No reason to stay around, she told herself. Especially since it was Christmas Eve and she'd heard there was a big party down at the new restaurant that Cade's friends had started.

But the main reason she couldn't stay was that Cade still loved his wife. Andi couldn't compete with Grace. And it was just too cramped in that cabin to live with a ghost, let alone the shadow of the house Cade and Grace were to live in together just up on the hill behind it.

While Cade knew his wife had been Starr Calhoun, he still believed Grace had been the part of Starr that was good, the part he'd loved and was going to have a family with. Andi knew he was hurting all over again at the loss of that woman—and his child.

If Andi left now, she could be back in Texas and settled in by the New Year. And it would make Christmas easier since she had no family to celebrate it with anyway. Better to be busy finding a new place and getting moved in.

The bell over the front door of the newspaper jangled, bringing her head up.

Cade came in out of the storm, brushing snow from his hat and coat. She felt her heart take off like a shot.

He looked shy and uncertain standing there, so different from the man who had saved her life. The sheriff had told her that it wasn't like Cade to ever ask for help. It had taken a lot of faith, but Cade had called his brother and told him everything long before the meeting at the fishing shack.

"You can't understand what a big step that was for Cade to do that," the sheriff had told her. "That says a lot about how he feels toward you."

Andi had nodded, touched that Carter had told her, and thanked him.

"I know I told you that I don't do holidays," Cade said now as he stepped up to her desk. "But tonight my brother's going to ask the woman he's been in love with for years to marry him and I promised I would be there."

She couldn't have said anything even if he'd asked.

"Everyone is going to be at the restaurant—Laci and Bridger—they own the place, my father, Loren, and his wife, Lila Bailey Jackson, my brother, Carter, and Eve

Bailey, she's the one he's in love with, her sisters, Faith and McKenna." Cade stopped to take a breath.

Andi waited, not sure what he was doing here or why he was telling her this.

"I went to the house site this morning," he said, the change of subject practically giving her whiplash. "I burned it down. In the spring, I'll get a backhoe in there to take up the foundation. It will take a while for the grass to come back in. That spot will never be exactly as it was before Grace came into my life, but in time…"

He held up his hand as if he was afraid she might speak. No chance of that.

"What I'm trying to say is that I can't pretend Grace wasn't a part of my life. I can't say I'm sorry that I ever met her. But in time, like that hillside, I'll come back, too. Not the same, but maybe richer for the fact that I loved her."

Tears welled in Andi's eyes. All she could do was nod.

Cade took a long breath and let it out. "What I'm trying to say is that—"

The front door of the newspaper office opened, the bell jangling as Andi's boss came in. He looked surprised to see her.

"I was hoping I would catch you before you left," Mark said. "I just wanted to congratulate you on that story you did. Saw you on television and said to my wife, 'That young woman was a reporter at the *Milk River Examiner*,' at least for a few days," he said with a laugh. "Best of luck in Texas." He shook her hand and left again.

"So you're leaving tonight," Cade said, nodding as he backed toward the door.

"I thought there was something you wanted to tell me." Andi knew if she let him leave, she would never see him again. She could see how hard it had been for him to come in here tonight, how hard it was for him to burn down the skeleton of the house, destroying the last remnants of the life he'd planned with Grace.

"You probably have to get going."

"No. Please. What were you going to say?"

Cade met her gaze and held it. "I can't let you stay in Whitehorse, not knowing how you feel about your career. I saw you on television. You are damned good at what you do. You deserve the best. I just wanted to tell you that."

He turned to leave.

She wanted to call him back, but she knew the moment was lost. Whatever else he'd come to tell her tonight was lost.

At the door, though, he stopped and turned back to her. "It *is* Christmas Eve. If you're not leaving tonight, maybe you'd like to go to the party with me."

She smiled through her tears. "I'd like that a lot. But I will have to change. Can I meet you at the restaurant?"

She'd seen the dark blue velvet dress in the window of the shop next door. Unless she was mistaken, it was her size. She knew the dress would fit perfectly.

He smiled. "I'll be waiting for you," he said as he pushed his Stetson down over his dark hair, reminding her of the first time she ever saw him.

"I'll see you soon," she said to his retreating backside as she picked up the envelope containing her resignation and dropped it into the trash.

* * * * *

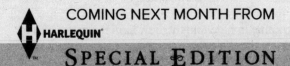

COMING NEXT MONTH FROM

HARLEQUIN®

SPECIAL EDITION

Available November 17, 2015

HSECNM1115

SPECIAL EXCERPT FROM

H HARLEQUIN®

SPECIAL EDITION

*Quiet librarian Celeste Nichols doesn't expect the
success of her children's book. But even more surprising
is the family she finds under the mistletoe this year with
childhood crush Flynn Delaney and his daughter!*

*Read on for a sneak preview of
A COLD CREEK CHRISTMAS STORY, the latest book
in RaeAnne Thayne's fan-favorite series,*
THE COWBOYS OF COLD CREEK.

"Okay," Olivia said in a dejected voice. "Thank you for
bringing me down here to meet Sparkle and play with
the puppies."

"You are very welcome," Celeste said. "Any time you
want to come back, we would love to have you. Sparkle
would, too."

Olivia seemed heartened by that as she headed for the
reindeer's stall one last time.

"Bye, Sparkle. Bye!"

The reindeer nodded his head two or three times as if
he were bowing, which made the girl giggle.

Celeste led the way out of the barn. Another inch
of snow had fallen during the short time they had been
inside, and they walked in silence to where Flynn's SUV
was parked in front of the house.

She wrapped her coat around herself while Flynn
helped his daughter into the backseat. Once Olivia was
settled, he closed the door and turned to Celeste.

"Please tell your family thank-you for inviting me to dinner. I enjoyed it very much."

"I will. Good night."

With a wave, he hopped into his SUV and backed out of the driveway.

She watched them for just a moment, snow settling on her hair and her cheeks while she tried to ignore that little ache in her heart.

She could do this. She was tougher than she sometimes gave herself credit. Yes, she might already care about Olivia and be right on the brink of falling hard for her father. That didn't mean she had to lean forward and leave solid ground.

She would simply have to keep herself centered, focused on her family and her friends, her work and her writing and the holidays. She would do her best to keep him at arm's length. It was the only smart choice if she wanted to emerge unscathed after this holiday season.

Soon they would be gone, and her life would return to the comfortable routine she had created for herself.

As she walked into the house, she tried not to think about how unappealing she suddenly found that idea.

SPECIAL EXCERPT FROM

ⒽHARLEQUIN®

I N T R I G U E

When a beautiful computer expert working with the
Kansas City Police Department Cold Case squad
stumbles upon information that could bring down a
serial killer, the only one she trusts to keep her and her
young son safe is the handsome detective who's been in
her heart for as long as she can remember.

Read on for a sneak preview of
KANSAS CITY CONFESSIONS,
the exciting conclusion of USA TODAY
bestselling author Julie Miller's miniseries
THE PRECINCT: COLD CASE

"I won't let him hurt you, Sunshine. I won't let him hurt
Tyler, either."

She nodded at the promise murmured against the
crown of her hair. But the tears spilling over couldn't
quite believe they were truly safe, and Katie snuggled
closer. Trent slipped his fingers beneath her ponytail and
loosened it to massage her nape. "What happened to that
spunky fighter who got her baby away from Craig Fairfax
and helped bring down an illegal adoption ring?"

Her laugh was more of a hiccup of tears. "That girl
was a naive fool who put a lot of lives in danger. I nearly
got Aunt Maddie killed."

"Hey." Trent's big hands gently cupped her head and
turned her face up to his. His eyes had darkened again.
"That girl is all grown up now. Okay? She's even smarter
and is still scrappy enough to handle anything."

Oh, how she wanted to believe the faith he had in her.
But she'd lost too much already. She'd seen too much.

She curled her fingers into the front of his shirt, then smoothed away the wrinkles she'd put there. "I'm old enough to know that I'm supposed to be afraid, that I can't just blindly tilt at windmills and try to make everything right for everyone I care about. Not with Tyler's life in my hands. I can't let him suffer any kind of retribution for something I've done."

"He won't."

Her fingers curled into soft cotton again. "I don't think I have that same kind of fight in me anymore."

"But you don't have to fight alone."

"Fight who? I don't know who's behind those threats. I don't even know what ticked him off. It's just like my dad all over again."

"Stop arguing with me and let me help."

"Trent—"

His fingers tightened against her scalp, pulling her onto her toes as he dipped his head and silenced her protest with a kiss. For a moment, there was only shock at the sensation of warm, firm lips closing over hers. When Trent's mouth apologized for the effective end to her moment of panic, she pressed her lips softly to his, appreciating his tender response to her fears. When his tongue rasped along the seam of her lips, a different sort of need tempted her to answer his request. When she parted her lips and welcomed the sweep of his tongue inside to stroke the softer skin there, something inside her awoke.

Don't miss
KANSAS CITY CONFESSIONS
by USA TODAY *bestselling author Julie Miller,*
available in December 2015 wherever
Harlequin Intrigue® books and ebooks are sold.

www.Harlequin.com